Praise for Jane Linfoot

'For those that like Sophie Kinsella style books, this is a cute story about a guy determined to prove he won't fall for a woman...'
Cosmochicklitan on *How to Win a Guy in 10 Dates*

'A hot as hell, sexy and enticing story.'
fter the Final Chapters on *How to Win a Guy in 10 Dates*

'Flirty, sexy and impossible to put down.'
Becca's Books on *High Heels & Bicycle Wheels*

'A delightful romance.'
The Book Lover's Best Friend on *High Heels & Bicycle Wheels*

'Funny, fast-paced and emotionally fulfilling, this book has firmly placed her onto my must read shelf.'
I am, Indeed on *The Right Side of Mr Wrong*

'I freaking LOVED this book!'
Crystal Blogs Books on *The Right Side of Mr Wrong*

JANE LINFOOT

I write fun, flirty fiction with feisty heroines and a bit of an edge. Writing romance is cool because I get to wear pretty shoes instead of wellies. I live in a mountain kingdom in Derbyshire, where my family and pets are kind enough to ignore the domestic chaos. Happily, we're in walking distance of a supermarket. I love hearts, flowers, happy endings, all things vintage, most things French. When I'm not on Facebook and can't find an excuse for shopping, I'll be walking or gardening. On days when I want to be really scared, I ride a tandem.

The Vintage Cinema Club

JANE LINFOOT

Harper*Impulse* an imprint of
HarperCollins*Publishers* Ltd
1 London Bridge Street
London SE1 9GF

www.harpercollins.co.uk

A Paperback Original 2015

First published in Great Britain in ebook format by Harper*Impulse* 2015

A catalogue record for this book is
available from the British Library

ISBN: 9780008119362

Automatically produced by Atomik ePublisher from Easypress

Printed and bound in Great Britain

This one's for Sophie...

1

Wednesday Afternoon, 4th June

IZZY, LUCE & DIDA

Vintage at the Cinema, Matlock

Birthdays and Bubbles

'So a few words, to celebrate our achievements, before we get on to the cake.' Dida gave a toss of her head as she cleared her throat. Then she stamped her foot to get the attention of the people gathered in the shop, although to be fair, most of them already had their eyes fixed on this powerhouse in red, standing up there, on her makeshift soap box. Waving her bubbly in the air, she grinned down at Izzy and Luce.

Izzy glanced up at the banner high above Dida's head, fluttering in the breeze from the open door. *Happy Third Birthday to Vintage at the Cinema,* and that retro turquoise font they'd gone for looked fab.

Dida might well have had a champagne flute grafted to her

hand at birth. Whatever the occasion, she managed to involve Moet & Chandon. It was the same with her ever present high heels. Izzy grimaced at the wooden box Dida had grabbed as her temporary stage. Good thing it was already distressed, as Dida's Manolo Blahniks were stabbing a hundred tiny indentations in the top as she teetered on her five inch stilettos.

'So Vintage at the Cinema is three today, and it's been an amazing journey. Three years since my other half accidentally acquired the cinema building...' Dida paused for the fleeting grimace that passed over her face every time she mentioned awful Aidie, the husband from hell. She certainly had her hands full being married to that guy, even if they'd all benefitted from this particular impulse buy of his. Getting hold of a building he had no interest in, in some very dodgy deal, was Aidie all over. Dida snatching and commandeering the abandoned cinema building had been a gift for all of them.

She took a slurp of champers, and carried on. 'Three years ago, Luce, Izzy and I decided to set up a pop up shop in the empty cinema, selling the vintage things we all love so much.'

Luce gave Izzy a nudge, and slipped her a sideways smile. Izzy swallowed down the lump that always came in her throat when she thought how proud she was of her best friend Luce for nailing being a single mum, and launching her vintage dress business at the same time, all thanks to the lucky break of Vintage at the Cinema. Before that they'd both come back from uni, armed with their art degrees, Luce with the additional bundle of baby Ruby, and slipped straight back into their default setting jobs at the coffee shop, where they'd worked before they left. Before the cinema, the furthest Luce and Izzy had got with their creative careers, were occasional stalls at craft fairs. But somehow with Dida, the three of them together had found the momentum to do amazing things. A pop up shop had been much less scary than committing to a lease, and given a risk free opportunity, they'd finally dared to do the things they'd been dreaming of for years.

2

'And the rest is history.' Dida paused for dramatic effect, neatly fast forwarding over all the slog and toil that had gone in along the way. 'But we couldn't have pulled this off on our own. Our success is also down to all of our lovely friends and fellow sellers, who joined in with us to make this the fabulous emporium it is today, and of course all our wonderful customers.' Dida waved her glass towards the crowd in an expansive arc, before knocking back another gulp.

Dida had come a long way too, even if the income made less of an impact on her domestic finances than those of Luce and Izzy. It wasn't that she'd ever grumbled previously about being a stay at home mum, managing a home which might have been super-sized on steroids, and a husband as capricious as a stormy day in spring. But Vintage at the Cinema had given her something else to focus on by taking her away from the hell that was her home life. These days Dida glowed with a new found confidence and zest for life she'd never had three years ago.

Looking around the shop now, Izzy knew she'd personally excelled herself with the preparations for this birthday bash. Flowery bunting mingled with the twinkly chandeliers, soaring across the lofty space, above the gorgeous creams and greys of painted cupboards and dressing tables and dressers below. Artful piles of trunks and suitcases nestled against cascades of vintage fabric, and every shelf was decked out with an array of beautifully displayed objects, like a series of arty still life paintings. There wasn't a corner of the shop that didn't look as if it had come from the pages of a glossy up market country homes magazine.

Izzy and Luce had first met Dida at art college, when they were eighteen, and she was a thirty something, desperate to find some sanity after having her first baby. The friendship was cemented when Dida and Luce rocked up at the same ante-natal class, having Lolly and Ruby, who were sitting together on the counter now, fingers entwined, swinging their legs. Ruby caught Izzy's eye as she gazed around, and her little wave made Izzy's tummy turn over.

Ruby was so like Luce, all pale slender beauty, in her flowery shorts, snuggled in next to the vision of frills in pink fluo net that was Lolly, Dida's daughter. Whereas Dida got the champagne flute, Lolly had exited the birth canal complete with diamanté tiara. Izzy knew without asking the battle that would have gone on at Alport Towers, Dida's home, this morning, over Lolly's insistence on day glow pink and orange glitter wellies.

Her friend was in full flow now. 'We were the first vintage shop, and as others followed, Matlock has become *the* retro shopping destination in Derbyshire.'

Izzy and Luce exchanged indulgent smiles. Dida was extending the short and punchy she'd agreed on for her speech, but they had pulled off something spectacular here, and just for once Izzy was enjoying a few minutes of basking in the glory. After the way her dad had treated her mum when he left, all Izzy had wanted was a means to make her way in life, without having to rely on a partnership with a guy who might up and leave at any moment. What seemed at the beginning like a happy accident of a retro shop, had gone a long way to giving her that independence, and she had her wonderful friends Luce and Dida to thank for that.

'So thanks to Byron from Corks, for the wonderful cocktails we love so much, Gigi at Amandine's Patisserie for keeping us supplied with delicious tarts especially the blue berry ones, to Evan at Majestic Wine, please don't count the Moet bottles...'

Izzy gave a wry grin, and noted that Aidie's name didn't appear anywhere on Dida's ever growing list.

Dida bashed on. '...and huge hugs to my mum and dad, I am so, so, so grateful...'

Talk about out of control at the Oscars. Izzy knew Dida's mum was a total nightmare. Dida was doing a Gwynnie here. It was time to cut to the cake.

Izzy put on a five hundred watt beam, and chimed in. 'So, shall we raise our glasses, and do confectionary?' She gave Dida's hip a large nudge, and nodded in the direction of the glorious tower of cupcakes, decorated with roses and lace, in sludgy blues and pinks and creams.

Luce had Izzy's back. 'Great idea.' She added with her own wide grin.

'Okay, so to sum up...' Dida took a deep breath, her voice wavering now. 'Vintage at the Cinema represents three women – Izzy, Luce and I – and we have worked our butts off to create something truly unique, that surpasses all our hopes and dreams.' Dida wrapped her arms around Luce and Izzy, and pulled them against her.

Tears welled up in Izzy's eyes at that last bit, and despite her best attempts to control it, her bottom lip began to wobble, as all the love she felt for Luce and Dida burst up in her chest. She was only saved from full blown howling by an overpowering blast of Dida's Diorissimo, and the pain in her shoulder, as Dida squeezed her tight enough for the linen of Dida's jacket to graze her skin.

'So let's raise our glasses, to the very awesome Vintage at the...'

Dida held her glass high, but before she could say the final word, a loud mechanical sound reverberated through the shop.

A shadow flickered across Dida's beatific smile. 'What the hell is going on out there...? Can someone please tell whoever that is, this is not the time for hammer drills.'

Izzy, peering past the crowd, could make out a ladder propped up on the pavement beyond the shop doorway.

As the crew moved towards the door and peered out, Luce got there first. 'What are those two huge for sale signs propped against the window for?' Her brow creased into a worried frown.

Dida staggered down from her trunk, and elbowed her way out onto the pavement. Then she grabbed an umbrella from a flower pot, rapped hard on the ladder with the handle, and shouted to the man above. 'Excuse me, what exactly do you think you're doing?'

'98 Derwent Street, Commercial Freehold For Sale.' The man said, glowering down from ten feet up and sounding casually confident.

Dida's jaw dropped, but she squared her shoulders, ignored the collective gasp behind her, and shouted up. 'I'm sorry, there must be some mistake.'

Izzy's heart plummeted. She knew Dida's husband, Aidie, was ruthless, but surely he wouldn't do this to them. Although on second thoughts, this stunt had Aidie written all over it. From his snarky comments whenever he was around, which happily wasn't that often, he clearly resented Dida's growing independence. His wife's success was a direct threat to a control freak husband like Aidie, and selling the building was a fast forward way to wrestle back his power, simultaneously wiping the floor with all of them. And if he was hell bent on bursting Dida's bubble, in the most spectacular and public way possible, his timing was impeccable.

'Definitely no mistake.' The workman up the ladder sounded very sure of himself. 'Don't blame me, I'm only doing my job.' His shrug and weary sigh suggested this happened a lot, then his tone became conciliatory. 'Best ring the agents love, they'll clear it up for you.'

Izzy, feet welded to the pavement, by a mixture of shock, and panic watched Dida bristle. She hated being called 'love'.

'Eldon and Trellis. Right. I'll do that now.' Dida's growl was ferocious. 'I hope you realise you're wasting your time up there, you'll be back in half an hour to take it down.'

Fighting talk, and good on Dida for not taking it lying down, but Izzy, whose stomach was languishing somewhere at pavement level, wasn't so sure.

Dida bustled back through the shop waving her mobile. 'So sorry about this, carry on with the cupcakes. One minute, I'll sort this out.'

Nice try, but nothing flattened bubbly faster than bad news. Realistically, this party was over.

Izzy, Luce and Dida threaded their way past the customers, as they discarded their plastic champagne flutes on the counter next to the untouched cupcake tower, and discretely began to disperse.

Izzy's heart was racing, and she wasn't sure if her shaking knees were due to anger or pure fear. Dida might have pulled off an upbeat exit to the kitchen, but Izzy had caught the wild whites of her eyes as she passed. The gash of her red lipped grimace reminded Izzy of the face in Munch's The Scream, and it was enough for Izzy to know that Vintage at the Cinema was in big trouble here. And that had to be awful news for all of them.

2

Wednesday Evening, 4th June

IZZY

A building site in Bakewell

The downside of upcycling

'Hey, you! Get out of my skip.'

Izzy froze, rammed her shoulder against the rusty metal container side, and crouched lower, cringing as the male voice resonated above her head and echoed across the building site.

Damn it. She kicked herself for coming back for one last look, when she should have got away. In some ways this afternoon's bombshell news that the cinema building was up for sale made it more important than ever for her to get her hands on stock. They weren't going to give up, they were going to fight to survive, and tonight's skip raid was a symbol of that determination. Ever since she, Dida and Luce had launched Vintage at the Cinema, they'd dreamed of a time when business would be booming, and it was ironic that now it was actually happening, it looked as if it might be snatched away.

Something about tonight's desperation spun Izzy back to the time when she'd first discovered the joys of skip scavenging, when her mum walked out on her dad. With four kids and an empty flat, skips had provided Izzy with most of her bedroom furniture. Those fledgling finds had kick started Izzy's love of rescuing what other people threw away. It turned out she had a flair for making old, unwanted things beautiful. At least one good thing had come out of her parents' break up, and the talents she'd discovered back then had exploded with the opportunity of Vintage at the Cinema.

A stripped out cinema building was a big place to fill, especially when the furniture you put in there was flying out as fast as it went in. But ending up on a building site, in a skip, with some guy yelling at you, wasn't the best of places to spend a Wednesday evening.

'Oi! I said move it!' He was still there then.

Izzy shuddered. Luce, always teased her about her compulsion for searching through skips, but it was true that Izzy found it very hard, if not impossible to pass a skip without diving into it. In her experience, there was often treasure to be found, but right now, with an angry man bearing down on her, she was wishing she hadn't let that last glance into the second, almost empty skip, entice her. She closed her hand around the small carved plaster cherub she'd found lurking at the bottom. Dusk was no time to get caught in the act, even if she had okayed it with the builders earlier.

'Think you can come round breaking my windows do you, just because the house is empty?' Enter one apoplectic guy, who'd totally got the wrong end of the stick. He didn't sound too close, but he only had to walk across, and peer over the skip edge, and she'd be done for. 'Did you hear me? I know you're there.'

Fierce and well spoken – they were the worst sort. Izzy grimaced, braced herself for trouble, and began to unfold her legs. Time to face whatever was coming her way. It was a daily hazard of skulking round skips – sometimes it was inevitable, you pissed people off. And Izzy couldn't bear to see old pieces with the potential to be pretty being tossed away. It broke her heart to think of lovely old things being smashed up by ignorant people who didn't know any better. As she saw it, she was on a rescue mission here, and no one in their right mind would object to that, once they saw reason. Although from the way Mr Shouty was limbering up, she wasn't sure reason was going to have much to do with this.

Slowly, she unfolded, to get a peep at what she was dealing with here, and as her nose drew level with the skip edge, she got a full frontal view of the man she was annoying. Talk about chiselled cheekbones. Add in eyes the colour of darkness, a body that would have made most women she knew ache to peel off his well-cut clothes, and for a fraction of a nano second she fell resoundingly, heart-stoppingly, scorchingly in love. She'd always wondered what her friends meant when they talked about thunderbolts, and now she knew. Before she could say "oh my sweet Jesus", her lips had parted, and she was letting out a long, wavering sigh.

Smitten or what?

'You little vandal.' The guy's scowl darkened as he whipped his growl into overdrive. 'I won't tolerate trespassing scumbags, get off my site, and I mean now.'

Phew. That went some way to blasting away the cupid dust.

Izzy straightened, poked her head and then her shoulders above the edge of the skip, and watched with satisfaction as the guy's jaw dropped. That would be surprise. And then his gaze honed in on her cleavage. That would be...

Oh shit. Nothing like eye-glue stuck on your boobs to give a girl yet another reality check. And her reality was the one where love and men were top of her Things-To-Avoid list. Yay! to Awful Alistair, who had messed with her heart for three years before stomping on it with the "it's not you it's me" thing, throwing in the added rider of "but you are coming over quite possessive" when what it turned out he really meant was he'd been shagging someone else for months. Enough said about that one.

Meanwhile, there was no point wasting her time explaining to this perfect specimen in his impeccably cut suit that she had okayed all this with the builders here earlier in the day. She shuddered to think what his reaction would be, if he knew her van was round the corner, full of things she'd dragged out of his other skip, only minutes before. Driving a van plastered with signs saying "Vintage at the Cinema, Everything Retro" might be great for publicity on a day to day basis, but it was hardly going to help her make an anonymous getaway.

The knot in her stomach tightened. She liked to think of herself as cool in the face of provocation, not that Luce would agree with that, but his unwarranted verbal attack had sent her almost as apoplectic as him.

Behind him, parked next to the house, she glimpsed the overblown tank of a car he'd just arrived in. Nothing like a gas guzzler to add fuel to her fire. So, not only was he rude and aggressive, he was also that arrogant type who thought he could rule the road, as well as the world, by swanning round in one of those "the rest of humanity can fuck off" vehicles. Izzy always saved her most savage contempt for that kind of guy.

She might be in his skip, behind his hedge, on his building site, but he had it coming to him.

'If you weren't such a wasteful and ignorant prat, people like me wouldn't have to go round rescuing the perfectly good stuff you'd discarded, would we?' Catching another glimpse of the half renovated house in the background, with piles of discarded floorboards in front of it, gave her a second wind. 'People like you, who rip the guts out of everything, with complete insensitivity, deserve a lot worse than thieving vandals.'

As she paused for breath, teeth clenched, she noticed he was scrutinising her, and that the thunder on his face had moved on like a passing storm. Wonders never ceased, but she suspected it was her chest popping into view that was responsible. Sad to say,

11

she found her D cups often smoothed the way, although she always preferred to make her progress on a gender neutral footing, on the basis of her own merits. It was a depressing fact of life that *some* men were remarkably a) shallow and b) susceptible, and Mr Shouty was obviously one of them.

'So, it's a female dumpster-diver – and dressed for a party too.' His tone had morphed from angry to mocking, as he strode across and peered in at her.

Izzy glanced down at her frock. Okay, maybe her flowery fifties tea dress was a bit close fitting, and it might be incongruous, but was there really the need for the attitude? She was only picking up a few bits and bobs – well a van full actually, but that was beside the point. It should have been a piece of cake, in a skirt and heels, without this unwelcome spectator.

'So what? Are you telling me there's a dress code now?' She swished her skirt, and an unintentionally vigorous jerk of her head dislodged her hair comb, and next thing her unruly curls were cascading across her face. Damn. Now she was essentially fighting with one eye.

'Marilyn Munroe curves, *and* a red head? Who'd have thought?' He was almost laughing now.

One raised eyebrow? Curves? She needed to close this down.

'Whoa, can we cut the sexual harassment?'

Her protest seemed to work, because he baulked momentarily, blinked, and when he looked up again the lust had reverted to bad temper.

'You're on my land, you're invalidating my insurance cover.' His glare sent her insides onto fast-spin. 'Just get out before I throw you out.'

Izzy took that as a dismissal. Great, time to go.

She put her hands on the skip edge and pushed, but nothing happened. She tried again, scrabbled with her feet, and winced as the lemon leather of her pointy shoes scraped down the skip side. Authentic fifties footwear hadn't been the best choice.

She'd got into the skip by climbing on a pile of pallets, then dropping over the side, with no thought to getting out. Now the sides of the skip had her trapped, like a hedgehog in a cattle grid. Clenching her teeth, and forcing her shoulders down, she let out an exasperated sigh.

The guy's hands were on his hips now, resting on his high end leather belt.

'Get on with it then.'

Could he not see she was trying to? His attitude was definitely not attractive, she noted. Except he was. He was horribly attractive in fact. Everything about him, from his stubble shadowed jawline to his muscular thighs tensing against the grey wool of those über expensive suit trousers, screamed SEXY, with the caps lock on. She gave herself a mental kick. What the hell was she thinking? After Awful Alastair, she was steering clear of men. Especially men with choppy brown hair, and definitely arrogant gits like this one. Her resolve was strengthened now she was well on her way to the financial independence she'd always craved. She bit her lip, and blew again.

'Well, what are you waiting for?'

His gravelly voiced query sent goosebumps scurrying up her arms, hotly pursued by a large dose of self-disgust. She was in the shit here on every level, and it was time to admit defeat.

'Actually, I can't get out.'

She lowered her eyes, tried to swallow the shame-faced words, desperate not to acknowledge the gleeful sneer chasing across that disgustingly beautiful face of his.

'Not so stroppy now, then.' He gave a low grunt that might have been a laugh. 'What do you suggest? Shall I come to help you, or will I get accused of sexual harassment?' His tone was lazy, and he didn't move, but the flash of humour in his eyes had Izzy's heart skipping a beat.

'Just sling me a pallet, stop gloating, and shut up. Please.' She watched him stroll forward, grasp a pallet, and swing it high into the air with brutal ease. A hollow clang rang out as the wood thumped down on the skip base, and sent reverberations through the soles of her feet.

'Thank you.' She pulled herself up to her full five foot four inches. Then grasping the pallet, she heaved it into position against the skip side, and checked out its stability with one foot.

'Careful. If you've invalidated my public liability cover, I don't want any accidents.'

God, this guy was a stuffed-shirt. She let out another impatient snort. 'If you don't stop going on about insurance, I might have to squash you on my way down.' And it was bad news that he made her even more insolent than usual, but at least she hadn't sworn at him yet. She already owed Luce, and her Customer Service Initiative swear box a bomb as it was.

Izzy clambered up the pallet, nudged her way onto the skip edge, and it was just too bad that her skirt was riding up somewhere around her bottom as the guy looked up. She really hadn't planned to give him an eyeful of underwear.

He staggered backwards, clearing his throat and looking away quickly. 'Alright up there?'

She dreaded to think what kind of acreage of her knickers she was showing, but frankly she no longer cared. Two kicks sent her pumps flying through the air, then as she splayed her legs, ready to jump, she heard a rip. Crap. The last thing she needed here was to leave her skirt behind her.

'Hang on...' The guy sprung towards her with a strangled squawk.

'Okay, keep your hair on.' Izzy gasped. Two strides later his hands closed around her waist. The breath left her body as he spun her through a glorious crazy arc, before setting her lightly and neatly on the ground beside him. For a moment she wobbled against the soft fabric of his jacket, getting a blast of aftershave that was way too delicious for someone so bad tempered. And then he stepped away, and she was the one left with wide eyes, and a sagging jaw.

3

DIDA

In the kitchen at Alport Towers

One husband, thinly spread

NEW MESSAGE TO: THE CREW @ VINTAGE AT THE
CINEMA... LUCE, IZZY, OLLIE, LYDIA, DAMON,
HENNI, DECLAN, SUZIE, ARTHUR, LEIGHTON,
MAGDA, THOM, ALLIE

Dida checked the names on the email, crossed her legs, and gave
a heartfelt sigh. Even if Aidie had slammed the cinema building
on the market, it was doubly important to carry on as normal.
However determined Aidie was to put a hatchet through her
proverbial baby, not to mention her success, she was ten times
as determined not to let him succeed. Though she hadn't yet
managed to track Aidie down to actually speak to him in person,

or at the end of a phone, she was certain that her husband's motivation for selling the building was as much about trying to limit her new found success, as it was about making a profit now the property market was improving. Although Vintage at the Cinema had started out as a tentative experiment, so much creative energy and talent had gone into making it what it was now, no way was she giving it up without a fight. Even thinking about it made her feel like her head was about to implode with rage at Aidie for doing what he'd done, and rage at herself for being so powerless to stop him. Whereas she should have been floating around on a champers-induced cloud, basking after a fabulously successful celebration, she was instead grinding her teeth in frustration, and biting on the bitter taste of humiliation.

Tonight she'd already bustled her youngest child, Lolly, off to bed in a blur, and now she was ready to sweat the bigger stuff. The disembodied roar of a football crowd meant that Eric was fully engaged with FIFA14 in the breakfast room.

Dida scowled round her apple green kitchen. The vile green paint was another reminder of Aidie's tyranny. That Aidie flatly refused to let her get the fifty seven kitchen units repainted in a more appropriate colour sent her round the bend on a daily basis and it was so typical of him to make this into a battleground. Now, her perpetual fuming about the argument she referred to as Granny Smith-gate only aided her incandescent rage about what had happened today at the cinema.

It was alright for Aidie, he was hardly here long enough to get tired of anything, even something as extreme as vommy green paint. He flew in, then he flew out again. Right now he was in Lithuania, working on "something big" to do with pipes, and as usual she had zero idea what. In fact some weekends he was home so little, they had barely enough time for an argument. Unfortunately for Dida there was always enough time for sex, and that would be sex not once, but twice a day. She gave a rueful eye roll at the thought of his whale-like bulk grunting on top of her, and thanked her lucky stars it was only Wednesday and so she didn't have that to look forward to. Although given what he'd pulled today, she'd be withdrawing that privilege until further notice. As far as the kitchen repaint went, if there was any excuse to wield his power over her, Aidie grabbed it with both his chubby hands. It was time she gave him a taste of his own medicine in the bedroom.

Her husband hadn't always been bloated. The twenty something guy she first hooked up with at the office Christmas party back in '94 had been relatively slender, albeit in a chunky kind of way. She'd first noticed him because he was the only one in the office with his own house, and she had an idea his sense of humour had been better in those days too. But years of expense account dining had pushed his BMI through the red zone, and straight on out the other side. His success had turned into one big power trip and now he pretty much claimed to be in charge of the world as far as the pipelines industry was concerned. He got his rocks off all week, ordering people around at work, and at weekends he brought his testosterone excess back home, and slammed them all into submission here too. And today he'd even managed to exert his power remotely, in the most awful of ways.

Aidie and his control issues. Dida gave a grimace. She was well used to them. It was an ironic twist that if Vintage at the Cinema hadn't dropped into her lap to take her mind off the most difficult thing in life, i.e. her husband, she wasn't sure she'd even still be here, despite the gorgeous home she'd thrown herself into creating. Ice cream was a crutch she leaned on in her struggle to stay cheerful. Usually, at ten o' clock, in a mere seventy six minutes from now, she'd be having a two scoop helping, and tonight she should be dipping into dark chocolate and raspberry, and pralines and cream. But this evening she was so wound up, she had no appetite at all, not even for ice cream.

'Mum, I just went up a league on FIFA, have you got any cake?' Eric, PlayStation controller in hand, wandered into the kitchen, his floppy fringe only partially masking his glazed expression, and walked towards a large pile of plastic containers stacked on the work surface.

'Nope, hands off those, they're Vintage at the Cinema ones, and I'm delivering them first thing.' How much of a bad mother did it make her that she had cake for work and not for home? 'How about ice cream. Toffee chip okay?' She slid off her stool, grabbed a dish, trundled to the fridge and dolloped out some soft scoop, pushing it towards Eric, who gave a grunt.

'It would be nice if you could say thank you properly.' She knew she had to insist on the manners thing, although she'd be lucky to get anything as complex as two syllables out of Eric in his current PlayStation induced trance.

'Thanks.' He mumbled and waggled his spoon at her.

'Bed by ten, alright?' She was talking to Eric's back as he sidled away, sighing as she saw how he even shuffled across the marble floor in the same way as his dad.

One of the many problems with Aidie was, as her Granny used to say, the all fur coat and no knickers thing. He boasted long and hard about his six figure salary, but when it came to housekeeping she simply couldn't get him to part with his money. Vintage at the Cinema kept her sane, by giving her something other than the warfare with Aidie to focus on, but, more importantly, it gave her access to cash. For the first time since she gave up work and had the kids, so long as she fudged the figures she showed to Aidie, she had some kind of financial autonomy.

The morning after Aidie came home from Corks Bar saying he'd got his hands on the old cinema building, she'd got straight on the phone to Luce and Izzy, and, as she'd said in her speech, before she'd been so rudely interrupted, the rest was history. And as Vintage at the Cinema emerged, so had the new independent, happier, Dida. There was no way now she could go back to being who she was before. Vintage at the Cinema had made her into a new person.

18

Dida looked at the names on the email again. Everyone already involved with the cinema was there on this week's email, although should she really *still* be including Ollie? Ollie, who'd waltzed off to the other side of the world five months ago at a moment's notice, leaving his sister Izzy to fill his shop space as well as hers, and do a double share of the shifts? Dida was very fond of Ollie. He'd been hauled on board at the start to help with painting, and proved so useful he never left. He also made the most fabulous one-off metalwork pieces, and had brilliant contacts on the industrial side. Dida tapped a thumbnail on her teeth as she deliberated. No doubt Izzy would have emailed Ollie to tell him the awful news from today. Not that she was in denial, but somehow Dida couldn't actually bear to type the awful physical words in the weekly rota email, because that made the whole nightmare seem too real. Losing the business just wasn't an option she could contemplate.

Even though she was pretty much in charge of the business admin, and it gave her a fab excuse to organise to the nth degree, she liked to think of this as a cooperative venture. Everyone pitched in, they played to their strengths and helped each other. True, they paid her rent, but mostly this was all about everyone benefiting, and having lots of fun along the way. And Ollie was fun, and he was dependable, when he was around, and she had an idea that it wasn't just his sister who was feeling his absence. Luce was missing him a lot more than she was letting on. So she'd leave him on the list for now, in the hope that if he read the email, in some far flung internet cafe, he'd remember to miss them, and remember to come back soon.

She flipped the screen to take one last look at the rota, then hammered out the email.

The rota for week beginning June 9th is attached. FYI we have a guy with very deep pockets who'll buy ANYTHING by Susie Cooper.

Come back soon Ollie, we're missing your industrial pieces.

The week's cake of the week is cocoa and banana :)

Dida xx

PS. Vintage at the Cinema is ready for the fight - we WILL survive!

That would do. She hoped the last line was enough of an acknowledgement of today's disastrous events. She liked to send the email out at nine exactly, not that she was obsessive, but if you were consistent, everyone knew where they were. The sky might be falling in on her own personal world, but she could still stick to a timetable.

Ten minutes to spare before nine then.

Just enough time to make the daily updates to her Aidie Special spreadsheet. She opened his email account, and tapped in his password, grimacing at the double bluff. Aidie's email account was the nerve centre of his life. He knew she knew his password, and he also knew she scrutinised his emails, which was his way of proving to her that he had nothing to hide. Quite how the negotiations for the sale of the cinema had slipped by her, she had no idea, but from now on she'd be doubly vigilant.

Dida never failed to be amazed at Aidie's meticulous management of his email account, given that dotting the "i"s and crossing the "t"s wasn't Aidie's natural way. His approach to life was usually way more sloppy, which was probably why he'd failed to spot the fatal flaw in his plan. It was a constant source of amusement to Dida that Aidie deleted all the emails he didn't want her to see, but just the same as at home, he never bothered to empty the trash.

Now for today's deleted mail. She clicked on the dustbin icon and leaned closer to the screen as she flipped through the list, and read intently. Wow. This was going some even for Aidie. A breakfast meeting with someone called Bambi, an eleven o'clock with Viktorya, then dinner with Dominika, Elvira and Albina.

Two minutes, and Dida had copied and pasted the names into her spreadsheet of Aidie's misdemeanours, and added times and locations.

Had this been anyone else's husband, she might have been impressed by the stamina of the guy. Some weeks he appeared to be keeping the sex industry of Lithuania in business single-handedly. When he managed to get any work done, she had no idea. Given today's developments, she may well be using the ammunition she'd been collecting sooner than she thought. The way she felt about Aidie now, after he tried to crush her dreams, she couldn't imagine being able to look at the man, let alone live with him.

Now nothing mattered, except what Aidie was trying to wrestle from her and her friends. It was too late to do anything more this evening. First thing tomorrow she was seeing Luce and Izzy. They'd have their emergency meeting. And together, they'd get their proverbial boxing gloves on.

4

Wednesday Evening, 4th June

LUCE

At her flat

Lace, sweat and tears

'Thanks for being so patient, I'm almost done.' Luce paused as she fingered the satin hem of the dress she was pinning, smiled up at Steffie, the soon-to-be bride, and took a minute to sit up, wriggling the ache out of her shoulders. 'These full skirts take an age to get around, but they're worth it.'

Steffie shifted slightly. 'No Ruby this evening?'

'It's my lucky night. I think the cupcake sugar rush from this afternoon's party knocked her out.'

Steffie laughed. 'It isn't the same without Ruby entertaining us whilst you pin.'

If Ruby hadn't fallen asleep by the time Luce's evening fitting appointments arrived, her bedroom was so close to the living room she invariably heard the chatting, and crept through in her pyjamas. The flat was such a good deal, and so close to work and school, the compromise on layout was one Luce was happy to live with, for the time being anyway. All her other vintage clothes and textiles were at the cinema, but she kept the wedding dresses at home because the fabrics were fragile, and so easily marked. Right now her bedroom was so full of lace and tulle, some nights it was hard to find the bed.

Luce did a mental double take and she gulped so hard she almost swallowed a pin, as she remembered in a sudden rush, that work might not be at the old cinema for much longer. She tried not to think how scared that made her. Vintage at the Cinema had brought a lot of things to her and Ruby's life. She was so lucky to have found a way of working that gave her satisfaction, an income, and which let her be here for Ruby too. The thought that it might be whipped away from her made her spine go rigid. And even though she knew that Izzy and Dida would go to hell and back for her and Ruby, for some reason the sheer, unadulterated fear of losing the livelihood she'd worked so hard to establish, made her feel very alone.

Luce tried to push that thought away with a smile, but the most she managed was a grimace. 'No, once Ruby comes through, it's impossible to get her back to bed again. At least I won't have a sleep deprived grump to deal with tomorrow.'

'She's such a cutie though.' Steffie looked wistful. 'Hard to stand up to, I guess.'

Too true. There were times when Luce wished that the random guy who'd accidentally donated his genes to her child, via a broken condom the last night of her second year at uni, had been slightly less good looking, and way less good at sweet talking. Soulful brown eyes and a penchant for fast come backs proved hard to handle in an offspring, and neither of those things came from Luce.

It wasn't that Ruby was naughty, because she wasn't especially, but Luce often found there just wasn't enough of her to go around.

She couldn't work and constantly keep her child entertained.

However high her ideals on bringing up children had been before she had one, now she was in the thick of it she often felt she failed on every level. And it had been much worse since Izzy's brother, Ollie, left to go travelling. It was only since he'd been away that she'd realised how much she'd grown to depend on him. Lying awake in the early hours, she kicked herself for how much she'd taken him for granted. And she kicked herself too for letting everything get so out of hand between them, and it being completely her fault that he'd left. In the first three years of Ruby's life she'd been determined to go it alone. She still was. But the friendship with Ollie had kind of crept up on her as they'd worked together. And tonight, when she was feeling scared and very alone, she knew it was wrong, and she knew it was weak, and she knew it was against everything she'd ever intended, but she could really have done with leaning on Ollie. Except he wasn't here.

Luce grabbed a few more pins, rammed them between her lips, and bent down to secure the last yard of silky hem.

'You look beautiful sweetheart.'

Steffie's mum, perched on the arm of Luce's sofa, finally broke their silence. Since she'd been working with bridal wear, and more importantly, brides, Luce had noticed that taking on the role of Mother of the Bride seemed to transform reasonable women into a) control freaks, and b) emotional wrecks.

'Hankie?' Luce caught the tremor in Steffie's mum's voice and offered her the flowery, fabric covered tissue box.

'Thank you.' Mrs Beeston plucked out a tissue, gave a loud sniff, and dabbed at the corner of her eye.

In her sleepless times, not that she enjoyed the luxury of many of those, given she usually fell into bed exhausted, Luce was already rehearsing her own "give this wedding lark a miss" speech to Ruby, to circumnavigate that particular minefield, and save herself from what had to be the last piece of hell in a mother's line of duty.

But she couldn't help herself but say, 'you do look amazing,

Steffie. The antique lace is so pretty over the champagne satin.'

Despite the fact that Luce just couldn't see the point in getting over emotional about weddings, by the time they'd all been to hell and back together over the wedding dress, Luce invariably loved her brides and their mums.

'We've done so much work here. All the changes, and then you've dropped three dress sizes or more.' Luce thanked her lucky stars that not every bride who chose one of her one off vintage dresses was going to put both the dress and herself through the wringer in quite the same way as Steffie and Mrs Beeston had done with this one.

'I know we've changed our minds on the shoes three times now.' Steffie said as she rolled her eyes. 'But the first pair of Rachel Simpson ones were so high, and we were sure the second pair were perfect right up until the moment I saw the Charlotte Olympia ones.'

Luce tried not to think that each discarded pair had a price tag in excess of her monthly food spend. And despite the fact that Luce had been on her hands and knees three times realigning this particular roll edged hem, her smile was genuinely warm. 'Let's hope it's third time lucky then.'

What Izzy and Dida couldn't get their heads round, was that someone as anti-marriage as Luce should end up dressing brides. Luce's true feelings on matrimony for herself – no fucking way – were a well-guarded professional secret, and they all kept their mouths firmly zipped for the sake of their joint commercial venture. Dida and Izzy were big on loyalty as well as support, although they did rip the piss out of her too at times, especially about her customer service ideas and her sex life. Definitely no link between the two of those things.

Luce managed her sex life meticulously, and it had nothing at all to do with being a mum. When Ruby went to sleep over with her granny some Fridays, Luce went out on the town, and sometimes brought a well-chosen guy back home. Well chosen as in nice, and not wanting any more than the one night, because no way could Luce allow a guy into her life. She'd never had a relationship, and it wasn't fair to make her mistakes and involve Ruby too. Ruby being used to having Luce to herself was the final decider.

Ollie had been different somehow. He'd come around the back way, almost letting Ruby coax him in, when they'd been thrown together at the cinema. Ollie and Ruby had this perfect understanding, and Luce had known Ollie since Izzy turned up at school in sixth form. But once he dropped firmly on the Ruby side of the fence, that automatically disbarred him from the Friday night area of Luce's life. It was non-negotiable. There was no crossing that divide.

'Okay, I'm finished, Steffie,' Luce put in her last pin, and sat up. 'Try a gentle swirl, and we'll see if it's level.'

Not that she was a religious person, but a tiny part of her was pleading to the god of beaded sashes that this was the last time she was going to be on her hands and knees in front of Steffie's dress.

Luce half closed one eye, and studied the dress as Steffie slid across the carpet, hands clasping a make-believe bouquet in front of her waist.

Luce turned to Mrs Beeston. 'What do you think, Betty?'

'Yes, it's lovely.' Mrs Beeston was dabbing her eyes frantically again, as Steffie stopped in front of the full length mirror.

'Steffie?' Luce, smiled at Steffie's reflection, and Steffie gave the kind of definite nod she'd given so many times before, but Luce *had* to sound optimistic here.

'Well I reckon that's a wrap. I'll get the hand sewing done and you can pop around same time next week if that's okay.' Luce reined in her grin, and mentally punched the air, for now at least. 'Lucky we've still got a couple of weeks before your big day. Fingers crossed we won't need any more changes.' Luce folded out the screen for Steffie to change behind. 'I'm going to miss you once the wedding's over. Wednesday evenings aren't going to be the same without you two and your dress.'

No doubt about it, she'd also miss the money too. Another eeek to that, in the light of this afternoon and the 'For Sale' sign. Steffie and Betty's mind changing had kept her and Ruby in luxuries this last six months. Hell, who was Luce kidding about the luxury part? In reality they'd probably kept them solvent. She'd dreamed of working with vintage clothes ever since she did her final degree show, which she'd somehow dragged together against all the odds a couple of months after Ruby was born, but the income was still precarious.

As she waited for Steffie to change, Luce heard her phone ping, and looked at her watch. 'Hmmm, nine o'clock on the dot. That'll be Dida, sending out the work rota.'

And how much longer would that be happening for? That thought alone was enough to make her heart jump against her rib cage, and kick up the beat rate to double speed. She tried to make her eyes less wide, before Steffie and her mum noticed she was sporting the saucer eyed loon look again. In the morning she'd meet up with Izzy and Dida, and together they'd find a way through this. But before then she had a whole night of worrying to get through. And for the first time since forever, she wished she didn't have to spend the night alone.

5

Wednesday Evening, 4th June

XANDER & IZZY

His building site in Bakewell

A vandal would have been so much less trouble

'At least lads would have legged it by now.' Xander was muttering under his breath, not that it was helping any.

As he rubbed his hands absently on his biceps, he stared at the wobbling girl he'd just dropped onto the ground. Somehow he couldn't shift the warmth of her off his skin. Broken glass might well have been preferable to a stroppy woman, who was so small and weedy she couldn't even climb out of a skip. Given the appalling state of the house, a few more smashed windows would hardly have mattered anyway.

He'd bought what he thought was a house needing slight refurbishment, in an up market area on the outskirts of Bakewell, and thanks to the combined efforts of builders and vandals, he was now the proud owner of what passed at best for a shit heap. Even if Bakewell was on the Telegraph's *Top Ten Places To Live In The UK* list, he was failing to see the attraction himself. Served him right for buying a place for the wrong motives, and shutting up your sister was no kind of good reason. Christina might be kicking his ass big time, but one land registry transaction was never going to transform his life from dysfunctional to socially acceptable. Although he hated to disappoint her, some leaps were too big to make.

He'd given up on relationships, stable friends, and places to live so long ago he'd forgotten what normal was. Glossy women throwing themselves at you came with the territory, when you were in film production and finance, but he had his avoidance tactics honed. One glance at the wasteland of a building site was enough to show anyone that even as a seasoned developer he was currently lacking the necessary motivation to push this large family house renovation to completion on his own behalf, let alone move into it. Now it was actually happening, it was going to be just another place to turn over, the same as all the rest.

'Thanks for that.' The words interrupted his thoughts. Her voice was smaller now, momentarily less objectionable.

Presumably she was referring to him putting her feet back on the ground. She was flapping her hands over her skirt, and the buttons on the front of her dress looked set to bust with every gasp. Worse still, he couldn't take his eyes off her.

Today just got better and better. Not.

'Okay, the show's over.' She said, attempting to straighten herself out. She jutted her chin at him. 'I'll just get my shoes and I'll be off.'

So that was good news. Right now his priority was to get her as far away from here as he could, and fast.

Shoes.

If he grabbed her shoes she could go. To his untrained eye, the pointy yellow heeled shoes he picked up looked completely inappropriate for scrabbling around on a building site, but what

29

did he know?

'There you go.' He picked them up and tossed them in her direction, then turned away quickly.

'Thanks.'

From the corner of his eye he saw her make a lunge to retrieve them.

'Ouch.'

Xander heard her sharp cry, and pivoted in time to see her jack-knife to the ground.

'Okay, what now?' This time he made no attempt to hide his exasperation.

She crouched, then slipped back to sitting and grasped one bare foot, and a mile of thigh slid into view as her skirt bunched-up.

Christ. Not what he needed.

'Damn.' Her fingers were dark as she pulled them away from her foot.

He leaned in for a better look. 'Is that blood?'

Ignoring both him, and the scarlet smears all over the lemon leather, she rammed her shoes on, got up, and began to hobble past him.

'Wait.' Somehow he'd already stepped into her path, and was barring her way. 'Let me take a look?'

As she screwed up her face and hesitated for a minute he suspected she was about to argue. Then she thought better of it, and stuck out her foot.

He'd take that as an okay then. Crouching, he grasped her ankle, and her weight wavered against his arm. 'You might want to grab my shoulder if you don't want to fall over.' Given her scowl, he'd let her decide for herself.

'Right. Now bend your knee so I can see the bottom of your foot.' Brushing away the blood with his thumb, he closed his eyes to the view straight up her skirt and focused on the wound. 'It looks quite deep.'

'I'm fine, it's nothing.' She was rifling through her skirt pocket

30

now, sending a shower of sweet wrappers past his cheek. 'You don't have a hanky do you?'

'Sorry.' He gave a helpless shrug.

'I thought men in suits always carried them.' She let out a snort of disgust, and yanked her ankle away. 'In that case I'll go.'

He was on his knees, her dress so far in his face he was breathing in the scent of fabric conditioner, and more. No matter how much he wanted her gone, no matter how fast his heart was pumping, he couldn't let her go when she was hurt.

'No.' He was already on his feet. 'There's a first aid kit in the car, I'll get you a plaster.'

She hesitated, then began to shake her head.

'How about I'm not taking no for an answer?' Part of his brain was telling him he should never have touched her, and another part was telling him he *had* to touch. 'I'll carry you so you don't get more dirt in the wound.'

'I don't think...'

There were times when you had to overrule an argument, even if it made you look like a caveman. He sprang forward, and this time he grasped her under her arms and knees.

'Hold on tight.' A curiously strong, sweet scent drifted up from her hair. No way was he going to enjoy the feel of her body, hot and heavy, bumping against him with each stride. Judging by her squirms and squawks of protest, she'd decided the same.

He supported her easily with one arm, as he undid the tailgate, and slid her onto the carpeted floor of the Range Rover. 'Can I smell bubble gum?'

'Oh, it's probably my tutti-frutti kiddy de-tangler, I use it when I've got paint in my hair, and I don't have time to wash it.'

'Right.' That information dump left him none the wiser. 'Lean up against the back seat if you like, pretend you're in Holby City...'

He grabbed the green plastic first aid box and flipped it open. He rested her dusty calf on his hand and set about examining the base of her foot before tearing open an antiseptic wipe.

31

'Sorry, this may sting.' He felt her flinch with the first touch, then he began to clean away the blood, determined not to look above her ankle.

'You don't have to do this.'

Xander carried on wiping. 'I'm responsible. You trod on my broken glass after all.'

'But you're a Range Rover driver, and by definition, Range Rover drivers don't know the meaning of responsibility.'

He gave her ankle a tug. 'And you're more stupid than I thought, making comments like that when I've got your foot in my hand.'

She gave a snort and sank back down.

'I don't think you need A & E. There was a lot of blood, but I think an Elastoplast will do the job. Maybe a dinosaur plaster to go with the tutti-frutti?' If he talked seamlessly there would be no space for her belligerent comments.

When she didn't reply, he dared to look directly at her, taking in the flecks of freckles across her nose. Her cheeks were paler than he'd remembered, she almost looked...

Shit. He slapped the Band-Aid into place. 'Are you feeling okay? If you're going to pass out you need to lie flat.' From back here she almost looked green. 'Lie down, breathe deeply, you'll be fine again in a minute.'

Her face was an unearthly white now. He needed to sound reassuring not exasperated, because exasperation would only prolong things.

He gently pushed her back flat, and began to fan her with a map he'd grabbed from the back seat, trying to ignore how small and helpless she looked. He winced as he caught sight of a slice of a bright pink bra between buttons, and rammed his spare hand firmly in his pocket. He flapped the map harder.

'Don't worry, just lie still, and you'll be fine again soon. There's some water here for you to sip when you feel better.'

Jeez, he spent his life avoiding women who were vertical, the last thing he needed was a horizontal one, in the back of his car. She gave a low groan. With any luck, she'd be insulting him again at any moment. He waited, and the silence stretched to what felt like forever. Perhaps conversation would drag her back to consciousness.

'So did you bring anything out of the skip in the end then?'

'I left it...'

A mumble, but at least she was conversing. That was a good sign.

'You're telling me you didn't get whatever you went in for?' He shook his head. All this for nothing. How stupid was that? 'What was it?' He leant in towards her to see if she was moving. The scent of tutti-frutti engulfed him again, but there was another, indefinable, delicious overtone, that set his heart on edge. Warm woman. How long was it since he'd smelled that?

'I was rescuing a cherub.' She was almost coherent again.

'Save a whale, adopt a tiger, rescue a cherub... Would you like some water?'

Xander held his breath as she lifted her head, pushed back her hair, and stuck out a hand to grasp the bottle he was holding towards her.

'Please...'

She lifted the bottle to her lips, and the way the column of her neck moved as she swallowed sent his stomach into spasm. As he waited, he counted broken window panes in the garage, and shut out the knots in his gut. She was sitting up now.

'Stay there.' He wasn't sure that she had any choice about that. 'I won't be long.'

One impulsive thought, and he was heading off towards the skip. At least it was an excuse to put distance between himself and the girl, and good thinking on that. What he didn't understand was the sense that on some deep and hidden level he wanted to please her.

He vaulted over the skip side, found the elusive cherub in the dirt, and twenty seconds later he was putting it into her hand.

'Thanks for that.' She examined the cherub, rubbing the dust off it. 'But why throw it away in the first place?' One coherent reply he could have done without, and, grateful might have worked better than an insolent pout.

'I only hope you think it's worth a cut foot.' He wasn't up for a wastefulness lecture.

She shrugged, and her mouth curved into an involuntary smile as she turned the cherub over in her hand. 'He's beautiful. I love cherubs. Are you sure you don't want him?'

As her face lit up, Xander's pulse raced, and he gave himself a hard mental kick for that. 'No, rubbish really isn't my thing. How come cherubs are always male?'

He watched her smile stretch further at this, and when she turned to look up at him, he caught the smoky blue of her eyes, and something about her raw vulnerability shot him through.

Shifting, she tossed him a grin. 'Not sure, just a fact of angel life.' She began to scramble out of the back of the car.

Result. Or maybe not.

Because now she was pointing at his thigh and wailing. 'Oh no, I've got blood on your trousers...'

'It's nothing.' He looked down at the splodge next to his fly, not sure he could stand the scrutiny.

'I'm really sorry.' Her eyes had locked onto his cock. 'Can I pay for dry cleaning?'

'Really, not a problem.' Except there would be if she didn't stop staring.

She raised her eyes at last and looked at him. 'I'd better be going then. Thanks... for the stuff... and for looking after my foot.'

Was she hesitating? Fleetingly Xander wondered where she was going next, what she was about to do, who she was going to be with. Whatever, it definitely had nothing to do with him, and he really didn't want to know.

'Wait. Do you need a lift anywhere?' He heard himself make this polite query, and was appalled by his sudden reluctance to see her leave. Any excuse to prolong the contact?

34

'Thanks, but I've got my own transport round the corner.' As she limped away she shot a grin over her shoulder. 'In any case I'd rather have my finger nails pulled out than travel in a Range Rover.'

Xander watched her uneven progress across the site. Just as she was about to reach the gateway, he raised his hand, and shouted after her. 'Just don't let this happen again, okay.'

If a voice inside his head was insisting that he wouldn't mind one bit if it happened again, he really wasn't going to listen. Automatically he stooped to pick up the rubbish she'd scattered across the dirt when she'd gone through her pockets earlier. Tidying up was futile, but maybe someone needed to start. There was one tattered card in amongst the sweet papers. *Vintage at the Cinema.* That faded retro font might have come straight from one of his sister Christina's colour boards. The address rang a bell, probably from a property alert. Due to his spending power, he was first in the agents' email firing line when new properties came up. The card was in his pocket before he realised. To pass on to Christina, obviously.

When he looked up again, the girl had reached the tall stone gate post. She turned to give him a last defiant smirk, and then a second later she'd disappeared into the dusk.

6

Thursday Morning, 5th June

DIDA

On the school run

Lunch bags and swear boxes

'It's really important to go as fast as you can, please Lolly.'

There were many times when Dida regretted her decision never to use the word "hurry" in the presence of her children, and this morning was one of them. She just had that idea that if she did include it in her vocabulary she'd over use it to the point where no one would take any notice anyway, and somehow she wanted her kids to have the kind of idyllic life where they didn't ever feel rushed or pressured. This early in the morning her high ideals were still in place for the day, whereas by six o'clock in the evening it was a whole different ball game. She'd barely slept the night before, kept awake by the double adrenalin rush of anger and anxiety about the cinema. Then at six am, just as she was dropping off, a text had come through from Aidie about the cinema sale, that had her wide awake with rage. The derogatory way he talked about Vintage at the Cinema as her "playing at shops" made her want to stamp on his head all over again. The only vaguely positive news was that it didn't sound as if he actually had a buyer in the pipeline, which at least gave them a bit of breathing space. But however shite she was feeling, she must try not to pass her fatigue and irritability on to the kids. She was failing.

'Who the hell thought it was a good idea, or even possible, to set off on a school trip at eight in the morning anyway. It's bloody inhuman.' Damn. Her swear box account for today was already long open and showing a large and unhealthy deficit. 'Lunch boxes are your responsibility. If you forget them, I won't be bringing them. Right, jump into the car, and make it snappy.' Waving her keys in the air as she ran, she clicked the button, and heard the clunk as the car unlocked.

Eric was onto her as he arrived. 'That's your fifteenth swear word this morning.'

Dida bristled. 'You're counting well for someone who was barely awake enough to eat their Weetabix. Remind me what you're doing on this trip?'

Eric gave a shrug as he clambered into the front seat, and pulled out an earphone. 'How should I know, you were the one who was supposed to read the letter.'

Eye roll and head shake to that one. Dida hurled her bag and the lunch boxes onto the seat, then flung open the back door, and shouldered Lolly onto her booster.

Lolly's squawk of protest left Dida's ears ringing. 'Hey mind my wings...'

'Isn't that tiara a bit ornate for school?' Dida grimaced at the Barbie pink crystal clusters as she clicked Lolly's seatbelt into place and made a dash for the driver's seat.

Her daughter's withering stare flagged up the stupidity of the question.

'Hills and caves.' Eric sent her a grin as she pushed the key into the ignition.

'What...?' Sometimes this boy was so random.

'Hills and caves, that's what we're going to see.' He fished a crumpled bit of paper out of his bag. 'The impact of tourism on the physical landscape around Castleton. Remember?'

'Yes, of course.' Not entirely.

Dida swung the car around on the gravel drive, then, as it slid between the gateposts, she braked, flipped down her sun visor mirror, and whipped a lippy out of the door pocket. Regardless of how late they were, her first and last rule of the morning was never to leave home without lippy. While Marilyn Munroe said "Give a girl the right shoes and she will conquer the world", Dida put her faith in lipstick. In her experience you couldn't underestimate the power of a perfectly applied pout. Not so much of the perfect this morning, but it would have to do. This morning she needed every bit of help she could get. Pursing her mouth onto the red slick of Mac Ruby Woo, she flicked the sun visor back up, then glanced into the rear view mirror, for her second affirmation of the day – a flash of the front facade of Alport Towers. That glimpse of tall sash windows, the mellow coursed stone, and the gently carved parapet, never failed to fill her chest with warmth. This house gave her both a direction and an identity, and this one fleeting snapshot, caught in the mirror each time she left home, reminded her why she was carrying on, and somehow rebalanced her. Today more than most she needed that view, to remind her why she was still here, when Aidie was such a bastard.

She drew in a long breath, and then she nosed the car through the monumental gateposts, and out onto the main street of Alport. She'd scoop up Luce at school, and head off to Izzy's to discuss the sale of the cinema. And together, they'd work out a fight strategy.

One lamp post later, Lolly was onto the next thing. 'Mum, can I have a falabella?'

Dida accelerated through the village, momentarily blocking the thought of the local speed vigilantes, twitching their lace curtains. 'What the hell's a falabella?'

'Sixteen swear words.' Eric's triumphant cry morphed to a whine. 'If she's having a falabella, I'm definitely having Black Ops...and a new pair of Vans.'

'No one's having a bloody falabella, okay?' Whatever it was, Dida wasn't about to buy one. Full stop.

'Seventeen...and it's not even half past seven. You may be heading for a swear record here.'

Dida took a deep breath, counted to ten, and reached to push on the stereo. She wasn't used to being under fire from Eric. She viewed the weekdays as ceasefire time. Hopefully Radio One might shut them up. Calvin Harris, she could cope with. As for lyrics about falling in love and lying cheats...

Talking of Aidie, there was something niggling her which she needed to get onto as soon as she had a minute. So many of the names of the women Aidie saw were full of V's, and they all sounded vaguely similar. Logged on her spread sheet like some Soviet birth register, they were bound to become a blur. She'd have checked it last night if she hadn't been so preoccupied, but thinking about it this morning, she had a feeling she might have seen one of the names before. Not that there was anything for her to worry about, it was completely feasible for two women in Lithuania to have the same name. But one area where Aidie was completely reliable, was that he always dated a different woman every time – that was his trademark thing – and she derived some strange kind of security from knowing that he wasn't deviating from the norm.

Dida zoomed through the lights on amber, slowing down as she turned along Derwent Street. Snatching a sideways glance, and checking out the shop windows of Vintage at the Cinema gave her a thrill every time, but this morning the monster For Sale sign hanging high on the wall above the door turned her heart to ice.

'What the hell...?' Three shops further along the road she

jumped on the brakes, and the car behind screeched to a halt inches from her back windscreen. The spray tan shop had changed overnight. Yesterday it was a plain shop front albeit one that was adorned with tacky ads for fast bronzing. Now there was brown paper on the windows, but, way, way worse, was the sign that said *Heart your retro home? Watch this space!*.

'You need to learn more swear words Mum, Miss Raymond in English says repeating yourself is a sign your brain is stagnating.'

'Thanks Eric, I'll bear that in mind.' Ball ache bastard fucking assholes to Miss Raymond. And ditto to whoever was taking over the tanning shop with what looked like more competition, right under their noses. That was all they needed, as if they didn't have enough problems already.

Lolly piped up from the back. 'A falabella would stop *my* brain smating.'

'Definitely not proven, Lolly.' Dida banged the car into first gear, and with a squeal of tyres that left the passing postman on the pavement open mouthed, they roared off in the direction of High Hills School.

Somewhere along the line, preferably later rather than sooner, Dida was going to have to find out for herself what a sodding falabella was.

7

LUCE, DIDA & IZZY

At Izzy's house

It sounds like a plan

'Brace yourself for fighting talk, I hope Izzy's got the coffee on.' Luce took a deep breath, as Dida swung the car into Albert Street, and pulled up next to an ornate lamp post. Luce and Dida got out of the car, turned in at the smart grey gate, and picked their way along the neat herringbone brick path. The lofty Victorian semi's, with their tight plots, and steep patches of garden were popular for divorcees, offering lots of space at half the price of the more desirable family areas. Izzy's mum had landed here years ago, along with her four kids, and this was where they'd stuck.

Knocking on the door, they watched Izzy's shadow approach through the frosted glass. The number eight, cut out on the fanlight etching, impressed Luce whenever she came here, with its clean modern lines, but then Izzy's whole place was like that. It was so obvious that Izzy's absent mum was a whizz at interior design. What's more, Luce never failed to be amazed that Izzy managed to have so many of the rooms full of junk in the course of her renovations, without appearing to make a mess of anything except herself.

'How's you? Half past eight, and already painting I see.' Luce, bobbing towards Izzy's ear, got a blast of candy-sweet scent from her hair. Air kissing might be frowned on, but for today it was the only way to avoid the paint smears on Izzy's cheeks.

'Pretty pink geraniums.' Dida said, strangely quiet this morning, stroking the petals in the planter, as if she was on remote control.

Izzy stood by the open door, ushering them in with the wave of a paintbrush. No doubt she was using work to take her mind of the bigger problems.

'I got the plants from the market in the park yesterday.' Izzy nudged her visitors further into the hall. 'That bright fuscia colour reminded me of the prom dress you made me Luce. That giant peony print was *so* awesome wasn't it?'

Izzy had arrived in sixth form, traumatised by being forced away from her prissy private school. It had taken a month of working with Luce at the local coffee shop before she'd thawed out enough to dare to speak, but shortly after they were best-friends-forever.

Izzy raised an eyebrow at Luce. 'I got up early to paint. I'll tell you about last night's haul later.' As Izzy led them down the stairs to the basement kitchen, the scent of warm baking met them head on. 'Don't worry, the kettle's on, caffeine's on its way.'

'Something smells delish.' Luce was regularly in a state of open mouthed awe at Izzy's drive, and her capacity to obsess over both work and home. Whereas Luce had one small girl and a tiny flat to look after, since Izzy's mum had headed off on her extended four year holiday, Izzy had been in full charge of this big house and her three brothers. And it wasn't just the brothers Izzy ran around after. She invariably ran around after everyone else too, including Luce and Ruby.

Today, most of Izzy's rampant strawberry blonde curls were caught up in a high ponytail that left her dimples on full show. Standing at the work top, in faded T-shirt, thumbs looped through the straps of her gigantic dungarees, she looked particularly child-like and vulnerable, which just showed you shouldn't be taken in by appearances. Izzy's inner Rottweiler was something she channelled on a regular basis.

'New cups on the dresser too I see.' Dida made more distracted comments, as she raked her hands through her hair. 'What's the khaki coloured stuff on the table?'

Izzy picked up a square plate. 'They're Susie Cooper, like you asked for on your email, unearthed from the back of Ollie's garage. I think they came from that house clearance he did with you Luce, just before he left.'

'Possibly.' Luce gave a shrug, and took in the familiar calm shades of the long spacious kitchen, which all looked as if it might have happened entirely by accident, except Luce and Dida both knew better. Luce tried to ignore how it felt a little bit sadder and so much emptier now Ollie wasn't here, with his blustery banter, and boyish grin.

'Wow, lovely detail on this.' Dida ran her hand over the carving on the half pained sideboard which stood on a dust sheet at one end of the long kitchen, then sank onto one of the cream painted chairs.

Three guys to run around after, and Izzy still managed to keep the place immaculate. At least there had been three before Ollie headed off so suddenly. If only Luce had handled things differently, and hadn't stuffed up so spectacularly, he'd be here to help them now. It wasn't that Luce ever felt the need for a guy. But Ollie not being here made her realise that if he had been, she'd have been very grateful for his reassurance. Something about his broad shoulders and laid back attitude had made him a very comfortable person to share her troubles with.

'Thanks for that, I bloody need it.' Dida took the steaming mug Izzy handed her.

'Anyone fancy a cronut? They're what happens when a croissant meets a donut.' Izzy didn't wait for a reply, but slammed two down in front of each of them. 'The holes in the middle are calorie free, and I'm hoping they'll help us with our brain work.' She licked a flake off her finger.

Luce broke off a piece of pastry to nibble. 'These taste amazing.'

'So...' Dida swallowed as Izzy sat down, and her chest heaved under her topaz cashmere cardi.

Luce braced herself as Dida began to speak.

'First I need to say sorry, this fiasco is my fault for so many reasons.' Dida puffed her cheeks out. 'If I hadn't made a fuss about the birthday celebrations, Aidie would never have noticed how well we were doing. And I should never have let the peppercorn rent go on long term, I should have negotiated a proper lease with Aidie a lot earlier. So I'm truly sorry for all those things.'

Izzy's nostrils flared. 'This is like bloody déjà vu, it's taking me right back to when my dad left – it's all about one guy with money, who is calling the shots, and having the control, and the power to take everything away. Only this time instead of my dad screwing the family over, it's Aidie ripping Vintage at the Cinema away from us.' The volume rose as she spat out the words. 'I hated it then, and I hate it now, but this time I'm older, and I'm damned if I'm going down without a fight.'

Luce took in the thunderous look on Izzy's face. The fiery anger, that so often got Izzy into trouble, could be just what they needed.

Izzy was in full rant mode. 'I can't believe I've let it happen again. If anyone should have learned, it's me. All this time I've been congratulating myself, and thinking I was standing on my own two feet, when all the time our happiness was in the hands of someone like Aidie, who only cared about the bottom line and who is now about to take it all away.'

Luce chewed her lip. 'Good points, but we need to move

forwards. So what are we going to do?'

Dida gave a grimace. 'The good news is, I reckon we might have a month or two before Aidie finds a buyer, and after that the conveyance will take time. It's possible that anyone who buys might give us a lease, or, if we put together a really attractive offer, Aidie might even be tempted to give us one himself instead of selling. But we need to get our act together, and we'll need to sort out a business loan.'

'Right.' Izzy and Luce both nodded.

Dida opened her iPad. 'So, we need to pull out all the stops, maximise the income from the business, and get our hands on as much cash as we can.' She leaned back in her chair. 'Any ideas?'

Izzy sat up, and folded her arms through her dungaree straps. 'We need to do everything we can to get more customers in. I'm thinking stand up signs out in the street, pushing the Facebook page, improving the website ... and we could also do free coffee.'

'Great. Free coffee is a brilliant idea. It'll pull people in, and they'll buy cake to go with it too.' Dida's lips, pursing into a determined red line, gave Luce the idea this was only the start.

'I'll need to do more analysis of our figures, for a loan application.' Dida narrowed her eyes. 'It would be great to know the seasonal breakdown of turnover for different types of stock too. That way if we survive long-term, we can make sure we're providing what the customer is searching for. That would work for sales, as well as happy shoppers. How's your customer service thing going Luce?'

Luce looked up. 'Well, what about broadening out and offering extras, like deliveries? There's other stuff we could do too.'

When they'd first moved into the cinema building, they were only the second antique shop on the road, but as more shops selling old stuff opened up, filling the cluster of un-let units on the street, the customers had arrived too.

Luce went on. 'These days Derwent Street on a Saturday afternoon is swarming with thirty somethings with their designer push chairs, out trawling all the shops. We're a retro destination, but we need to make sure the hordes come to us.'

Dida took a swig of coffee. 'What was Ollie's name for them?'

Luce remembered, with a twist in her stomach, how often Ollie had made her laugh about this.

To her relief Izzy chimed in. 'He called them DRRABs. Dressed up, Rabidly Running After Bargains, or something like that.' Izzy gave a grimace. 'Geeks in tweeds and designer specs, scouring the shops for the perfect piece to complement their retro styled lives. Not that I'm knocking them, their tweedy pounds are phenomenal for business.'

Dida tapped her pen on the table. 'The point is, the more we offer people, in terms of service, and variety of what we sell, the more likely they are to spend with us rather than the other shops.' She frowned as she considered. 'That's the other news, this morning I spotted another potential vintage store opening in the tanning place.' She added a huge eye roll. 'I'll send an email to the rest of our crew and see if anyone knows any more.'

Luce hesitated, then decided to take the plunge. 'Talking about quality stock, are you going on a buying trip to France this summer Izzy?'

There was a long silence. Luce knew this was something Izzy usually did with Ollie.

Her friend pulled a face. 'I hadn't thought of going on my own...' She hesitated. 'But I'll see what I can do. In the meantime I promise to keep my motor mouth under control with the customers, although the swear box takings might drop.' She sent Luce a wry grin.

Luce drew in a breath. Pushing the business was going to mean them all pushing themselves out of their comfort zones. It was going to be a challenge, but wasn't challenge supposed to be good for you?

'One more thing...' Dida turned to Luce. 'I know your clothes and textiles do really well, but it would be brilliant if you moved the bridal side out of your flat, and into the cinema. Wouldn't the projection room work brilliantly as a Vintage Bridal Studio?'

Luce opened and closed her mouth without any sound coming out. Her bridal sideline had been growing, but she wasn't sure she was ready for such a big step.

Izzy cut in. 'That's a fabulous idea. It would be great for the business, and for you too Luce.'

'I'm not sure.' Luce was hesitating, although she didn't know why. It was a great opportunity, and another step back towards being a real person, and not just a mum. 'I have some "vintage look" wedding dress designs that are almost ready too, but...' There were times when she kicked herself for not daring to be more ambitious and confident. So much for moving out of their comfort zones.

'I know your bedroom is bursting with wedding dresses, you've definitely got enough.' Izzy grinned at her. 'There's only one way to beat Aidie, and that's by being bloody marvellous, and that's what your vintage bridal line will be Luce. Seize the day, spread your wings, you know you can do it.'

Luce blinked. Maybe she could do it, for the team.

Dida, typing furiously on her iPad, came to the end of what she was writing, and her lips curved into a smile. 'So you could say we've got a plan then.'

'Too right.' Izzy sounded jubilant. 'All we need now is a name.'

Dida's head jerked up. 'For the three of us here, fighting to save what we love?'

'Exactly.' Luce smiled. 'We've been a team for years, but a title would make us stronger somehow.'

Izzy pushed one paint splattered thumb against her chin. 'At half past five this morning, when I was stirring my Farrow and Ball Cinder Rose, it hit me that three of us really are a club.'

Luce grinned. Izzy and her paint colours. But it was a fab idea.

Dida's lips curved into her first smile of the morning. 'It's obvious. We're The Vintage Cinema Club aren't we?'

'That's it.' Izzy thumped her fist on the table so hard the Susie

47

Cooper tea set rattled.

Luce chimed in. 'And we're not going anywhere.'

Dida's mug was already in the air. 'Let's drink to that. Here's to us, here's to The Vintage Cinema Club, and here's to a battle we're going to win...'

There was a clunk as their mugs clashed, and they all shouted.

'To The Vintage Cinema Club!' 'To saving the cinema!'

Luce only hoped they could.

8

Thursday Morning, 5th June

To: THE VINTAGE CINEMA CREW
Subject: RED ALERT

As if we don't have enough problems, there's another home
shop opening in the spray tan place. If anyone hears/knows/
discovers any info please shout IMMEDIATELY. Forewarned
is forearmed. As for "the other problem", Izzy Luce and I,
a.k.a. The Vintage Cinema Club are working on "a plan".

Dida xx

9

Thursday Morning, 5th June

IZZY & LUCE

Vintage at the Cinema.

Flapjacks and post mortems

'That's the outside displays set up, and the geraniums sorted. Oh, and there's no change in the shop along the road.' Izzy wandered back into the old cinema, watering can in hand, wincing slightly as she caught her bad foot on the step, and looked around to see what job to tackle next. 'But as I was saying before, it's just such a waste.'

Izzy knew she was repeating herself, but as Luce seemed miles away, sorting through a huge pile of buttons, the repeating part probably didn't matter too much today. They were still in shock about the cinema, but throwing themselves into work seemed like helping the cause. Izzy had blurted out last night's skip story to Luce when they'd first opened up, but a customer searching for the perfect vintage summer dress came in before Izzy got past the main headlines. Then two elderly ladies had come for coffee whilst they deliberated over which of two art deco lamps to buy. In the end they'd bought both, more power to Dida's chocolate and banana cake, and high five to the free coffee idea.

Izzy moved over to dust a dresser full of plates, and tried another tack. 'Are we going out tomorrow tonight then?'

Luce looked up at last. 'Ruby's going to Dida's, so I'd say that's a yes.' She gave a slow smile. 'So long as I can summon up the energy.'

Now Izzy examined Luce more carefully, she was definitely lacking something in the sparkle department, and it was more than just worry about the cinema. Luce had been flat even before the birthday party.

'That's not like you.' Izzy flicked her duster. 'Whatever happened to Lucy paint-the-town-red Morgan?'

Luce being reluctant to go out had Izzy's alarm bells clanging. This was the girl who'd been dancing on a table as she went into labour, but she was taking pale to a whole new level this morning. Izzy admired the way Luce embraced single motherhood, yet still managed to treat herself to some no strings fun on her fortnightly Friday nights out. Izzy steadfastly refused to follow her friend's lead, as her own disillusion with men, which had begun with her dad, was pushed off the scale by Awful Alastair. And whereas Izzy was short and curvy, edging towards dumpy on a bad day, Luce rocked the whole blonde and delicate thing, despite being five eight and rising. She had the kind of totally uncalculated appeal which had men falling over each other to try to do things for her, and that didn't stop at buying her drinks and taking her to bed. They would literally fight to open doors, carry her shopping, put petrol in her car, and if they put sugar in her tea, they invariably stirred it for her too. Frankly Izzy had never known anything like it. Anyone else with Luce's looks and fan hoards would have been totally insufferable, but Luce's saving grace was her older, even more attractive sister, who had gone on to have a super duper career as a model, and who had given Luce the impression as they were growing up, that Luce wasn't that pretty. As far as Luce was concerned she was just another ordinary girl, who barely noticed the trail of gawping guys she left in her wake.

Luce gave a shrug. 'Too much sewing, and working Saturday morning is what happened...'

Izzy shook her head. 'Jeez, that's what the rota is for. We should never need to come to work after a big night out.'

'True, and ideally I don't work weekends, but I've got two brides booked in for this Saturday, so my mum's having Ruby. Great for business, but...' Luce gave a long sigh.

Izzy jumped in, to ensure Luce didn't wriggle out of what they'd planned earlier. 'I'll help you move your dresses over tomorrow, then you can take those appointments here in the cinema. The projection room will be perfect for you, and we can move some mirrors and a sofa up there too.'

The projection room refurb had been Ollie's last job before he went AWOL, which, to Izzy, although technically not quite correct, was a much more appropriate way to describe a guy of thirty two shoving off with no notice on a so called gap year. To Izzy's mind, gap year implied a lot more planning and forethought, not to mention youth. Despite the fact it had given her the opportunity to expand her own business, on a personal level, the break neck speed of Ollie's departure had left Izzy feeling distinctly huffy.

Rearranging the plates, she gave them a final flick. 'I'm guessing coffee and some of my special flapjack might help?' She made a point of never leaving home without a large supply, given that Dida's cakes were supposedly for customers not staff. Oats and sticky golden syrup, gave the perfect combination of slow release and rocket fuel energy burst. People might laugh at her, but times like this proved how right she was.

Luce gave her friend her first proper grin since they'd arrived. 'Did I ever tell you I love you, babe?'

Izzy gave a laugh and dived off into the kitchen.

* * * *

'So what's this about waste again?'

Izzy peered around the chandelier she was twiddling with. She wasn't big on post mortems, possibly because she never did anything out-there enough to warrant one, but right now she really did need a debriefing with Luce.

'It's a complete waste for an awful guy like him to get looks like that.' Izzy mentally crossed her fingers, hoping for five minutes without interruption from customers, while she got her thoughts straight about the guy with the skip.

'If we're talking about the guy on the building site I may need more flapjack,' Luce said as she sank her teeth into another piece. 'So, just tell me again, how come you knew about these hidden skips in the first place?'

'I spotted some builders coming out of the Butty Box in Bakewell, so I followed them.' Izzy clocked Luce's eyes rolling skywards.

'Have you been hanging round sandwich shops again?' Luce was tutting and giving her a hard stare.

Izzy was well known for stalking anything in overalls and work boots in her mission to find skips. Saving old furniture gave her a warm feeling inside. She knew it wasn't logical to most people, but for Izzy it was a throwback to the time her family collapsed. Back then every item Izzy had rescued represented a step towards domestic stability, and rescuing other people's cast offs, and using them to make the family home pretty had been a way in which she grappled back control in a situation where she had very little. Even last night, when the threat of losing everything they'd worked for was hanging over her, she'd found it immensely soothing to dive into a skip. And that was where her fledgling obsession for all things vintage had begun.

Izzy heard her own voice rise in protest. 'I just happened to notice a builder on the street so I followed him, and hey-presto, there were two skips on his site. It's a cut-throat world out there, I make no apologies for my methods, especially now.'

'You get worse.' Luce shook her head, and wiped a flapjack crumb off her chin. 'So later, when you go back for your stuff, that's when you get stuck in the skip, and meet the fit guy...'

Izzy chimed in. '...the rude one whose looks are wasted on him. You got it.'

Luce's cogs were obviously turning very slowly today.

'So let's get this straight.' Luce licked her finger. 'This spectacular man finds you stuck in his skip, on his building site. He drags you out, looks after you when you cut your foot, then offers you a lift home. So remind me, how does this make him a bad guy, because from where I'm standing he sounds like a great guy who fully deserves to be drop dead gorgeous?'

Izzy pursed her lips, and let out a long breath through her nose. 'You'd need to have been there to understand. We just didn't get on, simple as. And incidentally, he wasn't a normal drop dead G, he was kind of totally exceptional.' Izzy wasn't going to elaborate, especially about on the stomach on fast spin thing.

Luce considered for a moment.

'Izzy, you weren't by any chance being difficult, were you?'

'Me?! Difficult!'

Izzy knew Luce despaired of her tendency to tell it like it was. Cue Luce's special customer service initiative, which everyone knew was directed straight at Izzy, full stop. As far as Izzy was concerned, if a customer was out of line, someone needed to tell them, and to hell with all that customer always being right shit.

'I might have been...slightly stroppy...perhaps.' Izzy decided to come clean. 'But in my defence, he was driving a hideous tank thing...and you know how that winds me up?'

It was all down to one bloody deserting dad, driving off in a blingy four by four, not only leaving the family destitute, but whipping all the assets off to where the divorce courts couldn't touch them. Who wouldn't hate four by fours?

'Does this mean you might be about to get back in the saddle again, Iz?'

Luce had heard enough ranting about Izzy's dad, especially in those sixth form years, when every day brought some new parental horror story, so it was only to be expected that Luce would head onto Luce's favourite soapbox topic – fixing Izzy up with a guy. Somehow, according to Luce, the answer to every problem Izzy had was man-shaped.

'Definitely not.' Years of practice, and Izzy had the excuses ready to roll out. 'After home and work, I have no time for dating. You know this already'

Since her ex, Alastair, Izzy had made her life so full that dates were out of the question, and that was how she liked it. It wasn't because he'd smashed her heart into teensy pieces either. Actually, he hadn't. It was just that in the end, like the guys who drifted through her life before him, he'd been ultimately disappointing in every respect. Given today's reminder that she never wanted to have a guy controlling her life, staying well away from them was doubly important. With her brother Ollie away, and the extra urgency to maximise income, she had to be entirely work focused. Now more than ever.

'I'm constantly pointing out hot guys, who you resolutely ignore.' Luce's tone of complaint lightened. 'It's the first time you've mentioned a man since forever. You can't blame me for encouraging you.'

'Thanks, but no thanks.' Izzy tried to breeze past it. 'Well-spoken really isn't my type.'

'Well-spoken? You can't dismiss a whole section of the popula-tion like that Izzy.' Luce's face was stern then her face cracked into one of her grins. 'I sense a chink in your man repelling armour. Just be sure from now on I'll make it my business to bring any hot guy around to your immediate attention – not that I don't already.' Luce's grin widened. 'So did you find anything good in the skips then?'

Hopefully that was Luce's man hunt lecture over for today. 'It was a brilliant haul. I was up at five working on it. There are some lovely frames, and lots of cupboards and little bits which don't need much doing to them at all before they can go on sale. It's a real boost, especially now.'

It wasn't only the panic over Aidie's threat – since Izzy had taken over Ollie's section as well as her own, she was under pressure. If your brother went off, it was a no brainer that you'd cover for him, but lately she'd felt like she'd been running to stand still.

'If it's quiet today, I can cover here for you this afternoon, so you can get to work at home on all your new finds.' Luce raised her eyebrows. 'Your new stuff will keep things looking fresh here. You'll be doing it for The Vintage Cinema Club.'

Izzy considered. Luce was right, so long as she didn't mind.

'Thanks, I'll do that.' Izzy looked up to see Thom and Declan, two other twenty-something Vintage Crew members, wandering in from the street. 'Here comes the muscle. I'm guessing they'll be here to help you out too, if there's anything you need.'

Meanwhile Izzy had to make sure that mind reading Luce didn't twig exactly how much the awful guy from the building site was distracting her. 'If that's all out here, I'll go and sort out the kitchen.'

Izzy had no idea what was going on with the skip man. Even now could still feel shivers on her skin, where he'd touched her foot. If Luce had the slightest inkling there was still a trace of his smell on Izzy's jacket, and worse, that Izzy kept breathing it in, Izzy would never hear the end of it.

10

Thursday Afternoon, 5th June

Subject: RE: RED ALERT!!!

To Dida and the cinema crew,

Quick tan central has been taken over by someone local called Joe Kerr, according to my mate who works in traffic at the council. Watch this space. Will send more info as I get it, the spies are out,

Ollie, sent from Goa, India

11

Friday Afternoon, 6th June

IZZY

At home

Nirvana

Back home, Izzy dived into her painting dungarees, and pushed her jacket firmly out of reach to stop herself from breathing in the scent of that insufferable man. Under her pillow, in her bedroom, two floors up from the sunny terrace outside the kitchen where she was going to be painting, seemed like the best place. That way she definitely wouldn't be tempted to bury her face in it – two days on and the scent of the hot guy was still vaguely there, and she still wasn't even sure what it was. Paco Rabane? Soap? And a hefty smudge of testosterone, no doubt.

Izzy had spent the morning helping Luce transfer her wedding dresses across to the cinema. Given Luce's reticence, she had decided that direct action was the only way forward to ensure the Bridal Studio idea became a reality. A few well-chosen accessories transformed the projection room, and another part of their Vintage Cinema Club Plan was in place. Luce's pale anxiety had been replaced with flushed excitement by the time Izzy left her.

As far as Izzy was concerned, the fastest way to reach Nirvana, apart from burying your head in fabrics that smelled of someone delectable, was to paint. The moment she had the brush in her hand, the real world around the edges melted out of focus, and all she concentrated on was her brush strokes. It soothed her, it calmed her, it took her to another level. Better still, the giant endorphin boost of satisfaction for whatever transformation she'd just pulled off, made her feel like she was flying. Talk about afterglow. And better still she got paid for the end result. Who wouldn't have been obsessed with it?

Three years ago, when Vintage at the Cinema began, Izzy majored in white and cream and pale grey, but the huge public demand for all things white was turning. Fifties brights were very popular now, and rich aubergines were also going down a storm. As for sludgy pink chairs, they were flying out so fast, she could barely keep up with demand.

Izzy had hauled lots of bits and pieces from her storage shed lower down the garden, onto the terrace, which she had swathed in dust sheets. Sitting in a splash of sunlight, by the open kitchen French windows, she began to paint. Today, despite the air being filled with the scent of early-summer lilac, her mind refused to wander any further than yesterday's grubby building site, and guess who...? It was as if her brain had the whole action replay on repeat. It was like when her younger twin brothers played on their FIFA game on Xbox, and the snippets of commentary kept coming round again and again. Except each time she heard her own voice in her memory, she cringed, and kicked herself, wishing she'd said something different. Talk about torture.

By four o'clock she was exhausted and bemused, but at least she had a satisfying array of transformed tables, cupboards, chairs and frames, drying in the sun. Just looking at them made her insides go all warm with a glow of well-being. Every time she made something perfect again, it reinforced that she was in control of her life. She was just about to head inside to wash her brushes when her phone rang.

She grabbed her handset. 'Luce, shouldn't you be picking up Ruby?'

'No, I'm at work, Ruby and Lolly are at Dida's.' Luce gave a husky laugh. 'And I'm ringing to tell you about a hot guy, at six o'clock.'

Automatically Izzy scanned the horizon, as she did whenever Luce tipped her off about talent in the vicinity. 'Thanks for the heads up, but I'm definitely too far away to appreciate him from here.'

'I'm not talking six o'clock positions.' Luce sounded as if she couldn't believe Izzy hadn't understood. 'Six o' clock is the time for the delivery I've organised for *you* to do. Remember the new initiative? And this delivery is to the yummiest guy ever, who's just walked out of here. I'm setting you up, okay?'

Or how about not okay. Izzy was kicking herself now, but she'd brought this on herself, when she should have known better. The merest mention of a man this morning, and Luce had launched into a full blown "grab a man for Izzy" offensive.

'Why didn't you grab him first?' Izzy queried. It was a fact of life that the male shoppers honed in on Luce, and she was exceptionally up for fun times, so long as it wasn't any more than that. What's more, sometimes flirting sold furniture, simple as.

'I've got someone else in mind for now...' Luce didn't elaborate. 'And to be honest this particular guy didn't seem that interested in me.'

Not interested? Izzy couldn't see that being true. As for whoever Luce was thinking about, Izzy didn't always keep track of the string of guys who Luce saw. Sometimes she hooked up with Josh, who was a dead ringer for Henry Cavill, guaranteed any girl a great time in bed, but shied away from anything more permanent since his mum died. Or Cal, who was similarly gifted, and up for no ties, whilst working past a break up. The others came and went. End of.

A while back it had maybe seemed like Luce was going a bit more crazy than usual on her Friday nights off. But now Izzy came to think of it, lately she'd barely been aware of Luce's liaisons at all. Luce passing over the guy with the delivery was maybe a sign of a bigger trend Izzy had been a) blind and b) stupid, not to notice.

Luce carried on. 'There's only a couple of bedside cupboards to deliver to him, and that small rocking horse of yours.'

'No...' Izzy let out a groan. 'I know I have to sell things, but I love that horse, it'll be a real wrench to let it go.' She knew she shouldn't complain. Sales were sales, and getting attached or sentimental in this business was not an option, especially now.

'A rocking horse is definitely a better bet than a falabella pony.' Luce complained. 'Honestly these falabellas are all we hear about at the moment, Ruby and Lolly are crazy about them. Daisy Benson from school's got one, unfortunately for Dida and me. They're the size of a dog, but they're actually a horse, in perfect miniature detail - they even smell of horse apparently.'

'Sorry, but I'm with Ruby and Lolly on this one, they sound adorable.' Izzy gave a smile.

'Exactly, that's the whole trouble.' Luce let out a wail. 'Daisy's pony is just big enough to pull a little cart with a can of lager in. Ruby isn't so bad, because she knows there's no chance of getting one in the flat, but Lolly's making Dida's life a misery, pleading for one.'

'What a pain.' Izzy had so much admiration for the way Luce handled having a child.

'Anyway, at least some lucky child is getting your rocking horse.' Luce switched back to business. 'I got the impression that yummy guy is looking to buy a lot, which is another reason I offered him one of our new Vintage Cinema Club special deliveries. He left written directions by the till, but remember, you need to be nice to him.' Luce paused, supposedly to emphasise that last point. 'You can thank me for the date you get, later.'

Date? As if. 'As of yesterday morning I'm on my best behaviour, but I should point out I was only ever rude when it was warranted.' Izzy had to stand up for herself on this, and she was having to ignore that Luce wasn't agreeing with her here. 'Fine, I'll be round soon to pick up the things. And try not to devour any more male customers in the meantime.'

Izzy could imagine Luce's eye roll here.

'This one's worth the drive, I promise.' Luce wasn't giving up. 'Stop resisting, go and enjoy the view. If I miss you, I'll see you later in the bar, okay?'

12

Friday Evening, 6th June

IZZY

Ashbourne

Special delivery, fully loaded

Batting along country lanes towards Ashbourne, Izzy was driving a vehicle that was a dead ringer for a dustbin and which was both noisy and bumpy. She suspected an actual dustbin may have been slightly more comfortable than Ollie's battered old Citroen Tube van, affectionately known as Chou-fleur, but at least it had started without a problem. Ollie had spent months on a total rebuild of Chou, working outside in the back lane, with his welding gear. Izzy was very grateful to her brother for leaving her Chou, but at times Izzy found the mechanical idiosyncrasies hard to work with. What with flagging batteries and dying starter motors, leaving home at all was a game of chance. Perhaps the clunky engine had sprung into life without complaint because Chou-fleur appreciated an outing on this sunny evening, and the bursting hawthorn blossom on the hedges, much the same as Izzy did.

She yanked on the wheel, and attempted to coax Chou-fleur round a sharp bend. Steering wasn't that easy in the van, but then braking wasn't her strong point either. But the up side was that with *Vintage at the Cinema, Everything Retro* written in large letters across both the grey sides, Chou-fleur was very distinctive, not to say eye catching, and free mobile advertising was a fab way to spread the word. And if you were entirely without transport, as Izzy had been since her last car died a few months back, you were damned appreciative of anything with an engine and some wheels.

Izzy pulled the scrap of paper with directions on, out of her pocket. She was looking for a large pink house, at the end of Carrington, which was the chocolate-box village north of Ashbourne, which she was driving through now. So much for Luce's promise of jaw-dropping talent here. She didn't want to pre-judge, but surely there was a teensy chance that a man who lived in the only pink house in the place, wasn't going to be interested.

Izzy's eyes widened, and she let out a low whistle, as the pink house came into view. After a slight disagreement with Chou-fleur about the exact course they were going to take as they left the main street, Izzy swung the van through between high gateposts. She made herself ignore the profile of a large four-wheel drive vehicle which passed through her sight-line as she wrestled the van around the sweeping drive, and thought instead about the satisfying scrunch of the tyres on the gravel, as she pulled to a halt in front of an exquisitely pretty Georgian house.

For a minute, Izzy's stomach tightened. Something about the proportions of the facade were so like the house she used to live in, a lifetime ago. She stamped on that thought. No point revisiting the past. Strange how today had raked up a lot of the old pain. She always tried not to think of how things used to be. It was way better to live in the here and now. Their family may have had an amazing home when they were small, but the anguish that the family went through when they left it all behind was something Izzy preferred to blot out entirely.

But her mum had made it okay. In the end. Her beautiful, amazing, lovely, talented mum, had picked up all the pieces, and, with the strength and determination of a superhuman, she had glued them back together again. Their new life was very different from the life they'd left, but, all credit to their mum, it was definitely not worse, and in some ways it was a whole lot truer, and maybe better than what had gone before. Izzy had learned so much, hanging on in there with her mum, as they started again from zero.

And a lot of what she'd learned was that you didn't have to have a house like this pink one, or that other one she'd once lived in, to be happy. Being happy was about many things, and what her mum had taught her was that the last thing on earth being happy was about, was splashing money around. Her mum had made everything alright, and her mum had made everything good again, and now they were all okay. Different yes, but definitely okay.

Once she'd moved on from that thought, she took in the understated grandeur of the house in front of her. Something about the pink stucco made her smile. Without giving herself any time to think about what she was going to find inside, she thumped her shoulder into the van door, which was the only way to guarantee that it opened, and jumped to the ground. Damn. A stab of pain, shooting through the sole of her foot, reminded her she should have been more careful getting down.

The house door was already open a crack, so it looked as if someone was expecting her. She took a deep breath, and imagined the huge potential sales that Luce had been banging on about. Right. Definitely no swearing, regardless of the four by four she'd spotted parked outside. A big house like this would take a lot of filling, which could mean a shed load of sales. Izzy tweaked the corners of her mouth into what she hoped was an acceptably agreeable smile. She tucked in the bit of vest that had accidentally hitched up to reveal her midriff, smoothed down her oversized dungarees, and adjusted the belt that clinched them in at her waist. If she'd realised she was coming anywhere this upmarket, she might have changed into something less paint spattered. As it was, she hadn't wanted to be seen to be making too much of an effort. Much as she appreciated Luce's efforts on her behalf here, going phwoar over hot guys when she and Luce were bored at work was a whole different ball game from being set up. Izzy *really* wasn't interested in joining in that game, no matter how much Luce had her best interests at heart. If her friend was trying to set her up against her will, she sure as hell wasn't going to cooperate by trying to look pretty, hence the 'take me as I am' dungarees. As she walked, a little unevenly, towards the beautiful six panelled front door, with the worn stone surround, her heart did a teensy flutter, not for who she might meet inside, but simply because the doorway was so perfect. She took a moment to admire the deep midnight blue of the paint, the original detailing, and the white china door knob. But the door was already swinging open.

'I've brought a delivery...' Eyes lowered meekly, she heard her own voice, sounding sweet enough to be someone else entirely, and gave the imaginary Luce, who was lurking, barely three feet behind her, a mental thumbs up.

Beyond the doorstep Izzy caught a glimpse of luxurious polished boards. Then bare feet, tanned and male appeared, sticking out below frayed jeans. She assumed this must be HIM. Had she been at all interested in Luce's hunk, she would have called that initial view promising.

'A delivery from Vintage at the Cinema...'

She pressed on with her announcement, as she slowly lifted her gaze, and prepared herself to take in the full glory of what Luce had enthused about, confident that it would leave her completely unmoved.

Her eyes skimmed up impeccably-muscled denim clad thighs. So far so good, Luce, but still not interested. Past a perfect six pack beneath a tattered Superdry t-shirt, beyond a jaw with just a brush of stubble, to a chiselled cheekbone with a tiny scar. Then the words died in her throat, and her smile crashed to the floor, as she met a horribly familiar, dark brown gaze, coming through a flop of straggly brown hair.

'Bloody he...'

Izzy zipped her lips, in a dual effort, to keep her mouth under control, and stop her wildly jolting heart from escaping, and landing somewhere, far along the hallway.

The guy from the skip. The guy who had been hammering round her head all afternoon. And now he had teleported, changed his city suit for something way more casual, and re-appeared, behind the front door of the pink house. And he was looking disgusting. Better than anything Luce could have expressed. Completely disgusting. Completely disgustingly, amazingly awesome. Drop. Dead. Gorgeous.

'Did you know you've got paint on your face?'

He was laid back, cool, laconic even, and giving nothing away through that steady, narrow eyed gaze of his. And shit, shit, shit to the way his impossibly low dusky voice sent shivers scattering down her neck. Her hand had risen in slow motion, and now she was rubbing her cheek, trying desperately to locate the offending paint, but without a mirror there was no chance. And somehow this caveman didn't look at all surprised that the girl who'd been rooting through his skip had rocked up at his very own front door.

'And you've got paint on your vest...'

Another useless observation from him, and definitely no need to look that pleased with himself about it. *Great. Whatever...* She resisted the urge to say the words out loud. Uncomfortable under his scrutiny, she shuffled her shoulders, fiddled with her vest strap, and shoved her hands deep into the pockets of her dungarees.

If he was trying to pull off a snarky smile, he'd just failed. Epically.

'So... Vintage at the Cinema?' He sounded vaguely bad tempered. 'Does this mean I've just bought back what you took from me yesterday?'

From somewhere she found the fire to reply to his taunt.

'Well you'd only have yourself to blame if you had bought everything back – given that you threw it out in the first place.' Shit, she was jutting her chin out, and that meant she was careering towards out-of-line, at a hundred miles an hour. Future business. Right. Keeping that thought firmly in her head, she sweetened her tone. 'But, I'm equally happy to assure you, nothing here was pre-owned by you.' She was cringing at the saccharine here, but the fact it was starting to sound like she was taking the piss, made it easier to carry on. 'And incidentally, I also apologise profusely for any paint in the wrong places, but this is an out of hours delivery, and some of us have actually been working elsewhere before coming here.'

Izzy was wincing at the grammar of the thing, but she hoped this speech would lick the requisite number of boots. Given the teensy size of the items, and the fact that this glowering man had his Range Rover languishing in the drive, she was questioning why she'd had to make this delivery at all. She suppressed her exasperation, and reverted to detached, ultra-professional mode.

'Okay.' Time to bring on the no nonsense approach. 'I'll bring the items from the van, and you can tell me where you'd like me to put them.' If he couldn't have been bothered to stick these few things in the back of his car when he was at the cinema earlier, he was hardly likely to want to carry them in for himself, was he?

She marched across to the van, flung the back doors open, grasped a cupboard, and arrived back at the house. The door was open, but the guy had disappeared, so she dumped the cupboard on the doorstep, and returned to the van for the second one. She was on her way to the house with the rocking horse by the time he re-appeared.

'Just went to get some shoes...'

'Sure.' Damn she shouldn't have said that, even though that might have been the hint of a shamefaced grimace on his face.

'Too late now, this is everything.'

Shit, his feet looked sexy in those flip flops he'd put on. She gave a shudder. Feet, sexy? He grabbed a cupboard, and headed off inside. 'Come in, follow me.' He'd already set off down the hall.

She stepped, tentatively, into a light echoing space, kicking off her converse as she hit the floorboards. Lugging the rocking horse past an elegant staircase, she wrinkled her nose at the sharp smell of paint and newness. If the house had looked impressive from the outside, now she was inside, she could see it was to die for. Not that she would have personally. But she knew high quality when it smacked her in the face. Even though she'd only seen the hall, she could already tell from the impeccable finish, from the plaster-work to the perfect wide oak floorboards to the brushed stainless electrical switches, that this was a stylish, luxurious, money no object renovation.

Izzy knew from working with her mum, that for a finish like this, you were talking serious dosh. As for the man of the house, if his jeans were slipping down over his bum as he made his way into the next hallway, she, for one, was not going to notice.

'It's all newly done.' He offered an unexpected burst of conver-sation over his shoulder as he went. 'All that's left to do now is the furnishing.'

Stating the obvious here, obviously.

Izzy always found it strange plunging into the heart of people's homes as she carried furniture in. One lucky family, moving into this place, although she suspected that houses like this had a lot less to do with luck, and more to do with hard work on someone's part.

The guy thumped down his cupboard on the hallway floor, opposite a doorway.

'Dobbin's going to live here.' He pushed open a wide panelled door, and stepped back, and gestured for Izzy to walk through first with the rocking horse.

She hesitated slightly, trying to take a line through the doorway, to ensure she made it into the room, without knocking into either the paintwork or the customer. Her heart lurched as she arrived in the huge space, and saw toys scattered across the floor.

'A playroom...' Of course, why wouldn't it be a playroom? Her mouth went dry, and her gut dropped. Why the hell did she feel as if she'd been thumped hard in the stomach?

'Are there children?' It came out as a croak, but she had to say something to fill the space until she started breathing again.

She kicked herself for being ridiculous. Of course he'd have children. Why wouldn't he? Hunky, virile, thirty-something men like him did. He was hardly going to live in this big family house on his own was he? She'd had no expectations at all in his direction, so why the hell should it matter to her if he had children or not.

'Two, actually.'

His gravelly confirmation echoed around the room, stamping on the hopes she hadn't even know she'd had. Not just one child then, but two. That was doubly resounding. She took a deep breath, and asked herself why she even cared that he was spoken for. Of course he'd have lovely children, and a beautiful wife. A life and a family to go with the perfect surroundings.

She needed to remind herself. She was making a delivery to a resoundingly unfriendly, arrogant customer, who was too idle to take his own purchases home, who she happened to have encountered the day before. Who was completely and utterly unavailable. It was nothing more, or less, than that.

'I hope Dobbin will be very happy here with them.' She lowered the rocking horse to the floor, gave the horse a pat on his dappled grey velvet rump, tugged his woolly mane for the last time, and turned to leave.

Izzy had to get the hell out of here and fast, before she made any more of a fool of herself. She arrived at the door, expecting the guy to have already melted away down the hall, but instead she came to an abrupt halt, faced with the faded grey of his t-shirt.

'Excuse me.' She looked up at him, close enough to see the stubble on his jaw, the creases on his lips. He smelled just the same as the other day. She shuddered, then reminded herself to get a grip.

He hesitated, staring straight at her, with those eyes full of darkness, his head inclined, for what seemed like an age, as the blood rushed through her ears, and her heart clattered against her chest wall.

Then he cleared his throat loudly.

'S-sorry. I was miles away.' He shook his head, stepped back, and turned to walk down the hall.

Izzy followed him, her hands scrunched into tight fists, her nails digging into her palms, her breath coming in shallow bursts. She had the strangest feeling that he had been about to kiss her back there. It was only half a feeling, the kind that makes you feel totally wrong, and stupid all at the same time. Perhaps she'd completely misread the moment, which she had every reason to have done, given how out of practice she was. The immediate thrill that had pulsed through her was replaced by a seeping revulsion. What a sleaze. A great looking guy who thought he could, literally, have it all. Well that went some way to compensating for the fact that he was taken. Not that she was in the slightest bit interested, because she wasn't. Who would want a guy who behaved like that?

'Thanks anyway.' She hurtled towards the open front door, overtaking him half way down the hall. Remembering Luce's firm instructions, she yanked herself to a halt at the door, and as she shoved her feet into her shoes, she forced out a sickly smile. 'You know where we are if you need anything else.'

Vaguely aware of his slightly bemused expression as he squinted after her, rubbing his chin, she stumbled over the cabinet on the doorstep, and fled for the sanctuary of the van.

71

13

Text from Luce to Izzy:

And...?? Was the hot guy hot enough for u Izzy? Did you nail a date? Need deets!!!! :D xx

*

Text from Izzy to Luce:

Already spoken for xx

*

Text from Luce to Izzy:

OMG!!! Really???? :(xx

*

Text from Izzy to Luce:

Married with two kids. Also loaded. You KNOW I'd never do loaded xx

*

Text from Luce to Izzy:

Eeeek, sorry :/ XX

*

Text from Izzy to Luce:

Give you deets l8r ok? xx

*

Text from Luce to Izzy:

Might give Corks a miss 2nite...need to do Steffie's dress :/ x

*

Text from Izzy to Luce:

Me too. STACK of painting height of house. Catch u 2moz then, hugs xx

*

Text from Luce to Izzy:

(((((HUGS)))) for you 2 Izzyboots :) xx

14

Saturday Afternoon, 7th June

LUCE

The Bridal Suite

Coup de Kerr

'So, do you have anything special in mind?'

Luce put down the mugs on the table next to the chaise lounge, and waited for Jules the bride, who was tentatively flipping through the wedding dresses hanging on the rails. So far, so good, with her very first Bridal Studio appointment. Even though she'd done it lots of times before at her flat, something about being in her own studio made her heart beat really fast. It was scary, yet at the same time, exhilarating.

It was so strange how life worked out. If it hadn't been for The Vintage Cinema Club needing her to do this, she'd never have taken the plunge. As it was, Izzy had kind of fast forwarded it, so Luce hadn't had time to put out the mental anchors, and resist. She hadn't even had the time to feel how far out of her comfort zone she was going, and like so many things, once you were there, it wasn't half as uncomfortable as you thought. In fact now it was done, and she was into her first appointment, she was feeling incredibly happy about it. Whatever happened with Aidie and the cinema, she'd always be able to say she'd had her own Bridal Studio. Luce mentally mouthed OMG, then punched the air with an imaginary fist.

Luce looked back at Jules. She was small, with a neat figure underneath her oversized shirt, and most of the dresses Luce had in stock would be an option for her. And not your everyday bride either, given she'd said no to the chilled cava in champagne flutes, which had been Dida's contribution to Luce's new venture, and opted for tea instead.

'You know I'm really not a wedding-y kind of person.' Jules sank down on the grey velvet chair. 'I hated it the first time around, and at forty it's even worse. I really don't want anything white and pouffy, but the guy I'm marrying loves vintage, so here I am. I really hope you can sort me out.' Jules gave a hopeless shrug, and a sigh.

Oh dear. Somehow Luce was used to more enthusiasm in her brides. 'Is there anything on the rail that catches your eye at all? You're not having a "coup de coeur" moment?'

A lot of brides said they knew instantly, the moment they saw "the dress". Often it was a love at first sight thing, but Luce definitely wasn't sensing any love here.

'To be honest, I can see all those dresses would be beautiful for someone, but for me they're all a bit lacy, or satiny, or beady...' Jules trailed off, and pulled a face.

At least she was being honest. Was this her first anti-wedding bride? If so Luce was completely sympathetic.

'Lace and tulle and beads tend to go with the territory, even for the vintage dresses.' Luce gave her a smile that came right from her heart. 'But don't worry, we can easily do something different.

What kind of wedding are you having?'

Jules took a sip of tea and gave a desperate grimace. 'It sounds awful, but I'd really rather not be doing it at all. I'd much rather just wake up one day and find I'm married, but it's really important to Joe, so here I am.'

'Oh dear.' Luce had never had anyone this reluctant before.

Seeing someone else mortified at the idea of a wedding was almost like looking in a mirror. Somehow it spun her straight back to Ollie, and the way she'd reacted to him, when he'd started suggesting they should take things further. At the time, the idea of Ollie crossing the great metaphorical divide, from being friends, to landing in her bed, had sent her right up in the air. Looking back, she wondered if she hadn't over reacted. There was something about today's bride and her reluctance that reminded Luce of herself. She'd always kept Ollie firmly on the friends side of the divide, not because he wasn't hot, but because she valued his friendship too much to lose it. Breaking her own very rigid rules would not only make things complicated, but there was too much at stake to risk it.

It wasn't as if Ollie had done anything as extreme as proposing marriage, and it hadn't come totally from out of the blue, but it all went horribly pear shaped all the same. What began with hints that he was thinking about her differently, had blown up into a full on explosion one Friday night, as she was leaving Corks Bar with a guy she didn't really give a fig about. The next thing he was saying was he couldn't bear to watch her with other guys any more, and if she didn't want to go out with him, and only him, he was going to have to leave. For Luce, being pushed into a corner only made her more determined not to bend. If Luce had been like Jules, and not over reacted, but instead tried to overcome her fears and work something out with someone she cared a lot about, the outcome might have been very different. Because in the end she'd lost Ollie anyway. And although she'd been desperate to prove to herself she didn't give a damn, now she was just left kicking herself. Very hard.

Jules went on quickly. 'Don't get me wrong, I am happy about getting married really, I just hate being the centre of attention, and it's all a bit last minute, I haven't even got an engagement ring yet. Joe's brother and his wife live in the states, so the ceremony's in Las Vegas. I'm hoping it won't be too brash. It's all tied in with the business Joe and his brother are doing together.'

'I'm sure a Vegas wedding can be tasteful.' Luce tapped her thumb nail on her teeth, sounding a lot more certain of that than she was, and desperately burying thoughts of Ollie back where they belonged. If she was in Jules' place what would she want to wear? 'Lots of brides are going for short dresses now, how would you feel about that? Maybe something with an American swing, like the dresses in Grease?'

Jules' face lit up. 'It was seeing those lovely fifties dresses on the rail downstairs that made me finally book in to see you. I've noticed them every time we've passed on the way to our new shop. Joe's taken the lease on the quick tan place just along the road, do you know the one I mean?'

Luce felt her spine stiffen, and her mouth dropped open. Joe who liked vintage? Wasn't it Joe on Ollie's email? That unexpected email from Ollie that had made her almost drop her phone, and sent her heart leaping right to the other side of the room. Joe, opening a "We heart home" store.

'Err...' Luce tried to act casual. 'You mean the place near the Italian, with brown paper on the window?'

The future Mrs "Heart your retro home – watch this space" was the first customer in her new bridal room? What were the chances of that? All Luce could think was OMG.

'That's the one. Joe's been negotiating for months, but he finally got the keys this week. It's a brilliant area for antique shops isn't it, it's getting quite a name for itself.'

Funny how they'd noticed that too. Not.

'Yes. It certainly is... Great.' Luce faltered. So what now? Should she pump Jules for all she was worth, or was it more professional to just get on with the dress. 'Sounds like we'll be neighbours.' Luce cringed, and threw out a grin. What a corny thing to say. She hurried on. 'You know, if it was me getting married in Vegas, I'd go for a dress like the ones downstairs. I could make you one up in whatever fabric you like, maybe in white or cream. We could always add in a really special belt.'

She'd blurted it out, to fill the space and move the job on, and only then remembered she should never be imposing her own views on her brides. She always tried to let them take the lead. It wasn't even as if what Luce was saying were true, because if Luce *was* actually in Jules' shoes, well, frankly, you wouldn't see her heels for dust. Talk about runaway brides. If it were Luce, she would be legging it faster than the speed of light.

'Wow, that's a fab idea.' Jules, suddenly brighter, sat up straight. 'I love those off the shoulder necklines. One of those would be lovely, and white cotton would be great. We were in the states recently checking out the vintage American things we're going to be importing for the shop here.'

Vintage American. Two words that made Luce's heart plummet. A uniquely different shop was a lot worse than more of the same.

Luce blurted out the first thing that came into her head. 'Wow, GI Joe is having his own Home Store?'

'The whole thing is pretty exciting.' Jules gave a grimace. 'Joe's brother is going to get the stock, and ship it over. You can pick masses of stuff up over there for next to nothing.'

Worse and worse. Luce shuddered at the information dump. 'Wow, it all sounds so amazing. I'll just grab the fabric samples, then you can try some dresses on to check out the sizes. The nipped in waist will really suit you.'

'Thanks.' Jules stood up, and smoothed down her shirt. 'All we need now is a name for the shop. He was thinking of The Diner, but I'm not sure that's right. Come to think of it GI Joe's would be a fabulous name. Would you mind if we used it?'

Oh no. Luce wished she didn't have to say. She was already kicking herself for having said it at all. Shit, shit, shit.

'You can call it whatever you like, really you can.' Right this second Luce wished she had Izzy's ballsy attitude, instead of being wet and weedy, and so damned polite.

'I can't believe that by the end of August I'll be Mrs Kerr. I'm so pleased I came in here. I'm about to find the perfect dress, and I've maybe found a name for the shop too...' Jules looked suddenly doubtful. 'Of course, that's if you don't mind me using what you said.'

Effing hell. How many mental effs could Luce get away with, before she was owing the swear box?

Luce gritted her teeth, and made her voice so light, it was almost a shriek. 'Mind? Of course I don't mind.' It wasn't poor Jules' fault, and at least she'd been decent enough to have a qualm about it. Luce composed herself and smiled at her. 'It must be your lucky day.'

As for Luce, she'd got a sale underway, dropped the clanger of the decade over the rival shop name, and found out a whole bunch of stuff she'd maybe rather not have known. She just wasn't sure how this was going to go down with the rest of the crew.

15

Monday Morning, 9th June

IZZY & LUCE

Vintage at the Cinema

What's in a name – expletives, implosions, and introductions

Subject: Tanning shop

To Dida and the crew,

Just heard on the bush telegraph that the Retro American shop is going to be called GI Joe's - obvious for someone called Joe Kerr, but a damned good name, unfortunately for us. Was hoping they were going to call it American Tan - geddit??

Ollie   Sent from Bangkok, Thailand

'Oh crap bloody asshole shit.' As Luce let out a stream of expletives, her phone smashed down onto the polished teak counter top, bounced off, traced a perfect arc through the air, and landed in a basket of jugs.

Izzy had been propping up the last of the Free Coffee and Bridal Studio signs she'd hurriedly painted yesterday evening, when the email had arrived on her phone, but she had managed to get to the end without going postal. She stared at Luce until her eyes wouldn't go any wider, then blinked, and stared again. What *was* going on? Luce swearing? And not once, but a whole colourful string.

Oh crap bloody asshole shit – what the hell?

'Are you okay sweetie?' Izzy swooped in and put her hand on Luce's wrist. By rights, her first move should be to pass Luce the swear box, given the way Luce jumped on Izzy if she swore in front of the customers, but something told her she needed to cut Luce some slack here.

'No I'm bloody not alright as it happens. Look at that bloody email.' Luce's pale cheeks were uncharacteristically pink.

Izzy flinched. She didn't think she'd heard two bloody's in one of Luce's sentences, ever, not even when she'd been in labour, having Ruby. 'Yes, I *was* looking at the email, isn't it mostly what we know already...?'

Luce hammered her hand on her forehead. 'You don't understand, I was the one who handed them the bloody GI Joe name on a plate. I didn't say before, I was hoping they wouldn't use it. They were going to call it The Diner, which is completely lame, and would have ended up with everyone being cross they weren't being served burgers.'

Izzy raised her eyebrows, then knitted them into a frown. 'Whatever, at least we've got a couple of weeks before they open, that should give time to raise our game. As Ollie says, GI Joe's is a damned good name.'

'That's the other thing...' Luce was taking through gritted teeth

82

here. 'What the hell is bloody Ollie doing in bloody Thailand? I thought he was in Goa.'

'And this matters because...?' As far as Izzy was concerned, all that mattered was that Ollie was away, which meant he wasn't here. He sent her emails now and again, mentioning where he was, but one foreign destination sounded very much like another. That was the thing with far flung places, they only became significant when you were actually there yourself.

Luce's eyes were flashing, and she was tossing her head. 'Everyone knows Thailand's the sex tourist capital of the world. What's the tagline..."Land of Smiles"? Those smiles are for one reason only.'

Luce looked ready to implode.

'I thought Thailand had jungles and pandas?' Izzy was puzzled. It was hardly like Luce to pass judgement, especially on someone who definitely wasn't on her Friday night list. Ollie and Luce hung around with the rest of the crew. They were friends, that was all. Izzy had once seen Ollie flare up on a night out and tell Luce she was worth more than some guy she was about to leave with, but apart from that, as far as Izzy knew, that was it. Izzy knew Ollie had always had a soft spot for Luce, ever since they made friends at school, but Ollie was punching above his weight as far as Luce was concerned.

When Izzy first brought Luce back home, back in the day, which must be twelve years ago now, Ollie had followed Luce around the house like a doe eyed puppy. Even if Luce had laughed a lot at Ollie's jokes, Ollie didn't have the rock star looks to make him a serious contender. That was the one time Izzy had to get fierce with Ollie, and insist that his sister's best friends were totally off limits.

That was when Izzy was sixteen and prickly, and mortified at having to leave her upmarket school, and go into the sixth form at the local comprehensive. Izzy got a job at the coffee shop, to help with the dire family finances, and Luce, who worked there too had seen beyond Izzy's growling, and befriended her. It helped that they were both doing art. A shared, if unhealthy, obsession with Busted and Robbie Williams cemented the deal. Luce, whose calm exterior was a front that hid a riotous sense of humour, considered Izzy, with her rarefied girls' school background, to be underprivileged, and took it upon herself to fast forward Izzy's real world education.

Since they'd all worked together at the cinema, Izzy was aware that Ollie sent Ruby into fits of giggles on a regular basis, and sometimes helped Luce out with babysitting, but as far as she knew, that was the extent of it.

'Apart from anything else, think of the STD's.' Luce's voice was verging on a wail.

If Izzy needed anything to prove Luce was off kilter today, this was it.

'Yuk, this is my brother we're talking about, *please* can we not go there.' Izzy cringed. 'Ollie's old enough, he's miles away. And it's nothing to do with us anyway...Is it?'

Izzy watched, as Luce's mouth froze in the open position, as Izzy posed that last question. It was almost as if someone had put Luce on pause, as if she'd suddenly been reminded it wasn't anything to do with her. Which it wasn't.

'Errrr...' Luce appeared to be struggling to pull herself together here. 'No... You're totally right... I wouldn't have even mentioned it if I wasn't kicking myself over that GI Joe thing.'

Right, Okay. Why might Luce be suddenly interested in Ollie's sex life? It didn't make sense at all. Even if Luce hadn't been out of his league, the kind of one night stands Luce dealt in weren't Ollie's style at all.

Izzy had a sudden thought. 'Have you emailed Ollie at all since he left?'

Luce pulled the corners of her mouth down, and shook her head. 'No.'

Exactly as Izzy imagined. So there was no reason at all for Luce to be getting her thong in a twist over this then.

Izzy's phone beeped, and she looked away from Luce as she opened the text. It was Dida. No surprise there.

GI Joe's? Let's have a Vintage Cinema Club Progress Meeting

Izzy banged off a return text,

Good idea - tomorrow before we open? xx

When Izzy looked up again, Luce was already half way down the cinema, and disappearing behind a large wardrobe.

16

Monday Afternoon, 9th June

IZZY & LUCE

Vintage at the Cinema

Hand signals and hidden messages

Pssst. Stop messing about with cushions and get over here quick. Talent in the grey section x

Izzy hooked the ribbon garland she was hanging on the stepladders, took out her phone, and read the text message from Luce.

Luce could arguably have walked across the shop and said the words to her, in the time it took to send the text, but Luce had been playing hide and seek all morning, and still was this afternoon. Wherever Izzy had been – and actually she'd been everywhere, desperately assessing ways she could make things better – Luce had made sure she was somewhere else. Izzy wasn't quite sure why Luce was avoiding her. It was obviously something sparked by

Ollie's email, but although she wracked her brains, Izzy couldn't imagine what it could be, other than that Luce was feeling mega guilty about the tanning shop name.

As for Luce's messages about talent, after Friday's delivery fiasco, Izzy wasn't sure she wanted anything more to do with Luce's particular brand of talent spotting. The wave of crashing anti-climax that had engulfed Izzy since Friday evening made no sense at all. A guy she had no interest in was flagged up as unavailable, end of story. Right now, there was no space for romance in her schedule, regardless of whichever hot guy popped his head over the parapet. The radical re-styling of the stock she was working on in response to the Vintage Cinema Club crisis was a welcome distraction, that kept her mind off a certain man she shouldn't be thinking about at all.

'What do you want?' Izzy squinted across the store to where Luce had now bobbed up behind the counter. She was handing a receipt to a customer who was propping up a gigantic mirror, by the main desk.

Luce gave a nod in the direction of a monumental grey armoire, and held up five fingers. Izzy got the message. Hot guy, five star rating.

But then Luce flashed her fingers again. And again.

In hand signal terms Izzy read this as a cross between a red alert and a mayday signal. She craned her neck to see, but despite being half way up a ladder, she failed to get a view past the massive butler's pantry piece. Luce's hands were both flapping now, so Izzy untangled herself from the ribbons, climbed down, and went across.

'He's here.' Luce was hissing excitedly. 'Over there by the chiffonnière, looking at the daybeds and the chests of drawers. It's the guy you delivered to.'

Izzy felt her heart fray, and her stomach lurched, and landed somewhere down by her knees 'Forget the hot. I told you, he's taken.'

One unavailable guy elsewhere, she could cope with. Having him dangled under her nose, yet again, seemed downright unfair.

Luce brushed away Izzy's protest. 'Whatever, he's doing just what he did on Friday. Taking pictures on his phone, then talking to someone. Look out, he's turning this way.'

Izzy chewed, narrowing her eyes to get a better view, then as the broad shoulders turned towards her, she snapped her head away.

Luce breathed in Izzy's ear. 'Wow, from the look of pure lust he's just given you, I'd say you're in big trouble, of the best sort. I know a come on when I see one, and that's the hottest one I've seen from twenty yards in ages.'

Izzy plunged down behind the counter.

'Hide if you like, but I'm going to see what's going on.'

Luce might look waif-like, but once she decided something, there was little point in arguing.

Izzy, crouched on the floor, grabbed a strawberry Hubba Bubba from her pocket. Whenever the going got tough, it always helped if she chewed. She began to rearrange the boxes on the shelves under the counter. Now she came to look, there was enough chaos to keep her down here for most of the afternoon. That sounded like half a hot man avoidance plan, but with Luce racing around the store in trouble shooter mode, there was no knowing what might happen. Izzy might be better to make a run for it. Through the slice of space between the counter side, and Luce's rail of dresses, Izzy had a view straight through the shop doorway, to where Chou-fleur was parked, out on the road. She was just contemplating a dash for safety, when Luce's yell echoed across the shop.

'Izzy!'

Shit. What now? Izzy wasn't sure how Luce balling across the shop fitted in with the improved customer service initiative. Izzy didn't move. Sometimes if you stayed completely still, whatever you didn't want to face would go away.

'Izzy...' Luce was definitely persistent. It just goes to show that the quiet ones were always the ones you needed to watch out for.

Hunched down, in the shadows under the counter, it reminded Izzy of how she used to hide under her bed and freeze when she was younger, and hope the shouting would stop when her parents were having their worst slanging matches, in the last few weeks when their mum had decided she wanted out, and family life had imploded.

'Izzy... Where are you?' Luce's voice was nearer now. Definitely not giving up then.

Izzy looked up to see Luce's face peering at her over the edge of the counter.

'There you are.' Luce shook her head, and gave Izzy a scolding scowl. 'Can you come over here right now please, because Xander's interested in buying your bed.'

So it was Xander now. Xander somehow sounded a suitably arrogant enough name for him. As for Luce, she certainly didn't hang about, getting to know people.

To Izzy's horror, a second later there was a blur of choppy brown hair, and then the face of a horribly familiar guy was staring down at her too.

Skip guy? Pink house guy? Hot guy? Or how about none of the above, because this was the original Mr Smoulder, and he appeared to be getting a view right up her dress, yet again.

Izzy grabbed at the folds of her skirt, scrabbling to pull it down. Somehow her footless tights offered very little cover at all the way she was sitting.

'Xander, this is Izzy, she's busy doing a spot of undercover tidying.' Luce beamed down at Izzy. 'I think you two already met.'

Izzy chomped furiously to steady her nerves. Nerves? That would include heart leap frogging out of her chest, too.

'I think we have.' Xander was talking in his best, husky, spine shivering drawl, and gazing down at her. He cocked one superior eyebrow at Izzy, from on high. 'So hello Izzy, or rather, hello, again. Can I smell bubble gum?'

Bubble gum? Cheeky sod. As for her meeting him scrunched

up on the floor, talk about setting off at a disadvantage. Again. Izzy gathered her legs together, and she pushed herself to her feet, but even when she pulled herself up to her full five foot three, and took a deep, deep breath, somehow both Luce and Xander still seemed to tower over her.

'Right. Interested in a bed? Which bed would that be?' And dammit that Izzy had just given a defiant flounce of her skirt. She really didn't want to come across as pouty and head tossing and petulant, but something about this guy made her horribly fighty.

Luce butted in. 'Xander's shopping with a stack of interior magazine pictures on his phone showing exactly what he's wanting, and the bed in your room at home is just what he's looking for. And technically it is for sale, isn't it Izzy, even if you're using it right now? It's the least we can do, given the amount of things Xander needs to buy.'

Luce gave Izzy a fierce "don't you dare refuse, think of the sales" glare, then turned to Xander with one of her more melting smiles. 'We always like to go that extra yard for our customers.'

Izzy's heart sank. She wasn't sure about extra yards, this felt like an extra mile at least, and definitely a mile too far.

But Luce was on a roll here. 'Fine, that's organised then, I'll cover for you here Izzy, whist you whizz Xander round to yours, so he can check it out.'

Izzy gave a groan. 'Fine. Looks like we're going then.'

Not what she wanted, not what she'd planned. But the faster she did it, the sooner it would be over, and, as Luce knew, Izzy could do with turning the bed into cash. She only had it at home because it had been on display for ages and hadn't sold.

As for Xander, the name sounded pretentious enough for the guy. Xander. Still unsmiling. Still unavailable. Still drop dead...

Whatever.

At least that got the introductions out of the way.

17

Monday Afternoon, 9th June

XANDER & IZZY

In his car

The only way is up

'Take a right, then a left, then it's as far up the hill as you can go.'
Xander watched Izzy out of the corner of his eye, waving her
hands, as she rattled off the directions. Izzy was a name that kind
of suited her. Small, dizzy, unpredictable, prone to explosions...
And here she was filling yet another of his cars with the smell of
sticky candy, except this time she was jammed up against him,
in his dad's ancient Aston Martin, as they made their way up an
impossibly steep road, towards high altitude Matlock. Come to
think of it, today the bubblegum was overlaid with a very different
scent that was somehow making him want to inhale incredibly
deeply. Something sweeter than sugar, more like burning roses.
'I'm liking your old car by the way.' She wrapped her arm

around her light tangerine curls, which were flapping wildly in the breeze from the open window.

Typical that she'd like something faded and worn and somewhat past its sell-by date, and he'd have said as much if she hadn't carried on without pausing for breath.

'A lot of people don't realise how cost effective it is to pick up an old banger for a couple of hundred quid, and run it until it dies. It's good to meet someone else who's in on the secret.'

Xander wasn't sure, but she seemed to be gabbling randomly, in fact she'd barely stopped talking for a moment, since they left the shop. But Izzy assuming this was an old banger had Xander suppressing an amused smile, and raising an ironic eyebrow. He'd temporarily liberated the Aston from his dad's vintage collection, simply because it seemed a shame for it never to see the light of day, and frankly his dad had so many cars tucked away, he probably wouldn't miss it.

'I once had a Nissan Micra called Shirley that someone gave me for free. I didn't open the bonnet once, and she lasted for three years, and my younger brothers both drive Corsas, because they're pizza delivery drivers.'

Xander let the words wash over him. Her one sided conversation was going fine without any replies from him.

No point asking himself how exactly he'd let this happen, when he knew it was all his own fault, and that in reality he'd engineered the whole thing. Dropping by first with the lame excuse of checking out the building – at the price it was on offer, it still looked like a good deal – and accidentally building up to buying furniture for The Pink House along the way. Hadn't this been the kind of end result he'd secretly imagined, when he'd dived on the card she dropped on the building site?

It had taken one waft of that crumpled card in front of his sister Christina, currently stuck at home with her leg in plaster, and she'd come up with a long list, just as he'd known she would. Christina always helped him furnish the properties he developed, and more often than not, the hugely profitable corporate lets she organised were a viable alternative to selling properties on. Solid quality, over laid with shabby chic style was currently proving very popular for letting, especially to the American clients. Though shopping by proxy, with a list so long it would scare a props department on a full length feature film, was hardly his idea of fun. In fact it was his all-time nightmare, given how much he hated shopping, but it had been made bearable, by the constant tingle of anticipation, that he might bump into the woman from the skip.

'Don't forget, you're turning left here.'

He had forgotten. 'Fine.'

When Izzy had actually turned up with the delivery on Friday, the shock had sent his pulse off the scale. But mixed in with the whole crazy thrill that he'd found her, there was a kind of horror at what he was doing, an anger with himself. If women pursued him, he always pushed them away, so he had no idea at all why he was technically being the pursuer here, other than the inexplicable attraction that coursed through him every time he saw her. Like the way his stomach was tied in knots now made no sense at all, given she wasn't even his type. And it really wasn't like him to be this out of control.

'The van I drive is called Chou-fleur, but it's my other brother's, not mine. By rights it should have died years ago, and it would have done if my brother hadn't been a whizz at metalwork.'

Sounded like she had a whole lot of brothers. On a need to know basis, Xander didn't need to listen to any of this. As for chasing around after a woman who made his car smell like a cross between a sweet emporium and a perfume counter, who seemed to flip from obnoxious to vulnerable in seconds...

'Turn right, watch out for parked cars, it's narrow.' She was barking the orders now. 'I don't usually take people to see stock at home, but we're in the middle of a special customer service initiative, so you're in luck.'

'So you said in the shop.' Xander gave a sigh. Because that was

93

another thing. How they'd got from there to here, on the basis of one picture of a bed, in one of Christina's magazines, he didn't know, although the main guest bedroom at The Pink House was still in need of furnishing, so if there really was a bed it could only be good. 'Would that be customer service, as in no skip too deep to search in?'

'Very funny. Not.' She gave a disgusted sniff. 'Talking about skips, where's your gas guzzling tank today?'

Xander gave a "whatever" shrug. Looked like someone came out without their sense of humour this morning.

'It went back to the film company that owns it.' Easy as. That was one Range Rover off his conscience. That should take the huff out of her.

'Do you work in film then?' She picked him straight up on that.

'Yep, I'm a Producer.' Dropped in. Casually. And even though he might sound like an arse, he never got tired of saying it.

'Which means...?'

He didn't usually have to explain, most people got it first time around. 'If I can persuade a whole lot of people to do everything I want them to, and make the books balance, the end result is a film.' And sounding even more like an arse with every word.

'So that's where you get your habit of ordering people around?'

Whoa. People were usually way more impressed than this, not to mention complimentary.

'My personal charm usually gives great results.' Not that it was cutting it today.

'Nothing at all to do with being a control freak then?' Her snort managed to be derisory and dismissive, simultaneously.

'You could say I'm a bit of an entrepreneur I guess.' Something about this straight talking woman told him it might be best to admit to being a secret shopper, with an interest in the cinema building, and now was as good a time as any. 'And I sometimes dabble in property development too.' That pretty much covered it.

'Entrepreneur?' Her voice rose half way to a shriek. 'What kind of poncey claim is that?'

He'd walked into that, and she had a point. He shouldn't have expected anything lass derogatory.

He gave a half laugh. 'It comes from the French word enterprise. It simply means I inject cash into projects, and then extract it later, along with a healthy profit.'

The huge snort she gave had to be disgust. 'I knew it.' All wrapped up with a derogatory sneer that told him she was looking down on him, as if he was some kind of worm.

All the more reason for him to clear this up now. 'The main reason I was in the cinema on Friday, was to look at the building.' He kept his voice calm and level.

'What?' A banshee would have been proud of the yell she let out.

He winced. This woman was certainly the queen of overreaction.

Tapping his fingers on the steering wheel was definitely not a sign of nerves. 'Early tip off from the agent, it would make an ideal space for a gym and upmarket coffee shop.' It had definitely been best to come clean, if this was her reaction.

'A high end gym? Why does that not surprise me?' She made a strange choking noise. 'It's about as acceptable as fracking in the park, but you've probably considered that too.'

He gave a shrug. 'I was actually also thinking it would be pretty awesome to re-open it as a retro cinema. They're very popular now. But you can't fight it, if it isn't me, it'll be someone else. '

'Well see about a fight.' Her brow descended like a thunder-cloud, and she closed her hands into tight fists. 'Pull in anywhere along here.'

Xander reeled. Nothing like touching a nerve. Given the freckles on her cheeks were now clearly visible, she was definitely several shades paler than when they set off, and he bit back the guilt about that. The thought of upsetting her made his stomach squelch in the strangest, most uncomfortable kind of way. As for parking, good luck with that one.

'What is this, boy racer central?' Given the line of cars with spoilers, fat exhausts and decals, he might have arrived in a scene from a Fast and Furious movie.

'It's band practice this morning.' She gave an "I don't give a damn" shrug, jutting her chin so far out it almost grazed the windscreen. 'Take it or leave it.'

Xander squeezed the car into the tightest of spaces at the end of the road. Part of him had jumped to grab a view of this woman's home, when the blond girl had offered the bed viewing, thinking it was a fast forward way of finding out about who she was. Now he was here, running behind her along the row of semis, and having upset her a lot more than he'd anticipated with his attempt to be honest, he was starting to feel like a gatecrasher. Dammit that his eyes had widened in surprise, when she turned into the gate of the smartest house on the row. Somehow it didn't fit with the girl in front of him, with, as he was noticing now he was standing behind her waiting for her to open the door, her ginger waves full of tangles.

'Have you brushed your hair today?'

That thought turned itself into words, and was out before he could stop it. Now who was gabbling stupidly?

'What's that got to do with anything?' Hand on the door handle, she jerked around, and stared over her shoulder at him accusingly.

Shit. He opened and closed his mouth. 'Nothing, it was just a random, passing thought.' That obviously shouldn't have happened.

'You might as well come in now you're here.' If this was customer service, this customer's reaction was "could try harder". Although with the bombshell he'd just dropped inadvertently, it was understandable.

As she swept along in front of him, he sauntered into a neat, white, hallway, with coir flooring, acres of white walls, pale grey skirting boards, and a smell of new paint. There was just enough judiciously arranged vintage paraphernalia to carry off the effect of being simultaneously stylish and homely, with clever splashes of colour that stopped it from feeling clinical. He had no idea why he was pulled up short by all this classy neatness. Through an open door he caught a vista of a crowd of pink painted chairs on a dust sheet.

'Hold on, what's with the Barbie chairs?'

Izzy carried on up the stairs. 'Last night's paint job.'

He called up after her. 'Mind if I take some quick pictures?' Even though he hated this kind of stuff, he knew they were ideal for Christina's up market rental clients.

'Help yourself.' Izzy paused on the bottom step, to wait for him.

Xander pulled out his phone, and began to click. A dozen mismatched dusky pink chairs. Regardless of how the bed worked out Christina was going to be ecstatic about these. Xander could see the edges of another perfect, vintage chic room, underneath the dust sheets.

How come Izzy had such an impeccable place here?

As he came back into the hall, the jarring noise of a sudden twangy chord drifted down from somewhere much higher in the house.

Izzy was waiting for him, swinging on the newel post, at the bottom of the stairs. 'Sounds like the band are tuning up. Festering Flesh are death metal, and they've been known to burst ear drums. It's an occupational hazard of living with brothers.' The wry grin that somehow escaped from her came as a relief.

Then she began to move on up, talking as she went. 'And no I haven't brushed my hair, do you have a problem with that?'

Problem? Him? Watching the way the hem of her dress danced around on the back of her thighs, as she took the steps two at a time, reminded him he might have had a problem – if he stopped to think. As it was he'd decided the only way to deal with this was to stop thinking completely, get the whole damned thing over as fast as he could, and get the hell out.

18

Monday Afternoon, 9th June

IZZY & XANDER

In her bedroom

Forty shades of white

Izzy was trying to ignore the fluttering in her chest. She'd thought at first that Xander looked as uncomfortable as she was, but then he'd gone and proved her totally wrong by marching on in and taking pictures of her chairs, as if he was totally at home. Nothing like a man on a mission. As for him checking out the cinema building, that shock would have made her vomit, if she hadn't been so furious. As it was, it made it all the more urgent to extract every penny from him that they could.

Grimly she made her way along the landing, yelling up the attic stairs to the band.

'There's freshly baked cupcakes in the kitchen guys, and fresh orange juice. Help yourselves.'

Xander had reached the top of the stairs now. Did he raise his eyebrows expectantly at the mention of refreshments? So much for free coffee. Looks like this taker was ready to extract everything he could. If he was expecting juice and cupcakes too he could forget it. Customer service had its limits, and she was already way beyond the call of duty. Later he'd be screwing her down on price too. That's what bastards like him did, wasn't it? If he thought she was going to give stuff away, he could take a running jump. Except they needed the sales more than ever now, if the pressure was on so soon from a potential buyer.

Given the racket that was about to begin over their heads, she shot him a grimace of apology. 'We need to make this fast, no way you want to hear the boys getting musical.' In other words, hurry the fuck up. Please. As far as she was concerned she couldn't get this over fast enough.

Xander, apparently not getting the hurry up message at all, paused, and ran his hand along the rail of the balustrade. 'It's all very white in here.' He sounded puzzled.

'I like white.' Izzy's nose shot high in immediate defiance, even though she hadn't meant it to. 'People think white is just one colour, but there are forty different shades of white on my favourite colour chart.'

He lingered, looking at the pictures, hanging in their recycled frames. Not everyone got the multi-layered collages of scraps of fabric and paper that Izzy made.

He pulled out his phone again. 'Christina would love your pictures, do you mind if I...?'

Izzy's chest lurched. So it was "Christina" now. Not just a wife, but a wife called Christina, which made her even more real, and that could only be a good thing. Izzy really needed to get her head round this wife thing, and fast, although what was she thinking anyway, having the hots for a guy who got his rocks off with profit extraction. Confirmation of what she'd suspected all along should have been enough to send an ice shower cascading onto her lust,

99

but the electrical charges coming off him, zapping around like lightning in a summer storm, were completely wiping out the chill.

'You carry on, take all the pictures you want.' Now they'd got this far, there was little point in refusing, however uncomfortable it made her.

She sidled into the bedroom, and wafted past the dressmaker's dummy and the chaise longue to look out of the slatted blinds at the window, in an effort to detach herself from what was happening. A man in her bedroom. It had to be light years since that had happened.

'The bed's in here, when you're ready...' Sometime today would be good, ideally. After all, she was supposed to be at work.

The tell-tale creak of the floorboards outside the door, told her that Xander was almost here. Fleetingly, she allowed herself to imagine his tanned feet, not in the scuffed leather deck shoes he was wearing today, but flat and bare and beautiful, on her white painted floor boards. And then she gave herself a mental kick. By the time Xander wandered in she'd blocked that thought, and dispatched it for good.

'Great room.' He stared around slowly, then nodded as his eyes came to rest on the bed. 'And this is brilliant. Exactly what Christina wants. Are you okay about photos in here? I'm sure when she sees it, Christina will want the whole room.'

Phone at the ready. Again. And why did Izzy feel so exposed, when he was simply staring at her bed, and worse still when her gaze accidentally collided with his, and stuck.

She braced herself, ripped her eyes away from his, and hesitated, not entirely sure that she was comfortable with the thought of Christina swallowing up huge chunks of her home, but she bashed on regardless.

'Okay, here's the low-down on the bed – it's not that old, but I've painted it to look as if it is. That way it's less rickety than an old one, and also less expensive. I'm assuming it's just the frame you're buying, then you can add your own mattress to suit.'

She was struggling with the idea of Christina hi-jacking her whole bedroom.

Xander narrowed his eyes. 'It's just the style Christina was looking for, and age isn't that important. Sit on it for me, will you?'

His hand was resting idly on the cabbage-rose print quilt cover. He was close enough for her to see the dark hairs on his forearm. It sounded like another one of his orders.

'Sorry?' She hid her shock behind an impassive expression. What was it with these well-spoken people who were too arrogant to say please? Did they really teach you to have your head so far up your arse at public school? She gave an involuntary shudder. If her dad hadn't left, and she hadn't crashed down in the real world at the comprehensive, she might have ended up like that. Funny how as she got older, she was more and more thankful for her life working out the way it had.

'Sit on the bed, or better still, kneel and bounce, unless you can think of a better way for me to gauge the creak level. I'll be dead in the water if I turn up with a squeaky bed.'

Izzy shuddered. That couldn't be a hint of smoulder in his eyes...could it? There were times when his eyes were so dark they were hard to read. She wondered how happy the much-mentioned Christina would be, if she knew her husband was in another woman's bedroom, discussing creak level, shooting glances like that. As for herself, she was pretty far out of her comfort zone here.

An ear-splitting roar crashed the silence. Yay. That would be the start of Festering Flesh's latest rehearsal. Izzy had never been so pleased to hear death metal. No point in pursuing creak tests now. She gestured to Xander wildly, pointing towards the door.

*   *   *   *

Izzy was hugely relieved to take refuge outside. In the dappled shade of the roadside cherry trees, was a great place to discuss any

101

other business. She was pleased she'd had a good excuse not to offer him coffee. Given she'd already spent too much time thrown together with this moody guy who she found strangely disturbing on every level, she didn't need the strain of entertaining him in her kitchen. She remembered hearing, that in some far flung places, natives refused to have their photographs taken, because they believed the camera would steal their souls. After the last twenty minutes, she appreciated how they felt.

Xander was on the phone by the car, talking to Christina, discussing the pictures he'd sent her, talking about which part of Izzy's life they wanted to buy. Izzy kicked herself for her reluctance. Hell, with the Vintage Cinema Club up to their necks in trouble, she was in no position to be choosy. She should be welcoming anything which was going to lead to sales.

Xander called to her across the pavement. 'Okay, jump in the car, and I'll run you back to the shop. I'll explain what we need as we go.'

Izzy got in without a thought. What had he said, about relying on his personal charm to achieve results, she reflected, as they roared off back into town? His methods had the finesse of an earth shifter, but here she was, back in the car, listening, taking mental notes, just like he'd told her to do.

'Okay, I hope you've got a good memory here, because you're going to need it. First, Christina would definitely like the daybeds I was looking at, back at the shop. And all your pink chairs. They'll be great for the summer house, along with a large round table please, if you can find one, and a floral cloth to go with it.'

What? Izzy could barely believe what she was hearing.

'All twelve of the pink chairs?' Izzy gave a squawk.

People bought pink chairs singly, to go in bedrooms. Who bought a dozen all at once? But obviously this was some kind of mega bulk buy, given Xander was still in full flow.

'Yes. And all the cream chests and all the other things in the room with the pink chairs.'

Bingo. The alarm clanged in Izzy's head. And he'd just done it. He was buying things she'd hauled out of his first skip, albeit now transformed to shades of white and grey and pink. And everything in the room? Who were these people, buying roomfuls of pieces rather than single pieces?

'Are you sure? It seems rather a lot?'

Xander wrenched the car around a tight corner, and Izzy heard the tyres squeal in protest. She wanted to squeal like that herself, but faced with Xander's seemingly unstoppable buying tirade, she didn't dare.

'Big house to fill, not much time to do it, and Christina adores your "look". Personally, I don't go for florals or frills, or ratty-tatty rubbish come to that. But then, what do I know?'

Say it like it is, why don't you? Izzy reeled. What a thing to have a hunk of a husband, who adored you so much, he'd let you decorate with the fraying and the florals he hated.

'Hardly the best time for her to break her ankle, but hey ho. I'm doing my best to stand in.'

So that explained it. Izzy gave a sigh, and tried to think of something suitably sympathetic to say. 'What a shame.' That seemed to pretty much cover the whole damned situation.

'Thanks to your customer service being above and beyond, she's managing quite well by phone. She'd definitely like the bed from your bedroom, squeaks, or no squeaks...'

Izzy suspected he might have been taking the piss early on there, and he might also have paused for her to giggle at this point, but she was in no mood to laugh.

'And she'd like everything else from your bedroom you are willing to sell. As for the things you can't spare, she'd like replacement items which are as close as possible to the originals, right down to the last picture, scarf and string of beads. Oh and an extra wardrobe, as large as possible, to fit in with whatever you select. Have you got all that?'

The gasp Izzy let out was more one of dismay, than ecstasy. She knew she should be doing back flips of excitement on the business's behalf. This was going to run into thousands, but somehow the hefty order left her cold. It felt more like someone was taking over her own persona.

'Right. What about timescale?' She floundered to find her cool professional self, but that person appeared to have gone A.W.O.L. around the time they left the cinema. Was it even possible that it was only half an hour ago?

'We were rather hoping that as much of it as possible would be ready for collection by tomorrow evening. It's just a matter of sorting out the items. You should be able to manage that.'

Izzy flapped down her panic. No way should her stomach screwed up like that, just because she heard him say the word "we". And neither should she be letting her eyes linger on his knuckles on the steering wheel. He sounded scarily efficient, and horribly demanding. That's how people like him were. That's how they made their money.

'I should be able to arrange it.' It was a reckless promise, made in a voice a hundred times lighter than her heart.

He carried on, seamlessly. 'I'll send a van from the production company. They'll pack it all when they pick it up. Oh, and it goes without saying that we'll be expecting to pay top whack for this kind of service, so don't worry about the bill.'

That had her sitting like a gulping gold fish. What happened to nailing her down on price?

'Are you sure about the van?' Izzy looked doubtful. Somehow this didn't fit in at all with her having to dash across to The Pink House in Ashbourne on Friday with two bedside tables.

'If you're thinking of last week's delivery, I could have easily thrown those things in the car, but the blonde girl insisted you would bring them. Said something about you wanting to say "goodbye" to the rocking horse?'

Izzy grunted. Silly how she'd assumed that the delivery had been down to him, when it had been Luce's fault all along. She'd deal with Luce later, if she ever had a minute, which to be honest, given what she had to arrange, sounded doubtful. Izzy took a deep breath, and leaned back, against the cracked leather seats, as the car swooped down the steep downhill sections, leaving her stomach somewhere much higher up the bank.

Wow. Great. She'd made the sale of her dreams, and there really wasn't a catch. She should be dancing here. This was exactly what she, Dida and Luce needed.

Xander accelerated round the roundabout, went through the lights at amber, tore down the road, and screeched to a halt outside the cinema.

'There's only one stipulation.' He turned towards her, ominously. 'And this one's non-negotiable.'

Izzy held her breath.

'We need you to come to The Pink House, to help me arrange it all.'

Izzy's stomach landed back into place with a jolt.

'I'll pay top rates for your time.' Xander carried on. 'Usually Christina's department, but seeing as she can't do it, I'll have to make do with you.'

19

Tuesday Morning, 10th June

LUCE, DIDA & IZZY

Luce's flat

Happy shoppers and sweating men

'It's fine for us to come to yours instead of the cinema Luce, it's only round the corner. Hey, nice frocks...' Izzy stopped and stroked the flowery dresses hanging in Luce's hallway, then made a dive for the living room.

This morning Izzy looked even more dishevelled than usual, and Luce could tell from her slightly far away expression, that she wasn't entirely in the room.

'If you'd been here earlier, I'd have got you to try them.' Luce, balancing a tray of tea and mugs, followed her in to find Dida settled deep into the sofa.

And it wasn't like Izzy to be late either. Maybe the huge order she got yesterday was stressing her out.

'How's Ruby anyway?' Izzy perched on the edge of the tub chair, as if she wasn't fully committed to staying.

'Ruby's got the squits, nothing serious, but I thought I'd better keep her at home.' Luce passed Izzy a tea. 'She's curled up in my bed watching Peppa Pig on my laptop, it must be riveting, or she'd have been through by now.' Luce handed a mug to Dida, and passed around the flapjack box that Izzy had brought – go Izzy, never without flapjack – and pulled up the foot stool that doubled as a table, and sat on it.

'So, how was it with Aidie at the weekend?' Luce had to ask.

'Bloody awful.' Dida rolled her eyes. 'He refused to discuss the cinema, and spent the whole weekend huffing on this exercise bike he had delivered, which is linked into a computer screen. I swear he was only seconds away from cardiac arrest by Sunday evening. He was so knackered, I never got the chance to punish him by withholding sex, because he never asked, and that's very unlike him.' She paused to pull a face. 'He's got some personal trainer called Elvira apparently, although Aidie being into fitness is unlikely to last.'

Luce and Izzy exchanged frowns. They had no idea how Dida stuck it out with Aidie. 'So no news at all on the sale then?'

'Nope.' Dida gave a helpless grimace, and waved a piece of flapjack, seemingly anxious to move the subject on. 'So what about the GI Joe's thing?' Dida frowned.

So far Izzy was the only one who knew that Luce had provided their main competitor with their name, and Luce was hoping it would stay that way.

'We'll have to see once they open, and pray that they attract a whole new set of customers rather than poaching ours.' Luce pondered. 'Obviously we need to redouble our efforts to be the best we can, especially after Izzy's news yesterday.'

Izzy gave a dramatic groan. 'Xander the bloody entrepreneur, eyeing up the building. I knew he was bad news.'

Dida tapped a pen on her teeth. 'His plan about the retro

cinema gave me an idea though. Maybe we could play old films on a laptop, and project them onto the back wall. That would be something different. I'm sure we've got the necessary gadgetry at home somewhere.'

'Wow, awesome idea. That'll be so cool.' Luce was trying to put a positive spin on Izzy's dismay. 'Well at least you managed to get a massive order out of the man.'

Dida joined in the praise. 'Yeah, that was a huge amount you sold, all on the basis of taking one guy to see stuff at home. It shows that extra customer service really pays off, and now you're getting paid to style too, it's brilliant.'

Luce couldn't help smile at Izzy's scowl.

Izzy groaned again. 'From where I stand, apart from the cash, it's bad news all the way. You all know I hate dealing with customers, *and* I'm crap at it. And it's way worse when they're in their own homes. Clients and their "attitude"...' Izzy made a mocking comma sign with her fingers. '...they drive me right round the bend. Let's face it, bloody clients are the whole reason I didn't take over my mum's business.'

'But this is totally different.' Dida rubbed her chin thoughtfully. 'Your mum's interior design projects involved builders and decorators, and they're such a pain to have around, frankly there's no wonder the clients get grumpy. But with this, all you are offering is to style a room, with stock you supply from Vintage at the Cinema.' Dida was thinking as she spoke, and sounding more and more excited. 'It's simple, and it's brilliant. If we can offer that whole "sell and style" package, we get to provide everything, and we squeeze out the opposition altogether.'

Izzy slumped in her seat. 'Maybe...'

'And the other great thing is...' Dida raised her eyebrows. 'If you're working with Xander, at least you can keep an eye on him, keep tabs on what he's up to. You know what they say, keep your friends close, and your enemies closer...' She was wiggling her eyebrows now.

Luce watched Izzy's expression turn from mildly grumpy to pure horror as Dida spoke.

Izzy broke in. 'You surely aren't suggesting...?'

Dida blew out her cheeks. 'You just need to hang on in there with Xander for as long as you can. Desperate times and all that. The closer to him you are, the more likely he is to tell you what his intentions are.'

Izzy's squawk of protest was long and loud. 'But he's a profiteer and a rich git, not to mention total dickhead. If he was on a desert island I'd have to take the swimming option.'

Luce chewed her cheek to keep herself from smiling. However much she was protesting, Izzy was definitely more susceptible to Xander's magnetism than she was admitting. Swimming? More likely she'd be climbing into his hammock.

Luce let her smile go. 'You might have to do it for the sake of The Vintage Cinema Club.'

Izzy gave that the eye roll it deserved.

Dida broke in again. 'Well, we mustn't forget Luce's bridal thing is bringing in new clients too.' Obviously moving on swiftly here. 'It's funny, but for you two, since the start Vintage at the Cinema has been about pushing yourselves, and developing your talents and your careers, whereas for me, it's always been a way of escaping from my less than perfect home life.'

Luce knew that was true. Even when they met on the art foundation course, whilst she and Izzy were honing their artistic futures, Dida was only there because she was climbing the walls at home every day, looking after a toddler.

Dida carried on. 'The cinema crisis has resulted in you two making another quantum leap with your career achievements. But what it's done for me is to pull my relationship with Aidie into focus. For the last three years I've put up with things at home because Vintage at the Cinema has taken my mind off all my problems. But what Aidie's doing now changes everything. You two are daring to do new things. Maybe it's time for me to stop burying my head in the sand, and dare to change some things in my life too.' Dida gave a wistful sigh.

'Oh Dida, we're both here for you.' Izzy reached over and squeezed Dida's arm.

Dida drew in a breath. 'The trouble is, I've always been a bit of a material girl. I married Aidie because I knew he would give me the lifestyle I wanted, I just hadn't counted on the downside of living with a tyrant in the long term. I've always been so certain I was going to hang on in there however hard it got, but now I'm not so sure.'

Luce took a deep breath at that. That was pretty monumental for Dida who so far had soaked up everything Aidie threw at her, with barely a complaint. But they were in this together, and she and Izzy would support her, as best they could. Strange how Dida was the one with the massive house, stuffed with possessions, and the highest standard of living, not to mention the husband, and yet she was the one who, when you scratched the surface – in fact even when you didn't – was most unhappy.

Luce looked up, to see Ruby peeping round the edge of the door. 'Okay Rubes?'

Ruby came in with a beam, waving a card in her hand. 'Look what the postman just brought, please can you help me read it?'

A post card from Ollie? Bad timing or what? Ten minutes later, and Luce and Ruby would have been alone. Although Ollie had removed himself from Luce's life pretty effectively, he'd made sure Ruby didn't feel he was running out on her, and his post cards for her had been arriving every week.

Luce had been so careful to keep the Ollie thing under wraps, what with them hanging out being so much of a big fat nothing anyway. When the three of them had gone out, they'd chosen places where they wouldn't be noticed, or places where they might have accidentally bumped into each other. Or if Ollie had come around to the flat, he came when everyone else was busy working. And now one post card was going to bust the whole thing out into the open. Luce's saliva ran sour at the thought.

If she kept her cool, she might get away with it. One post card didn't show anything. She needed to stop panicking. They didn't even know who it was from.

'How about we look at it in a minute, when it's just the two of us.' Luce could only hope Ruby was open to persuasion. 'We could have juice and chocolate.'

Luce could see Izzy and Dida were bursting to ask, but politely examining the ceiling.

'Nice shorts Ruby.' Izzy gave Ruby a grin.

Luce picked up the lifeline, and ran with it. 'You love those shorts don't you, Rubes. She even insists on wearing them with tights in winter.'

'Well talking of post cards and far flung places, don't forget Aidie and I are away next week.' Dida changed the subject again, with a neat flip, and gave a seismic groan. 'His mum and dad are coming to look after the kids so I can't get out of it without a diplomatic incident.'

'Where are you going again?' Luce picked that up and ran with it.

'I don't have a clue, Aidie revels in the control.' Dida groaned again, and shook her head. 'Although right now I'm done with Aidie and his nasty surprises.'

Izzy gave a grunt. 'Wherever he chooses, it can't be anything as bad as last week's shock.'

Sometimes Dida's life seemed so far removed from Luce and Ruby's, it was strange that they were friends at all. It was the ante-natal class where they'd really bonded, and somehow having their girls together, and watching them grow up transcended all their material differences. And Aidie failing to make it to the delivery room when Lolly had arrived, had made their "women doing it for themselves" bond even stronger.

'Ollie's sent another card from that Go place, Mum.'

Damn.

Ruby tossed it into the first open space that had cropped up in the talking, and oblivious of Luce snatching her breath, she was carrying on. 'This one's got palm trees on, and he's done another funny drawing, of a man with drips coming off his head...'

Okay. Luce was officially stuffed here. She braced herself, and waited for the fallout.

'Ollie's sending cards from Goa?' Izzy's mouth dropped open.

Dida gave a shrug. 'What a great idea, cards from round the world really help kids with their geography.'

Luce had no idea why Dida had handed her that lifeline either, but she capitalised. 'Yes, you put stickers on the map, don't you Rubes?' Luce and Ruby poured over the big map on the wall, tracing Ollie's path with sticky blue sparkling stars. The fact that what had been Luce's totally private vice, was now being offered up to two surprised faces, made Luce's stomach wither.

'I've got sixteen cards with this one.' Ruby, was playing to the audience, lapping up all the attention.

Izzy's smile was uncomfortable. 'That's nice.'

Dida pushed herself up from the sofa, and was sweeping her iPad into her capacious bag. 'Is that the time? Come on, we are going to have to run if we're hoping to open up at ten.'

Izzy didn't get up. 'So how many cards has Lolly got then?'

'Sorry?' Dida pretended not to hear.

Luce's heart sank. Izzy had always warned Ollie off a relationship with Luce, and if Izzy ever found out the whole truth about what had gone on between Luce and Ollie, she was going to go ape shit. But maybe only a part of the whole sordid tale needed to be dragged out here.

'How many cards has Ollie sent Lolly, to help with her geography?' Izzy definitely wasn't backing off here. 'Just out of interest.'

Dida screwed up her face and rolled her eyes. 'Ollie hasn't sent Lolly any cards.' She gave Izzy a glare. 'Now can we go please?'

And just for once Luce was glad that Dida, in decisive mode, was not someone that you messed with. Two minutes later Dida had swept Izzy out of the flat, and she and Ruby were left there alone, listening to the sound of Dida's high heels clattering down the stairs, and staring at a cartoon drawing that was making Luce's heart squish.

20

Early Wednesday Morning, 11th June

XANDER

The Pink House

Pole vaulting, objectives and swishy dresses

Xander leaned against the door frame, squinted down the road, and gritted his teeth against the wrench of anticipation that twisted his stomach. He slid his phone out of his pocket. Seven thirty. Izzy wouldn't be here for at least another ten minutes, and that would be if she was early. He resisted the urge to flick the camera on. Pouring over the photos he'd taken of her standing in her bedroom was really not that healthy. Pretending he'd been studying the furniture had only cut it for so long.

And what would she be wearing today? He tried to pretend that he hadn't been asking himself the same question, repeatedly, since he woke up at four thirty, with the hard on of the decade. One of those swishy dresses maybe? Or those dungarees that showed the smallest patch of pale skin, where her T-shirt slipped when she lifted up her arm. He stamped on that thought, as firmly as he'd taken himself in hand earlier.

As for the pangs of self-doubt, he knew he was putting himself in a difficult situation he might not be able to handle, but what the hell. Reckless didn't begin to describe it. Perhaps he had allowed it to happen, engineered it even, because he had some crazy subconscious macho need to prove that he was strong enough to resist. This was the first time in eight years a woman had penetrated his defences. So much for breaking through the barriers – this woman appeared to have pole vaulted straight over them, and short circuited all his sensible brain function.

Objectives. That was what he should focus on. So long as he reminded himself there was an objective argument for every decision he'd made, he was fine. He was here to finally get The Pink House sorted and let. It had been standing empty for years, ever since his mum had died. Before, he'd always found it too painful to come back and tackle the work that needed doing, but having decided he couldn't put it off any longer, the builders blitzing the place had, in the end, proved cathartic. And now here he was, standing on the doorstep in the morning sun, with a rush of anticipation in his chest he hadn't felt in years. With Christina out of action, bringing Izzy along to sort out the finishing touches, was the best way to push the project through to completion. Simple as. It was a problem-solving solution, which he'd put in place, to get the job done. And he hoped that would put the ghosts of the past to rest along the way. Having Izzy here was the best way to achieve the best results. Nothing more, nothing less.

Except early indications told him that today was going to be very hard work.

And he hadn't even seen her yet.

21

Early Wednesday Morning, 11th June

IZZY

On the way to The Pink House

High hedgerows and cocktail shakers

'If I didn't need the money, I wouldn't be doing this.'

Izzy muttered her pacifying mantra for the day, and scowled to herself, as she drove. Possibly mantras should be more positive than this, but whatever, it was going to have to do. In her head Luce was telling her she was doing this for everyone in the crew, especially The Vintage Cinema Club, reminding her there was nothing she loved more than making homes, especially stylish ones. Both these things were, arguably, true, but, Luce and her disembodied voice needed to butt out. All in all Luce had a lot to answer for. As for whatever was going on with Ollie, Izzy still hadn't got to the bottom of that one. She'd been rushing around so much yesterday getting the order ready, and Luce's brushed-under-the-carpet explanation, had been given as Izzy dashed away, at a run. Sixteen cards in as many weeks. That Ollie and Ruby hit it off just wasn't cutting it somehow.

It was so early that the sun was only just slicing over the tops of the high hedgerows, but already the sky was deep blue. Last time she came she hadn't twigged exactly where she was going, but this time she recognised it as pretty close to the most significant night of her life to date, when, at sixteen, she'd been allowed to tag along with Ollie to a house party, and they'd left their parents arguing at home. In the morning they'd gone home to find their parents were getting a divorce. Kind of figured as a big night in her history.

No way should Izzy waste a glorious summer day like this arguing with herself, stressing, or brooding about the past. She looked around at the baskets and boxes, and the piles of fabrics, and bits and pieces, crammed into the van, and smiled at the potential. She was here to do a job, and she'd make sure it was spectacularly good. And hopefully, after this, she wouldn't come into contact with any more guys, who made her feel like she was permanently in a cocktail shaker. She noticed the four white cut out letters, sliding around on the van floor, next to her bag. She'd grabbed them as an after-thought this morning. Now suddenly the way they spelled LOVE, made the cupcakes she'd stuffed down as breakfast, taste much less sweet.

She edged the van up by the front of the house, yanked on the break, took a very deep breath and dug in her pocket. No way was she going to make it through today without bubble gum.

22

IZZY & XANDER

The Pink House

Poncey excuses, and crashing and banging

'Bubble gum?' Xander stared at Izzy as if he couldn't quite believe the audacity.

'So?' Her reply bounced along the hall, where she'd dropped her box to the floor, and was now standing, with her hands firmly on her hips. And Luce would have a fit if she knew that Izzy was thrusting out her chin before she'd even got into the house.

'I'm just not sure how Christina would feel...'

What sort of poncey excuse was that? The least he could do was to man up and admit it was him that hated her chewing.

Izzy screwed up her face to think. She always chewed when she was nervous. Today was going to be hard enough. She couldn't do it without gum.

'Sorry, but it's a deal breaker.' And echoing his challenging words from the other day gave her a snarky sense of satisfaction. She hitched up her boyfriend jeans, gave a mental curse for not putting a belt on, and wrenched down the hem of her T shirt, to make sure all gaps were covered. Then she darted towards the door to carry on unloading.

From the depth of Xander's sigh, he knew he was onto a loser here. Result for Izzy. As for how frigging hot he was looking – same old faded jeans, ripped T-shirt – that she was going to have to blank, on every level, other than general generic admiration from a very long way off.

In the end Izzy had largely managed to find enough pieces from the stock at the cinema, to keep her home bedroom intact, apart from the bed, of course. She was confident that she could create a room which would give a similar look, without the need to ransack her own private space. She wouldn't usually have minded, but she simply didn't feel comfortable with the idea of planting her personal things in this particular home.

'It's all a bit chaotic here, the builders have mainly moved out, and the furniture's arriving bit by bit.' Xander apologised, as he led her through the house. 'Yesterday's delivery guys put your things into approximate position. We may have to move things around a bit ourselves.'

She wobbled behind him up the stairs, basket in her arms, eyes anywhere but the stretch of tanned skin on his back, where his T-shirt didn't quite meet his low slung jeans. They pushed through a six panelled door, and arrived in a first floor room, containing the furniture she'd piled into the back of the film company van yesterday.

'I really appreciate your coming to help. I've really no idea what to do after this point.' Xander shot her a disarming, sideways look. Izzy, off her guard, felt her legs melt, and let her eyes slide to meet his. Her breakfast lurched dangerously, her pulse hammered in her ears, and still he didn't look away. Yanking her gaze onto the pieces of bed, stacked in a pile on the newly laid grey wool carpet, she chewed like crazy.

Except why should he look away? She was the one who needed to feel guilty here. They were both adults, doing a professional job, and she couldn't believe she was allowing herself to over react like this.

'Christina's very particular, she's a bit of a perfectionist when it comes to the finishing.'

There. That booted Izzy firmly into her place.

'Really.' Izzy knew there was a distasteful expression on her face that shouldn't be there, but what the hell. Izzy already knew Christina insisted on quality. She'd chosen Xander hadn't she? And this only went to underline Izzy's theory about the impossible nature of clients.

Xander hesitated. 'Now the work's completed, a lot of the character has gone...'

Izzy stared around at the impeccable flat walls, and the perfect paintwork. 'It does feel a bit clinical.' A familiar problem her interior designer of a mum faced, with her loaded clients, and she couldn't help pointing out that if he really was the successful entrepreneur he boasted about being, Xander should have known better. 'Typical rookie developer mistake – excessive cash injections can wreck these old places. Play's havoc with your capital extraction.'

Izzy watched Xander's eyes widen in shock, then a shadow passed across his face.

'This isn't a profiteering scheme.' His stare was stony, and his tone cut her to the core. 'This is the house my mum lived in. Before she died.'

Shit. Izzy wished that the shiny, wide boarded, oak floor would open and swallow her up. A dead parent pretty much top trumped everything. Xander already had a height advantage as he glowered down at her, but she felt about an inch tall. How the hell was she going to claw her way back from this one?

'That's why you're here.' Xander gave a shake of his head, as if he didn't get it himself and thought better of fighting with her. 'To help bring back the magic.' He finished softly.

Izzy blinked, hardly believing she was off the hook. No way would she have expected him to wade in and haul her out of her chasm of embarrassment.

'No pressure there then.' Izzy gave a shrug and tried for a cover all smile, which didn't come out properly due to nerves. 'So, I take it this is a guest room?'

Given they were at the back of the house, this was probably not the principal bedroom.

'Yep, the master suite is at the front, it's bigger.'

He sounded completely at ease. She needed to make a super-human effort to get over herself.

'The wardrobes look nice, and they fit well where they are. Good thing too, because they weigh a ton. They don't completely match, but they really go with the house somehow.'

'Yep. Good choice.'

He'd picked himself up after her blunder about his mother, and he was staring at her again. In the most undressing kind of way. This time she knew she wasn't imagining it. Like back in her own bedroom at home, only now it was worse. Damn that she hadn't thrown her long sleeved shirt in the van either, because she could really do with taking cover here, given how flimsy her T-shirt was. There was only one thing she could think of to make the situation better here. She chewed harder, and as prickles bristled on the back of her neck, she dragged the scarf that was tied around her hair, and pulled it free, and rammed it through the belt loops on her jeans. Now at least one of them had their jeans firmly secured, even if his were sliding towards indecency.

'I'll go and get my spanner, then we can sort the bed out.' She made a dash for the door, but even as she left the room she could have sworn he was checking her out.

* * * *

'Is there a reason for all the crashing and banging?'

Xander sent Izzy a hard stare, across the scuffed metal curls of the bed head that they were propping between them. They'd already got the bed head and foot into place, and now she was struggling to get the side bars attached.

Izzy paused, dragged the new ribbon out of her hair, grappled her hair into a pony tail again, then retied the bow.

'Trying to put a bed-frame together is a balancing act at the best of times.' When you were trying to work with a dumb ass, whose main contribution was to stare at your boobs, it was bloody impossible.

She was bending down now, trying to twist a nut onto a bolt, and he was still staring. Damn. The nut span right out of her fingers.

'Shit.' Her spanner thudded onto the carpet after the nut.

Grrrrrrrr... And shit for swearing too.

'That's the third time you've dropped your spanner.'

So Xander could count. Great. They could put the flags out to celebrate that.

'Izzy...' He'd never used her name directly before.

The gravel in his voice made her breath catch. Shit. She watched as slowly he walked all around the bed frame, and came to a halt. On her side of the bed. Shock waves zithered down her back. This *so* was the wrong side for him to be.

He was behind her now, and her legs wouldn't move. She was welded to the spot, frozen by an equal mix of horror and anticipation. She could feel his warm breath now, grazing the skin beneath her ear as he bent his head towards her neck.

'Izzy?'

The note in his voice had changed, and out of the corner of her eye she could see his hand lift, to hover by her shoulder. Enough. She had to stop this. Now.

For a fleeting second she was so damned thankful for every scrap and fight she'd ever had with her brothers. A big thank you to Ollie, for beating the shit out of her when she was little when she always refused to give in, and for developing her natural left hook.

She jived, reeled around, and bang. Xander staggered backwards as her fist smashed into his shoulder.

'What the…?'

Good contact, just a shame she missed his jaw.

He shook his head, doing a good impression of open mouthed shock, and she hung on to her stinging hand.

'What the hell are you playing at?' Her question ripped through the air. 'What about your wife?' Her furious roar was inflamed by the imploding pain in her knuckles. 'Not to mention your children, what about them?' She was standing square in front of him now, anger bursting out of her chest.

He rubbed the side of his chin, slowly, screwing up his face, like he somehow didn't understand. Stubble. She'd definitely have done better with this whole episode if he hadn't had the stubble.

'I don't know what you mean. I don't have children, I don't have a wife – well not any more, I don't. What are you talking about?'

As he glared at her, she could feel herself shrinking, backing onto the bed frame.

She hesitated, before she let loose her next tirade. 'No wife? Well if you don't have a wife, who the hell is Christina?'

Even with the furniture in, the room was horribly echoey.

He raised his eyebrows, exhaled, and shook his head. 'Christina is my sister. She's involved because she helps me furnish my places.'

Oh crap. Izzy felt the blood drain from her face, and her stomach descended like a lift. How the hell could she have…?

'And her children are my nephew and niece. If you have a problem with that, maybe next time you'd be kind enough discuss it before you start hitting people?' He snorted with disgust, as he marched out onto the landing. 'I'll leave you to get on.'

If there hadn't been so much riding on this job, she'd have done a runner already, but she wasn't just here for herself. The whole crew stood to benefit from this job, and she had to remember that. Grabbing her spanner, she set to work, tightening the endless nuts on the bed-frame. There were certainly enough of them to give her ample time to cringe at her stupidity. She'd been here all of an hour, and already she'd made two major blunders. All she wanted to do was to crawl into a hole and die.

*   *   *   *

Izzy was tightening the last nut when Xander reappeared, and by the looks of him, half an hour hadn't been anything like enough time to cool off.

'So what sort of a guy do you take me for?'

Irate and well spoken. How was that familiar?

Never apologise, never explain. Dida's words flashed though her brain. Followed by Luce, insisting she should explain every time.

'I took you for a bad guy, obviously.' And dammit that she couldn't put the brakes on the explanation. 'I assumed you were a married guy, hitting on me, I had a valid reaction to an honest mistake.' Somewhere down the line she had to justify this, but was there actually a way to put a good spin on trying to sock a client in the mouth?

'I wasn't hitting on you, and nor would I.'

Looking grave, he sounded horribly sincere and final, cutting her down to two inches tall, in one breath. Again. This guy certainly knew how to make a person feel small. Her jaw sagged, but something inside her made her desperate to crawl and apologise.

'I'm sorry I got it wrong.' Not really sorry for smacking him. Somehow she didn't think he was quite as blameless as he claimed. He'd definitely been on the wrong side of the bed back there, and there was no explanation about that part. She didn't hear him apologising for being so close he was practically blowing in her ear. But she was very sorry there was still a whole day left to work here. And how the hell was she going to explain whacking him to Luce?

23

Wednesday Afternoon, 11th June

IZZY & XANDER

The Pink House

Four...five...six...seven...maybe

Izzy wasn't sure if it was due to guilt or thirst, but Xander disappeared, and came back with fresh coffee. She threw in some flapjack, and after that they skipped lunch and worked through the afternoon, mostly in silence. Izzy dipped in and out to the van, while Xander looked on, or helped if she asked.

'We don't make a bad team.' He stood back, with his hands on his hips, assessing the eau-de-nil taffeta curtains they had just put up, which, to Izzy's mind, perfectly framed the small paned sash-windows.

Izzy, still crouching at the top of the step ladder, wasn't going to let Xander get away with that one.

'What kind of team has me doing all the work and you

watching?'

His face split into something half way towards a smile. Izzy was relieved that the tension was diffusing. Thumping him may not have been great for customer relations, but at least it had moved them onto a less awkward footing. She'd found it unbearable being near him, when she'd thought he was married, and had guilt coursing through her for having the hots for another woman's guy. Hots like this had never happened to Izzy before, and unlike Luce, Izzy didn't eye up anything and everything in trousers.

The bizarre attraction Izzy felt for Xander was somehow misplaced and muddled, and had nothing to do with the man himself. More to the point, no way was she ever going to act on it. Yes, he was a looker, who'd accidentally got a triple dose when they were dishing out the sex appeal, but he was also damned arrogant, with a lot less charm than he seemed to think. Xander's superior attitude alone would have pretty much ruled him out of the running with Izzy, had there been any running, which, of course, there wasn't. And that was before she got onto the fact that by his own admission, he was extracting cash at every turn. So she had no idea why she felt so much better now she knew he was single, because really it didn't matter a jot.

'If you want to be useful, get a duster, and give that chandelier in the corner a final rub.' Izzy climbed down the stepladder, and crossed to a basket by the wardrobe.

The list Xander gave Izzy on the first day included lacy dresses, to be hung around the room, and Luce had come up trumps on that one. Izzy began to sort through the pile she'd sent, to see which worked best.

'So whose house is this then?' Izzy asked as she shook out a cream silk chemise, and slipped it onto a padded hanger. She hadn't been able to face asking about the ins and outs of who exactly she was working for before, but now she needed to know, if only so she could get the styling right.

'It's mine, but we're furnishing it to let.'

'Right.' Izzy pondered. 'So why did I deliver a rocking horse then?'

Xander's sigh was slightly embarrassed. 'I bought that for Christina's kids, to keep them quiet when she's here sorting things out, not that she will be, with her leg in plaster.'

'So how old are they?' Izzy was aware she should possibly be avoiding small objects.

'Four...five...six...seven, maybe.' Xander's shrug gave him away. 'They're rocking horse size.'

Not crucial about the accessorising then, but Izzy was onto him anyway. 'You don't know do you?'

'What?' He gave a squawk of protest. 'I work in film and property, not child development, and their ages keep changing. Their birthday cakes have quite a few candles on these days if that helps.'

'I hope you're not such a rubbish uncle as you sound.' She sent him a grin. 'So how much time do you spend here?' If she was sounding embarrassingly inquisitive, it was too bad.

'I've dropped in, between films, to check the progress on my other place – the one with your favourite skips – and pull this house together. Doing what Christina would be doing if she wasn't hobbling around on crutches.' His face relaxed into a smile. 'Then later we're all off to France together, to their barn conversion. They're having a holiday, and I'm checking out some locations for a film that I'm hoping to get finance for.'

Izzy stared hard at his bare feet. It was the only part of him she had allowed herself to look at since this morning. Still looking off the scale sexy, which she knew was ridiculous in every way.

'And it's Christina who loves the whole vintage thing, not you?'

She knew this was strictly more than she needed to know. She didn't even know why she wanted to get to know more about him.

'Me? Not my thing.'

'You have your old car.' She couldn't overlook that.

He dismissed that quickly. 'The car's not mine, I borrowed it from my dad, and if I was decorating, which happily I'm not, I definitely wouldn't go for the old tat look.'

Nothing she didn't know already. Polishing the chandelier obviously wasn't loosening his tongue.

'So what sort of style do you go for?' She walked over to adjust a folding screen she had set up next to the dressing table.

'I don't have a house. Not that I live in anyway. Only the one where the skips are.'

She thought of the broken windows, and the building site.

'But that's only half finished. What about your place?'

He looked as if he was giving the question full consideration.

'Nope, I really don't have one.'

She tried to conceal her surprise. For Izzy, her home was so crucial to her whole being, she couldn't imagine living without one. Home was what made her feel secure, where she expressed her creativity, and it was a huge part of her identity, all tied up with who she was. Ever since her parents' divorce wrenched them out of their family home, home to her had been a symbol of safety.

'But where do you sleep then, where do you keep your things?' She found this so hard to believe, she no longer cared if she sounded nosey.

'Sometimes I stay over at the office. Film production is time consuming, so I spend most of my waking hours working. I'm here and there, work away a lot, have my clothes in a couple of holdalls, stay in hotels, on location, or at friends places sometimes. And when I need somewhere to crash, Christina catches me. She's never given up being the big sister, we're very close, especially... well...now.'

Izzy suspected he was going to mention his mother again, but thought better of it. Phew to that, but there was something immensely puzzling about Xander. What was he? An itinerant workaholic who didn't actually live anywhere at all? So much for the image she had of him as a happily settled, family man, with a beautiful Georgian home. How was he so different to the guy she had him down for?

She couldn't hide how horrified she was about the idea of being essentially homeless. For her, being without a home would be the worst thing in the world. 'Don't you think you're a bit old to be sleeping on people's couches?'

Xander gave a hollow laugh, apparently amused at the extremity of her reaction. 'Thirty four isn't old.'

'It all depends what you're doing at thirty four. That's not a good answer, and you know it.'

Izzy sensed she'd accidentally stumbled on a crack in Xander's arrogant shell. Sometimes if you broke through a tough exterior, you might find humanity underneath.

'So why all the work? I'm sure that film production is all consuming, but I've heard of film producers who managed to have a life as well.'

He considered for a moment, as if he realised a flippant answer wouldn't be acceptable. From the furrows of concentration on his brow, it was almost as if he were asking himself the question for the first time. 'I guess the work fills the spaces.'

One short, succinct answer, but Izzy knew exactly what he meant. In her own life work definitely filled spaces, and it was definitely a substitute for something – she just hadn't quite worked out what yet. With her own work, she drove herself until she couldn't do any more, until she was dropping with fatigue, and then she did just a little bit extra. When she was done with painting she cleaned the house until it was immaculate, and then she found something else to organise, or bake, or renovate, and then she started all over again. Stopping meant slowing down, and when you slowed down the past had a nasty habit of catching up with you. And she packed her days full, because when she was busy there was no space for the doubts and bad thoughts to creep in, and she carried on the whole treadmill of her life, because she was too scared of what she'd find if she stopped. But one thing she did know was that it takes an unhappy person to know one. She wondered if Xander had any idea how much he'd given away with those few words. She'd expected to peer through a chink in the armour, to see through to what might be the tiniest glimpse of the real guy, yet one small tug, and the whole lot had come crashing down, and laid him bare before her. Just what she hadn't expected.

'Work fills spaces?' Her tone was low, as she tilted over her basket, and pulled out a lace chemise. 'You aren't kidding there.'

'Without the work, maybe there wouldn't be anything there at all. That's the bit that's really scary.' His voice was gruff, scraping like sandpaper on a board. 'Yet how would you know?'

He tilted his head on one side, and there was a faint hint of triumph in his voice.

'You only know, because you're the same. Aren't you, Mrs Paint-All-Night?'

24

Wednesday Afternoon, 11th June

DIDA & LUCE

The Swimming Pool Viewing Area

Every grimace leaves a wrinkle

Luce wiggled her way along the row of spectator tiers, flipped down a blue plastic seat, and edged onto it with a sigh, dropping her bag onto the floor. She held out a can to Dida.

'Iced tea, not sure what it'll taste like, but it's way too warm for proper tea today.'

'Thanks, it looks fab. I'm having a whole day of firsts.' Dida ran her finger over the condensation on the ice cold can appreciatively, popped open the ring pull, and made sure she kept her voice cheery. 'I know we're used to our weekly dose of chlorine fug sauna up here, but now we're in the grip of flaming June it's unbearable.'

Dida peered over the balcony edge, trying, just for a minute, to blot out the double whammy of blows she'd suffered that afternoon. Two things had come hurtling out of nowhere, and she was still mentally gawping, trying to get her head around them.

Way below, Lolly and Ruby were wriggling around with a huddle of children on the pool side, listening to Tilly, their swimming instructor. Dida crossed her legs, smoothed out the creases in her taupe linen trousers, un-peeled her lawn shirt, where the sweat had stuck it to her back, and wished she'd worn something lighter. Luce looked way more comfortable in her capri pants, cropped polo, and flat pointy pumps, but then Luce always looked effortlessly chilled. Whereas Dida's chunky build meant she could spend a fortune at Mint Velvet or Toast, and still end up looking like she was wearing a sack, you could put Luce in a bin bag, and she'd look like she'd walked out of a Vogue shoot. And given Dida's bird's eye view, it was obvious even at this stage, that poor old Lolly, sticking her bum out down below, had inherited Dida's shape exactly, whereas Ruby, beside her, was as willowy as her mum.

Genes were one thing you couldn't fight, whereas Aidie...Well, he was different matter altogether. The Vintage Cinema Club were already pulling out the stops to defeat him. Dida had dragged together a stonking business loan proposal, which would be ready to drop into the bank before she went away. But Aidie just kept giving and giving, and not in a good way. With the stunt he'd pulled today, Dida was going to see to it that he had the mother of all battles on his hands.

Luce pulled a face, as she held up her can to scrutinise the contents list. 'Brrr, it's a bit strong on the lemon.' She took another swig, and shuddered. 'Let's hope your other first is better than this one. I think this might be the vilest thing I've tasted since root beer.'

'However bad it tastes, I reckon I have a top trump of awfulness for my other.' Dida drew in a breath. She knew her mouth was set in the kind of grim line her mother had been warning her against all her life, made all the more obvious by the lippy touch up she'd slapped on as they'd left the changing rooms. "Smile and the world smiles with you", and "every grimace leaves a wrinkle" were two stalwarts of her mother's mission statement.

'So would I be right to think Aidie is responsible, yet again?'

One thing Dida loved about Luce was how perceptive she was, although, in fact, that statement might actually have applied to most things in Dida's life, on any day.

'You got it in one.' Dida punched the air. 'The "first" is, that he's broken his habit of eighteen years of top secret holiday destinations, and told me where we're going on Saturday.' Dida decided whatever her mother had drilled into her to the contrary, this was a moment so awful, she was completely entitled to blow out her cheeks. Quite why Aidie had broken with convention was something else Dida hadn't found an answer for. That was the thing with her husband – he worked in mysterious and convoluted ways, and the origins of his actions weren't always immediately obvious. He was like every smoke cliché rolled into one. With Aidie smoke screens were an everyday occurrence, there was rarely smoke without fire, and he was a living embodiment of smoke and mirror deception.

'I take it you aren't happy?' Luce pushed back a strand of hair. 'It's not a cultural holiday then?'

Dida shook her head. Talk about a bloody understatement. 'The sod texted me the link as I came out on the school run.' She flashed her phone at Luce, who blinked as she took it in.

Candi, holiday deets, get yourself some kit, AD
www.Fit-Italy/cycling/UndulatingUmbria

'Oh my...' A bewildered expression spread across Luce's face, as Dida clicked on the link. 'But you don't ride a bike...do you?'

Dida had kept a lid on it for the last hour during the school pickup and the swim change, but now her voice rose to a hissing growl. 'Exactly. I'm the least likely person in the world to ride a bike, and I thought Aidie was too, until he started on his totally ridiculous fitness kick last weekend. As for the kit, I refuse to put my bum and Lycra in the same sentence.'

'It's not all bad...' Luce was reading from the web page now. 'Sun-drenched terracotta, mediaeval Montefalco, private pools, and apricot orchards. Those bits sound nice.'

'If it was bike riding anywhere else in the world, I'd definitely stay home.' As Dida's hiss rose to a wail, the woman further along the row turned her head sharply towards them. Dida gritted her teeth, in an effort to keep the volume down, knowing deep down that Luce was the last person she should be grumbling to about luxury holidays. 'It sounds great until you realise it's all done on a bloody bike. We're supposed to ride from hotel to hotel for god sake. I have no idea how I'm going to handle this.' The thing was, Luce was always understanding about Aidie, and so sympathetic.

As for the other first, no way could Dida risk broaching that on the public balcony. No way she even wanted to think about it herself, until she'd worked out what was going on. There had to be some mistake, some sensible explanation, because yet again today, for the fifth day in a row, her regular trawl through Aidie's trash hadn't yielded the huge list of women's names she usually found. It was ironic that the first time she didn't find great lists of women's names her alarm bells were clanging. More than likely someone had told him he should be emptying his trash. Because as things stood, the happy hookers had gone, and the only name figuring in Aidie's emails was Elvira. And that would be Elvira the fitness instructor.

'You've got three days to come up with a watertight plan to get out of the cycling.' Luce sent her a calming "it's all under control" smile. 'We'll get the Vintage Cinema Club on the case, don't worry.'

Dida gave a grateful sigh.

'I love that I can always rely on you lot to help me dig my way out of a hole.' Which took Dida neatly onto the next question which had been playing round her head for a while. 'And talking of holes, is everything okay with Ollie?'

Luce's foot jumped as she went rigid, nudged her can of iced tea, and sent it clattering down to the tier below, where the liquid began to glug out over the floor.

Dida watched Luce scrabbling to retrieve the escaping can, and was ready for her when her face bobbed back to head height.

'I'll take that as a no, then.' Dida bowled Luce a reassuring smile of her own.

'It's nothing.' Luce was opting to breeze her way through.

'Sixteen cards seems like quite a lot.' Dida did her best to sound unconvinced. 'And you can't really talk to Izzy about this can you?'

Luce sank lower in her seat, and gave a loud sniff. 'Okay, I give in, I've really stuffed up. It's my fault Ollie left.'

So there was a problem. 'Sweetie, it can't be that bad...' Dida hadn't expected Luce to be this upset.

'We'd been hanging out together, and getting on really well, but he wanted more, and you know I always keep Ruby away from guys I sleep with.'

Dida sighed. 'That's only your way of protecting her.'

Luce rubbed her nose with a hanky. 'One Friday Ollie made this huge scene when I was leaving the bar to go home with a guy. And afterwards he said he couldn't bear to stay around and watch me go out with other people, and if I didn't go out with him properly, he was going to have to leave. And then he went, just like that.' Luce's bottom lip was juddering, and she swallowed hard.

Dida clicked her tongue, and shook her head. 'So that explains his quick exit, but it's great he's not letting Ruby down. Sending all those cards is Ollie all over.'

Luce's voice was barely a whisper. 'The thing is, since he left I've missed him more and more. I thought it would get easier, but it just gets worse. And now he's in Thailand, and we all know what happens there. I can't bear to think of him with anyone else.'

Dida, seeing Luce's shoulders shaking, slid her arm around her friend. 'Ollie's not like that.' As far as Dida knew. She hoped for Luce's sake he wasn't.

'It serves me right. It's karma. Now I know how he felt with me, and it's awful.' Luce was mumbling into her tissue now.

Poor Luce. Dida struggled to find something comforting to say. 'At least it's good that the break has showed you how you really feel.'

Luce blew her nose loudly. 'Izzy would be beside herself if she knew Ollie went away because of me. And I've got to be strong, because he's only been away five months. He isn't coming back until next February, and who knows what will have happened by then.'

And who knew where they'd be with the cinema by next February too? Dida wiped a slick of perspiration off her forehead, and tried to ignore the way that thought made her chest implode.

She took back her arm, and gave Luce a pat on the leg. 'Remember, I'm always here if you want to talk about it.' Dida gave Luce a nudge. 'Hey, from the way Tilly, the instructor, is filling in forms, it looks like they're getting another badge. More sewing, if they get many more badges there won't be any room for them on their swimsuits.'

And then the kids were piling out of the pool, and next thing Luce and Dida were on the stairs, in the crush of mums, jostling down to the changing rooms.

25

XANDER & IZZY

The Pink House

Natural breaks and crazy invitations

Izzy pulled a bow into shape, tried it against the curtains, and squinted at Xander over her shoulder. 'So why *don't* you get a home sorted out? You could easily rent a flat?'

Xander let out a sigh, and let go of the chandelier he'd been told to rub. What was it with women and their home obsession? 'You sound just like Christina. She's the reason I bought the house with the skips.'

'Because you wanted a home?'

'No.' His reply to that question was filled with the scorn it deserved. 'Because I wanted to get Christina off my back.'

Izzy's wide eyes suggested she couldn't believe what he was saying.

'Having that house renovated will give me a few months respite from Christina's nagging. I'll most probably sell it once it's finished.' He'd settled on the biggest wreck he could find, counting on years of building work, but thanks to a scarily efficient builder, even if it still looked like a disaster on the outside, the inside was all coming together scarily fast.

'It looked like an amazing place, although I'm not sure you needed to rip the guts out of it as much as you obviously have.' Her brows descended into a dark frown.

'It's a load of trouble I don't have time for. I'll be pleased when it's over. End of.' That about summed up his thoughts on the matter.

'Sometimes rebuilding can be very cathartic.' She gave him a loaded stare.

'Meaning?'

'When we did up our house after...' She stopped, shaking her head. 'I mean, once, we had to start over again with nothing, and that taught us a lot along the way...if you let yourself, you might find the same.'

Xander snorted. 'Thanks for the analysis.'

She was fiddling with her hair again. Unknotting her bun, throwing her curls forward, before she regathered them. One escaping tress hung messily over her forehead, tempting him to reach out and tug it gently.

'You could always come and have a look round the site. See what you think.'

One random, ridiculous thought, and the words had tumbled out before he could stop them. From her sideways stare, it looked like she thought he'd gone mad, and she might not be wrong there.

She didn't reply, just went on fixing her bow on the curtains, and when she'd done she stood back, hands on her hips, assessing the room. 'Right.'

Xander put down the duster and stepped away from the chandelier. He'd had enough of crystals for one day, quite apart from not having spent so long in a bedroom with a woman since he couldn't remember when. Maybe that's why he was coming out with the crazy invitations. Maybe he needed to get out of here, and fast. No way did he want a rerun of earlier on, when he'd somehow fucked up on the personal space thing entirely. He wasn't quite sure what had happened back there with her, and he definitely wasn't as innocent as he'd protested, given that he'd probably have liked nothing better than to grab her and kiss her. Something about her made him leap in, every time, overruling his better judgement. Her underlying vulnerability switched on the caveman in him. It certainly had nothing to do with how pleasant she was, because let's face it, at times she couldn't have been more truculent. Even when she was acting all sweet and amenable, stroppy and difficult was only ever a breath away, bubbling under, waiting to break out. He glanced pointedly at his watch.

'If you've reached a natural break, we could call it a day here. How about we grab some tea and I'll show you how your pink chairs look in the summer-house?' There, another random idea that came out of nowhere.

'Just to get this straight, is that a suggestion, or an order?' Izzy studied him quizzically.

He thought for a minute. 'Maybe both.' He sent her a grin, and headed for the door. 'But I'll definitely order more flapjack if there's any going.'

*   *   *   *

'Roses and honeysuckle and cornflowers, all tangled and beautiful. Walled gardens are my favourite thing, and this one's as perfect as the house.' Izzy, apparently having left her strop upstairs, had already kicked off her shoes, snatched the ribbon out of her pony tail to let her hair go wild, and thrown herself down on the grass.

Xander sauntered across the lawn and stopped in his tracks, struck first, by her enthusiasm, and second, by the way she was arching her back and – worse – her boobs, right towards him. Bloody hell. He blinked for another double take. In this light that T-shirt was damn near translucent.

'Aren't you coming to see the Barbie chairs in the summer house?' That should take care of the temptation, not to mention the full on nipples.

She folded her legs, and scrambled to her feet, grabbing the bag she'd brought from the house. 'Another non-negotiable suggestion?'

'Absolutely.' He walked up the steps to the summer house deck, throwing open the double doors as he reached them.

'Wow, this is more of a full blown pavilion than a summer house, and the dusky pink of the chairs goes perfectly with the old brickwork on the back wall.' Izzy stepped into the lofty space, looking around at the other horizontal plank walls. 'I'm loving the pale grey paint, and I can see why you needed all twelve chairs now. Cushions in a mix of prints will finish it off well. I'll check the swatches in a minute, and see if I can get onto those this evening.'

Tonight? 'Who's the workaholic now? What about your action packed social life?' He put the tray on the table, and began to pour the tea. And why was he holding his breath, waiting for her answer, to what was meant to be a throwaway comment.

She gave an airy smile. 'I've got lots on, I like to keep on top of the jobs as they come in.'

She carried on. 'And I won't be able to come here tomorrow, because I'm in the shop, but I can bring a few more bits around after work, if you like?'

'Yep, fine, whatever suits you.' He felt a strange surge of disappointment that she wasn't coming earlier.

Izzy offered him a piece of flapjack from her plastic box, took her tea, contemplated choosing a pink chair to sit on, then at the last minute veered away to squat on the steps. He got the idea she was deliberately keeping her distance, although he might have caught her staring at his legs back there. Or had he imagined it?

141

She squinted out at the garden. 'A mixture of spots and florals would work in here, and bunting would really finish it off.'

Xander pulled up a chair, and sat down. At least he only had to look at her back from here. He would close his eyes to the fact that despite the scarf she'd tied around the waistband, her jeans still stretched down as she leaned forwards, exposing the double indentations where her pelvis joined her spine.

'Sounds great.' He was munching, replying to something she had said that he hardly heard, and definitely ignoring the way his pulse was racing. He hesitated for a second, and then thought about casually dropping in the next question. The one he'd been itching to ask since this morning, but hadn't got around to. If he didn't do it soon, the opportunity would be gone altogether. He took a deep breath, and wagging his half piece of flapjack, he went for the jokiest tone he could manage. 'So, now you know about the wife you thought I had who isn't one, and the wife I used to have, but don't have any more, are you going to tell me about your husbands?'

For what seemed like forever, he cringed at the silence.

'What?' Then she screwed her head around, for another of those "is he crazy?" looks, and her face broke into an indulgent smile. 'This conversation is way outside the line of customer service, but I'll tell you for free, a husband is the last thing I'd have. Ever.' By the time she said ever, she'd gone all fierce again.

'Okay. Sounds pretty final.' However left field his question had been, he hadn't quite expected a response that shouty.

'I'm way too busy for all that stuff.' Her forced laugh made it sound like she was back tracking, covering up somehow. 'With Vintage at the Cinema and three brothers to run around after, another man is the last thing I need.'

Xander didn't know why he'd been compelled to ask the question in the first place, as for why relief was flooding through him, that was another mystery. He made it his business not to make moves, unless they were moves to stop the women who had him

142

cornered. So it was nothing to him, that Izzy had just implied she was available.

'Will you be dropping by the building site tomorrow?' Another stupid question, given she'd just said she was working.

She gave a short laugh, shooting him a smile over her shoulder. 'Depends if that's an offer, or an order?'

His stomach clenched as he registered the stretch of her neck as she twisted. 'I'd say an order...' He watched her back, focusing on the bumps of her spine sticking through the stretch of her T shirt, crossed by the horizontal line of her bra. Not the pink one today, probably petrol blue from the shadow at a guess. A shiver zipped down his spine. He pulled himself up sharply. Waiting, he prepared himself for the answer to the invitation he hadn't even meant to give, all ready for her to turn and say "no".

She raked her hair back, and let it fall again. 'I'll maybe have a few minutes round two. Shall I see you there?'

He tried to ignore the fact that the football crowd, on the story board in his brain, were jumping up and down, and yelling. He tried instead to sound cool, offhand even.

'Great. More flapjack might be good. If you have any...'

26

Wednesday Afternoon, 11th June

New message To: The Crew @ Vintage at the Cinema... Luce, Izzy, Ollie, Lydia, Damon, Henni, Declan, Suzie, Arthur, Leighton, Magda, Thom, Allie

Subject: Vintage at the Cinema... News and Rotas

The rotas for week beginning June 16th and June 23rd are attached. I'm away for a week, starting Saturday. Any problems, please let me know before I leave.

Vintage Cinema Club Fight Back Measures so far:
Free coffee
Exemplary customer service – going the extra mile, and then some
An exclusive, room by room, styling and supply service (thank you Izzy & everyone)
Bridal (thank you Luce)
Silent Film Projection

NEXT PRIORITY: TO SOURCE FRENCH STOCK, AND LOTS OF IT!!!!

Cake of the week is WALNUT AND CAPPUCCINO, the week after it's MOROCCAN ORANGE :)

Dida xx

27

XANDER & IZZY

On the building site in Bakewell

A thousand miles away

Xander stood in the doorway of his house, looking across the mud towards the skips. Yet again, the builders were largely absent, rather than at work, which he was surprisingly pleased about. One electrician's van, and the front door left ajar, was the sum of it today. He had no idea how they were making the astonishing progress when they never seemed to be here. Although the outside still resembled a bomb-site, inside things appeared dangerously close to completion. If he didn't watch out, Christina would soon be moving him in.

He didn't need to look at his watch to know he was hideously early. After yet another glance down the road, to assure him Izzy wasn't about to arrive, he wandered off up the glass staircase to the first floor bedroom, to follow up a query about the en suite, that had come through from the architect. Realistically, Izzy wouldn't be turning up for ages yet.

With a twist in his gut, he thought of the last time he'd sorted out a house. Years ago, with their home in Hampstead, Astrid had taken charge of everything, and all he'd had to do was sign off on the payments. Astrid, with her combination of drive, flair and efficiency, had made everything beautiful, and then he'd asked too much of her, pushed her to a place she couldn't go. When he'd come back home again, after going to hell and back with his mum, there had been nothing left. What had seemed like the perfect partnership when the going was good, had proved to be entirely empty under pressure. He still felt guilty for being the one responsible for doing that to the relationship, by making the choices that he did. It had been totally unfair of him to ask what he had of Astrid, and she'd been entirely within her rights to make the choices she did. But once it was broken there was no way back.

Occasionally he asked himself if he'd ever get his life together again, but if his life was still this upside down, eight years down the line, he doubted he ever would. The extreme working habits he'd thrown himself into after the break-up had become a way of life. No way would he think of changing them now, and they simply didn't allow for the kind of normal existence other people enjoyed. It was as if dysfunctional was the only thing he knew now, but the point was he was happy this way. Somewhere along the line, he'd become content to be like this.

One floor up, he chose the bedroom with the best view of the street, then automatically checked his watch again, unnerved by the spring-loaded sensation in his gut. He still wasn't exactly sure why he'd asked Izzy along today. Asking her because he didn't want to wait all day to see her again was totally illogical, and it wasn't how he operated.

'Hello...Xander?'

Xander's heart knocked against his chest wall as he heard Izzy's voice. All that hanging round the window, and she'd slipped in under the radar. Catching a glimpse of himself in the mirror as he headed out of the bedroom, he shocked himself with the width of his smile.

'Xander...the door was open...are you there?'

He dashed onto the landing, peered down through the galaxy of lights that twinkled across the huge void, and saw her, way below, squinting upwards, shading her eyes with her hand, against the glare of the bulbs. If ever he needed confirmation that the services engineer had gone over the top with the lighting scheme, he had it now. And he had to be imagining that sweet scent, wafting upwards on the air, didn't he?

'Come on up...I'm checking the bathroom cabinets.'

'I see you've gone for shopping centre style. If you had a glass lift, I might have thought I'd arrived at Meadowhall.' She was climbing the stairs, and the lilt of her lips told him she was enjoying the jibes. 'You've really done a great job of emptying this place haven't you? Bloody hell, this platform is hanging on nothing, is it even safe?' Her voice echoed as she eased off the top step, still hanging onto the stainless steel handrail as she slid along the landing.

'It's fine, it's cantilevered. Designed by experts.' Throwing in the technical bits here, to hide that he was suddenly breathless.

Xander blinked as he saw her full length for the first time, and dammit that he'd missed the details before. So much for the blinding lights.

'Well it looks like it's almost done.' She was wandering towards him now, hands deep in the pockets of her denim jacket. Perusing, inspecting, commenting. 'Completely insensitive, you must admit, but totally amazing all the same. So long as you appreciate empty space, that is.'

He shut his eyes, then opened them again, and something was jamming the words in his throat. She was still there, and she was wearing shorts with a liberal splattering of paint, and tights underneath. Thank god for the tights – how much worse would it have been if her legs had been bare? But still, there were the shorts. And she looked as if she owned the place.

'Wow, who'd have thought...' She flashed him a hundred watt smile he assumed was meant to go with the compliments. At least he assumed they were compliments – with Izzy it was very hard to know.

He shrugged. 'I can't take any credit, with this one I left it all to the architects.'

Xander rubbed the stubble on the side of his chin with his thumb, shaking his head to get rid of the blurriness, as she sauntered towards him.

'I pretty much feel like I've got vertigo though. Glass stair treads, then this hanging landing, punched with tiny holes, it's kind of dizzying.' She put out a hand sideways, narrowly missed his bare arm, diverting to the door frame at the last moment. 'Go ahead if you're working in the bathroom, anywhere less giddy than here would be good.'

Whereas his swimming head had less to do with heights, and more to do with sudden lack of oxygen.

'This is one of the smaller bathrooms.' He turned, and padded across the bedroom to the en suite he was supposed to be inspecting, his deck shoes squeaking on the polished boards. 'I'm just checking there's enough room in there, now they've put the fitted cupboards in.'

Her reflection appeared in the bathroom mirror behind his own, softened by the LED lights, as she followed him in. Damn, two of her only made things worse, and filling the air with sweetness too. He backed up against the basin unit, trying to pull out of the danger zone.

'Do you want me to shut the door, so you can see if the cupboards open okay?'

He wasn't sure being closed in was advisable at all, given that the closer she got, the harder he was finding it to keep his hands off her. 'Great idea, thanks.'

As the door handle clicked, he bobbed to try the cupboard door. Playing along with the charade kept his mind off the whole softness of her, made it possible to think he *could* make it out of here without an incident. He was just standing up again, when the lights gave a single flicker.

Oh shit.

And then they went out entirely.

Shit, shit, shit.

The sudden blackness engulfed them.

'Don't worry...it's probably just a power cut.' He made a lunge for the door in the dark.

His torso banged into something soft, and warm, and squirming. Izzy. Right in his face. No surprise there. Shit. Close enough for hair to be tangling in his stubble. He found her shoulders, tried to navigate past her. He had approximately two seconds to make a run for it. He bent his head, and then he was inadvertently rubbing his chin against her cheek, and breathing in her perfume which smelled of burning roses. Too sweet. Too late. Way too late to run now. He heard her drag in a breath as he felt his cheek bump against her face, but he didn't move it away. What the hell was he doing here, and more to the point why wasn't she knocking him out with that flaming right hook of hers? He waited for resistance, but it didn't come. Instead he felt her fingers close around the back of his head. She was pulling him in closer. Slowly, he let his lips meander across her skin, past her nose. When he found her mouth, it was hot and soft and open, and she let out a low groan as he feathered his tongue along the inside of her upper lip. He felt his own lips twitch. Ridiculous that he should be bloody smiling now. As he tasted the velvety depths of her mouth, she was kissing him back, hot and lethal, ramming her body hard against his, and sending thrusts of desire right through him. Not sure who was the hungriest here, he clamped his arms around her back, buried his fingers deep in the chaos of her hair, tugging, rubbing the softness of her neck. Her hands were digging into the

150

muscles of his back, her finger nails scraping delicious arcs across his skin under his shirt, winding around his ribs, sending spiralling shivers straight to his groin. Tasting like heaven, and that would be urgent, desperate, lustful, dizzy heaven, and grinding against him with a need...

A clatter somewhere down below in the house pulled Xander up. Then another. One more bang broke the kiss. As the lights gave a momentary flicker, their bodies parted. A second later, by the time the lights had blinked, then blazed, Izzy had her hand on her mouth, and her back pressed against the door. Xander, wobbling against the shower screen, let his gaze run up her body, as far as the paint smear across her left cheek. He had no idea what the hell happened there, but now it was over, it left him feeling like he had a gaping hole in his chest.

When he finally dared to meet her gaze, their eyes locked in one trembling flash of incomprehension and horror, then a shout from downstairs smashed the silence. 'Sorry mate, just knocked the power off, it's on again now...'

One absent electrician, making a timely appearance.

They both made a grab for the door handle, but Izzy got there first, hurled open the door, bolted across the bedroom, and was out on the landing before Xander could say bubble gum. Getting the hell out of here then.

She was calling out as she picked her way gingerly down the staircase. 'Thanks for letting me see the house, anyway.'

Obviously remembering her manners, despite the hurry. Xander couldn't fault her on her customer relations today, even if that kiss was the last thing in the world he'd needed. And pinning his hopes on her needing the cash so much that she'd come back to finish at The Pink House later. He'd get his head straight, and get the job done. End of.

'The mattress and bedding arrived this morning...' He leaned over the balustrade, and shouted after her. What kind of fool would think that by shouting domestic inanities, he might catch her interest, and hook her back? Only a no hope guy, who had no idea.

She did slow her run across the hall for long enough to give him one wild eyed, backwards glance.

'See you at The Pink House at seven then.' He was shouting louder now, just to be sure she'd heard him.

As for this house, having Izzy round, even briefly, had simply reinforced why he was a thousand miles away from wanting to keep it. This was no place for someone like him, someone with no hope of ever pulling his life back together. As soon as the summer was over, and the outside was straightened up, he'd be selling, for sure.

28

Flowers, spots, and generous euphemisms

Pretend it never happened.

Izzy stabbed the last stray cushions into plastic bags, and tried her new mantra out for size, now she was actually here at The Pink House.

Pretend it never happened?

Easy advice for Luce to dish out, but quite another thing to pull off, when Izzy's whole world was imploding after this afternoon's blunder. She hadn't even managed to get back home to make the chilli for dinner, and she'd had to text the boys to say she'd cook for them later. Her whole day had already been tipped upside down by bloody Xander, and his stupid suggestion of looking round his house, and that was before she'd even got into the sodding en suite.

She grabbed four bulging packs of sheets and cushions, and headed for the house. If she'd had the nerve to get this far, maybe she was managing to block out reality better than she thought.

As for what happened in the bathroom, she preferred not to go there. She suspected she was suffering from what Luce always termed "the post-snog washing-machine effect", because despite the fact that she hadn't been able to face eating anything, from the way her stomach was churning, she might well chuck up at any moment. She reminded herself not to be sick on the cushions. Or on the brand new carpets. Or on the new bed. She simply had to hide behind her bin bags, get in, get out, and away. Easy as.

So. She was here.

And so was he. The hot guy she'd failed to keep her hands off in the dark was standing by the open door as she approached, and giving nothing more away. Damn him, and his slightly raised left eyebrow.

'Hi there...' His voice even more gravelly than usual though.

He stepped back, widening his narrowed eyes slightly, as she barged past him. She couldn't risk lingering, because even though she was cringing inside, and mortified about what happened earlier, she couldn't be entirely sure her inner tramp wasn't going to go out on a limb, and make another grab for a repeat performance. Two of the bags she was carrying hit the polished floorboards, as she dropped them by the bannister post.

'I'd say help yourself, but I see you have anyway.' His slow, snarly comment followed her as she skittered up the stairs. 'The electrician has been to install the chandelier, by the way...'

Izzy made a dash for the sanctuary of the bedroom. So far, so good. It was uncanny the way this house reminded Izzy of the place where she had spent most of her childhood. Even though it had been recently done up, there was still the same quality to the creak of the floorboards. Something about looking through the sash windows catapulted her back in time. She'd been a happy, privileged child, living in a cosy family, with her mum, and her brothers, and the dad she now knew to be a disgusting excuse for a waste of space.

When her family had broken up, the sudden downwards trajectory for Izzy's mum and the children had been like sliding down a snake on the snakes and ladders board. And not just any snake. This was the huge one that caught you out when you got to the ninety ninth square, and whisked you all the way down the board, and deposited you unceremoniously right back at the start. There was nothing to compare with the whole numb shock of it.

Izzy guessed her mum had faced this before, working for clients who lived in the kind of large and affluent home she'd lost. Izzy wasn't sure how she felt about revisiting a house like this, in the guise of hired help rather than occupant. There were some memories which were better left to lie, simply because once you disturbed them they became just that: disturbing.

Upstairs in the bedroom the chandelier was twinkling above the bed, which now had a new mattress, quilt and pillows added. The chandelier was a simple one with a few, tear-drop crystals. Why the hell Xander had made such a song and dance about dusting it yesterday she had no idea. But then he seemed to have a gift for making everything more complicated than it needed to be, didn't he?

She switched her thoughts back to her old home, which usually she tried not to think about at all. They had been train wreck divorce years, when their dad had gone, and the rest of the family had been crammed into a small flat, struggling at new schools, with her mum desperately trying to keep her head above water from day to day, and fight her dad through the courts. It was Luce who had really helped Izzy to settle in, and assimilate into the completely different social structure at school. For Izzy who'd been used to an all girls education, negotiating corridors full of testosterone challenged fifteen year old lads had been a minefield, despite having a house full of boys at home. With a whole new social etiquette of the co-ed school to negotiate, having Luce as her wing girl had been a godsend.

The quilt cover she'd bought for Christina's bed was a similar print to her own at home, and she unpacked it now, slipped the new duvet in, and flung it into place over the bed. She spread a couple of folded silk quilts across the bottom of the bed, and the array of cushions she threw into place against the bed head completed the effect. As a final finishing touch, she arranged the letters that spelled LOVE along the top of one of the large chests. She ground her teeth as she looked back on the room from the door – all good, but if anything merited a vomit emoticon, those "love" letters did.

'All done up there.' She thundered down to the bottom of the stairs, and grabbed the bags she had deposited in the hall earlier, catching a view of Xander's back, as she sped past the kitchen, and out towards the sanctuary of the summer house.

Once there she began to tie the cushions onto the chairs. Finally, she grabbed a chair and got out her tools, to fix the bunting in place. Twenty minutes later, she was just stretching to attach the last flag when she heard the clunk of feet on the wooden steps outside.

'Anything I can do?'

Izzy lurched at the low burr of Xander's voice behind her, dropped the bunting end, and flashed round on the chair she was standing on. And damn him for arriving when she was so close to being finished.

'You can stop creeping up on people, for a start.' And making them wobble on their chairs. She knew she sounded snappy, but cross was good, because at least when she was angry it made her feel in control.

He crossed the summerhouse in three strides, taking in the new additions.

'Nice.' He nodded, with an air of satisfaction, which would have come across more convincingly, if his eyes had been on the cushions, and not apparently stuck on her legs.

Thank Thursday she'd swapped her shorts for a dress she'd

nabbed from Luce's rail before she set off, especially since she was wobbling up here on a chair. Not so good that she'd lost the tights. If she'd given a damn at all, she'd have been damned happy she'd shaved her legs though.

Izzy gave a snort. 'You don't even like flowers and spots.' Here he was, being patronising, and looking down his nose at the world again.

'Dots and flowers aren't my favourite, but I can see they might look good in this context.'

Still talking in that same drawly way then. How could he be so bloody superior and unsmiling about cushions?

'Well, thank you to our very own Gracious Living Interiors Expert.' The way he was sauntering round prodding and poking things she was ready to throw something at him.

'Health and Safety says you should stand on steps, not chairs.' He sidled in her direction, with what she took for a mocking swagger. 'You don't look particularly stable up there.'

He was in front of her now, and looking down into the dark pools of his eyes, she shivered. Close enough for her to make out the individual prickles of his stubble, was way too close in her book. What was the health and safety advice on guys making your blood pump fast enough to give you a heart attack then?

'I'm fine.' She was talking through gritted teeth, again, and given that she was inadvertently swishing her skirt, she was probably sounding like a spoiled child too. 'At least, I *was* all good until you came along.' There, she hoped that told him.

'You haven't got a brilliant track record on the safety thing, getting stuck in skips, cutting your foot, tripping up in bathrooms...' His lazy drawl slid to a halt.

Tripping up? That was a generous euphemism, considering the way she'd launched herself at him earlier. And he sounded almost expectant. Bloody hell, he surely couldn't think she'd make the same mistake again.

'I'm not going to throw myself at you now if that's what you're

157

thinking.' Important to make herself totally clear here, so she sent him her best scowl too.

He gave a low laugh. 'Not coming back for more of a good thing then...?'

He couldn't be serious. And to think five minutes before she was congratulating herself on a job well done, and thinking she was going to get away with this.

'Good thing?' Hearing her voice soar to a shriek, she yanked it down an octave, tried to cut the decibels, and ended up hissing. 'If you think I enjoyed being snogged within an inch of my life, actually I didn't.' Slamming him down felt good, except from the way his lips were spreading into a smile, he seemed to have taken it as a compliment.

'Oh, I almost forgot, Christina's been adding to the shopping list suggestions.' Great, it sounded like he was changing the subject. 'She'd like two more daybeds, for in here, and a daybed for the play-room, all with cushions and covers. And thirty metres of bunting for the playroom, and the same for the children's bedroom.'

Izzy blinked as she took in the list. It was a relief to move back onto a professional topic, but her mind blurred at the scale of what this one, domestic buyer, was consuming. 'What sort of bunting is it?'

Xander screwed up his face. 'Did she mention kites? It's on your website. A lot of her letting clients have children. A well decorated playroom can close a deal.' He took in her nod.

Another order tying her in to Xander and The Pink House? It was enough to make anyone dizzy. Izzy's heart would have sunk a very long way, if it hadn't been beating so damned fast. As it was it stayed in place, battering her ribs.

'Blue and yellow colour way, or red and green?' She pulled herself together, and stretched up to secure the last piece of bunting. She only had to loop the fabric end over the hook, and now she was up there, ideally the chair needed to be another six inches to the left, but she was damned if she was going to get down and move it with Mr Marvellous watching her like a hawk. She fiddled, missed the hook three times, then stretched a bit further. Got it. But as she made that final stretch to get the loop over the hook, she felt the chair tilt underneath her feet, then she was tipping, and the world went into slow motion. One second she was falling, the next Xander was leaping towards her, the second after that she thumped into his chest, and his arms had her clamped tight against his T shirt. Too shocked to even gasp, yet somehow the delicious smell of him was intoxicating her. And then she was clinging onto his shirt, and somehow her mouth had locked onto his, and her taste buds exploded with the dark coffee and bitter chocolate and hot, velvet man.

Her front brain was exploding, her body was on fire, but somewhere at the back of her mind, the sensible part of her brain was flashing up the danger signs, and reminding her a) she was locked in mouth on mouth combat with – ouch – a customer, who she'd just assaulted for the second time in a day, and b) she really should be home by now, making...

'Chilli...' Izzy gasped, broke away from the kiss, and struggled to get her feet back onto the ground. She pushed her fists against Xander's chest and broke free from his support.

Bloody hell. He leaps in to save her from a nasty fall, and she repays him by launching herself straight at his lips. And this time it had been light, nothing to do with the dark and confined spaces, and her blood was popping like shaken champagne. What's more, when she snogged him it made her feel as if she wouldn't be able to stop. Ever. And that wasn't good, in fact it was totally bloody terrifying. She had never felt so out of control. 'I need to go...'

As she bolted, she caught a sideways glimpse of Xander, eyebrows on the ceiling, jaw on the floor. He was suitably and horribly appalled as he had every right to be. If she was thinking of customer relations – and realistically given the business Xander had brought their way, that should have been her number one priority – she should have stayed and made a full and sincere apology. One jumping in a day was dreadful, but two was beyond reproach. But it was too late for that, because she was already hurtling across the grass. Already gone.

29

Thursday Afternoon, 12th June

LUCE & RUBY

Luce's flat

Drowning not waving

RE: VINTAGE AT THE CINEMA... NEWS AND ROTAS

Hi Dida, and the rest of the guys,
Cake of the week nearly had me booking my flight home...
almost!

waving from the beach Ollie

Ruby glanced up from the falabella family she was colouring in,
and fixed Luce with a quizzical stare. 'Why did you throw your
phone on the floor Mummy?'
Luce dragged in a breath, and tried to blink away the image

that was attached at the bottom of the email. Ollie, in the surf, surrounded by hot girls in bikinis. At least six of them. And the way they were casually draped all over him left her seething.

She always made a point of telling Ruby the truth, but this once she was going to have to go with a porky. 'Sorry, it slipped out of my hand, I need to be more careful.'

No question, she needed to watch where she opened her emails, ideally choosing somewhere that would cushion a falling hand set. She wasn't sure her phone would survive many more trips through space at seventy miles an hour, followed by a crash landing against the book case.

But this had to be the worst of Ollie's emails yet. If only she hadn't been so pig headed and self-righteous when he left. If only she'd answered that first email he'd sent her when he'd landed, fresh off the plane in Bali, instead of blanking it. At the time she'd been so up in the air and confused about what had happened in those two hours before he left to get the plane, when he'd called round to say goodbye to her and Ruby. Two hours when her sensible, responsible brain had a total by-pass that she'd been trying to blank ever since. Not replying to his email had been her way of pretending those two hours never happened.

Her denial about what they'd done had been so complete and all-encompassing at the time, she hadn't ever stopped to think how Ollie must have felt when she didn't reply. Somehow the very fact those two misguided hours had happened, were the reason she hadn't been able to face a year long, small talking, email correspondence, based on a boat that she'd very definitely missed.

Finding out that she and Ollie had the chemistry of the decade, when he was about to board a plane and go to the other side of the world was just plain bad timing. What hurt even more was that she'd known she only had to say the word that night, and he'd have been willing to stay. Even that close to getting on the plane, he was willing to throw away the trip of a lifetime, to stay with her and Ruby. But she hadn't been able to make herself say the words, because she'd been too scared. Too scared it might all go wrong. Too scared to commit. Too scared they might all get hurt.

Too scared. It was the story of her life.

And today it had come right back to haunt her, big time.

30

Making judgements and pointing fingers

Accidentally stopping a woman from falling was one thing, not being able to keep your mouth off hers was something else entirely.

Xander grabbed a handful of his hair, tugged very hard, and mentally collected the parts of himself which appeared to have been scattered across the summer house. And he'd managed to scare her off so much that she'd actually left at speed. He hurried to follow Izzy, but even before he got around the front of the house, he heard the door of her van clunk closed, the engine splutter, sounding, as always, as if it were never going to start.

Despite the fact that he wasn't religious, he made a silent prayer for it to fail. Then something beyond disappointment imploded in his chest, as he heard the engine roar to life. He forced himself to carry on, hoping, at least, to snatch a last view of her, as she headed off into the distance. One small woman, who'd blown through his life like a hurricane twice today, and now he'd driven her away. Well done with that one.

He emerged into the driveway, to see the van slewed across the gateway, and Izzy jumping down to the floor.

'Fuck, fuck, fuck fuck...'

Flailing her fists, cursing loudly, why did that not surprise him?

'Is there a problem?' He raised his eyebrows in silent question as he walked towards her, and tried to shut out the football crowd, that had erupted into cheering, in his head.

'Stuffing flat tyre on the front...'

He could see that now. He gave a mental high five, then remembered himself, and tried to feel less happy. Now he was at the front of the van, he could see where the wheel had gouged into the earth beneath the gravel. Better and better.

'Okay. Leave it to me.' He headed off towards the nearby garage, to collect what he needed to change the wheel, and returned a few minutes later, with a trolley jack and a handful of tools. He sprang into action, shoving the jack around, and wielding the wheel brace. The wheel nuts came off no problem, but the wheel was proving more stubborn to shift.

Once he'd brushed off Izzy's vague offer of help, she'd retreated, propped herself against the tall stone gatepost, and had quietly watched from a distance, as he worked. He got the feeling her immediate urgency for flight had ebbed away. She kicked the gravel with her scuffed converse resignedly, as she wandered back towards him now.

'Boys and their cars.' She rolled her eyes. 'This is just what my brothers are like – er, not that I'm knocking it, actually I'm really grateful.'

Nice afterthought there.

'The wheel nuts are off okay, but the wheel won't come free.' How much of a failure did this big macho caveman feel telling her that?

'Shit.' Izzy shook her head and grimaced. 'Just my luck...'

Xander had no idea why it was so important for him to appear like a mechanical whizz kid, other than the points he might gain on that invisible, yet vital, macho skill set scale. 'It's probably seized on after the winter. It'll need heat on it.' Instinctively trying to show he was bursting with testosterone, made him feel pretty pathetic. 'I'll get the local garage out in the morning – unless you have breakdown insurance that is?'

She scowled at him, obviously exasperated. 'Do I look like I have breakdown insurance?'

True. She didn't.

He attempted to sound breezy. 'It's fine, the van can stay here until morning, and you can too. I could run you back to town, but that would be a pointless seeing as you'll need to come back for the van first thing tomorrow. Unless you have something you really need to get back for, that is?'

Her brow furrowed. 'I need to get back, because...Well, I promised to do dinner for the twins.' Her hesitant grimace suggested she knew how pathetic that sounded.

Dinner for the twins? Now he'd heard it all. 'Excuse me? They play in a band. They drive. Shouldn't they be able to get their own dinner? How old are they anyway?' Xander couldn't hide his disbelief. If this was an excuse, it was a bad one. She surely didn't really think she had to cook for a couple of over-grown teenagers?

'Twenty-one.'

'Twenty-one?' He couldn't keep the rise of incredulity out of his voice. 'I think they should be able to sort out their own dinner, for once. Ever heard of take-away pizzas?'

She gave a groan. 'Pizza delivery is what they do. It's just, well... they're my responsibility. It isn't healthy to eat pizza all the time, so I like to look after them.'

His response was firm. 'Text them, let them take responsibility for themselves for once, I'm sure they'll understand. They might

166

even be happy to get a break from their suffocating surrogate mother.'

Izzy still looked unsure, and he grimaced, suddenly aware that she may be covering for worries of a different kind.

'You'll be quite safe here. Seven bedrooms should give you enough space to stay well away from me, and whatever may have happened before...' Hoping that covered it, in a "less is more" nutshell. 'I'm really *not* going to jump on you, okay?'

He noted that her usual fuck you "attitude" had turned to quiet resignation, and wasn't sure he was comfortable with that.

'I guess it'll have to be.'

On balance, he probably preferred her rude and ballsy incarnation.

'No need to sound so enthusiastic.' He heard himself sniping, and switched to a more conciliatory tone. 'A cool beer, stir-fry, and a DVD. How does that sound?'

'Do you have rom coms?'

'Sure.' Fingers crossed that somewhere amongst the lifestyle props Christina had already installed, he could source some.

Xander tried to keep the triumph out of his voice, although he wasn't clear what he had to be triumphant about. Dinner with a girl who he'd failed to keep his hands off, not only once, but twice, who'd tried to leg it, who patently, would rather not be here? And who was going to make him sit through rom coms.

Perhaps it had more to do with the disappointment that had engulfed him when he thought she'd gone. More to do with the fact that when he started something, he liked to finish it. He was about to face an evening when he obviously needed to be on his best behaviour, and he couldn't remember a time in his life when he felt more like being bad.

*   *   *   *

'I can't remember the last time I sat and watched one DVD, let alone three, although I'm not sure The Hangover is strictly romcom.' Izzy sounded as if she were confessing here. 'In fact I don't often sit down at all.'

Xander looked across at her, curled up on the sofa opposite him, hugging her knees. She wasn't the only shocked one in the room. He could barely believe he'd just sat through Bridesmaids *and* He's Just Not That Into You, or more surprising still, that he'd enjoyed howling with laughter along with Izzy. He'd definitely drawn the line at Marley and Me though.

They were sitting in the snug beyond the kitchen, which had had sofas reinstated after the renovations, and was already a haven of stripes, and rugs in shades of grey and pale blue. He tried not to notice the haphazard flash of upper thigh beneath Izzy's bunched up dress, as she shifted her position.

'If you've never seen Marley and Me you're very behind on your girly films, so if you aren't watching films, what *do* you do in the evenings?' He asked, making conversation gently, because that was how this evening was.

'Mostly I prep stuff for the emporium, or I catch up with home chores, or run round after my brothers.'

She sounded laid back about it, but she was describing days and nights where she never stopped. In some ways it sounded as if her life was more full on than his.

'So how come you do all the work? Aren't you a bit young to be playing mother?' If he was gently teasing information out of her to satisfy his curiosity, he wanted it to seem totally accidental.

'It wasn't planned, it's just the way things worked out since our mum went away.'

'Something doesn't add up here. Your mother's gone off and left you holding the proverbial babies, also known as your brothers.' He was as surprised as Izzy to find himself wading in. 'So I don't suppose they even do the dishes? If you eat you wash up – that thought goes a long way.' He couldn't believe how cross he was on her behalf.

'Anyway, what about your dad?' He saw her flinch.

'My dad left. It's not something I discuss.'

That told him. She was definitely shutting Xander down here. He rubbed his jaw but stayed silent as she carried on.

'Now you mention it, the idea that someone who has totally disappeared should take responsibility is laughable, and pretty damned ironic too.' She gave a bitter snort. 'Actually I appreciate your concern, but I'm happy with things as they are. Our mum had a hell of a time bringing up four teenagers on her own, she did a great job, but it's time for her to live her life. She can't hang around forever now we're grown up, and we wouldn't want her to. When she had a second chance to be happy, we made damn sure she took it. Her new partner got the offer of a four year post in New Zealand, so it was a no brainer. She had to go.'

Xander thought fleetingly of his own parents, of losing his mother. Her illness had taken her away a tiny slice at a time, until all that was left was her wasted body. That loss had made him flip and had changed the course of his life. Before his mum was ill Xander had a marriage he assumed would last forever, and only after his mum died did he discover that it hadn't been as strong as he thought at all. And just like Izzy, Christina, the older sister, had always been there for him, trying to pick up the pieces as best she could.

'So what about your brothers?'

'Parker and Barney are the pizza delivery death metal guys, who only come home for band practice, meals, and to go to the toilet. And then there's Ollie, who's in Thailand. I've got his van and his share at Vintage Cinema while he's travelling. Ollie's not so bad, but the twins, given free rein, could total the place in seconds. It took my mum and I so much effort to make the house into a home, I couldn't bear to see them trash it. If I keep control, I make sure it stays perfect, because for me a perfect home means we're safe.'

'And you're so obsessed with home making, you've actually

made a career out of it.'

For someone like him that was a scary thought, but judging from the way her pout had flattened to a straight line, she wasn't going to agree with him on this.

'Okay, my situation is unusual, but it's mine.' Her eyes flashed. 'When your family has broken up, a stable home is very important.'

He'd guess from how jumpy she was, that "broken up" was a bit of an over simplification, whereas his own dad and mum had separated by default. They had lots of homes, and one day in his early twenties it had finally dawned on Xander that they never actually coincided in the same house any more.

'It may be nothing to do with me, but at your age shouldn't you be having a good time, not being a domestic slave?' He needed to tread carefully, but some things needed to be said.

Her chin was out now. 'It's my choice.'

Xander felt his frown growing deeper with every word she said. That was the trouble, down trodden people were the last ones to see it. 'So when was the last time someone cooked you a meal?'

'You did, just now, in case you've forgotten. I told you, it was wonderful.' She shot him a smile. When she wrinkled her nose like that, she had dimples in her cheeks.

He resisted the ridiculous thought that he'd like to put his finger in them. 'You know that's not what I mean, so tell me when.'

Her smile faded as she knitted her brow. 'Okay, you win, I can't remember the last time someone cooked for me.'

'There you go.' He rounded on her. 'This isn't good. Just because you paint things pink, and cover things in flowers and bows, doesn't make it all okay, you know?'

From the way her face darkened, she wasn't happy with that remark.

She sat bolt upright, obviously fired up. 'Well, you're one to talk. Look at you. You don't have a home at all, and just when it looks like you might be going to get one, you say you don't want it. If we're making judgements, and pointing fingers, what's that

170

all about then?'

He winced slightly at the onslaught. She wasn't pulling any punches then, and right now it felt like she'd got him on the ropes, but bowing out wasn't his way.

'Not everyone who loses a home reacts in the same way. We don't all turn into rabid cushion fetishists, who festoon our lives with bunting, and prop cut out letters spelling "love" on the dado rails.' He quipped back. As things had panned out, letting Astrid keep the house in Hampstead, and their place in France too, had seemed like the least he could do, given that their marriage had failed because of him. He didn't want anything to do with those places anyway. They would only have been a constant reminder of what he'd broken.

Xander watched Izzy's eyes fly open, and she stared at him, as if she couldn't quite believe what he'd said. Maybe he'd been too scathing, but hell, she had to appreciate that sprigs and pastels weren't the universal "fix all" solution she thought they were. A bit of pretty wouldn't scratch the surface of his own issues. For some people the problems ran a lot deeper. This house was loaded with painful memories of a different kind, which were agonising to revisit. At least the renovations had wiped the slate clean in some ways. They might be clinical, but in some ways clinical was like a breath of fresh air. Before, when it was full of his mum's things, the sense of the tragedy of the past had been so oppressive he couldn't bear to be here at all. He took a long breath, and braced himself for Izzy's return attack, but instead of the anticipated wrath, he watched as the scorching scowl sank from her brow. She was suddenly pale, except for a crimson smudge on each cheek.

'Sorry, I didn't think, I should have known better...' She gave an apologetic shuffle, and rearranged her feet. 'We all have baggage to deal with, I should have been more sensitive to yours.'

Xander wasn't quite sure what baggage exactly she was referring to, but he sensed that somewhere along the line, she'd rumbled him. But he didn't care half as much as he should have done, because strangely, he had an idea he'd rumbled her too.

This might be the perfect opportunity to dip out, force the conversation to an end, before she decided to dig further.

'I think it's time someone brought you another beer.'

As he stood up and stretched, he couldn't help noticing that her gaze had locked onto his abs, and her expression had gone all soft and gooey. And he couldn't help noticing he liked that.

31

LUCE & DIDA

At Luce's flat

Sex on the beach or a rainy summer in Matlock

'Hey, everything okay up here?'

Luce tiptoed into her living room, to find Dida pouring over her laptop.

Dida smiled. 'Yes, Ruby's been great. She dropped off really quickly, once she'd talked about ponies for half an hour. And I knew Aidie's parents wouldn't mind staying home with the kids, if I did beef stroganoff for tea. So did the wedding dress delivery go okay?'

'It was great in the end.' Luce wrinkled her nose and poured herself a coffee from the jug on the tray. In theory she didn't like weddings, but she had to admire the Beeston's total dedication. 'Steffie loved the dress, it fitted – thankfully, because I really might have jumped out of the window if it hadn't – and it was awesome to see the cake and the bridesmaids dresses, and her mum's outfit, and the shoes, and the serviettes, and the place settings, and the chair bows. Oh, and Steffie even read me her vows too.' Luce suspected her raised eyebrows might give away that it had all been a little bit over the top, but what the hell. 'So thanks for looking after Ruby whilst I was out.'

'Well before she settled down Ruby showed me every single one of Ollie's postcards, and gave me detailed descriptions of where he's been travelling.' Dida stirred the sugar into her coffee, and bit into a chocolate brownie. 'So I was right about the geography part.'

'Did you see that latest email from him?' Luce tried to make the question casual.

Dida pushed a crumb into her mouth. 'With the bikini babes?'

'Talk about bloody sex on the beach.' That came out as a whole lot more of a wail than she'd planned. The truth was, every time she thought about Ollie shagging someone else, it was sending her head to crazy places. She'd hoped that saying it out loud, rubbishing it even, might make it less of a biggie. She took a large bite of her own brownie, and let the sugar and cocoa pulse around her body. Anyone who thought eating chocolate didn't bring you instant comfort had it totally wrong.

'Or maybe not...' Dida's reply was level. She reached for another brownie, then tapped it thoughtfully on her plate. 'Maybe he's just trying to make you react.'

'What?' Luce supressed a grimace.

'As for the sex thing, I wouldn't worry. He'll be back before long. But you might need to send him a sign of some kind.'

That was exactly the reassurance Luce was desperate to hear, except Luce had no idea how Dida could sound so certain.

Luce gave a long sigh. 'Sex on the beach in Thailand, or a rainy summer in Matlock – I know which I'd choose if I was him.' It was a no brainer as far as Luce could see. Thailand won every time she chewed it around in her head.

174

'And I know too, and it wouldn't be Thailand...' Dida gave a low laugh and sent Luce a sympathetic smile. 'But you definitely need to drop him an email. Something casual, to remind him you haven't forgotten him. You could tell him about Ruby and her current obsession with falabellas. I think Ollie would like that.'

Luce gave Dida a grateful grin. 'I might just do that.' She would need to screw up every bit of her courage, but she was getting a lot more practice at that lately. 'So how about you. Have you sorted out how you're going to play this cycling holiday?'

Dida gave an eye roll. 'You know me. I'll handle it poolside, while downing huge quantities of Prosecco.' She gave a low laugh. 'And doing affirmations to make sure Vintage Cinema Club gets approval on that damned business loan.'

Luce laughed too, and crossed her fingers very tightly for the same end. Luce could definitely benefit from taking a life lesson or two from Dida.

32

Even Later, Thursday Evening, 12th June

IZZY & XANDER

The Pink House

The thought of cool beer

'Hey...' Xander turned on Izzy, as she followed him through to the kitchen. 'You're supposed to be sitting down whilst I get the beers.'

'Just thought I'd stretch my legs.' She'd had to move. 'I'm not used to doing the couch potato thing.'

As he crossed to get the beers, she wandered over to lean against the island unit, resting one bare foot on top of the other. She'd come through without her shoes, and the limestone floor was smooth and cool under the soles of her feet. She shivered as she saw his T-shirt ride up again and his jeans tighten, as he bent to reach into the fridge. Still as devastating as ever, from a distance. Just too explosive close up. And definitely out of bounds.

He'd kept his distance meticulously right through this evening, just as he'd assured her he would. Even though she'd been silently aching for him to close the space between them, there was something incredibly delicious about spending hours together, watching random TV, with a guy who was essentially a stranger. And damn it if she'd spent the length of three films wishing he would go back on his word, and jump her on the sofa.

He straightened to standing, holding two green bottles between the fingers of one hand, and clunked them onto the worktop. Even his elbows looked amazing. How was it possible for one person to be so mind-blowingly attractive in every area? She heard two clinks as the bottle tops flew off. He turned and rubbed his forehead with the back of his hand, scrubbed his fingers through his hair.

'One cool beer coming up.' He appeared to be assessing her, through half closed lashes, as he sauntered in her direction.

She felt her mouth water, not at the thought of cool beer, but as his scent reached her before he did. Whatever he smelled of, it turned her knees to jelly every time.

'There you go...'

Her eyes were a lot lower than his collar bone now she'd taken off her shoes, and her stomach gave a tiny lurch as her gaze locked onto the indentation at the base of his throat. He held out a bottle, gently grazing it across her bare arm as he handed it to her.

She jumped at the chill. 'Hey.'

He didn't reply, just raised one eyebrow, pursing his lips around his own bottle as he took a swig, and when his eyes finally met hers they were dark and guarded. She followed his gaze downwards, to where it honed in on her nipples, pebbling, and erect, with the shock of the cold bottle on her arm. Nothing to do with her skin tingling all over because of the hot guy alert. Honestly. As his gaze moved up, in the split second it met her own again, she saw his eyes had blurred, and she couldn't stop the trace of a smile. Then she felt her lips part as she drew in a deep breath, and stayed perfectly still, waiting, aching.

Slowly, slowly, his face moved towards her. Then just before his mouth met hers, he ducked out, slipped sideways, brushed his cheekbone against hers. No other contact. Just that. She heard a low groan from her own throat. He pulled backwards to look at her, and as she slowly raised her eyes to meet his, she could hear the thump of a heartbeat, but she wasn't sure whose. As she raised an unsteady hand to check where he'd touched her face, she saw the lines of his face change, then her insides turned to hot syrup, as she took in a disarming smile.

She felt the lightest brush of his lips on hers, the faintest tease of his tongue, then he pulled away. She shuddered. A ripple of white hot desire snaked through her.

For a moment he rested a steadying hand on her arm. Then, as if he was deliberately holding his body away from hers, he reached behind her head. Made tiny tugs on single pieces of her hair, before he cupped her head with his hands, and raked his fingers through the tangle of her waves. As his tongue made contact with the base of her neck, she wound her fingers under his shirt, but lightly he lifted her hand away, and placed it back by her side.

'No touching. Not yet.' His words were a grating whisper.

One tug, and he was pulling her head backwards, tracing a finger over her lips. 'Every time I kiss you, you run, so maybe we'll try without.'

So he thought he'd been kissing her, not the other way around, even though she'd...That thought came to a crashing halt as one bold hand slid up under her skirt, and slipped between her thighs. As she parted her legs, his fingers were already inside her pants, fluttering against her clit. Now was not the best time to decide this was a bad idea, not when he was doing what he was doing. She pushed onto his hand, moved with him, felt the mounting need surging through her. Spreading her arms sideways, she grasped hold of the edge of the granite work-surface, to hold herself, and stop her wobbling legs from collapsing, half closing her eyes to shut out the blur of the cabinets. It was so long since she'd done this, yet it was going so fast, as if he'd inadvertently released some kind of crazy chain reaction deep inside her, and there was nothing she could do about it, except enjoy it. Could it be any more embarrassing, to be on the verge of coming, with a guy she didn't know, in a kitchen...Then suddenly she didn't even care any more, as her whole body exploded and imploded all at the same time. Talk about rainbows, firework fountains, crystal mazes, falling off mountains. And that was no measly excuse for a mountain...that was a Himalayan peak. As she slid down onto the pale cream stone floor, she came face to face with Xander's jeans, and looked up to catch a view of an erection pushing against denim that reminded her she'd left him hanging.

A second later he was beside her, propping his back against the island unit, crossing his legs, casually, in front of him.

His eyes had a kind of impressed gleam she hadn't counted on, given the one sided nature of the pleasure. He dangled a bottle in her direction. 'Beer? For the intermission?'

She shot him a shy, sideways glance, and as she stretched out her hand to take the beer, he did that smile again. She twisted a strand of hair around her finger, and smiled back, as she struggled to steady her breathing again.

'Thanks. And thanks for...you know. It was epic, in a Himalayan mountain kind of a way.'

That put a kind of satisfied smirk on his face. 'I take it you're pleased you came, then?' She wasn't quite sure which arrival he was talking about, but whatever, it was a big fat yes to both.

She pushed him a grin. 'I hope you don't think I do that every time someone gives me a beer.'

His smile broadened. 'I'd like to see what happens when you drink it.'

'Actually, I don't actually do this at all, not usually.' It suddenly seemed important to let him know. 'I mean I don't make a habit of ending up in crumpled heaps on people's kitchen floors, with people I don't know, not on a regular basis. Well hardly at all... well, never, in fact.'

179

He was laughing at her now. 'Me neither. But I'm happy to make an exception, for you, just for tonight, okay?'

Somehow that made it better, so she gave a nod. Loving the way his thighs pushed tight against his jeans, she trailed out a finger, daring herself to touch. She traced a finger-nail along his muscle, and felt a curious tingling after-shock through the denim.

'It'll be pay-back time any minute.' She could hardly believe the throaty voice she heard was hers.

This time when she ran her finger along his thigh, the after-shock was juddering.

'Is that a threat? Or a promise...'

She didn't have time to get around to answering that. He finished his beer with one tilt of his head, jumped to his feet, and she heard the chink of glass on granite, as he put his bottle down. Then he was holding out his hand, and the next thing she knew she was being pulled towards the snug.

'Doesn't anyone think to provide cushions around here?' He gave a wicked grin, as he peeled off his T-shirt and bundled it up.

Izzy inhaled sharply. Smoothly defined muscles and powerful shoulders, all enhanced by darkly bronzed skin.

'Nice tan you've got there Xander.'

He brushed off the compliment. 'Perk of the job, location shoot in South America.' Then he threw himself down and was on his back on the rug, head propped on the makeshift T-shirt pillow.

Bloody hell. Horizontal. She was unsure what he expected next. 'Now what?'

'Your call.'

Her eyes followed the trace of hair, from his navel, down the perfect plane of his stomach, and her breathing sped up as she came to the sexy place between his hip bones where it disappeared down below the waistband of his jeans.

'That makes a change. Usually you're the one ordering everyone...' Her words tailed to nothing as her eyes slid to take in the slanting punch of an erection, which was growing as she watched. She swallowed hard.

For a moment she hesitated, not quite knowing what to do with this whole, beautiful man, lying in front of her. Then slowly, she lifted one bare foot, and rested it lightly on his thigh. She felt the flex of his muscles beneath her foot, heard him catch his breath. She moved her foot upwards, to his groin, and increased the pressure, feeling the heat of him through the sole of her foot. His low groan told her she was on the right track. She moved her foot around, daring to nudge the swollen bulge of his penis. More teasing nudging. Then another groan as she carefully moved her foot again, to rest along the length of him.

'Come and sit on me.' His voice was blurred and grating.

Hang on, wasn't she supposed to be the one giving the orders here?

'Now.'

She lowered herself to sit astride him, put her hands on his chest, and got a view straight into his eyes. As she shuffled to find a comfortable position, she felt the heat of him through her knickers and watched dusky shadows of pleasure passing across his face as she shifted.

'That's better. Now stay still, and don't touch.' He was back to ordering her around and suddenly she didn't give a damn.

He put his hands on her hips, and shifted her forward. 'Sorry, if you'd kept that up I'd have come straight away.' He cleared his throat. 'As for these buttons on the front of your dress, I've been itching to undo these ever since you turned up.'

He smiled as he undid the second button. 'Flowery bra. Why does that not surprise me?' He rubbed a thumb lazily across a nipple. 'Liking the silk by the way.' He carried on teasing, and just before she was about to die, he whipped down the bra cups.

He let out a shuddering gasp as he revealed her breasts, then stretched up to touch.

Izzy shifted, her brain fuzzy and confused by the pleasure. He dragged her towards him, cupped her breasts between his hands, and drew his tongue across a nipple, before he took it into his mouth. He kept up the torture, rubbing her other nipple, making her breath come in uncertain jerks, as her pelvis ground onto his stomach. Her sudden moan that grew to a gasp came out of nowhere, and felt as if it belonged to someone else. Her knees gripped the sides of his body and, as her eyes closed, her body disintegrated with waves of pleasure. She knew he was watching her every move.

He only looked away when she collapsed on top of him, but this time she recovered faster, and pushed herself up to sitting. She began to fiddle with the buttons of his jeans.

He sat up abruptly, and ran a hand through his hair. 'Jeez, I need to go and see if I can find a condom.' He gave a grimace. 'Although if there is one it's probably out of date.'

'It's okay, I've got some.' Deftly she slipped off him, crossed the room, and dug in her bag. Thank you Luce, for always making her carry her emergency supplies. She flipped a foil pack in his direction. 'They're Luce's, not...'

He cut her off in mid-sentence, with a half laugh. 'Right now I don't care whose they are.' He met her half way back across the room, pulling her dress up and over her head in one easy movement.

Her pants and bra hit the floor a moment later, and she watched as he peeled off his jeans, shuddering as she saw the size of him.

As he pushed her down to sitting, the velvet of the sofa crushed against the skin of her back. Then he stood in front of her, and took her hands in each of his, and placed one on each side of her.

'No touching, and definitely no kissing,' His voice was little more than a grating whisper. 'Not until it's over.'

She looked down at his dark scrambled hair, caught the shadow of the tiny scar on the side of his cheek as he parted her knees, slid his hand upwards, to where her thighs met. He was on one knee in front of her now, dragging her hips into position, gently nudging her clit with his dick, teasing.

'Steady...' He put a hand on her arm, and caught her eye. She stared, unable to look away from the intense, inky darkness of his gaze. He held her eyes there, welded to his, widening, for what seemed like forever. Until she was completely still.

And then he slid into her.

Her mouth dropped open, and she heard herself cry out. She lay back on the feather-bed softness of the sofa, and gave herself up to the twist and grind of pleasure, closing her eyes tightly, to concentrate on the chaos overtaking her. She opened them, as she heard a low growl lodging in Xander's throat, took in the beautiful grimace spreading across his face, and as he gave one final push, she let him take her with him. Whoever said the female orgasm lasted twenty five seconds had to have been underestimating. Xander let his head fall against her neck as she slumped. And then, only then, did he begin to kiss her.

33

Thursday Night/Friday Morning, 12th June

Subject: RE: *waving from the beach*

Hi Olls,
Pleased to hear you're having a fab time. Just to let you know
Ruby's so thrilled with your cards. She can't stop talking
about them – that and her latest obsession with falabella
ponies!

waving from Matlock Luce & Ruby xx

34

Thursday Night/Friday Morning, 12th/13th June

XANDER & IZZY

The Pink House

Caveman, out of practice

It seemed like a very long time later when Xander pushed his arm out from where it had gone numb underneath a sea of curls, to squint at his watch. He had no idea how he'd feel about this later, but he'd face that tomorrow. Right now, he knew it couldn't have been any other way.

'It's two thirty, is this the part where I carry you up to bed?' He was uncertain of how she'd react on all counts, but he'd float the idea and see where it got him.

'Thanks for the offer.' She rubbed her eyes blearily. 'But I can easily walk.'

He found himself smiling, uncontrollably, as he ignored her protests and scooped her up. Even as he had spoken the words, and now, clasping her body tightly against his, he realised that this was what he'd been wanting to do, ever since he had carried her across to his car, the night he'd found her in his skip. As he swung along the hall with Izzy in his arms, and turned up the wide stairs, he was filled with a curiously certain sense that this could be all he was ever going to want. Except that was crazy. He could never let that happen. He wiped that thought, and concentrated on her tangled hair flopping, the way her pale knees bent in the crook of his elbow, the burn of her fingers as she dug in, to cling around his neck.

Something in the way she curved her naked body into his told him he was carrying her to his bed, and not to another bed, in a room of her own. Downstairs, when he'd picked her up, he'd been thinking of the sheer comfort of falling into a deep sleep, with her tucked in bed beside him. But now, fifteen stairs later, he was screamingly aware of the sensuous friction of her skin on his own, the irresistible way her flesh yielded in his fingers as he carried her, and the thump of his growing erection, as it rose to bump the dip of her bottom, with every step he took.

This whole thing had taken him unawares. Out of practice didn't begin to cover it. He hoped he had some condoms in his bag upstairs, because they were damn well going to need them.

35

Friday Afternoon, 13th June

LUCE & DIDA

Vintage at the Cinema

Bits and bobs

'So Izzy's looking for three more daybeds?' Luce fiddled with the post it note announcing the fact. 'Her getting stuck in that skip turned out well for our cause, even if it means no child this side of Paris is going to be able to have a French bed because they're all in a pink house near Ashbourne. I was hoping I'd see her today, to ask how she'd got on with her building site visit.'

'There's a bit of a news blackout on that.' Dida looked up from her laptop. 'She rang me first thing this morning saying something about Chou-fleur breaking down, and asked me to cover this afternoon so she can work at home, which was fine as I was planning to be here in any case. She sounded a bit flustered'

Luce gave a laugh. 'Let's hope that's a good sign. If a hot guy like Xander was lusting after me like he's lusting after her, there's no way I'd leave him sitting on a chaise longue.'

Dida gave a shrug. 'Izzy definitely deserves some down time.'

Luce smiled at Dida's euphemism. Down time? Occasionally Dida really showed her age.

Dida carried on. 'Well, my news is that I've almost finished our Vintage Cinema Club business plan, and I'm about to email it to the Enterprise Manager at the bank, so he can process the loan application whilst I'm in Italy. How about you, have you emailed Ollie yet?'

Luce gave a shamefaced grimace. 'I didn't mean to, but I couldn't sleep, and I thought, what the hell, and the next thing, I'd written one and pressed send. Serves me right for taking my iPad to bed, I'd never have done it in the cold light of day.'

'Yay, well done for that.' Dida's whoop turned into a sympathetic smile. 'And now you're waiting for a reply?'

'Yep, checking my phone every five minutes as we speak. Nothing yet though.' Luce shook her head. 'Hey, see that guy over there by the brass bed, he's Mr Browntree, our Susie Cooper collector, who told me on his way in he's got an interest in Art Deco too.'

Dida stretched forward to see, then belted backwards so fast she knocked three standard lamps flying. 'Crap, you have to be kidding?'

Luce jumped to catch the tumbling display. 'Is there a problem?' A bit of a rhetorical question, judging by Dida's agonised grimace.

'That's David Browntree, my obs and gynae man. What the hell's he doing here?' Dida had taken temporary shelter behind a decoupage screen.

'At a guess, I'd say he's buying lovely things, and bringing us much needed takings.' Luce couldn't help but be amused. 'Even gynaecologists will have interests apart from...'

'Enough!' Dida's squawk silenced Luce, then her chest puffed out, as she dragged in a deep breath. 'When a guy prods your bits and bobs with your knees hooked in the air it's bad enough, but facing him across the counter, knowing what he's seen... I'm sorry, but there's no way I can do that.'

Despite her giggles, Luce entirely understood. 'Fine, you go and hide your fanny upstairs in the bridal room. You'll have plenty of time to finesse the business thing, because he's usually here for ages. I'll text you when he's gone, okay?'

Luce didn't get a reply, because Dida was already half way to the stairs, and as she turned back to the shop, it was to find Xander arriving at the counter.

Raking his fingers through his hair again, rocking up, cool as you like, in a suit too, despite the warm day. Could a guy be any more of a hot mess? And smelling divine too, not that Luce was sniffing on her own behalf here. Izzy had to be totally bonkers if she was passing this one up.

'Hi, can I help?' Another smile that Luce had to rein in, for all the right reasons.

The way Xander bit his bottom lip only went to accentuate that gorgeous wide mouth of his. Mentally Luce was shaking her head, hard, holding up her imaginary hands in despair. How could Izzy not?

He tilted his head on one side. 'Izzy in?'

'Nope, sorry.' Luce watched the light fade in Xander's eyes as he took in her reply. But no way was Luce going to allow Izzy to throw away a five star hottie, who was so obviously into her. 'You'll definitely get her at home though. You know where that is don't you?' She suspected that was another rhetorical question.

'Great, thanks. Albert Street?' Xander turned to leave.

Of course he damn well knew. 'Number eight.' Luce called after him with that detail, just to make it look as if she needed to, even though she knew she didn't. 'She'll be working down in the basement, go in through the garden, off the back lane.' Luce hoped he'd got all that.

One hot guy, for Izzy. On a plate. And if Izzy blew this one, Luce was going to blow her top.

36

Friday Afternoon, 13th June

IZZY

In the kitchen, at home

Pattern repeats

Izzy, hunched over her sewing machine, in the sun squares at
the kitchen table, next to the open doors, was thanking every
lucky star in existence that Dida was standing in for her at the
cinema. No way could she have faced Luce after everything that
had happened yesterday. She was finding it pretty hard to get her
own head around it, in fact she was doing her best not to think
about it at all, because whenever she did for a teensy second she
melted, just because of the whole awesomeness of it all. Then she
went hot with shame, then cold in case someone should find out,
then sweaty rivulets started running down her back. And she had
no idea what those rivulets were about.

Xander had woken her abruptly at six thirty with a shake, and presented her with a mug of coffee, and her clothes in a neatly folded pile. Definitely a guy who got things done. And more fool her for imagining it could have happened any other way. Problem was, she didn't even know how the etiquette of the one night stand thing went. Any hope of being woken slowly, with a snog, went right out of the window.

This morning he was already dressed in a suit, and champing at the bit to head off to a meeting. He must have been up for hours, because her van had already been collected by a tyre company, and Xander had apparently organised for it to be returned to her later, at home. Almost before she'd had time to open her eyes, let alone wake up, he'd zoomed her back into town, and left her standing on the pavement outside her house, whilst he disappeared into the sunrise, in a proverbial cloud of dust.

She'd dived in the shower, and rushed off to the cinema, and the refuge of the Luce-free morning shift. Once she'd got home again, Izzy had got straight on the phone and tracked down the three day beds she needed. Now she was losing herself in the mindless repetition of making bunting. Coupled with the fatigue, which made her feel like she had needles sticking in her eyes, the kites and spots and stripes of the bunting fabric should have been enough to bring her brain to a halt. But somewhere between the flags, the scissors, and the ironing board, rogue thoughts were creeping through. She never leapt into bed with strangers, but worse, Xander was such an arrogant know it all, and he annoyed the hell out of her.

She told herself to concentrate on the pattern repeats...

The trouble was he was one hell of a good kisser, not to mention all the rest. Talk about divine shagging. Which she definitely wouldn't be, especially not with Luce, who would no doubt try to prise it out of her if she got so much as a whiff of what had gone down. And last night hadn't been a mistake, whatever she pretended. She'd done it because she'd desperately wanted to, because her body wouldn't take no for an answer. She should have known better than to stay in an empty house with him. If she'd had a sensible bone in her body, she'd have called for a twin in a Corsa to airlift her out.

Spot, stripe, kite...

She should be feeling mortified, yet she wasn't. Xander was heart-stoppingly, sizzlingly gorgeous, and it had been earth shattering, mind boggling and amazing. But that had to be the end of it. Here she was now, desperately making bunting after rushing back from the cinema, then tomorrow first thing she had to check out a house clearance, then she was back at the cinema again. Every second of her waking hours, and more, were already spoken for. Where in hell would she find time to fit in even the occasional date, let alone something more? As for letting a guy into her life properly, men inevitably wanted to grab control, and she couldn't have that. Good kisser or not, she was going to have to let this one go. Plain, stripe, kite.....

In fact, given it was already mid-afternoon, in everyday dating land, she would already have entered the hell known as 'waiting for the next call/text', although now come to think about it, she wasn't sure Xander even had her number. Maybe she needed to take the initiative here, and get in touch with him, just to tell him she wasn't up for anything more of course. A kind of thanks but no thanks would at least be polite. Civilised.

A hammering on the glass door cut in above the clatter of the sewing machine.

Damn. She could do without interruptions.

Triangles of bunting floated in front of her eyes as she staggered towards the door, then they cleared to leave something so much worse.

'Xander?'

Her stomach plunged to somewhere near her knees, kick-starting her heart as it passed. What the hell was he doing leaning on her door frame, his hands in the pockets of his impeccable jacket, with a face like a storm?

'Van still not back yet? I've told them to put on new tyres all round, by the way.' He strode past her, and into the kitchen, leaving her blinking.

She hurried after him, steering him past the ironing board, and pushed him to a halt, with his back against the sink. Her heart was thumping now with a different kind of panic. 'I can't afford all new tyres.'

'The old ones are full of nails from the building site. It's my fault, I'm happy to take responsibility, I've covered it.' He was sounding incredibly matter-of-fact, and focussing on a spot in space, six inches above the top of her head.

She wasn't sure she was comfortable with him buying her tyres. 'I don't know...'

'Anyway, I'm here to talk about last night.' His voice was brusque, his expression unexpectedly grim.

It hadn't been that bad had it? She pushed to get in first. 'I hope you don't think I always put out on a first date, because I really don't.'

He hesitated, fiddled with his belt. 'I know we watched films, but really, it wasn't a date...'

'What?' She felt her eyes widen. She hadn't seen that coming.

He rubbed his thumb on his jaw, 'The thing is, I want to put things in context, so there aren't any misunderstandings.' He paused, and drew in a breath. 'Last night wasn't what I do either so it's only fair I explain. It isn't that I don't respect you as a person because I do, and it isn't that I don't find you attractive, because you are. Very.' The corner of his mouth jerked a little bit sideways, as he hesitated. 'But my lifestyle doesn't allow for commitment, and I'm more sorry than I can say, but I'm afraid it can't happen again.' The tension lines around his eyes relaxed once he'd got that lot out, as if he were relieved to have said his piece.

She gawped back at him. Maybe this explained this morning's high speed eviction too. At least he'd pussy footed around enough to avoid calling what was obviously a sodding huge mistake, by

193

its proper name.

She waited a few seconds, for the whoosh of shock to pass, and her anger to kick in. 'Thanks for that. I'm pleased you feel that way, because if you'd been polite enough to let me finish, I'd have pretty much said the same thing first. So that's alright isn't it? I'm pleased we both know where we stand.'

So why the hell did she feel like he'd smacked her in the face?

He turned slowly, disentangling a stretch of bunting from around his ankles. 'Anyway, I hope this won't affect our working relationship, or the outstanding work at The Pink House. I've got a lot on the next few days, so I'll trust you with a key for the front door.'

Izzy's eyes widened as he tossed it down on the table. Just like that. Chilled to the point of ice cold. At least that might explain why she was shivering hard enough to make her teeth chatter.

Except maybe she shouldn't be feeling as angry as she was, because the slight tremor of his voice gave the suggestion that he wasn't as completely in control as he was pretending. True, he had given her the hundred percent knock back, but for an arrogant git, if she stopped to think about it, he'd somehow surprised her, by choosing the most respectful words, and emphasising that he did find her attractive, and making this all his fault not hers. What's more, he did sound and look sincerely sorry, and not in a wimpy way. Something about the dark pools of his eyes made her heart screw up in her chest, to the point that it physically hurt her.

'Okay.' So that was that then. She really was off the hook here, but who'd have thought she'd have felt so deflated, when she'd just got exactly what she'd thought she wanted.

As he turned to go he paused. 'It's good to have cleared that up.' He hesitated in the doorway, almost as if he were reluctant to leave. 'I'm sorry if I gave you the wrong impression, I really didn't mean to mislead you.' And a second later he was gone.

37

Monday Afternoon, 16th June

IZZY

At The Pink House

No running in the corridors

Izzy told herself it would be like a stealth raid.

In. Hang the bunting. Get the hell out of there.

And then it would all be over. Then she could get back to her life. Her proper life. Not the life where she stayed out all night, being shaken with orgasm after orgasm, that made Niagara Falls look like a very minor wonder of the world. The life she'd go back to would be the one where she concentrated on home and work, dreamed about being totally independent, and stayed awake at night worrying what the hell she was going to do for income if Vintage at the Cinema collapsed. Her life as it was, before that evening in the skip, before The Pink House and its huge shopping list, and definitely before some bad news guy had turned her life upside down, namely Xander.

Today she'd been the one barking out the orders. She'd rung him, and told him. Told him to get the steps set up in the playroom, told him she'd let herself in, told him, in no uncertain terms, to keep out of her way. For goodness sake, if he didn't put so much effort into being arrogant and up himself, he'd have had time to hang the blasted bunting himself. Something about being the one giving him the orders for a change made her feel wonderfully empowered. This was a feeling she could get used to.

And now she was here in the house hanging the bunting herself, it seemed even more simple than she'd anticipated. There was a picture rail in the playroom. It was literally a matter of a few tacks, and at least it was good to catch up with Dobbin again. If Xander was anywhere around, he'd made himself scarce. Probably hiding in the summer house.

She really wouldn't be letting herself think about the mistake that was last Thursday night, or the way it made her feel like she had the entire London Philharmonic Orchestra playing symphonies in her chest. Not to mention other places too. The fact she'd thought of not much else since it happened was by the by. Right now she had her brain under very strict control. She wasn't even going to think about it as she was passing the foot of the stairs, smelling the familiar smell of the house, catching unnerving whiffs of Xander, which seemed to hang randomly in the air.

Even though she worked fast, after half an hour the job was still only half done.

Meanwhile it was best to concentrate on the "worst bits". The way he accused her of being home-obsessed. The sniping way he'd mocked her for her spots and flowers, for the bunting, and the cut-out letters. She was filled by a sudden need to take her cut-out letters back home with her. Leaving her six inch high letters saying LOVE on the chest of drawers, which he would sneer at whenever he visited, wasn't an option she was comfortable with. It felt like she was leaving part of herself behind.

On impulse, she made a mad dash, out of the playroom, and up the stairs to the guest room. She grabbed her letters from the chest, and rammed them into a bag.

Much better.

She careered downwards, two steps at a time, and was hurling herself back down the hall, when a familiar husky voice almost stopped her dead.

'Someone's in a hurry.'

Xander stepped swiftly out from the drawing room, directly into her path. Only the fact that he put out his hands and caught hold of her bodily, prevented her from hurtling right into him.

'No running in the corridors.' His voice was stern, but then, as she beat her fist on his chest, his lips began to twitch.

Damn that the full blown, close up scent of him had knocked the breath out of her, and holy shit to her collapsing knees.

Her indignation that he hadn't kept his side of the bargain arrived late on the scene, but it was enough to turn her shock into snappiness. 'You aren't even supposed to be here!'

Xander let one nonchalant shoulder drop against the wall. 'Your friend's completely right about you. You fast forward to angry every time.'

The prickles on Izzy's neck turned to spikes. 'Not that it's anything to do with you.' She glowered at him, and gritted her teeth.

What was this anyway? Hurling accusations about "every time" made this sound like some old married couple argument.

He gazed back at her steadily. 'It might pay you to channel your inner goddess instead of your inner rhinoceros for once. Shouting your mouth off isn't necessarily the way to get the best out of a situation.'

Izzy reeled. Could he get any more patronising? She decided to ignore that he might have a point. 'You're the one who went back on your word.'

He sighed, and looked up at the cornice. 'I'm aware of that, but I came in to tell you something important.'

Izzy managed what she hoped was a face saving mumble. 'Right... And?' This better be good.

Xander gave an "at last" kind of sigh. 'I came to tell you I've registered an interest in the cinema building, that way I get to know what's happening with the sale.' He paused, presumably for dramatic effect. 'I thought you'd like to know. It could be useful for you.'

Izzy opened and closed her mouth, but nothing immediately came out. She needed to pull herself together here, this was an opportunity she shouldn't stuff up. Xander was handing her something here on a proverbial plate, and she needed to concentrate, and grab it with both hands.

'So are you going to buy the cinema?' The words tumbled out. 'Have you even got that kind of cash lying around?' Suddenly she didn't care how rude she sounded.

Xander rolled on his heels, and she took a step backwards. No need to be standing so close. She had a fleeting flashback to how his stubble prickled her hands, as she'd rubbed his cheekbones between her palms, then melted her mouth onto his. She clenched her thighs to get rid of the sudden gaping ache between her legs, and closed that thought down fast. Ideally she needed to put several miles between them, not just a couple of feet, but this would have to do for now.

He cleared his throat to answer her questions. 'With equity and a good track record, as far as the bank's concerned, I'm a good bet.' A shadow crossed his face. 'Though I don't have cash coming out of my ears.' He went on. 'Most developers owe a lot more than they own.'

Izzy chewed her thumb. Talk about poker faced. One economics lecture later, and he still hadn't told her if he was intending to buy.

Xander narrowed his eyes. 'So where are you planning to move to?' A note of concern cut into his voice. 'You do have a plan?'

Something about the way he asked that sent Izzy's stomach into free fall. Put into stark words, on a warm Monday afternoon, it made the whole awful situation horribly, scarily real. Suddenly The Vintage Cinema Club, and all their drives and initiatives seemed completely inadequate.

'We've applied for a business loan to buy the building...' Even as she spoke, Izzy's voice was faltering, because it suddenly sounded like such a long shot. 'Or possibly just the lease, if we could persuade whoever owns the building to sell us that.'

'Right. Yes…Great ideas.' Xander's deepening frown lines told a different story.

Izzy rushed in, her heart sinking lower by the second. 'You don't think we can do it, do you?'

'I didn't say that.' Xander sighed and rubbed a thumb across his chin. 'But it's damned tough out there.'

Tough meaning Vintage Cinema Club didn't stand a snowball's chance in hell of saving themselves. Izzy got the message loud and clear, and her chest was contracting so hard, she could be having palpitations.

'The thing is, Luce is a single mum, she'll find it tough but at least she can apply for benefits. Dida has a well off husband, even if he is a devil to live with. But I'm on my own, I'm self-employed, and if I lose my income I have nothing to live on at all.' Izzy knew she was almost wailing now, but she couldn't help it. 'I've worked really hard, and I have to make the business work. Failing simply isn't an option.' She wondered how the hell, and when exactly, failing had started to sound like a dead cert.

'I'm sure it will all work out.' Xander hooked his thumbs through his belt hooks.

Izzy could tell from the way he puffed out his lips that he didn't think anything of the sort.

Shit. What the hell was she going to do? She had to look like she was doing something constructive. She was going to stick her metaphorical neck out here. What was that thing, look like you mean it, and people will believe you?

She wrenched out a smile. 'I'm going to France for stock soon anyway, that trip should be enough to tide me over.' Lying through her teeth here. Going to France without Ollie to drive and navigate and be her sounding board was almost more scary than not having an income.

Xander's face crumpled into a grimace, and his eyes went horribly soft. For a moment she had that same feeling she'd had so often – that he was a nano second away from throwing his arms around her, and crashing his mouth onto hers, and yet again, despite every logical argument, she was disgustingly up for it. What the hell did he do to her that made her desperate to stick her tongue down his throat, within seconds of meeting him, despite knowing every logical argument to the contrary? Being snogged senseless would be the perfect antidote to take the fear and pain away. She gave in, took a deep breath, and let her eyelids drop closed. Whatever she'd said on Friday afternoon, right now she would not resist.

Seconds passed, as she trembled, waiting, aching for that delicious mouth to slide onto hers, anticipating the heat of it. Still nothing. Her work here was almost finished, and unless Xander dreamed up a whole new shopping list, which frankly was unlikely, this might be the last time she ever saw him. Not a good feeling. If this was her last ever chance, maybe she needed to take the bull by the horns herself, and make a grab for him herself. Time for a look. When she opened her eyes, instead of finding him a breath away, staring at her, ready for grabbing, Xander was already three strides down the hallway. If she hadn't known better, he might have looked like he was legging it. Another blink and he was diving for the kitchen, leaving her clamping her fist to her lips, with an empty hole the size of Tarmac quarry in her gut.

'Brilliant. I'll let you get on then.' He gave a breezy wave from the doorway.

A minute later she heard the door to the garden slam closed, and she knew she was on her own again.

38

Monday Afternoon, 16th June

XANDER

At The Pink House

It's a bird

Xander hared across the grass, and threw himself down on the steps of the summer house. Simply being close to Izzy again had made him smile, and he knew his sudden, impulsive ambush had been well founded. And he'd extricated himself just in time, although how the hell he'd resisted   that pout of hers, he had no idea. It was true, his sense of guilt at sleeping with her when he wasn't willing or able to follow through was well honed. But letting her know he had the cinema covered had been an inspirational excuse to chat to her, and he was congratulating himself on that, whilst doing her a good turn at the same time. He knew she'd want to get her hands on any information she could, and this was a good a reason as any for her to stay in touch, once her work here was over. Not that he had anything to give her in the long term, but the more he saw her, the more he knew he couldn't let her disappear from his life completely.

He hoped he'd avoided giving the impression of coming from old money, where anyone in the family could find any amount, given that the right strings were pulled, regardless of whether it was for a Grand Cru Domaine, a central London development, or a multi-million pound film. Instinctively he knew that cash strapped developer was a better face to show Izzy.

The trouble was, when he saw how eager, and optimistic, and hard-working Izzy was, it turned his gut into knots to know the bank would barely be considering their loan application, let alone releasing the money. Izzy came across so vulnerable and upset back there, that he was kicking himself for raising the subject at all. And when all he'd wanted to do was wrap his arms around her, he'd had to make the swiftest of exits.

It was doubly important that he kept his distance today, however much his gut, or rather the part below his gut, was telling him otherwise. When he'd gone crashing round to her house earlier, he'd be kidding if he told himself it was only out of concern for her. In reality he knew it was also his own self-preservation instinct, which had told him, that if he was going to have sex with anyone, it needed to be with someone he didn't feel anything for, someone who left him cold, detached, and above all safe. And Izzy didn't fall into that category. She fell so far out of it, it wasn't true. Further out than anyone he'd ever met, in fact. And spending the night with her only served to confirm that. There was no way he should have done that. It was completely unfair of him. But somehow, without even trying, she'd caught him, and he hadn't been able to walk away. He wasn't proud of what he'd done, in fact he intended to make it up to Izzy in every way he could. No way did he want to mess her around. He knew she was way too good for that.

Which was why, he was hiding out in the garden, watching the seconds tick by on his watch. An hour and a half since he came out, she should be long gone, and he should be safe to go back in. Making his way back into the kitchen, he let out a curse as he saw Izzy's van through the front window. Another plan gone belly up. What was taking her so long? Could she have fallen off the step ladders? His heart did a ricochet and bounced off his chest. Shit. He launched himself into the playroom, and when she wasn't there, he whizzed through the rest of the downstairs rooms, and finding them empty, he dashed up the stairs. He whipped around the first floor, and still hadn't found her. That only left the attic. Bounding up to the top floor, he saw that a door that should be closed was open.

'What the hell are you doing up here?' Xander's chest tightened as he approached the doorway, and he made no attempt to keep the annoyance out of his voice.

This floor was where all his mother's things were stored, no way did he want anyone wandering into here. Not only was Izzy still here when she should have left, she was also in a part of the house, which she had no reason to be in, and which was entirely off limits for everyone except himself and Christina.

He burst into the room, and immediately caught sight of Izzy, crouching under the sloping roof by the far wall, concentrating intently on something on the floor.

As she turned to look at him, her neck muscles flexed and he caught sight of the pale exposed crescent of skin, where her T-shirt and jeans had parted.

Her voice was low with concern. 'It's a bird. He must have come in through the open skylight.' She stretched a finger to stroke a crumpled pile of brown feathers on the floor in front of her. 'I heard him banging on the window just as I was finishing upstairs, but by the time I came up here, he'd stunned himself. I thought he was dead at first, but I think he's coming round now.'

'Bionic Vet meets Country File.' Xander gave a mental eye roll and the snarkiest comment he could, but only to fight back the lump in his throat, as he watched Izzy scoop up the bird, cup it gently in her hands, and walk towards him.

As she held the bird up for him to see, he took in a minute beak, quivering eyelids, and fine, wiry claws.

'He's so light.' Her lips curved into a smile, for the bird, not for Xander, then she nodded at Xander to open the window wider. 'I think he's ready to fly.' She stretched her arm out through the open casement, and flattened her palm, and a moment later, the bird spread its wings and blew away on the breeze.

She sent Xander a grin over her shoulder. 'All done.'

He told himself to look away.

'You weren't scared of holding it then?' He found her confidence puzzling. Didn't girls freak out at stuff like this? Not that he was comparing, but Astrid would have run the length of the village sooner than touch a bird.

He gave a sigh as he saw Izzy rubbing her hands on the bum of her jeans. Some people couldn't help themselves. They cared for, and helped, and looked after anything and everything. It wasn't Astrid's fault she wasn't wired like that. She'd come to see his mum once in those last months, and that had been enough. She hadn't come back again. As for Izzy, despite her shouting, she had so much heart, and her softness went right through her. Scrunched up over one injured bird. He was definitely not comparing, but if Astrid had had a tenth of Izzy's compassion and warmth, things might have turned out differently. As for Izzy, he was aching to press all that delicious softness and warmth against him, just one more time.

'Why would I be scared of holding a bird?' The incredulous look Izzy bowled him suggested she thought she was dealing with an imbecile. She gazed around the space with a grin. 'You've got some lovely things here, it's like a display from the cinema.'

Xander dragged in a slow breath. 'It's all my mum's stuff.' Eight years since she died and he still found it hurt too much to look at some of her things.

Izzy frowned. 'It seems a shame to hide them up here. Don't

you want to take them downstairs?'

He scrunched up his face. 'They're loaded with the past somehow...kind of heavy with the angst and pain of her dying.' He rarely talked to anyone about his mum, let alone her things, so no idea why he was opening up now.

'Is it still painful to think about her?' Izzy had moved right into his personal space now, almost close enough for her hair to be catching in his stubble.

Xander gave a grunt. 'I'm not sure.' He'd always preferred not to think about his mum, not to come here, not to face going through her things. Until the house had deteriorated so much he'd had to do repairs, he'd had it locked up. Blocking his mum out, closing everything away, had been the only way he could protect himself, after the slow and undignified agony of her dying.

Izzy looked straight into his eyes. 'If you bottle up all the memories of someone you love, it's as if they're gone completely, whereas if you can remember the happy times, and think about them every day, that way they live on, just differently.'

'I never really thought of it like that.' He ran his hand through his hair, where the wind from the skylight had tangled it. 'It's easier to be here now because the renovations have refreshed the place, and it feels different.' It was a relief that the grab handles and the stair lift had disappeared with the refurb. In some ways this had been the perfect house for someone ill, and at the stage when his mum had been confined to the ground floor, the doorways were wide enough to wheel her chair around easily. Even when she couldn't move or speak any more, he knew she still loved being in the airy downstairs rooms with their splashes of sunlight. It was the right place for her to choose, to die.

Izzy was right though. Maybe by shutting everything of his mother's away, he was actually cutting himself off from her more than if her things were around.

Izzy frowned. 'I can't say what it's like for other people, but I have my grandmother's bread board, and every time I cut a slice of bread, I think of the lovely times I had with her. I can't be with her any more, but remembering her every day is the next best thing to having her.'

He gave her a grin. 'Remind me of that, when I'm next at yours for toast and marmalade.' He went on, to hide the sudden chill of disappointment that thought sent through him. It was really not likely that he'd ever be at Izzy's for breakfast. 'My mum used to live in this house when she was a child. It was really special to her. Even though she lived here on her own at the end of her life, she said it always felt cosy, and never too big.'

Izzy looked around the room. 'It's funny, I can tell from her things here that your mum was a lovely person, and there's a wonderful atmosphere. But the things up here feel like they belong in the rest of the house somehow.'

Xander picked up a small angle poise lamp. 'Maybe I'll take this down for the desk while I'm here. She always used this to read in bed.' He smiled at Izzy. 'She was so dynamic, she loved searching round for vintage things – you'd have got on well. Come on down, we'll see how this fits in the office.'

Not that he was playing for time, trying to keep Izzy here. Except that's exactly what he was doing. There was something he needed to tell her too. Now that she'd finished all her work here, and was about to leave, his chest was tightening with a strange kind of panic. The thought he might never see her again left a kind of shell hole ripping through his chest.

Following her down two flights of stairs, watching the pale nape of her neck under the cork screw strands of her pony tail, and not touching her, was sheer hell, but he loved every damned step of it.

'I think we need to talk.' By the time they sidled into the office his voice was low, and grating.

He just hoped she'd be prepared to listen. He'd done the decent thing, and made his point, and told her straight that he wasn't having sex with her again because he had nothing to offer, and it was entirely unfair on her, and maybe him too. But right now a different kind of instinct had kicked in altogether, because no more sex wasn't something he could bear the thought of either. He clunked the lamp down on the desk, and spun around to face her as she accidentally jolted into him. He grasped his hands around the warmth of her waist, and she didn't pull away. As his fingers slipped across the silky skin under her t-shirt, he could smell the familiar sweetness of her hair.

'Talk? What about?'

He had a lot of ground to make up. 'About before. The things I said, at your house?'

'Mmmm?'

The tilt of her head, and the way she narrowed her eyes with only the merest glint of a smile, told him she wasn't going to be letting him off. At least she was still here, still listening.

'It all still stands. The things I explained. Except the last bit. I've changed my mind about that.' It wasn't exactly coming out as clearly as he'd hoped.

'Sorry?' If she carried on biting onto her pout like that he might just come on the spot.

'What I'm saying is I can't do relationships, and I don't do commitment, but seeing as we're here, like this, more of what we did the other night seems like a natural thing to do. If you'd like to, that is?' He was smiling now, broadly, hearing the absurdity of his words. He had a funny feeling that she was about to smile too.

As she leaned back against his locked arms he could hear her heart, clattering like a pneumatic drill in her chest.

'Same as the other day, I'm pretty much with you on all of that.' She was smiling like a girl who'd just been offered the only thing in life she wanted right at this moment. 'One last time, just before I go, might suit me too.'

He raised his thumb, grazed her cheek bone, and felt her shudder. Sliding his hand around her head to clasp a tangle of waves, he tilted her face upwards. She had those smoky flecks in her eyes again. And dark, dilated pupils that made him catch his breath. Made his stomach double-flip.

His words were husky. 'You wouldn't happen to have another condom in that bag of yours?'

He heard her ragged inhalation, as her lips parted, and he saw she was nodding.

39

Thursday, 19th June

Postcard from Dida in Assisi to The Crew, Vintage at the
Cinema

*Snatching a delicious day alone in Assisi... Sitting on the steps at
the Temple of Minerva, in the Piazza del Comune, eating a gelato.
Company wonderfully civilised, hotels fab, food yummy, scenery
sensational, oregano AMAZING. Best hols ever! Wish you were all
here too. Love D xx*

40

Friday Afternoon, 20th June

LUCE & IZZY

Working at the cinema

Loose change and a ton of bricks

'How's the unloading going, and are you ready for a drink yet?' Luce, perched on a high stool at the counter, work box in front of her, was sewing as she looked after the till.

'Almost done, a tea would be awesome thanks.' Izzy's reply came from somewhere behind the Lloyd Loom chair she was lugging down the shop. 'I'll keep an eye here if you get drinks.'

For the last half hour Izzy had been dashing between the shop and van, bringing in the immediately saleable parts of a house clearance she'd done this morning.

Luce eased herself down from her seat, and when she came back with the drinks, Izzy was propping some step ladders by the doorway.

'I wonder how Dida's getting on.' Luce plonked the mugs on the counter. Talking about Dida might just bring the conversation round to Ollie.

'Poor Dida, she really didn't want to go.' Izzy frowned. 'Do you think she's heard back from the bank yet?'

'Probably not.' Even Luce, with her non-business brain, knew it was too early for that.

Given she'd asked the same question every day this week, Izzy was definitely anxious about the bank though at least she seemed to have forgotten about Ruby's postcards. Luce was desperate to find out if Izzy had heard from Ollie lately, because since Luce sent Ollie that damned email in the early hours she'd been checking her inbox every five minutes, and eight days later, he still hadn't replied.

Izzy took a slurp of tea, and began to write down stock numbers. 'I can't imagine Dida on a bike, but knowing how Dida pops life's lemons straight into her g and t's, I guess she'll have made a bee line for the nearest pool and won't move for the week.'

'So did you finish all your bunting?' Luce knew the dark circles under Izzy's eyes were a giveaway. No doubt she'd been working round the clock to get it done, and maybe that also explained why she was less bouncy than usual. The fact she hadn't heard Izzy swearing or sounding off at all yet today was a definite indication that Izzy's energy levels were low.

'I took the bunting round on Monday, and that's the end of The Pink House cash cow.' Izzy gave a visible shudder.

'That's it? Really?' Luce put down the needle she was threading. 'And what about Xander then? You should so get in there girl, he's one dream boat that's too good to miss.'

Izzy gave a diffident shrug. 'Ship's already sailed...back to London.' She hesitated. 'Not that it's anything to do with me.' She stuck her chin in the air just to underline the fact.

'Well, fuck me...' The f-word was out before Luce could stop it, but it was simply a measure of her frustration. 'Sometimes you drive me right around the bend, Izzy Mellor, do you know that?

211

On a plate, and you let him go? I know you'd have had the hottest time with Xander if you'd given it a go, don't ask me how, I just do.' It needed saying, and now Luce had done it.

'Fifty pence.' Izzy's face was expressionless.

'What?' Luce didn't understand what she meant. She might be wrong, but wasn't that the faintest flush on Izzy's cheeks, between the freckles?

As Izzy waggled a jar of change under Luce's nose, a smile was spreading across her face. 'The f-word costs fifty pence, believe me I've said it enough times to know. This whole swear box thing was your idea, and if you can't take the heat, keep out of the kitchen.' Izzy began to giggle.

One of Izzy's giggling fits was the last thing Luce needed.

'Okay, you got me.' Luce dipped into her skirt pocket for change, and clinked some coins into the jar. 'But you'd better keep the manic shrieking down, there's a customer on the pavement, you don't want to scare them off.'

As Izzy looked over to the door her laughter faltered, then turned into a groan. 'Shit, shit and double shit.'

'If we're talking swear boxes, that's another sixty...' Luce said grabbing the jar and watched as Izzy's face went pale. 'Oh my god, it's Xander. I thought you said he was in London.'

Izzy, putting a hand to her forehead, wilted visibly. 'He was. But the only possible reason for him to come in now would be to tell us there's a bid coming on the cinema.' She looked as if she was about to faint, and she grabbed Luce's arm as her voice rose to a squeak. 'What the hell are we going to do? If there's an offer, we're finished.'

Although Luce's stomach was about to disintegrate, she knew one of them had to stay calm.

'Right, breathe!' Luce rapped out the instructions. 'And don't start to panic until we hear what he's got to say, okay?'

Izzy gave some sort of strangled croak in reply, and thankfully when she turned around again she'd composed herself, stuck a fixed smile on her face, and moved into full, if slightly shaky, professional customer-meet-and-greet mode. 'Hello Xander, what can we help you with today?'

That's better. For a minute Luce was very proud of how far her she'd brought Izzy. And then she forgot all about that, as it dawned on her that whatever Xander was about to say, he was looking at Izzy as if he'd like to devour her. Whole.

As Izzy brushed her hair out of her eyes, she sent Luce a worried look, then hit Xander with her question, no messing, straight between the eyes.

'Is someone buying the building? They are, aren't they? You have to tell us...'

Xander looked as if he didn't know what she was talking about, then his lips curved.

Something in the warmth of Xander's smile was patently only for Izzy, but Luce was close enough to catch the way his eyes went dark and very squishy when he looked at her. For a fleeting moment, Luce couldn't help wishing she had someone to look at her with adoration like that.

He gave a strangely nervous cough. 'No, it's nothing to do with the building.'

Izzy almost collapsed in a heap beside Luce. 'Holy crap why didn't you say that, we were literally bricking it here.'

So much for being polite to customers. Luce rolled her eyes, and let her own long sigh of relief go too.

Xander's face creased, apparently with amusement, but he pushed on anyway. 'Christina loves what you've done at The Pink House, and she'd like you to go to France to do some styling on her barn conversion. I don't suppose you'd consider....coming down...? Maybe combining it with that trip to France to get stock you mentioned the other day?'

'Wow, absolutely, that sounds brilliant, we're crying out for French stuff, of course she...' Luce started to tail off when she could already see the frown spreading across Izzy's face. If Izzy blew this she was going to personally throttle her.

'No...I'm sorry, I couldn't possibly.' Izzy's answer was flat, and horribly decided. And very customer unfriendly. Not at all in the spirit of the Vintage Cinema Club, which was weird, because she was usually so enthusiastic about it, and committed.

Luce, mentally took back everything she'd thought earlier about Izzy's progress. There were times when Izzy needed someone to knock her out and drag her away, just to stop her ruining her own chances in life, and this was one of them. 'Izzy, you don't need to decide this minute, think it over.'

He was with Luce on this. 'Good idea, I don't need an answer now, take as long as you need.'

Xander was sounding keen, but at the same time there was an air of quiet determination about him, that Luce liked a lot.

'No, I don't need any time, because it's completely out of the question,' Izzy replied, steadfastly determined to shoot herself in the foot. 'I'm, sorry, but you know I have the business, and three brothers, well, two at the moment, seeing as one's travelling, but I'm not sure he's enjoying it that much. And whatever *your* opinion, *I* know they still need me to look after them...' Izzy gave Xander a hard scowl at this point. 'I'm completely over stretched, and I can't take on anything else. End of.'

What? A tiny piece of unexpected news about Ollie had Luce's heart flipping. She clamped her mouth shut, to stop her jaw sagging, and hugged her arms around her waist. One little throw-away sentence from Izzy, that probably meant nothing, but it was the best news she'd had in the five months since Ollie left, and dammit if she was a selfish cow for being pleased he wasn't having the ball she'd imagined he was.

And meanwhile Izzy was talking herself out of...Maybe it wasn't the opportunity of a lifetime, but it would mean French stock for the cinema, which could only be good for all of them, and if it meant Izzy got another crack at Xander, it looked all good from where Luce was standing. And she'd be keeping the so called enemy close, although Luce wasn't sure if he still qualified as that.

'I understand...' Xander narrowed his eyes at Izzy. 'I knew it was a long shot.'

Please don't give up on her that easily. Luce's immediate instinct to wail and shout in protest really wasn't in line with everything she preached. But somehow Luce didn't have Xander down as a quitter either. His gooey eyes had gone now, and his mouth had hardened into one straight, determined line.

'We definitely don't have to say "no" now, we could talk about this some more.' Luce knew she was sounding desperate, but then she was.

Izzy gave a head toss. 'It's always going to be "no" I'm afraid.'

Luce looked around, wishing there was someone who could leap in and gag her friend. She jumped forward. Sometimes there was nothing else for it, you had to be rude, to be radical.

'Let's talk about this on the way back to your car.' Luce gave Xander a meaningful nod. 'Are you parked anywhere near?' With any luck he would get where she was coming from.

'Just outside actually.' Xander took the opportunity and ran with it. 'Sorry, I don't know your name?'

'Luce, I'm Luce.' She was already out on the pavement, arms flapping, willing Xander to come away from Izzy.

Luce blew her fringe into the air with relief, as he stuffed his hands deep into the pockets of his jeans, and ambled out into the sun.

'No definitely isn't her final answer.' Luce was aware that she might be gabbling now, in her efforts to make her point before Xander drove off in a cloud of diesel fumes, taking Luce's hopes with her. 'Give me a day or two, and I'm sure I'll change her mind.'

Xander eased himself into the driving seat. 'I get where you're coming from, thanks for giving me the heads up.' He raked his fingers through his hair. 'Leave this with me. I'll work something out, and I'll be in touch.'

Luce hoped he was serious.

41

Saturday Afternoon, 21st June

To: Vintage at the Cinema Crew
Subject: Coup de Coeur

Hi guys,

The future Mrs Joe Kerr has been in for a wedding dress fitting. If we thought GI Joe's was going to be bijou i.e. a teensy shop the size of a tanning booth we were VERY wrong...They have BIG PLANS – three floors, AND the basement, which will be bifold doors leading out onto a terrace by the river, with an outdoor sales area for garden furniture and statues. :(

Love Luce xx

42

Monday Afternoon, 23rd June

LUCE & DIDA

At the cinema

No flirting at all

Wow, it was clear that the boss was back in town. Luce, taking refuge behind a rack of clothes, and making a big deal of checking every label, could hear the regular stomp of Dida's heels on the wooden floors, as she careered around the cinema, checking everything out. Except it wasn't checking up, it was more reconnecting. Readjusting to being home again. That was what Luce called it. And even more important to reconnect this time, given that the cinema might be ripped away from them any day.

'Luce...?' Dida, was back behind the counter, her circuit completed, slamming through the various ledgers, and obviously in need of a sounding board.

'Over here.' Luce popped her head over the parapet of dresses, negotiated an ocean of dressing tables, and arrived next to the counter.

Dida looked at Luce expectantly. 'That *For Sale* board outside turns my heart to stone every time I see it.' She gave a long body shudder, before she pulled herself up, and carried on. 'So first, did you hear from Ollie?'

Luce's shoulders sagged. 'Nope.' Although she was checking her inbox every ten minutes now, instead of every five, the thought of exactly what Ollie was doing out there in Thailand still kept her awake late into the night. At times, like at three in the morning, she wished she had a less vivid imagination, and she truly regretted having seen the ping pong scene in Priscilla Queen of the Desert.

Dida gave a grimace. 'There's no news on the business loan as yet either, but what about GI Joe's?'

Luce opened her mouth then realised she wasn't expected to reply, as Dida ploughed straight on with her tirade. At least she didn't sound as if she was gunning for Luce, who had wondered if, as the email messenger, she'd be in the firing line.

'Three floors and an outdoor sales area is insane. It's all I bloody need on top of everything else.' Dida flung back her hair, readjusted her layered linen top, and let out an ominously large sigh.

Luce was on the verge of a) pointing out it was four floors not three, and b) grabbing the swear box, but decided, on balance, it was safer not to do either. If this was holiday blues, it was a damn bad case.

'Thanks for the post card, it just arrived.' Luce examined the picture of a fresco, and turned it over to check again that she hadn't misread Dida's bold pen strokes and happy words. 'Sounds like a lovely place.'

Dida rolled her eyes. 'The holiday was great in parts, but my problem is Aidie, and it's not just the cinema. He's losing it right across the board.'

Aidie's extremes were nothing new.

Dida raised one carefully painted eyebrow. 'The painters are

218

coming in to re-do the kitchen tomorrow.'

'Wow.'

Dida took in Luce's astonished stare. 'Exactly. Totally unexpected. Those hideous bright green cupboards are on their way out and if Aidie's backing down on Granny Smith-gate, he's up to his ears in guilt about something. It's completely unconnected to the cinema. I accidentally came across pictures of some woman's boobs on his phone whilst we were away.'

Luce gave an eye roll. 'Aidie's always been a boob guy. Didn't he wanted you to have implants for your fortieth?'

Dida gave a sniff and looked down at her already ample chest. 'That's the thing, the tits on his phone were tiny, and there were lots of pictures, all of the same ones. And he still isn't wanting the sex I'm withholding.'

Luce shook her head, as sympathetically as she could. 'So did you confront him about the pictures?'

Dida shrugged. 'Confrontation isn't really an option with Aidie. I accidentally drowned his phone in the bath. But the fact he's going so far off piste is a bit of a worry.'

From the way Dida was thrashing her hands through her hair, Luce got that "a bit of a worry" was a bit of an understatement.

'So how did the cycling go?'

Dida considered. 'Put it this way, I'd go again. As it turned out, with the right company, bike riding can be great.'

Luce couldn't believe the turnaround. Company though, could only mean one thing, not her husband, but somehow that didn't fit with Dida. 'Did you meet somebody?'

Dida smoothed down her trousers, and Dida running her hands over her thighs was a sure sign she cared about something. A lot.

'It was nothing.' Dida's throwaway denial obviously meant it was huge. 'There was a guy from Newcastle, he was very kind and calm and reasonable, we were thrown together, and it was pretty nice, that was all.'

So maybe this explained the "best hols ever" bit. Luce wasn't letting her leave it at that. 'And...'

'He liked opera.'

That *was* a biggie. Dida was the only person Luce had *ever* met who could stand it.

Another biggie coming up. 'Was he single?'

Dida gave a sniff. 'Newly divorced, but it really wasn't like that, there was absolutely no flirting at all. In fact, he was so well behaved, Aidie had him down as gay.'

That answered Luce's next query, as to how this had gone on under the nose of the most insanely possessive guy in the area. 'But was there a spark?'

'It's hard to say.' Dida screwed her face up. 'He was very hunky, and divinely civilised, but he was definitely keeping his distance.'

Luce's lips twitched into a smile. Good to know that was who the post card was talking about then. 'Are you still in touch?'

Dida's chin went up a degree. 'No, everyone said their good-byes at the airport. We didn't exchange email addresses, and it's probably for the best.'

'That's a shame.' Luce gave her friend a sheepish grin.

Dida laughed. 'What? Is Ms Shag 'em and Leave 'em going soft in her old age? Is selling all those wedding dresses bringing out your romantic side?'

Luce ignored that jibe. 'There's only one decider – are you missing him?'

'Since you ask, yes, I bloody well am,' Dida gave a rueful smile. 'But if you're going to ask me if I'm going to do anything about it, no, I'm bloody well not.'

Luce decided the time was right to pounce. 'Swear box, you had two bloodies in one sentence there.' She waggled the jar under Dida's nose, mildly aware that beyond the faded chintz of the window display a Range Rover was manoeuvring outside the shop. That could well be Xander on his way in.

'Fine.' Dida, nostrils flaring, dived into her bag. 'I hope your swear box takes foreign currency, euros are all I've got.'

As Dida fiddled in her purse, Luce watched as out on the street she saw some tell-tale faded jeans jumping down from the car.

'I think we're about to get a visit from Xander from The Pink House. That's something else you need to get up to speed on – he asked Izzy to go to style his sister's place in France, but Izzy turned him down.'

'What?' Dida was back to her "incensed of Matlock" voice. 'Izzy can't say no to an offer like that, especially not now.' There were rare times when Dida's red glossy lips looked like they belonged to Cruella De Vil, and this was one of them. 'When was this?'

Luce decided to 'fess up before she got the full brunt of Dida's frustration.

'Last Monday. I know I should have been firmer, but Izzy's stubborn, and it's not always practical to fight her head on...'

Xander wandered in, and came up to the counter. 'I don't suppose Izzy's in is she?'

Luce was counting this as her lucky day. If Izzy had been in, she'd most likely have turned down Xander and his offers point blank, whereas if Dida was on the case too, they had a better chance of steam rolling Izzy into being sensible.

'I'm sorry, she's out on a delivery, is there anything we can help you with?' Luce gave a double strength smile. Even if Xander only had eyes for Izzy, it still wouldn't hurt.

He gave a shrug. 'Well Izzy seemed very reluctant to come to France to help with Christina's new barn conversion, but she did mention wanting French stock.'

'What was that about French stock?' Dida was at Luce's elbow now, her breath hot on Luce's neck.

'Xander, this is Dida.' Luce felt she had to do the introductions, given Dida had already joined in. 'Dida owns the cinema.' Luce hoped that the hierarchy thing would excuse Dida's conversation crashing.

'Nice to meet you, Dida, it's an amazing place you've got here.' Xander said charmingly. 'And it's true, some French stuff would go down really well here, wouldn't it? If Izzy came to France she could stock up, and by way of an incentive, I'm happy to bring a large load of furniture back to the UK for you.'

Dida gave a surprised gasp. 'Bloody hell. Sounds like our Izzy's made a big impression.'

If Dida hadn't been wearing vintage Dior shoes, Luce would have stepped sideways onto her toe to get her to butt out. As it was, the best she could do was to shoot her a "look".

'Wow that would be amazing. It's so generous of you.' Luce stepped forward. 'We'll certainly do our best to persuade Izzy. She's a bit of a home bird.'

Despite caring very little for the bottom line, even Luce had excitement rippling through her at the thought of how much cash and custom a load of exclusive, highly sought after French furniture would bring in. It would all help towards getting their hands on a lease, at the very least.

'Leave it with us.' Luce's smile was more confident than she felt. 'She'll be there.'

'Great.' Xander's grin suggested he'd got exactly what he came in for. 'Give me a ring if there's anything else you need to know.'

Luce shadowed Xander as far as the pavement, and by the time she came back, Dida was already back behind the counter scrutinising the books.

'Now there's a guy who's used to getting what he wants. And what a stunner too.' Dida tapped her pen against her teeth, obviously impressed on all sides. 'As for his offer, bloody hell, a load of French vintage might just save our bacon. Izzy's certainly come through on keeping that particular enemy close, hasn't she?'

Luce hated to bring Dida back down to earth, but it had to be done.

'Don't forget – we need to persuade Izzy to go.' Luce frowned. 'Any suggestions how we're going to do that?'

Dida propped her pen on her chin. 'I think our Vintage Cinema Club might need a girls' night in. How are you fixed for Friday?'

43

Friday Evening, 27th June

DIDA, LUCE & IZZY

At Dida's House

Big guns and reading between the lines

'I can't believe how different the kitchen looks already with one undercoat. Pale grey is definitely the way to go, from the look of the door they've already done. But there's a lot to paint isn't there?'

Luce was chatting and holding the tray, as Dida loaded her up with dishes, ice cream, a jug of apricot puree, and finally, the delicious cream filled almond meringue, Dida's favourite fast-yet-fab dinner party sweet.

'I agonised over the colour.' Dida gave a grimace and grabbed another bucket of ice and more chilled wine. That understatement barely expressed the sleepless nights she'd had, or how many test doors the painters had done. 'Hopefully, if we down enough Prosecco we can drown the paint smell.'

Dida would never usually have entertained midway through a paint job, but this was a full blown emergency, and it was only the girls. She'd been right when she'd predicted that Aidie wouldn't be back until Saturday. Yet again. Head shakes to that one. She'd shoved the painters' dust sheets into a cupboard, shoed Eric out of the conservatory, and stuck Lolly and Ruby in front of a My Little Pony DVD in the bedroom. The canapés and seared tuna had gone down a storm, and the four empty wine bottles already lined up in the kitchen hopefully meant that Izzy was now going to be open to suggestion.

'So have you heard from Ollie recently, Iz?' Dida dropped the question casually, as she unloaded the tray onto the long table in the conservatory.

They were sitting by the doors which opened onto the garden, and the candles Dida had placed along the table were flickering in the evening breeze as it wafted in.

From the way Luce leaned in, she was pleased Dida had asked.

'I haven't heard for a while.' Izzy took a slurp of her wine. 'Last email, he said he was going to stay offline for a bit. Funny, reading between the lines I'd say he was a bit homesick.'

Dida noticed Luce's anxious expression relax into a half smile. Dida sent her a private "Go Luce" grin, and risked a wink.

'It must be hard to strike a balance when you're travelling.' Dida needed to grab this opportunity, and steer the conversation round to Izzy's trip. 'But holidays are great, a short break makes you feel *so* much better.' Not speaking for herself here, obviously, given she'd had the shittest week ever since she'd come back. Worrying about Aidie, up to her ears in painters, and kicking herself for letting Hamish from Newcastle slip out of her grasp, not that he was ever actually in it. Dida caught Luce's eye, and narrowed her own, giving her the nod to launch Operation Ambush Izzy.

Luce came straight through with the goods. 'When you go to France it will be like a working holiday, won't it?'

Good on Luce for saying it like it was already decided, and for prettying it up with a smile that should make it irresistible, but most of all for omitting Xander. They'd decided that Xander was probably more of a sticking point for Izzy, than leaving the twins.

Dida chimed in. 'And you won't have to worry about anything back here. We're all going to help whilst you're away. I can call in every morning, and sort the boys out, and do their washing, and make sure they don't trash the place.'

'I'd never inflict that one on you Dida.' Izzy gave a shudder.

Dida flinched and kicked herself for putting her foot in it. Given they were trying to sell this to Izzy, a trashed house was the last image they needed to plant in Izzy's mind, no matter how likely it was in reality. And given what Dida knew of Parker and Barney, Izzy's twin brothers, it was most likely a dead cert.

'Well, I'll promise to keep them supplied with more cakes and lasagnes than they can possibly eat too, and I've already got more than enough volunteers to cover your shifts, and everyone has agreed to put money in for the load.'

As Dida waited to gauge Izzy's reaction, she began slicing the almond meringue, and as she slid the loaded dishes across the table, she received a series of ecstatic groans in return.

'Here, have some apricot coulis.'

Dida pushed the jug to Izzy first, then watched as she drizzled the orange liquid onto her sweet pavlova. Dida couldn't work out if Izzy's impassive expression was because she was reluctant, or drunk, but she decided it was time to bring out the big guns anyway.

'You know this could be make or break for all of us. A haul like this could make the difference between buying a lease and losing it. We wouldn't be asking, but all our livelihoods are on the line here, yours too, and Ollie's when he comes back.' Dida's words shot across the table with such force, she almost blew out a candle.

Izzy gave a heavy sigh, and it was a bad sign that she'd put down her spoon without taking a mouthful.

'I know I have to go, it's just...' She sounded resigned rather than drunk.

Dida hadn't anticipated Izzy giving in so easily.

'Just what babe?' Luce was on the case, but treading gently. 'Is it Xander?'

Izzy's flush, which began as two bright patches on her cheeks, and gradually worked its way as far down as the dippy bit of her low cut vest, was enough for them all to know the answer to that.

'What is it? You like him, you're cross you let him get away, or you don't want to spend time with him because you like him too much, or you don't like him, and he's too hot to handle...?' Luce's guesses came out in a rush.

Sometimes less was more. Luce's list somehow gave Izzy the time to regroup, and now she wasn't going to give anything away.

'No, it's fine, I'm a big girl. I'd rather Xander wasn't going to be there, but if he is, I'll deal with it. At least he can do the driving.' Izzy gave a shrug, and drew in a breath. She suddenly seemed to be sitting a whole lot taller. 'Don't worry, I know how desperately we need this opportunity, and I'll do whatever I have to, to make sure we get it. But first I'm going to get stuck into this sweet.'

Dida glancing around the table, and saw spoons were poised tantalisingly close to meringue.

'Great, let's drink to Izzy, to France, and a long hot profitable summer.' She grabbed the nearest bottle and filled their glasses to the rims. 'Bottoms up for the Vintage Cinema Club.' Before Izzy had time to change her mind.

44

IZZY & LUCE

In Corks Bar

Pickled Bears and a passion fruit allergy

'So you remember that snog you had in the bathroom at Xander's house?' Luce, legs swinging from the bar stool, poked at her Cuba Confidential cocktail with the little accompanying umbrella, and swirled the contents of the jam jar glass with her straw.

Izzy's own jam jar came to a halt in mid-air, half way to her mouth. Spilling the beans to Luce about the snog that afternoon had been a mistake, especially given the hugely bigger blunders with Xander that had come afterwards. How she'd been able to keep the lid on the whole double shag fest, Izzy would never know, although with the girls, if you could keep something under wraps for twenty four hours, there was often something else happening that took the heat off you.

As it was, Happy Hour at Corks on a Saturday had been a left field suggestion from Luce, who, by rights, would normally have been having tea with Ruby. Given that Ruby was otherwise engaged with Lolly, Izzy suspected there might be more people involved here than just Luce. Sold to Izzy as a hangover cure after the heavy intake of Prosecco at Dida's the evening before, it was beginning to look a lot more like a continuation of Luce's interrogation about Xander and the French trip, which Izzy had only avoided by the skin of her teeth last night.

As for snogging in the en suite? 'Ancient history.' Izzy slurped up a gulp of her Pass The Basil, and kicked herself for choosing that, instead of the Pickled Bear cocktail she'd been going to have. She hoped that would put an end to the Xander talk. As much as she'd enjoyed the interlude it had all come to a firm and consensual end last Monday afternoon.

'History so ancient, you went purple at the merest mention of Xander last night then?' Luce pursed her lips, and left the question hanging.

'Probably an alcoholic flush.' Izzy replied quickly, heat seeping from her chest up to her cheeks, she racked her brain for a total change of subject, and cursed when it went blank.

'Same as the flush you've got now you mean?' Luce wasn't giving up.

'No, that's just a passion fruit allergy. It happens sometimes.' Izzy was clutching at straws here. 'I knew I should have had a Margarita instead of this.' She nodded at her cocktail.

Luce jumped straight onto that one. 'Hell no, last time you had two Margaritas on an empty stomach, they laid you out, and we had to get that off-duty fireman to carry you to the taxi. And a crying shame you were too far gone to see him, because he was sizzling. Shame I missed him too, because I would not have minded a piece of that one, but hey, someone had to take you home.'

Great. Izzy let herself breathe again. A discussion about post-cocktail disasters could go on all night, given how many there had been.

'Anyway, we're not here to talk about cocktails.' So that was Luce coming clean. She did have an agenda after all. 'I wanted to clear up the Xander stuff, because two weeks on your own with him in France is a long time, especially when his sister is as hell bent as I am on getting you two together.'

Izzy's stomach took a high speed lift ride, and came to a halt, somewhere a long way under her stool. 'Shit, you *have* to be joking me?'

Luce shook her head, and her lips twitched with amusement. 'Nope, she's convinced a bit of homey Izzy is just what Xander needs.'

Izzy's appalled face gave way to one of her hard stares, which she turned on Luce. 'And you found this out how?'

Luce's eyes went skywards. 'Long story. I thought I'd better check things out, and when I looked back at the account details, I realised Christina's had quite a bit of stuff from us before. So I rang her for a little check-up chat.' Luce's lips curled into a "told you so" grin. 'Apparently Xander's had a rough time for quite a few years, but last week he started smiling again. I think you're being credited with that one.'

Izzy was wailing again. 'So why didn't you let *me* in on this?'

Luce shook her head. 'Every time I tried to tell you, you hijacked the conversation.'

And that was true. The merest mention of Xander by Luce, and Izzy had bounced the subject *anywhere* else.

'Happy hour was my last hope of telling you.' Luce gave Izzy a sideways grin. 'I can't pretend I'm not pleased you're getting a second chance with Xander, because he's a peach. But you are doing all of us a monumental favour with this trip, when I know you'd rather stay at home. You're stepping right out of your comfort zone for us. If you insist you want to keep Xander at arm's length, we *should* lay down conditions with Christina, in advance. So she knows not to meddle too much.'

Good old Luce. Izzy could barely admit to herself, let alone her best friend, how fast her heart had raced when she'd heard there was a chance she'd be thrown together with Xander again. And the fact her first refusal was over ridden, and wrapped up in a way that meant she had no alternative, well, that brought out her goosebumps. She tried to shut out how amazing that night with him had been, and then there had been that amazing swan song of an afternoon, which they both went into knowing it was a one off. At the time, she'd just been desperate to jump him, full stop. He couldn't have made it clearer that he wasn't available in the long term, which was absolutely fine, because she definitely wasn't available either.

So although she was reluctantly resigned to going, it still had her waking in the night and mouthing OMG into the darkness. What she hadn't begun to work out was how she was going to handle hanging out with Xander in France, after what had happened between them. *Mental note to self: hands off the hottie.* But spelling it out, loud and clear, in advance of their trip was one inspired idea that let everyone know where they stood. And what's more, it made her sound like she meant business. Which obviously she did.

'You think that would be okay?' Izzy wanted to hug Luce for this.

'You're calling the shots here, and I know from the relief on your face, that you'd be happier if we spelled it out.' Luce grabbed Izzy's hand and gave it squeeze. 'We all owe you big time for this, so it's our responsibility to know you're comfortable. Leave Xander and his sister to me, I'll make sure they get the message.'

And a big phew to that. 'Thanks, do you know how brill you are?' Izzy flung her arm around Luce's neck and gave her a kiss on the cheek. 'You're the closest I've ever got to having a sister.'

'Real life sisters aren't always that great, but thanks yourself.' Luce, cheeks all pink, paused, played with her ice some more. When she next looked up at Izzy, her eyes were clear and sharp, and her tone was altogether different. 'Did you sleep with him?'

Izzy gulped, and inhaled a lungful of cocktail. As she finally swallowed back her coughing, she knew she was opening and shutting her mouth like a goldfish, but no sound would come out. Eventually she croaked out a mumble. 'Er, who, er, what...me...?'

Luce was straight onto her. 'From the speech hesitation, I'll take that as a yes.'

Shit. No chance of secrets with Luce around.

Izzy suspected that despite Luce's ear to ear beam, she was toning down her delight.

'Bloody hell.' Luce was hugging her again, this time so enthusiastically Izzy could barely breathe. 'I knew there was an information black hole when you were at The Pink House. Good for you, you little tart.'

Except Luce was missing the point here.

'We *both* agreed it was a one off.' Izzy strategically missed out the "both times" bit, or the fact they were both clear about the last time being exactly that.

'Neither of us want to take it further, but how the hell do I face him again now, every day for two whole weeks? I mean I nearly died that day he came into the cinema, and he was only there for a few minutes.'

Luce pulled down the corners of her mouth. 'If I was bothered about meeting the guys I'd slept with, I'd never set foot outside the front door.' She gave a low chuckle. 'Having sex with someone is in the moment, it's a bit like drinking a milkshake with them – it happens, you both have a great time, then it's over. End of.'

Izzy wasn't being deliberately dense, but she wasn't getting this. 'I can't see where milkshakes come into it.'

Luce gave a shrug. 'The point is you enjoy it at the time, but then you move on. And the knack is, you don't think about it ever again, *especially* not if you meet the person.'

Izzy pursed her lips. 'So you're saying I go to France with Xander, and I just blank the sex bit?'

'Exactly, and believe me, I should know.' Luce gave her a superior, serial-shagger-and-proud-of-it grin.

'Right, thanks for that one.' Izzy wasn't sure she could pull it off, but at least she had a tactic now.

'So how was it?' Luce was waiting, expectantly.

There was no dodging it, so Izzy answered fast. 'Absolutely fucking awesome. Ten plus four. Next question.'

Luce gave a suitably satisfied nod. 'This definitely calls for another cocktail.' She hoovered up the last of her drink, and shoved her empty glass onto the bar. 'Now do you need any more dresses to take? We want you to look very pretty.'

45

Sunday Afternoon, 29th June

XANDER & IZZY

In Izzy's back garden

Something less corporate

'Now you're here, and you've crashed my Sunday afternoon completely unannounced, what I want to know is why the hell you're doing this whole damned France trip thing in the first place?'

Xander stood back, and watched Izzy. Hands on hips, head tossing, voice revving like a Ferrari. All very familiar. He was kicking himself, because this could have gone so much better. Yes, he should have told her he was coming, but that would have made it all too formal, and after Luce's call he was only trying to get things clear before they set off. Better to have the shouting here than in France.

He tried not to show his disappointment. 'A trip to France – wasn't that what you wanted?' Only with Izzy could he have got this so wrong.

As for why he was doing this, he'd asked himself that question a lot of times too. In his head he maintained that he was doing it all for Izzy. Because she was so upset and worried that last day at The Pink House, about losing her livelihood, and the cinema. This trip was something he'd dreamed up to help her.

Izzy's eyes flashed. 'You waft in, waving a fait accompli offer that no one will let me refuse. Don't you realise how much I hate being controlled?' Her heartfelt complaints were pouring out. 'I feel like a beetle that's been picked up, and no matter how hard I'm waggling my arms and legs, someone else is deciding where I go.'

Damn, damn, damn. How could he have got this so wrong?

'Beetles don't have arms,' Xander pointed out. What a stupid thing to add, but for the moment sensible was evading him.

Izzy gave that the eye roll it deserved. 'You do realise that the clever little incentive package you put together meant I couldn't possibly say no.'

It had taken him a few days to come up with a deal he knew she wouldn't be able to resist, especially after her shock refusal first time around, which he really hadn't been ready for. How like Izzy to wrong foot him, and do exactly the opposite of what he expected. Still he was pretty proud of coming up with an offer she couldn't wriggle out of, especially one that everyone at the cinema would rally round and pressure her into. The important thing had been that she – and her business – stood to benefit in the long run. That's all he'd wanted to achieve. Hopefully she'd get that eventually.

Xander looked at her steadily. 'You were the one who said you were relying on French stock to save the cinema. I took that and ran with it, to say thank you for all the work you'd done at The Pink House.' That last bit was an impromptu addition. 'And to answer your question, there isn't just one reason why I'm doing it.' That at least was true.

'Right.' Not sounding convinced, but she'd stopped jumping

up and down. That was an improvement.

He tried again. 'It's a combination of reasons that all coincide, and are beneficial to everyone.'

Izzy gave a dismissive snort. 'You're talking producer-speak here Xander. Could you possibly be less corporate?'

Xander drew in a breath, and counted to ten. Who was doing who the favour here? He had so much to learn about going the right way about things with Izzy.

'I'm hoping it will help you and your business. Free travel, free accommodation, all you need to pay for is whatever you bring back.' Important point, clearly made. On that basis alone, for anyone other than Izzy, it would be a no brainer. 'And it's a way of helping Christina, to pay her back for everything she's done for me over the years. Her leg is broken, she can't sort things out for herself, and she loves what you do. It's a perfect coincidence of circumstances which...'

Izzy butted in. 'You're veering into the boardroom again.'

He carried on, making mental notes for future challenges. 'And it'll help all your friends at Vintage at the Cinema too. Supporting local artists and artisans is always a good thing.'

'Supporting local artists?' Another query, marked "Incredulous". 'Everything you've mentioned is about helping other people.'

Xander gave her a searching look. 'Do you have a problem with that?'

Izzy gave a puzzled frown. 'It just doesn't quite fit with your image as a hard-nosed developer, that's all.'

Xander broke into a grin. 'Developers don't *have* to be hard-nosed. Maybe I'm a philanthropist.'

That made her laugh out loud. 'Now I've heard it all – a philanthropist *and* an entrepreneur.' She picked up a handful of petals that had fallen off the clematis that was rampaging up the garden wall, and began to let them fall to the floor, one by one. She was so hot when she was furious, but when her anger melted away, it left a vulnerability which made his gut wrench. As for his caveman drive to crash her straight up against the wall, that was something he had to learn to block, and fast.

Xander had to admit this offer was really about his guilt. The guilty as hell feeling he had for inadvertently dragging Izzy off to bed when he knew he couldn't offer her anything more. By doing something that was good for her and her friends at the cinema he hoped it was a way to right that wrong.

Although deep down he knew that it was also about him being completely selfish, because although he didn't do commitment, and his life was a dysfunctional mess he couldn't add anyone into, since he'd been around Izzy, he'd felt so much more human. Almost happy at times. There was just something about her – ordinary things were transformed when she was there. She had this goodness that shone out of her, and when she was around, it made him feel like a better person. And he hadn't felt that for such a long time, if ever.

The thing about Izzy was that even though she was impetuous, and just like today, she was liable to chew his head off as soon as look at him, she had an honesty and wisdom about her. In a few minutes, in his attic, she'd turned his pain and grief for his mother around, and made it something he could deal with. That kind of person, and this kind of connection hadn't ever happened to him before. And although he knew he had nothing to offer her in the long term, he couldn't let her slip away. Not yet.

Right now, he could bear not to have her in his bed, but he couldn't bear not to have her in his life. So he was entirely happy to agree to a hands off scenario, because that way he wasn't deceiving anyone. Even though he had a whole set of screwed up ulterior motives here, he hoped he was still being honest with her. Long term, he'd have to wean himself off her in some way, extricate himself, but he'd face that later. And it was important that he didn't let her get involved, and ultimately get hurt, although she was adamant that was the last thing she wanted anyway.

'So Mr Philanthropist, what's really in it for you then?' She was

236

gazing at him with her head on one side now. 'Or is it all about the welfare of others?'

Now it was Xander's turn to laugh, but more with relief that she'd gently lowered him off the hook. 'I'll take the wine, and the sun and the scenery. It's an idyllic spot. You're going to love it.'

And that seemed like the ideal place to leave things. They both knew where they stood on the hands off thing. That blueprint had been established when they'd snatched that last delicious, yet ferociously hot afternoon, which already felt like stolen goods, even when they were wrapped around each other. It was Luce, and the stern talking to she'd given him, that had sent him scurrying round here, but no one was making any moves today. It was for the best.

'I'll see you at the airport then. Bordeaux. 11th July.' And with that he backed out of her garden, and left her to get on with her day.

46

Monday, 7th July

Izzy's To Do List

Before I go to France... eeeeeek!!!!
Teach boys to make spag bol
Show boys sink and Fairy liquid
Remind boys how to wash up
Tell boys where Sainsbury's is
Teach boys to use washing machine
Write backup washing machine user instructions
Ditto Dyson
Remind self not to make out with you know who
Show boys how to empty bins
Show boys recycling bins
Leave list of bin and recycling collections out
Do outstanding washing
Do outstanding ironing
Pay car tax on Chou-fleur
Sort out house insurance

Email Ollie
Print out plane ticket
Clean house from top to bottom
Pick up pill prescription
Get Euros from post office
Finalise deets of order wish list from Vintage cinema peeps
Buy bulk supplies of factor 50 suntan cream (or risk speckled hen
look)
Buy plane friendly mini cosmetics bottles
Pick up suitcase on wheels from Dida
Buy apple & bubblegum supplies
Remind self AGAIN not to make out with you know who
UNDER ANY CIRCUMSTANCES
Buy paperbacks/fill up kindle
Buy new bikini
Buy paint brushes to take
Wash painting dungarees
Pack

47

LUCE

In her flat

A postcard from Thailand

Luce, sitting at her sewing machine, pausing at the end of a seam, lurched as she heard the click of the letterbox downstairs. Summer dresses made up from vintage patterns were flying out of the shop so fast she could barely keep up with demand, especially since Izzy put them in the window display. Luce heard the click, and this time she was determined not to react.

Every day when she heard the postman come, she careered down the stairs like a crazy loon, and every time she'd been disappointed. It seemed like forever since Ollie's last post card had arrived. Looking back, those postcards arriving every week for Ruby had been like a connection to Ollie, and more fool her for a) taking them for granted and b) coming to rely on them. There really wasn't any point in dashing down stairs again today. Snipping off the loose ends of thread, she put the skirt section of the dress she was sewing to one side to press later, picked up the next pieces of fabric, and eased them under the machine foot. Except she really wasn't going to be able to concentrate. Not until...

Ten seconds later she arrived breathless at the bottom of the stairs, and wrenched at the letter box on the back of the door. And damn her, there was a postcard. If her heart had been high jumping it would have cleared two metres, and her mouth stretched into a smile with no input at all on her part. Ignoring the picture she grabbed the card, whipped it over, and took in a Thai stamp.

Yay! She thumped her fist in the air. Then her heart did another extra lurch, as she saw her own name. Lucy Morgan. Not Ruby, but Lucy. Ollie was writing to her. Her heart was galloping in her chest now. How many times in the last month had she'd opened her inbox willing there to be an email from him, only to be disappointed, and now it didn't matter at all, because he'd written to her anyway. Except the writing was maybe neater than Ollie's... And it was too small... And Ollie would never use turquoise ink, would he? And Ollie would have called her Luce, not Lucy? And this postcard wasn't from him at all...was it? How could she have been so damned stupid? Her stomach sagged as she read the message.

Having a fabulous honeymoon here in Thailand. The dress was SO perfect. Thanks for making our wedding day wonderful. Will be in touch with the pictures when we get home, love Steffie and Brin, aka Mr and Mrs Johnson
nee Beeston x

P.S. Still can't believe I'm actually married!!!

Luce turned the card over. Something about the bride and groom on the front of the postcard, hand in hand, on a sodding Thai sea shore, complete with inky silhouettes of palm trees, and the dark orange sunset reflected in the water, made her want to bring her breakfast straight back up.

She ran upstairs, and was about to throw the postcard straight in the bin, when she remembered her customer service initiative. Damn. She'd better file it with her happy customer letters instead.

48

XANDER & IZZY

At the flea market in Vaunac, France

Fast work

'So, is this enough French junk for you then?' Xander smiled at his own understatement, as they rounded the bend in the narrow street, and the high stone buildings opened into a huge square, rammed with antique stalls.

'Wow...' Izzy came to an abrupt halt, and gazed at the multi coloured chaos spread out in front of them. 'It's beyond amazing. A whole village covered in everything from tractors to dining suites.'

It was true. There was barely space to fit your feet between the crates and piles and stalls of what Xander could only describe as rubbish, but which he assumed would be a treasure trove to Izzy.

'However I'd imagined it, it's a hundred times bigger.' Her voice was breathless with excitement, as she fiddled, trying to recapture

243

her escaping hair into its pony tail. 'It's so exciting, I barley know where to begin.'

Xander gave a laugh, for Izzy's burst of childlike enthusiasm, and because this was the first sign of the real Izzy he'd seen since he'd picked her up at the airport earlier this morning. She'd been like a frightened, rather grumpy rabbit the whole journey, trying to put as much space between them as the hire car would let her, which frankly wasn't a lot.

Despite the fact that her grunts and eye rolls had strangled all his attempts at conversation, her heady scent, and the curves of her body, pushing against the riotous flowery print of her dress, had made his head swim. It was like overdosing on some glorious raspberry sundae, and getting the brain freeze to go with it. Two weeks of keeping his hands off her was going to be hell, but somewhere along the line he'd got hooked, not to say obsessed. How following one woman round a crowded, noisy French market could make his insides feel like warm syrup, he had no idea, but it did.

Although there was no reason why he should have expected anything else from her but distant. He'd pretty much press ganged her into coming, and even if the trip would give her finances a boost, committing to this long with a virtual stranger, even if you had slept with them, was a bit of a leap of faith. She was damned brave to have done it at all. As for him, his life had bumped along the same dysfunctional and solitary road for eight years. He'd hauled one woman out of a skip on a building site and the rut he'd been trudging in for so long had morphed into some exotic kind of tropical rain forest.

'So this is a *Vide Grenier*.' Xander was taking it upon himself to talk like a guide book here. 'It means An Emptying of the Attic, and I can see that no-one's held back. I can also see this might be a long job.'

And it hadn't been anything like as awkward as he imagined it might be, going back to hands off, given what had happened between them. Izzy was treating him like just another guy from the office, in fact she was being so professional, that what they had together might almost never have happened. It was almost as if she'd taken lessons.

'This could only be France.' She glanced round at him, as they went into the square. 'The shimmery heat and the sun that makes you feel like passing out the minute you step out of the shade, and the lovely accents.' Izzy was definitely loosening up here.

'You aren't feeling faint are you?' He jumped in, then felt stupid when she snuffed out his sudden anxiety with a half shake of her head. 'Can you understand the locals at all then?'

'I can get by, but my French is nothing like as good as yours. It must be totally awesome to be bilingual.'

He took it she was impressed with his earlier banter with the guys manning the car park in the large field, who were already a good way through a crate of Kronenbourg, despite it only being ten in the morning.

He wouldn't go as far as to call his French fluent though. 'Speaking French happened by accident – I've been coming here every summer since I was small. That explains why random people keep saying hello to me too.'

It might be best not to expand on all those childhood memories. Thanks to his dad's local empire building, the family owned several prestigious vineyards in the south west, and he had an idea Izzy might just have kittens if she ever got a glimpse of the size of the chateau they owned nearby. Given she was so touchy about wealth, he'd done his best to play down his links with his loaded family. In the past he'd fudged the details about his background in order to avoid hangers on, but this was the first time he'd ever had to pretend because someone had been running scared of rich guys.

As for the memories of his mum, coming here every summer had illuminated her failing health. The year on year comparisons were inevitable, and it had been not only profoundly depressing, but it had scared the bejesus out of his teenage self, to see how she deteriorated more each year. And yet that had only been the start of the nightmare to come. Since he'd been in the attic at The Pink House with Izzy, he'd been thinking about his mum a lot more. The strange thing was, although Izzy wasn't physically like her, Izzy's energy, and openness reminded him a lot of his mum. They both had a warmth that spilled out and somehow extended to wrap up whoever was around them.

When he caught up with Izzy again, she was already picking her way along boxes overflowing with linen and books and crockery. He gave her a tap on the shoulder and she turned.

'It's heaven here, but it's really hard to know where to start. Remind me exactly what Christina wants?'

Xander gave Izzy an encouraging smile. 'Christina, in her words, wants you to "make her house into a home", by "buying for yourself". What could be easier? You doing this is my present to her. She'd have done it for herself if it hadn't been for her ankle.' If, as he suspected, Christina was also counting on Izzy to tame, domesticate and house train him, she could forget it.

'Jeez, I just hope Christina won't be disappointed. The barn is already beautiful as it is.' Izzy dug deep into her skirt pocket, and pulled out a bubblegum, unwrapped it, popped it into her mouth, and began to chew, vigorously.

Izzy with cold feet? Izzy quaking? Izzy, her bolshie confidence whooshed away, with that vulnerable grimace that put a tourniquet on his insides every time.

'That makes two of us.' He cleared his throat, and told himself to get a grip. 'Only joking, Christina's very easy to please, especially where your stuff is concerned.' And Xander wasn't kidding there either. Christina had been gushingly enthusiastic about everything Izzy had done at The Pink House.

'It's just a huge responsibility, from all sides.' Izzy shoved her hands deep into her pockets again. 'I'm not clever like the rest of them at the cinema, I'm only good at sloshing paint on stuff. I feel like a fraud and I'm not sure I can do this.'

The way her voice was all low and croaky made him want to

wrap his arms around her, and not let go. Damn the "hands off Izzy" policy. There were times when verbal reassurance wasn't enough, but it was all he had to offer here.

'Don't be so hard on yourself.' Xander stretched out to squeeze her hand, then, deciding he shouldn't, he turned the movement into a head scratch. 'You go into a room, tweak a few things, and the whole space springs to life. I've never seen anyone else do that before.'

It was true, although these days she barely needed to bring in the accessories. As soon as she'd stomped into Christina's echoing hallway this morning, swishing her skirts and doing that whole stroppy wiggly shoulder thing of hers, she'd lit up the whole damned place.

He coughed, and carried on. 'So hell, I *know* you can do it, and I'm here to do anything I can to help too.' He watched her scowl ease. 'So no pressure, but seeing as you have a furniture lorry to fill, *and* a large barn conversion to pretty up, I suggest we need to get shopping. Fast.'

'Okay. As soon as I've bought something I'll be better.' Izzy pulled the elastic out of her pony tail, shook her head, and recaptured it again. Had to be her default "nervous in France" setting. 'That is a pretty quilt over there.'

Xander gave a sigh of relief that she'd finally begun. 'One more thing. You'll get better deals with private individuals than with the traders, and bargain hard. Begin with a ridiculously low price, and if you need me to translate, just shout.'

Izzy spun around, puzzled. 'Great, and you know all this how?'

'Years of practice shopping for French antiques with my mum.' She had spent her summers trawling flea markets to find bits for the chateau, always dragging Xander with her.

'Of course.' Izzy's face softened to a smile. 'A lot of the things in the attic were French weren't they?'

Xander gave a low laugh. 'I reckon she bought every damned available wire basket in south west France.'

Izzy's eyes were shining, as her hand landed on his wrist. 'I can never resist a wire basket either.'

Xander ignored the way his pulse had gone up a notch when she touched him. 'And I can also spot a garden trug at a hundred metres.' He gave a wry smile. 'She had a thing for those too.'

Izzy gave his arm a last squeeze, then released him. 'So what would you suggest I offer on that chandelier then?'

'Go in at ten euros, and we'll see if they'll do a deal for two. And as soon as we've spent two hundred and fifty euros, we'll have a drink.' Thinking of the last time they had drunk beer together, his pulse started to race. And more fool him for walking – or running – away from that.

49

IZZY & XANDER

At the flea market in Vaunac, France

They both knew who she was talking about

'Good thing we came in the hire van.' Xander leaned back on his chair in the shade of a parasol, on the terrace of the local bar, tilted back his head, and took a slug of cool beer.

Izzy, pushing her sunglasses up on top of her head, prodded the lemon slices in her Perrier water. Xander and Christina had thought of everything, including hiring a large left hand drive transit, which Xander had taken charge of. Xander liking to take control? No change there then. And his excuse – "it's a boy thing" – was one she'd heard a thousand times before too. Eye rolls to that one.

It had been strange arriving at the airport, walking towards the most drop dead gorgeous guy in the place, knowing he was waiting for her. It was a good thing her case was on wheels, because when she caught a first glimpse of him, leaning against a pillar, all cheekbones and tangled hair, she thought her legs were going to give way. It was all she could do to stop herself, ripping off that Superdry T-shirt of his, and all the rest, and leaping on him there and then. Somehow knowing the glorious extent of what was underneath it made it all the worse. The way her blood had been fizzing ever since she got here, she had a feeling she may either spontaneously ignite, or expire with high blood pressure, well before it was time to fly home. She was handling it...just. A lot of the time she was having to pretend he wasn't actually there beside her.

Following Luce's instructions to blank the sex, she was finding her only way through this was to blank the guy as well. Far from the stuck up guy she'd half expected, Xander had been nothing less than considerate and helpful since she'd arrived. What's more, as far as their new hands off rule was going, he was behaving like a perfect gentleman. He wasn't even perving on her boobs, not even when she inadvertently pushed them in his direction, which, sad to say, she found herself doing more often than she'd have liked to admit. Mother Nature, and her need to ensure the survival of the human race had a lot to answer for. Because however logically Izzy knew Xander was entirely off limits, her body just hadn't got the message. The lust part of her brain was sending out a million messages a minute, telling her to grab him, and jump him ASAP.

From opposite, Izzy had a view of Xander's throat, which moved with every swallow as he drank his beer – no surprise there, that's what throats did wasn't it? Except she found it ridiculously distracting.

'So when was the last time you went on holiday?' Even though Xander's shades were firmly down, she knew he was watching her every move as he spoke, pretty much as he had been all morning.

Given that so many people at the flea market here were holiday makers of one kind or another, it was an obvious choice for Xander to make for neutral conversation, although her and Xander sitting here was too surreal to be anything like a holiday.

She squinted into her drink. 'Holidays aren't my best times.' Thinking about them almost brought her out in hives. There had been that family holiday in Biarritz, just before her dad left, and a wet week camping in Wales, with Awful Alastair, just before he dumped her. Izzy chewed the skin at the side of her thumb nail. 'My last one was six years ago, and it sucked, how about you?' Keep the detail to a minimum, and if in doubt, throw the question back. It always worked a treat.

Maybe she was projecting her own feelings onto him, but Xander's smile had dematerialised once the focus was on *his* holidays, and his hollow laugh suggested he'd walked into that one without thinking.

'Would you even believe me if I said my honeymoon with my ex?' The sound he made in his throat was a lot more bitter than a laugh. 'Ten years ago.'

'Bloody hell, I'm sorry.' That would teach her to be a smart arse. And shit to opening that whole ex-wife can of worms.

Xander sped on, and hauled the conversation back onto a lighter note. 'Actually everyone knows a film producer's life is one long holiday, but sometimes it's just plain tiring.' And today the weariness came right to the top.

'Seems to have given you a great tan, whatever you've been doing.' Damn. That had slipped out without thinking, and her turning the colour of a beetroot thinking how his tan faded to nothing around the small of his back wasn't the best idea either.

She decided to try again. 'Let's make a list to see how we're doing. Tell me what we've already bought.' Immediate blunder saying all those "we"s, but what the hell.

He watched her as she dug in her bag, and pulled out a pen and paper, a smile flickering over his lips. Surely he couldn't be thinking about the times she'd fished other things out of her bag... could he? The only upside was her cheeks were already puce from

251

a minute ago, so another rush of blood wasn't going to show.

Xander sighed, and then began. 'Candlesticks, sheets, straw hats, trunks, wheel barrow...are you keeping up?'

'Hang on...' She scribbled away. The focus and efficiency he brought to every task, however incidental, was astonishing, not to say scary, but at least he was following instructions here without complaint.

She finally got to writing down bike. 'Okay, you can carry on now.'

Chewing the end of her pen as she waited, after a few seconds of silence she glanced up to find him staring into the distance, looking as moody as a model in a Vogue photo. She followed his eyes in an effort to see what had grabbed every ounce of his attention.

Izzy's stomach clenched. He was staring at a woman. Tall, slender, and startlingly attractive. And his eyes followed her, as she meandered in the crowd.

Izzy swallowed down a mouthful of sour saliva. Bloody hell. If this was jealousy, she had no right to it, simply because Xander looked at someone else. She shouldn't give a damn who he looked at, given she had no claim over him, and nor did she want to have. But that was no ordinary look. And seeing how it didn't matter a jot to her anyway, she forced herself to ask.

'Do you...do you know her?' Her dry throat hardly let the words form. No need to say more. She and Xander both knew who she was talking about.

'You could say that.' Xander wrenched his eyes away, gave his head a slight shake, and sniffed. 'That's Astrid. My ex-wife.'

Izzy's breath hitched as he threw his head back and emptied his glass. Something about the tilt of his chin, the stretch of his throat, sent a bolt of desire ripping through her. Or would that be down to the jealousy too?

'We had a house here, Astrid kept it after the divorce. She's usually down here later in the summer, but she's obviously come early this year.' His grin was vaguely uncomfortable, as he put his

252

glass down on the metal table.

Crap. Why the hell did Astrid have to be so damned perfect?

Izzy bit her lip. 'She's amazing. Like a dark brunette Kate Middleton, only way prettier.'

It had never crossed Izzy's mind that Xander might have been hitched to a super model. If someone had popped Izzy like a balloon, she couldn't have deflated faster. She sat forward, looped her feet in their ripped converse, which had seemed like sensible option footwear this morning, around the legs of the chair. Tugging at her dress, with the torn buttonhole and one slightly detached pocket, she grimaced because her fuchsia pink nail varnish, applied less than four hours ago, had already chipped in several places. Hopeless. Then her heart, already at rock bottom, sank even further, because, despite slapping on most of a bottle of factor 50 sun tan cream before they left this morning, her arms were already a mass of freckles, and no doubt her face was too, which made everything ten times worse. Not that she was even thinking about going out with Xander, but at a stroke, he'd just jumped a thousand light years out of her league.

Xander gave a wry laugh. 'Astrid's a whole lot more ambitious than Kate Middleton.'

Izzy's mouth dropped open. 'What?'

'No, actually I'm being unfair.' Xander gave a sheepish grimace. 'Astrid's great. We still work together now and then. She's smart, funny, and scarily good at her job.' He propped his chin on his hand, and sent her a matter of fact grin. 'I think you'd like her.'

Somehow Izzy wasn't as optimistic as Xander about that. She looked back to the crowd again, where Astrid, almost a head taller than many people, was easy to spot. What an advantage for Astrid to look Xander straight in the eye, instead of staring at the shirt buttons half way up his chest. Maths wasn't Izzy's strong point, but even she could work out that Astrid's legs were possibly nine inches longer than her own. Even if he'd parted company with his ex, that was the type of woman that Xander would be heading for next time. Izzy was bloody grateful for the reality check. Small, stroppy and scruffy, from Matlock, was not going to cut it with Xander. No wonder he couldn't commit. To her.

He pushed himself to his feet, flexing his shoulders. 'Time to get back to work then?'

Izzy followed him up. 'Sounds like a plan.' Way too late to wish she'd gone for stilettos instead of the practical flats, which somehow hadn't looked scratty at all when she'd pushed her feet into them earlier. Not that heels were going to make a difference here. It took a whole lot more than shoes to elevate a girl from a five to a ten out of ten. Some leaps in life were simply not possible.

Xander obviously wasn't going to be hiding away from his ex in the bar then. It might have helped that he was heading straight for the rotisserie stall, where he queued while Izzy took time to haggle over some baskets, and bought them delicious roast lamb baguettes, which they ate as they wandered around the stalls.

Although Xander might have brushed himself off and moved on from seeing Astrid, Izzy found that harder to do. For the rest of the afternoon, Izzy saw her willowy silhouette lurking behind every armoire. But if Astrid had lingered at the market, they hadn't seen her again. What Izzy couldn't get out of her head, was how Xander and Astrid must have been a dazzlingly attractive couple. The thought of them together, looking like they'd stepped straight out of the pages of a glossy mag, made Izzy shudder.

'Your French is better than you think. You were bargaining like a pro back there.' Xander, coming back from another trip to the van, had stumbled in on her tussle with a local farmer.

'I had a lot of holidays in France, when I was younger.' Before her dad walked out on them, obviously. But it was true, simply being here, smelling the garlic smells drifting out of the cafes, seeing the sun bouncing off the orange pantile roofs, and watching people choosing postcards from the pavement displays, took her straight back to when she was younger.

As for ex-wives, the thing about broken relationships was that they left you with baggage. Not that she could count Awful Alastair in that one. On a baggage scale, with luck and a following wind, he possibly made it to the status of a small paper bag, and a crumpled one at that. But that was another good reason for staying right out of the relationship game. If you didn't participate, you wouldn't become a casualty. She would do well to remember that.

'I hate to say this to a relentless bargain hunter, whose energy is apparently unflagging, but I think perhaps we need to be heading back now.' It was a long time later, when Xander, dusty now, and flagging under the weight of a pile of suitcases, managed to look at his watch. 'We've got to unload when we get back, and I don't believe I'm saying this, but we can always come back again in the morning. They do it all again tomorrow you know?'

Who'd have thought Xander would still be this enthusiastic at four in the afternoon.

'Thanks, I may take you up on that.' Izzy grinned. 'Don't tell me you're getting a taste for vintage.'

'Never.' Xander gave an exaggerated grimace of disgust. 'But I've still had a great time.'

Izzy raised a disbelieving eyebrow. 'Really?' She failed to see how shopping for "rubbish" and an ex-wife mounted up to great in Xander's book.

The corners of his mouth twitched. 'Three things I've enjoyed especially.'

'Well?' This she had to hear, although she had a feeling from the way he was laughing that she might want to hit him when he told her.

'The complete concentration on your face as you shop, the way your skirt pulls across your bottom as I follow you.' His face broke into a full blown grin now. 'And the freckles that are coming out across your nose...'

50

Saturday Morning, 12th July

XANDER & IZZY

Christina's Terrace, Les Cerisiers, France

Exclusion zones

As Izzy emerged through the huge barn doors, onto the terrace by the kitchen, Xander clocked pale skin, and curving, delicious smoothness, all the way up to her shorts.

And beyond.

Izzy was wobbling towards him across the limestone flags, with a coffee pot and cups on a tray, frowning with concentration as she tried not to spill, and looking closer to undressed than dressed. He was so darned temped to adjust that bra strap, which had slipped and was slanting above the dimple of Izzy's elbow.

'That's a bit below the belt, under the circumstances.' He had to fight his corner here.

That much thigh on show was going to kill any guy.

'What?' She looked up at him as if she had no idea what he was talking about.

'Shorts, that's what, when I've been told in no uncertain terms that there's a strict exclusion zone operating around you.' It was the first time he'd properly broached Luce's terms and conditions, but realistically, how the hell was he supposed to keep his hands off Izzy when she wandered out, looking like that? 'Not fair.'

Her head shot up. 'Excuse me? You were the one who claimed "unavailable" status first.' Her chin stuck out, but just for a moment, then her face softened into a wide defiant grin. 'Hard luck, anyway. It's only eight o'clock and twenty six degrees out here already, you're going to have to get used to it.'

Great. Defiant grins were a lot easier to work with than silences, even if her shorts were giving him a hard on he'd rather not have.

Xander poured coffee, and pushed a giant cup across to Izzy, who was already tearing a croissant apart. He might as well take this opportunity to clear up something that was hanging over from yesterday, and had been bothering him.

'Just to put Astrid into context.' Xander saw Izzy's head shoot up.

'Mmmmm...' Izzy had already gone back to her jam spreading.

In his experience, ex-wives were always best brought out into the open. That way there were no secrets, and everyone knew where they stood. It was the best thing to put Izzy in the picture, and let her know he and Astrid bore no grudges, especially as they were still linked by the film company.

He cleared his throat. 'I was the one who messed up the marriage, Astrid was completely blameless.' He hoped that went some way to covering it.

Izzy was biting her lip, but she didn't look up enough to meet his eye. 'Okay.' She said it slowly, as if she had no idea why he was telling her this.

'It was entirely my fault, I asked too much of her, when I should have known not to. That we didn't make it was completely down to me.' More so now Astrid was in the area, wandering around in person, it seemed important to absolve her of any responsibility for a marital failure that had been all his doing. 'All break ups are hard, but this one was amicable, and we still maintain a good working relationship.'

Xander took the fact that Izzy had spread jam twice on the same croissant to mean she was probably listening more than she was pretending to.

He carried on, just to make certain he hadn't done badly by Astrid. 'She is an amazing person though, I wouldn't want you to think in any way that she wasn't.'

Izzy blinked, grimaced at her croissant, then looked up to meet his gaze with a smile that was possibly a shade too bright. 'Great, that's fab to know. Thank you for sharing that, Xander.'

Was Izzy's expression too brittle? There couldn't have been anything there for her to object to, especially seeing as he'd skipped over the bit about him currently working with Astrid.

So, now that was out of the way, they could get on with their day. 'What are we up to later? Today I'm in your hands.' He gave a smile in Izzy's direction. If she could push him with delicious acres of bare thigh, that were taking his temperature at least twenty degrees above the already hot morning, he could definitely retaliate a little.

While Izzy's narrow eyed glare told him to back right off with the innuendo, her reply was surprisingly cool and unruffled. 'Perhaps the market again this morning.'

Xander let out the loud token groan she was expecting, largely so he didn't blow his cover. No way did he want to go down as a happy shopper. 'Okay, but only on condition we make time for a proper lunch.' He wasn't sure either Izzy, or Luce for that matter, would be happy if they knew quite how much he was looking forward to following Izzy around the market for a second day. He'd been longing to spend more time with her, and yesterday hadn't disappointed. It was kind of weirdly, surprisingly comfortable, yet at the same time, all electric and zingy.

Izzy shared a passing eye roll with the barn door, and skipped over his plea for proper food. 'And maybe we can try some of the things in the house later on.'

Not okay. There were times when guys needed to prioritise their stomachs.

He wasn't backing down on this one. 'We can eat in Périgueux. Christina gave me special instructions to call in there for some towels for the pool.'

Breezing through, and sounding a lot more chilled about that than he was too. Markets were one thing, home shopping à deux, in what Christina described to him as Périgueux's premiere wedding list shop, was something else. He wasn't sure he was ready for it.

51

Saturday Afternoon, 12th July

IZZY & XANDER

In Chic Couleurs, Périgueux, France

Enthusiastic about towels

'You're definitely not railroading me out of a proper lunch tomorrow. Chips and mayo are all very well, but a guy needs to eat, and the food here is too good to miss out on.'

Xander's bemused expression, as they wandered through the town streets, shouting to each other over the roar of the early afternoon traffic, suggested the skipped lunch might almost have happened without him realising.

'You could have warned me you don't so much wind guys around your little finger to get your own way, as crack them over the knuckles with an iron bar.'

'Years of practice, living with brothers I'm afraid.' Izzy laughed at the truth of that. 'But those chips in boxes were delicious, and after spending so long at the market this morning, there really wasn't time to lounge around over lunch. And for the record, I never met anyone who grumbled so much as you.'

The dead eye she tried for failed when she didn't keep her face poker straight. She wasn't backing off here, but she was definitely regretting putting on those shorts for breakfast. Provocative was the last thing she'd intended at the time, but unfortunately for her, provocative was how Xander had interpreted it. Whatever, the shorts had kicked off an episode of sparring between herself and Xander, which through the morning, had ranged from gentle teasing, through to playful, to full blown wind up. While she knew she was as much to blame as him for keeping it going, somehow she couldn't not retaliate, nor could she simply make the whole thing go away, by not reacting. Even if they were jibing, it was way more relaxed now than when she'd arrived yesterday, when the atmosphere had taken stiff and awkward to new highs. She was also pretty certain she was nailing the sex blanking thing Luce had trained her up for, face to face with Xander, if not privately. On her own, was another matter. Xander being so close had her body strung like a piano wire, and the downside of that was her personal sex with Xander replay button had got stuck on repeat, and consequently it wasn't only the baking sun that was making her over heat.

Hopefully the man in question wouldn't guess there was no way she was going to a restaurant, because she couldn't face looking at him through a whole damned meal. In any case, the more time she hung round with him, the less appetite she had. She usually devoured her food, but with Xander around, her stomach did so much flipping, that hunger was the last thing on her mind.

'Well at least I'm not complaining about going to the towel shop.' Xander's brow furrowed. Wounded protest was yet another angle he had polished. 'I categorically don't do shopping, but I admit it'll make a change to look at something new, not old. We're turning here...'

As he steered her into a side street, he ended up so close to her they almost bumped hips. Dismissing that as an accident, she let it go.

'That's actually yet another complaint, just skilfully wrapped up.' She wasn't going to let him off that too, but she wished she'd chosen another word than "skilfully", given she didn't want to dish out compliments. And if she was truly amazed at his shopping stamina, she definitely wasn't going to weaken her position by admitting it.

'Here we go, this is it. Chic Couleurs. How's that for a shopping emporium?' He gave her a triumphant grin, as they turned in through the double height plate glass shop frontage, as if he were personally responsible for the amazing scene in front of them.

Despite feeling like she was bowing too much to the opposition, Izzy couldn't stop her smile stretching beyond her ears, as they walked into the cool lofty space, and she took in the sparse, yet beautifully stylish, shelves.

'Homeware in rainbow colours, this is beyond perfect.' She let out a long sigh. 'Aren't the displays immaculate?'

'Even I have to admit it's pretty impressive.' Xander slid her a sideways smile. 'Although somehow it feels like we should be holding hands here.'

Izzy gave a gulp. 'What...?' She watched his smile crack into a grin.

Dammit. She'd just reacted to another of his prods. With all her brotherly experience, she should know better than to rise.

'Wedding List posters and dinner services? It's married couples all the way in here. Don't forget, I know the signs, I've lived through it.' Xander gave a low laugh. 'If the other customers are anything to go by, they probably won't even serve us if we aren't snogging each other's faces off.'

Shit. Why the hell had her neck gone sweaty and prickly? Full blown panic about getting hitched was ridiculous, when he was only joking around, and his point about the couple bit was true.

Despite the array of zingy colours, the shop oozed Coupledom, with a capital C, and the coupley customers were jaw-droppingly "hands on" to say the least. Exactly the kind of place she avoided like the plague, because she was so far from wanting what it stood for.

He tilted his head and shot her a full on, dazzling smile. 'Maybe we should pretend we're married whilst we're choosing towels? Or set up a wedding list, just for fun.'

Now she'd heard it all. As for the way that smile of his was making her feel like she'd just jumped off a cliff edge... If this is where wearing shorts for breakfast got her, tomorrow she'd make sure she was in a long sleeved onesie, with feet attached.

The glare she shot him would have been enough to close down any one of her brothers in a nano second. 'Just get over here, and shut up, will you.'

'Whatever you say, Mrs Blackman.'

'Sorry? Mrs who?' For a moment Izzy didn't understand. 'Who's Blackman?'

'Me, of course.' He stared at her, his voice rising in surprise. 'How did you not know that?'

Izzy's insides dropped like a lift shaft.

'But your paperwork always said Porter...'

'Yep, Christina is Porter, I'm Blackman.' His matter of fact words hung in the air, and he smiled at her inscrutably. 'Oh, and for the sake of completion, Astrid is Duval, and always was, she stuck with her maiden name.'

Izzy reeled. 'I'm not happy about this.' Understatement of the century, for so many reasons. At least it explained why nothing had come up when she'd googled Xander Porter. But sleeping with a guy when she didn't know what he was called? Even Luce insisted on a name before she did the deed. As for his gravelly voice calling her by his name? Mrs bloody Blackman? *Damn to the way it made her dizzy too.*

'Do you know you've turned so pale I can count the freckles on your cheeks individually?' He was milking this for all it was

263

worth now. 'Come on, Mrs Blackman, what shall we choose then?'

She raised her hand, half threatening him to start behaving, half pretending she was going to slap him, then immediately regretted it, as he snatched her wrist from mid-air, and held it between his fingers.

Shivers zinged up her arm as he hung on to her, and radiated out through her body. For one tantalising moment she watched his eyes blur, and then she just knew he was going to bring that horribly sensuous mouth of his careering onto hers. Her heart jolted, and she held her breath, knowing she was daring him here, goading him – willing him? – to kiss her.

He stood, his hand welded to her wrist. Then suddenly, he let her hand drop.

For some reason, he was a few words in before he regained the same joking tone he'd had before. 'Watch out. That assistant over there couldn't look more disapproving if I'd thrown you over the counter and ripped your dress off.' Another achingly slanting smile. 'Which I'm quite happy to do, by the way. You just have to give me the go-ahead.'

Shit. She had to shut this down fast, even if they both knew it was all empty bluff.

'In your dreams.' She stuck her chin in the air. What the hell happened to unavailable Xander?

The sinking feeling in her chest had to be relief, not disappointment. No way had she actually wanted him to kiss her back there. Had she? She took a fistful of skirt in each hand – she refused to let him accuse her of flouncing – and proceeded as smoothly and unhurriedly as she could across the polished concrete floor towards the sweeping elliptical staircase. Then realising he wasn't following her, she turned and scowled at him over her shoulder. 'Come on Mr Whatever-Your-Name-Is, towels are on the first floor.'

His lips curved into another teasing beam. 'You're going to have to look at me more sweetly than that, or they'll think we're having a lovers' tiff.'

She tried to blank how irresistible he looked when he smiled like that. Irresistible? She had to be off her head to think that, when she had a hundred reasons to resist. a) He wasn't what she wanted, b) she knew after that other night with Xander that flings only flung her into total confusion, and she wasn't having any more of those, c) he'd told her he didn't want her, and when someone's rubbed your nose in it like that, you don't go there again, d) he was way out of her league, e)... She could go on all day, but now she needed to concentrate on picking out towels.

She sped up the stairs, focussed on the mental mood board she was building up for Christina's barn – vibrant pink petunias in the planters around the pool, colours from the quilt she'd found yesterday, a sludgy green watering can she'd picked up this morning – headed for the towel stacks, and honed straight in on the fuchsia.

She was still furious, with Xander for his teasing, still kicking herself, for wanting him when she should know better, but she forced her voice to be light, when five minutes later, she put her hands on the perfect towels.

'How would pistachio and cerise look against the cream pool loungers?'

'Pistachio and cerise?' Xander arrived at her elbow, suspiciously acting like a lamb now. 'Any chance you could translate that into English?'

Here we go again. Izzy was trying to limit the eye rolls, but she did one anyway.

'Pale mint green and bright pink?' She picked up some towels to avoid further confusion, and waved them at him.

'Great, yes, they'll look brilliant.' His broad grin wavered into a grimace. 'Shit, I don't believe I actually got that enthusiastic about towels. I think what I should be saying is I don't give a damn, now can we go home please?'

52

XANDER & IZZY

At Christina's, Les Cerisiers, France

Large doors and stone walls

Izzy rubbed her forehead with her knuckle, inadvertently smearing the sweat and the dirt into streaks, as she surveyed their work in progress. 'It's always amazing how a few pretty things can make a place so different isn't it? It already feels less stark in here.'

Xander stood back himself, and took in the changes in the vast living area, which opened straight onto the sun drenched garden.

'You know I'm not a fan of old stuff, but I reckon you've nailed it here.' Even he had to admit she knew how to transform a room into a home, although somehow he had a feeling it had less to do with the actual material things and a lot more to do with her. The way she rushed around, with her swearing and bubble gum and messy hair, brought the whole place to life instantaneously.

'Even those two ancient milk churns are looking great.' Seeing them here, he couldn't believe he'd given her such a hard time about those when she'd bought them, and neither could she, judging from her one raised eyebrow and full on glare.

'It helps that they're full of flowers.' At least she conceded that much. 'Agricultural really works here, and the features are wonderful.' She propped the ancient hay ladder she was carrying up against the exposed stone wall.

Although he was used to working non-stop, Xander had to admit that Izzy's work ethic was something else.

'It might be a barn but you do realise you can't reinstate the animals.' He threw that in and waited for her reaction, which turned out to be one finger, waved at him. 'Someone's got to curb your wilder ideas, I'm happy to take the job. Anyway, isn't it time we had that swim I keep talking about?'

'Later maybe.' And from the scrunch of her nose, he'd take that as yet another flat refusal.

He shrugged. 'Bit of a waste, to have a pool and not get the benefit.'

He hoped he sounded less obsessed about this than he felt. Cold logic told him that swimming would be scarily dangerous territory, but the lust side of his brain over rode the logical every time. What's more, his caveman head had taken the delicious recurring image of her, stretched out naked after sex, head dangling over the edge of the sofa, hair hanging down to the floor, and photoshopped it onto a sun lounger. In real life there would obviously be a bikini, but, whatever, the opportunity was too good to miss, even if he wasn't allowed to touch.

She gave that comment the attention it deserved, by marching out. Definitely big on the non verbal signals this afternoon then, whereas earlier she'd returned all his jibes, which began with payback for the shorts, getting more suggestive every time.

Izzy was definitely a fighter. However far he pushed her, she refused to back off, but what started as barbed fun had run away with him. He had an idea what the problem was, that lately around Izzy his dick was over ruling his rational thought process. But at the same time, what the hell *was* wrong with him? Two weeks ago, he'd been a sour and determined loner, this afternoon he'd been happily playing at wedding lists – albeit to take the piss wildly, but still.

Throughout his last eight wasteland years, Christina had maintained that all he needed was to meet the right girl, and he'd come right to heel. As for his sister's horribly smug grin, and her cringey "Izzy makes you smile" comment – as far as he was concerned she could stuff those particular hopes, and take her interference with them.

'So today's about instant changes, I'm saving the painting until later.' Izzy was back. Wafting through with yet another bucket and half the garden, her lips curling into a smile that was definitely more for herself, than for him. She turned to him, with a teasing stare. 'It won't be long before you're doing this in your house in Bakewell will it? Making it pretty before you move in.'

That was a sore point, or it would be when Christina heard about it.

'Actually the agent rang before to tell me he's finalised a let on that place. There was a bit of a bidding war, before it even hit the market, and someone made an offer that was too good to miss.' Which may also account for his good mood these past couple of weeks.

So that was that. Another potential home that had come and gone, all wrapped up, without him ever having spent a night there.

Izzy wrinkled her nose in distaste. 'I pity the person who has to get vertigo on that balcony every morning.' She began to strip leaves off a stem. 'It's very spectacular, but that house was never particularly "you" was it?' Not pulling any punches then.

Xander braced himself for whatever was coming next. 'Meaning?' He tilted his head, preparing to take whatever was coming on the chin. Some days it was like Izzy had taken a truth drug, and the insults just kept pouring out. He'd never admit, even to his secret self, that sometimes he actually enjoyed it. As for admitting she was ever right, that would be tantamount to treason.

'I only mean that you didn't really have much connection to that house. I fail to see how anyone as averse to retail as you, ended up embracing the shopping mall aesthetic so wholeheartedly. You'd *never* feel comfortable there.' Said with a smile, but a bit damning, even for Izzy.

He paused a second, to regroup. 'Thank you to our architecture correspondent and resident psychologist.' He definitely wasn't about to admit she might have a point.

The architects hadn't stinted on the wow factor, which had proved to be exceptionally commercial, and therefore a good call. But however he enthused about it publicly, in reality, the vast spaces there left him cold, even if they did have a lighting scheme large enough to illuminate a small city.

Izzy's tone was matter of fact. 'The Pink House suits you way better.'

'Sorry?' Xander blinked. That was the last thing he expected to hear.

She gave a shrug. 'You look like you belong there, that's all. You should definitely move into that instead.' She gave a satisfied grin, as she wiped the table. 'Sorry, I'm only stating the bleedin' obvious.'

'Right.' He shook his head. 'Thanks for that insight.' Out of the question, for every reason he could think of. He didn't want to move into any house, especially not that one, and why would he need a home, when he'd managed just fine for the last eight years without one. He was glad the subject was closed.

Except if he thought Izzy had finished, he was wrong.

She screwed round on him with another glare that bored right into him. 'If you're too short sighted to see it, and too stubborn to do it, you might need someone to knock some sense into that thick head of yours.' Only Izzy could be that rude, and get away with it, simply because she was so sincere and, more to the point, honest. Deep down he knew she had his best interests at heart, but more importantly, there wasn't a glimmer of self interest in anything she said.

Xander's lips twitched, as he held back his smile, and his voice rose. 'You're offering to hit me? Again?'

Izzy stuck her chin in the air and was about to whoosh out of the room when she jerked to a halt by a small desk, suddenly serious. 'Hey, not meaning to be nosey, but is this you in the photo?' Given she was peering at a small frame on the wall, nosey was the perfect description.

He made his way to the dark corner, squinted at the picture. 'It's Christina and me when we were kids.' Their gawkiness made him smile.

Izzy's breath was warm on his neck, as she huddled in for a closer look. 'All jaw and attitude even then, I see.' That nudge in the ribs she gave him was very close to being off limits. 'You look very alike, apart from Christina being blonde.' She was gently ignoring the third person in the photo. Tactful was possible for her then, even if she didn't normally choose that route.

'I can't have been much more than five.' Xander's voice grated. 'And that's our mum...' The innocent optimism of the faces in the photo, given what came later, sent a rocket of sadness through his chest.

'It's weird how you remember things from images in photos, isn't it? Even in colour, it all looked kind of sepia back then, didn't it?' Izzy's voice was dreamy, as she looked closer.

She did this a lot. Making random comments, as if she were coming at every subject from around the back, always taking him unawares.

He gave a half laugh. 'Everything was kodachrome coloured before digital came along.'

'Your mum looks so young, and so pretty.' Izzy's voice slipped to a whisper as soft as her hand, which fluttered across his. Just for a second. 'She's lovely Xander.'

It was true, she was.

The dull ache in his chest made him sigh. 'It's strange to think she'll stay fifty four forever now.' He'd never thought of that before.

'Is that how old she was?' Izzy's head was almost touching his shoulder, pressing close enough for her hair to be tickling his ear.

Xander sighed. 'Yes. She had this degenerative neurological disease, a bit like MS, but rarer. It simply wiped her out. She had her last year at The Pink House.' It wasn't something he often shared. Mostly people would run a mile rather than hear about it.

'I'm so sorry.' As her fingers slid onto his arm the warmth made his skin tingle. 'It must have been awful.'

When she didn't let go, he carried on. 'It kind of crept up slowly over the years, but at the end it went very fast.'

'Xander, your poor mum, poor you.' Her arm was around his back, sliding around his ribs, and he closed his eyes, as she pulled him in.

Merged in the darkness, dragged against her softness, he gave into a warmth that slowly permeated, and then totally embraced him. There was nothing sexual at all, just a wonderful enveloping strength, that he wished could go on forever.

When she finally eased away, the knot in his chest had gone.

'Oh, shit.' She was muttering in the gloom now. 'Talk about putting my foot in it. I'm so sorry, all that stuff about you belonging in The Pink House, I shouldn't have said it, I wouldn't have, not if I'd...'

'It's okay.' He gave her a sideways nudge with his elbow. 'You weren't to know.' He wasn't sure when he'd ever had a hug that sustaining.

Izzy's hands were still covering her face. 'I'm so sorry, I'll be more careful in future.'

Xander gave a low laugh. 'And there's a chance you might just be right too.' How come the woman with the motor mouth could hit the nail on the head, without even trying? 'Maybe I am more comfortable at The Pink House, despite all the sad stuff that

271

happened there.'

She'd been talking about him fitting in. But what was it about her that made her fit in here, because she did? As for why he felt so complete and comfortable whenever she was around, that was something else he puzzled over endlessly. His pulse banged uncomfortably, as he watched the pale skin at the base of her neck tighten, as she leaned forward to pick up the bucket she'd put down.

He checked his watch. 'It's almost five. Even a slave driver like you must see it's time for a swim by now.' He needed to cool down, even if she didn't. 'No point buying pool towels, if we aren't going to use them.' His pent up sexual energy had to be rechanneled somehow. A thrash in the pool might ease that problem.

'It's hard to stop, when there's so much to do.' She let out a long sigh. 'But okay, we'll swim.'

What? He'd expected more of a fight.

He narrowed his eyes. 'You haven't caved because you feel sorry for me?'

From the guilt on her face that was exactly why. The grin she tried for floundered. 'Maybe I'm just feeling cooperative.'

Izzy and cooperative didn't belong in the same sentence.

She turned, and tossed her head. 'Great. I'll go and get changed, see you at the pool.'

So many thoughts crashed into Xander's head. He wanted to tell her never to feel bad because of his mum, not to bend over, or make allowances, that there was nothing she could do, nothing any of them could do, how amazing that hug of hers had been...

But she was already half way across the courtyard.

53

Saturday Afternoon, 12th July

XANDER & IZZY

By the pool

Quick changes

When Izzy was concentrating on the house, she could largely shut Xander out of her head, but the minute she stopped, everything became more difficult. Lazing beside the pool, having his tanned, disgustingly attractive body, parading in front of her? That counted as torture in anyone's book. Which was why she'd ripped off her clothes in the house, and had the fastest shower in the history of the world, to ensure she could grab the advantage of arriving at the pool first.

Throwing down her sarong on the smooth stone pool edge – why the hell had she chosen a bikini this small? – she slid off the side into the deep end. Diving in and losing your bikini bottoms is something you only do once in life, and Luce still howled with laughter every time she remembered Izzy doing underwater ballet impressions in Matlock pool, trying to reconnect with her knickers. Thank god she'd got that life lesson out of the way back then rather than today.

The water closed around her, deliciously chilling, after the sticky heat of the afternoon. By the time Xander appeared she was fully occupied bashing a ball around the pool, bobbing down to keep her boobs under water, having every reason to keep her eye firmly on the ball, and no reason at all to ogle any random drop-dead gorgeous power packed thighs.

'You got here fast, considering how reluctant you were.' Xander stood on the side, staring down at her.

Izzy tossed back her hair, with a silent curse for the straggles. Damn that there was no place to hide her freckles either, but even more of a damn at what she was staring up at. Those tanned abs, and bulges in all the right places, were way more than a girl should have to cope with in the name of work. She hoped Luce and Dida appreciated the effort she was putting in here, not to mention the mental agony she was going through. One stroke of luck, he was wearing boxer shorts. She might have expired on the spot if he'd been wearing speedos.

Locking her eyes onto his ankle bones seemed like a plan. If she gritted her teeth very hard, and hugged her ribs tightly, she could just about squeeze the butterflies in her stomach into submission. It wasn't hard to think this was the same confident guy who hauled her out of the skip, and acted like he ran the world, but who would have thought the underneath of that expensive suit, and developer attitude, would be so full of pain and hurt? Back there, talking about his mum he'd looked so bereft, she'd simply wanted to wrap her arms round him, and never let go, and nothing to do with him being hot. All she'd wanted was to stop him from hurting. Getting in so close had not been ideal. Breathing in so much of his scent had left her aching for so much more, but as proximity wasn't on offer from either side, she'd have to block that too. And there had definitely been a life lesson for her back there, about being more careful about what she said, and not shooting her mouth off in every random direction.

In fact, the more she saw of Xander, the more certain she was that she should be keeping her distance. A two mile exclusion zone would still probably be too close. His commitment aversion probably wasn't only to do with his career and his nomadic lifestyle. The glimpses she was getting of his complex past only underlined why he wouldn't be up for emotional complications. If any man needed an "avoid at all costs" sign hanging around his neck, it was Xander.

There was a swish as he dived into the water, and Izzy's shoulders relaxed. At least when he was submerged there was less of him for her to swoon over. In fact he was little more than a line of splashes, as he sped through the water at the other side of the pool, flipping over as he reached each end. Ten lengths. Twenty lengths.

Eventually he stopped at the deep end, surfaced, shook his head, and through the volley of falling water drops, he shot a wide, deep grin at Izzy.

Then he disappeared and began to swim again. Definitely a man with a lot of issues, as well as a demanding fitness regime. A body like that didn't happen by accident.

Once he was safely underwater again, she swam off to the deep end, clambered onto the poolside, and slipped back into her sarong. Then she helped herself to a couple of pristine pistachio towels, went to sit on the edge of a pool lounger, and began to dry her hair.

'I think you might be able to stop rubbing now.'

Izzy, looking down inside her towel, saw Xander's feet facing hers on the stone flags, water puddling around them, as it ran off his ankles. His gravelly voice scattered shivers right through her.

'Look at you, your legs are all sun-kissed.' His voice was low, and horribly fluttery.

Izzy abandoned the hair drying, threw down her towel, and

examined her shins. She gave a snort, as she saw the effect the sun was having on her skin. 'Freckles, speckles, and more freckles. I know. It's awful.'

'They're all over your nose too.' He sounded like he liked them.

'Yep, well they would be, wouldn't they? A bit of sun and they're everywhere.' And shit to how flirty the word everywhere made that sound, because flirty was the last thing she meant to be.

'How's your foot anyway? After you stepped on broken glass by the skip? Let me have a look, whilst you're sitting down.'

Déjà vu or what? Here she was, letting him boss her around, all over again.

He knelt in front of her, grasped her ankle firmly, and gently raised it upwards, until he could see the sole of her foot. Brushing away the dust and water with a broad thumb, he brought his face close in to examine the scar.

'Nicely healed.' He gave a satisfied nod, but he didn't let go.

She gave an inward grimace at putting such a short and stubby leg in his hand. 'So much for my cart horse ankles.' Some days it seemed entirely unfair that she hadn't she got slight and willowy genes. Not that she was making comparisons. Astrid was so far up the scale, she couldn't realistically be used as a yardstick. It would be like weighing up a Ford Focus against a Formula One Ferrari.

Xander was biting his lip, apparently making a detailed assessment of her calf, and still hanging onto her heel. 'Nope, you're soft and curved, much more like a cherub, I'd say.'

She wasn't sure if chubby, as in cherub, was a compliment or an insult. 'I'd love to rock the waif look, but I like cake too much, and that's before we get to the gene part.'

He sent her a wicked grin, and gave a laugh. 'I know which I'd rather be in bed with.'

That comment had her gulping hard enough to choke, and luckily she caught her jaw before it dropped. Off limits. Below the belt. Out of line. All of the above. She wasn't going to give him the satisfaction of a reaction.

Still grinning, he added quickly, 'Not that I should even be thinking about it, but just saying.'

However much of her sympathy his achingly vulnerable alter ego deserved, there were times when the version of the man who had popped up here, deserved to be hit over the head. And hard.

He took a deep breath, and refocused, with a subject change. 'Sorry to cut this short, but people eat earlier here. If we're going out for Pizza, you might want to whip off to get ready. Dress code is casual, it's a relaxed kind of place. Not that I'm hurrying you, but now would be good.'

He was back into command mode then. And staring at her with a vague impatience, as if he were querying why she hadn't already leapt into action. 'Is there a problem?'

Izzy hung onto her lips, which were bursting to break into the broadest smile. Rookie mistake on Xander's part, chasing her off, when he was still hanging onto her ankle.

The look she posted him was silky cool. 'No problem at all.' She was fighting to keep the irony out of her voice, and biting back her giggles. 'The minute you give me my foot back, I'll be on my way.'

54

Saturday Evening, 12th July

IZZY & XANDER

Pizzeria Le Gourmande

Checked cloths and total wimps

'So, it's not too smart here, but now you've tasted the desert, you can see why the ex pats' all love it. The ice cream's to die for too.' The grin Xander sent Izzy across the table was teasing. 'Are you sure I can't persuade you to try it?'

Izzy beamed back. 'Fabulous deserts, I pushed the boat out with two, but even I can't handle three.' As well as the deserts, she was enjoying that the restaurant terrace, in a large cobbled courtyard off the market square, was so full and bustling, that it had been easy to keep the conversation light, and keep her eyes on everything but Xander. Two feet of checked table cloth between them wasn't a lot, but it was better than nothing.

Xander, gazing into the distance, leaned back on his chair. 'So much for being popular with ex pats, Astrid's just come in.' He drew in a breath. 'On her own.'

Remembering her skinny silhouette from the other day, Izzy doubted Astrid was here for the ice cream. She followed Xander's stare, past the relaxed family groups spilling around the tables, towards the bar. Even from behind, Astrid looked like she'd walked straight out of French Vogue. Izzy wondered how it was possible for a person's back to be so classy.

Xander's comment was loaded enough to beg the question from Izzy. 'Does she have a partner then?' Not that it was anything to do with anything.

'She has done in the past, but as far as I know, she doesn't at the moment.'

Izzy watched Astrid's perfectly regular features light up as she shared a joke with the waiter, and turned from the bar. There was no mistaking those long supple limbs, or the hair that fell in glossy waves, without the slightest blur of frizz, as she threaded her way between the diners. From across the restaurant she had made Izzy feel small and scrubby and invisible, but now she was coming closer, Izzy had the overwhelming sensation that she, herself, was about to shrivel up, like a slug in salt.

'Okay, I'd say she's definitely coming over.' It sounded like Xander was talking her in to land.

Despite Izzy having devoured a medium Pizza Provençale and a side order of fries, not to mention the double desert, as Astrid picked her way, delicately, yet deliberately, towards their table her stomach began to wither.

Xander's expression relaxed. 'She's probably coming over to have a word about the project we're working on, apparently it's all coming together faster than we anticipated.'

So this would be the fabulous working relationship Xander had talked about, when he was so determinedly putting her into context. More fool Izzy for not getting that it was quite this live and ongoing. And so many "we"s in one sentence too. She tried to ignore the way that brought her heart to a total standstill, with one huge jolt. Not that she could be jealous logically, because seeing Astrid only underlined to Izzy yet again, how far out of her reach Xander was. But there was something in the implied closeness that made Izzy wish she could be someone else entirely, and, at this moment, somewhere else entirely too.

'This is great, I can introduce you.' Xander was getting more enthusiastic by the second. 'You'll really get on.'

Izzy cringed, and slipped as low down in her seat as she could. Only another couple of feet, and she'd disappear right under the table.

He hesitated, narrowing his eyes. 'You are okay with meeting her, aren't you?'

And why the hell would Izzy not be okay with it? What possible reason could she give for not being okay? Apart from the Ford Ferrari comparison, which was going to make Izzy come out of any meeting with Astrid, looking only slightly more upmarket than a tramp, and the fact she felt completely inferior on every level, there was no rational explanation for her reluctance.

'She looks...well...a bit intimidating.' Understatement of the decade, and the best Izzy could come up with at short notice. Seeing the ochre shot silk of Astrid's dress, a mere three tables away, Izzy's throat was clenching up. 'In fact, actually, I'd rather not.' Rising panic had morphed her voice into a strangled shriek. 'If you don't mind.'

Xander's eyebrows rose. 'So you're really not happy about it?' He assessed the situation.

'I'd rather eat my own head.' Izzy sent him a wide eyed plea, hoping he might understand. 'If my legs hadn't totally frozen I'd run.' As Izzy watched Astrid's hips wiggling as she twisted between the chairs, her body went rigid too.

His frown was perplexed. 'I haven't made eye contact yet.'

'I'm sorry if I'm being a total wimp about this...' Izzy cringed. She hadn't meant to make this a big deal.

'It's fine, there's one way I can think of to divert her, but I'm not sure you'll like it.' He gave her a doubtful look.

Izzy shook her head. 'I'm desperate, do whatever you have to.' Anything would be better than dying in front of Astrid.

Xander was up on his feet, and swooping towards Izzy now. 'Sorry, but it's the only way I can think of...'

Izzy snatched in a breath as he zoomed towards her. Shit, he couldn't be. Her eyes widened to saucers, and her pulse started to bang as she saw he was heading straight for her. If she might have died meeting Astrid, this was ten times worse.

One growled excuse as his stubble grazed her cheek, then his mouth landed on hers. She tasted him, light and sweet as the crème caramel they'd just eaten, as he brushed her lips for a lingering moment and felt her heart banging hard enough to leap out of her body.

When he finally did pull away, he left her dizzy and quaking.

She sat there, stunned, rubbing her lips with the back of her hand. What she must look like? But as she dared to raise her eyes and meet the stares, she realised that no-one at all was looking at her, because everyone's eyes were on Astrid, in that sheath of a silk dress, as, with long strides only a five ten woman could make, she hurried out of the restaurant.

Occasionally, it was definitely an advantage to be small and ordinary, and "Yay" to being invisible this time, with no help from a Harry Potter cloak.

Xander leaned back on his chair, ran his thumb over his jaw, as a satisfied smile curled across his face. 'Thanks for that Izzy. I'd say that did the trick. Wouldn't you say so?'

Alongside her great goldfish imitation, for once Izzy had no words to add. All she could do was slump in her chair, as her torso had apparently collapsed, when she'd finally exhaled. And even though Xander was doing a good impression of a waiter with OCD, intent on tidying the table, she couldn't help noticing his beam was slightly blurred with smoulder.

Those smoky eyes almost popped out of his head as he sat back down, then returned to normal as he shuffled, and readjusted his jeans. 'Well, now that's sorted, how about we move on to coffee?'

55

Saturday Evening, 12th July

IZZY & XANDER

In the garden at Christina's, Les Cerisiers, France

Flailing in the dark

'Shall I light the lanterns?' Izzy, padding barefoot across the grass following Xander, could just make out the shadows of the loungers. Behind them in the barn, the windows glowed yellow against the stone, from the glow of the lights Xander had turned on as he got the drinks.

'Sometimes it's nice to sit in the dark, and listen to the noise of the crickets.' Xander let her take the first lounger, handed her a beer, then settled onto the second himself.

Izzy noted the exclusion zone. Still a meticulous three feet, and her sane self knew she was all the better for that, however much, after yet another taste of Xander, the need to grab him for a complete replay was distractingly strong. She hugged her arms around her middle, to lessen what Luce called the post snog washing machine effect, which this time had the spin set to very fast. Add in Xander's scent in the car, all the way home, and she was pretty much wrung out.

Izzy settled back onto her lounger, looked at the tree canopy above, and searched for a neutral observation to make. 'I love the way the leaves are all inky against the sky.' That seemed to do the job.

Xander gave a laugh. 'It's a walnut tree, if we were here in October we'd have walnuts dropping on our heads. Whereas the cherry tree the house gets its name from is on the other side of the barn.' He paused, and his voice dropped as his tone became graver. 'For the record, I'm sorry for pouncing on you earlier.'

'No need to apologise.' She shut up the part of her that almost added "anytime" and jumped on whichever bit of her said that, squashed a pillow over it, and held it there.

Xander took a swig of beer. 'Astrid isn't really that scary, either...'

Izzy finished his sentence in her head. "We're committed friends with a great deal of admiration for each other." He'd made that clear on two previous occasions as well as tonight.

She forced out a light laugh. 'Rocking the divorced friends thing, just like Gwyneth Paltrow and Chris Martin?' If he gushed any more about Astrid, Izzy thought she might just have to be sick. 'I've never seen anyone that much like a super model in real life. Talk about golden couples.'

'Not quite.' Another low laugh from Xander. 'Although we were quite a starry double act in film production when we got together. Maybe that was the problem. We were young, and talented, and ambitious, and our best chance of making it in a competitive profession was together, rather than singly.'

'Right.' Izzy supposed this was Xander putting in more of the context he was so keen on. He'd obviously missed the bit about not talking about your ex when you went on dates. Except, shit to that, and a big mental kicking too, because what was happening now, between her and Xander, wasn't a date, was it? And she'd do well to remember that. She needed to put a damn big sign reminding her about that, right at the front of her brain. Huge letters, bold font, caps, underlined. That might do it. Although at the same time, part of her – and she had an idea it might be the masochistic part – was dying to hear every last detail about him and Astrid. And there was something about talking in the dark that made it so much easier to spill secrets. And so much easier to devour them hungrily.

Izzy braced herself with a shudder, as he carried on.

'I guess we ticked each other's boxes.' He held his beer up to the light from the house, and looked through it. It was almost as if he were talking to himself here. 'She was clever and successful, I got her access to contacts she wouldn't ever have had otherwise. It should have been win win.' He'd neatly side stepped the bit about them both being stunning.

He took a deep swig of beer. 'I'm not sure love had anything to do with it either. Maybe if it had, we'd have survived me taking time out to look after my mum.'

Izzy's eyes widened in the dusk, and the question was out before she could stop herself. 'You looked after your mum?' It came out as a horrible shrill shriek, as if the surprise had pushed her voice up an octave. Mentally kicking herself again now for that. She'd been so determined not to blurt stuff out, and this question was just plain rude, not to mention intrusive. 'Sorry, you don't need to answer that, I really shouldn't have asked.' She hoped that second blurt would make the first one right.

'It was only for the last six months of her life.' Ignoring her, he carried on anyway. 'Christina was in Hong King, my mum and dad didn't live together any more, and as there wasn't anyone else, it made sense it was me. I'd seen it coming, so I took time out from the film sets, went to stay with my mum at The Pink House, and did whatever work I could from home.'

So that was why The Pink House held so many memories for

him, much more than just being where his mum lived, and died. All the hell of watching her suffer, day in, day out, was there too. That explained how jumpy he'd been in the attic that day.

'With work, Astrid and I were often in different places anyway. The idea was she could come up to my mum's between projects. She came a couple of times, but she couldn't wait to get away, she hated the illness. It wasn't her fault, caring just isn't her thing. I should have known better, I shouldn't have put her though it.'

It wasn't Astrid's thing, but it had obviously been Xander's. 'I didn't realise you had been looking after your mum. That's an amazing thing to have done.' Izzy was still doing a mental double take.

'Not really, I didn't do it all on my own. We had nurses who came in to help too.' And Xander was making it seem like it was nothing.

'But caring is so difficult, for so many reasons.' She knew that from her grandmother dying from cancer.

Xander's voice was low, and husky. 'It's tiring, it's relentless, but knowing you are making a difference helps. The toughest part was having to watch my mum go through the hell and indignity, not to mention the pain.' He swallowed hard. 'That illness strikes everyone slightly differently. As the muscles fail people lose their facial expressions, so it's very hard to tell how they're feeling. My mum could barely move, or speak, but we were lucky because she could still swallow. In the end she died of pneumonia. Apparently that's a good way to go.'

Lucky because she could swallow? A good way to die? The phrases echoed in Izzy's ears. The sheer bleakness of Xander's words in the shadows had tears pricking her eyes. Everything she thought of to say seemed inadequate, as she swallowed back the lump in her throat. 'I've never been there, but it must be dreadful.' As for Xander raging around the building site, the harsh aloofness she'd read as arrogance might have been something else entirely. Detachment, maybe a sheer disillusion with life? There was no room for arrogance when you'd been to hell and back looking after someone sick, who'd died of such a degenerative disease.

Xander went on. 'When someone disintegrates in front of you, no matter how well you look after them, you're left wishing you could have done it better. You can't help thinking, if only you'd done a little bit more, they would have lasted longer, or they might have suffered a little bit less.'

Her chest ached for Xander. Izzy screwed up her face, kicking herself for how wrong she'd been. It was strange how you could jump to conclusions, and make instant judgements. Once you knew more, your first impressions were proved completely false. Izzy's stomach was twisting into knots with guilt for how wrong she'd got Xander.

But he was still talking. Almost as if now he'd begun, he couldn't stop.

'Afterwards Astrid and I tried to pick up where we'd left off, but somehow there wasn't anything there any more. I guess the partnership was pretty superficial, and when I put pressure on a relationship without any real depth, it simply crumbled.'

Izzy shook her head at how empty Xander sounded. How sad must that have been, to go through the agony of losing his mum like that, and then to find he'd lost his wife and marriage too?

He gave a sigh. 'With nothing there, it was strangely easy to separate. Astrid simply took the houses in London, and the one here. My mum left me The Pink House, but I didn't want to be there, so I closed it up. I only went back when there were so many holes in the roof this year, I couldn't ignore it any more.'

There were so many reasons for him not wanting to be at that house, and Izzy had jumped in with both feet earlier, telling him that was where he belonged. She wasn't to know, but at the same time, what she'd said couldn't have been any more insensitive. Remembering how she'd forced her ideas on him made her want to bang her head against a wall with the shame of it. As for how he'd become homeless, almost by default, she could understand

287

why he wouldn't want the bother of making a proper home after everything he'd gone through. And somewhere down the line she'd sounded off at him about that too. Mortified didn't begin to cover it.

He let out a long sigh. 'I hope that explains.'

Not that he had anything to explain to her. Although maybe this was his way of putting a stop to her thoughtless interference. Perhaps he'd told her, hoping once he'd put her in the picture, she would back off. Izzy reached out to touch him, just to show him he wasn't on his own. Just because she was another human. One who cared. A lot. Because she did. But even outstretched, her arm got nowhere near, and her hand was left flailing in the dark.

At least she could apologise. 'I'm so sorry I was so opinionated about where you should live. I won't be in future.' She wanted to go on, to say sorry for his mum, sorry for his marriage, sorry for his whole life, but somehow that was too intrusive.

'Sometimes it's good to hear a different point of view.' Xander cleared his throat. 'As for Astrid, hopefully we won't bump into her again.'

Izzy hoped that too, for lots of reasons, not all leading completely back to Astrid. Even though right now her heart was swollen with sadness for Xander, Izzy wasn't sure she could survive another snog like that one. Maybe next time, if there was a next time, it would be easier for her to take the eat her own head option.

Xander stood up. 'Well, thanks for listening. Sorry to be going, but it's getting quite late and there are some scripts I need to look over before tomorrow.'

That had solved another immediate problem for her, of how they were going to get back to the house, without the inevitable awkwardness, and skirting around each other. 'I'll stay here a bit, if that's okay.'

As he left, the light from the house lit up his face, and the deep lines of sadness she saw there made Izzy's heart ache. She'd come here to style and buy furniture, but the man she was coming to know along the way couldn't have been more different than she'd thought. He was turning every preconception she'd had about him on its head. And she wasn't quite sure where that left her.

56

Sunday Morning, 13th July

XANDER & IZZY

In the kitchen at Christina's, Les Cerisiers, France

Making flapjack

'Are you cooking? At seven in the morning? Can I smell toffee?'

Xander arrived in the kitchen to find all the doors open, bright sunlight slanting across the stone flag floor, and Izzy in a dress the colour of buttercups, leaning over the stove. It had to be surprise that had his jaw dropping, and caused the ridiculous rhetorical questions.

'Yes, yes and yes.' The look Izzy sent him over her shoulder was a mix of impatience and pity, at a guess for him being so stupid.

He had to hold his hands up to that one.

She gave a rueful grin. 'I had a sudden craving for flapjack, so I raided the cupboards. I hope that's okay?'

He shook his head, because only Izzy would do something

weird like this. Flapjack, at this time? 'Fine.' He was feeling so contrite after last night, he'd be going with everything she said this morning, if not all day.

The point was, he'd dreamed up this whole trip to make up for messing her about by sleeping with her. His most private self would possibly concede that he'd also done it because he wanted to prolong the contact. But whatever, jumping in to snog her senseless last night had been completely wrong of him, given he hadn't changed his position on his overall availability, but also given her wishes for him to keep his distance, that both she and Luce had made abundantly clear to him. He had to admit he'd been aching to close the gap between them ever since Izzy had arrived, which made no sense at all, when the trip was to make amends for doing just that in the first place. But however unavailable she was, he knew she'd been in there, kissing him back, big time.

What was worse, he really hadn't needed to take that course of evasive action in the first place. Looking back now, he had no idea why he hadn't simply walked over to Astrid, and headed her off. Simple as. As for the way he'd come back and info dumped on Izzy later, well that had to be down to the fact he was totally wiped out after the unbelievable kiss.

Yet again, he'd wanted to put things right, and, yes, into context. But he never spilled like that, and why he'd done it so completely, and without holding back at all, he had no idea. Somehow, the way Izzy simply soaked up everything he had to say, and the way he knew she understood, even without her needing to say anything at all, was something he hadn't ever come across before. Having her there beside him, calm and quiet in the dark, made him feel whole again, which was maybe why he'd carried on talking for quite so long.

How one small, shouty woman could make him feel better, and absorb his hurt too, was something he hadn't worked out yet. As for how he was going to cope when they both moved back to their real lives again, that was something he hadn't yet addressed. In fact he was trying to block out that it was going to happen at all.

Across the kitchen Izzy looked up from scooping the flapjack mixture into a baking tray. 'I got a long email from Dida.'

News from home? He wasn't sure he wanted to burst the bubble they were in. 'Heard anything from the bank yet?' It had been impossible to miss that this was one of Izzy's preoccupations given she talked about it every day.

'Nope.'

No surprise there then. From what he knew of banks and the vintage business, their chances of getting a loan were approximately zero, although he couldn't bring himself to tell her this.

'Dida and Luce are planning a fancy dress retro film night though. Sounds like a creative way to sell and raise the profile at the same time.' She held out a sticky spoon to him. 'Want a taste?'

He took the spoon, and was about to comment on how exciting it would be to have films back at the cinema, but there was no time for that, as she'd just given him the perfect opening for something more pressing he had to broach.

'Talking of film, I got an email from Astrid.' He wasn't going to elaborate, that politely, Astrid hadn't mentioned the kiss, although quite what she'd have made of him making such an over enthusiastic public display of affection he had no idea. 'Probably what she was coming to talk about last night, but there's a proposal she wants me to look through, it's going to keep me tied up for the whole of this morning.'

Izzy pushed the baking tray into the oven. 'I've got lots to get on with anyway.'

At least she wasn't reacting, or rather overreacting, to him working with Astrid. That was one piece of good news. He decided to drip feed a bit more information. 'It's a project she's been trying to get off the ground for years. It's potentially huge, dystopian, with vampire dinosaurs. Looks like now might be the time it's going to fly.'

'Vampire dinosaurs? How does that not surprise me?'

He ignored that Izzy's breaking grin was overlaid with mischief, and licked the spoon instead. Unbelievably sweet and good. 'Very moreish.' He grinned at Izzy. A lot like her.

'Too true.' Her voice was thick with the sticky mixture she was eating from her own spoon. 'You can have the pan too if you want.'

Xander reached for it. Too good to miss. Although eating flap-jack mixture, out of a pan? How had he fast forwarded to this scene of domesticity, and more to the point, why the hell wasn't he legging it as fast as he could? A larger part of him than he was comfortable with wanted to admit that he was actually enjoying it. Maybe a bit too much. He was just relieved that Christina couldn't see him. Her smug grin and know-it-all look would just be too much.

57

Late Monday Afternoon, 13th July

IZZY & XANDER

Le Bac à Glaces, Brantome

The ice cream sundae scene

'We've got to sit right out on the street, because being seen as you eat your ice cream is an important part of the experience.' Xander steered Izzy through the pavement tables, and pulled out a chair for her when they reached a suitably prominent table. 'And after the number of armoire's I've looked at today, I'm claiming the most major sundae on offer.'

Izzy knew she'd tested Xander's patience to the limit and beyond, with a vintage trawl that had expanded like elastic, with shopping time currently standing at seven hours. Plus, with the bigger pieces they'd been looking at today, she knew she'd been banging on about margins to the point of making them both want to scream. Her real problem was the Vintage Cinema Club money was running out a lot faster than she'd anticipated.

Xander pulled away from the pavement edge, as a 2CV chugged by a little too closely for comfort. 'As for the cars going past our elbows, they're only usually crawling by, although once an old French guy did lose it on his mobilette. He scattered the tables and crashed straight through the plate glass window.'

'Wow, living dangerously or what?' Izzy laughed at him 'It's the only way to do it. Shall we look at the menu?'

Their waitress was less than helpful. Stroppy enough, in fact, for Xander to ask if she could possibly be related to Izzy, which was witty enough to almost win him a slap. In the end, Izzy went for triple raspberry with strawberry sauce, and Xander settled on chocolate rum mocha, with extra cream. He was half way down his when he stopped.

'My mum used to bring us here when we were kids.' He had a faraway look in his eye as he rubbed a drip of chocolate off his chin. 'You know, since we were in the attic at The Pink House that day, I've thought about my mum a lot. I think I actually shut her memory away when I locked up the house.'

Izzy sighed. 'And how is it since you've let her out?' She fixed her eyes on his stubble. It would be more comfortable if her heart didn't pound so much, when he looked so grave and serious.

He rested his chin on his hand. 'It's good. The funny thing is, when I think about her now she isn't ill any more. Now she's come back she's young again.' He hesitated. 'And happy.' His mouth twisted downwards for a second, then finally made it towards a half smile.

Izzy blinked furiously, as her mouth filled with saliva, staring at the crisscross pattern on her ice cream wafer, trying to make her tears go away. There was no point both of them getting upset here. She dived into her bag, dragged out a tissue, and blew her nose, cringing at how loud it sounded, not quite sure if this was sad crying or happy crying.

Eventually she gave another loud sniff, and deciding her

voice might not be too wobbly, she tried to talk. 'So that's good.' Encouraged, she went on. 'You look so like your mum you know.'

The grin he sent her was kind of rueful.

Izzy studied him over her melting ice cream. 'Especially when you smile.' It was something about their cheeks. A sudden thought flapped through her brain like a black crow. 'This thing your mum had, it isn't...?' Realising she was bang out of line, she slammed the brakes on her mouth.

Too late.

Xander picked up where she'd left off. 'Hereditary?' His grimace was enough. He drew in a long breath. 'There's a fifty fifty chance it will be passed on, yes.' He gave a shrug.

'What?' Izzy balked. Fifty fifty, that was one in two, like tossing a coin. Her stomach turned into an ice block, her heart came to a thudding halt, and all the colour seemed to drain out of the street. Xander couldn't possibly have it. This amazing, muscular, beautiful, fabulous, energetic guy couldn't end up like...It couldn't happen. Not to her beautiful Xander. It simply wasn't fair. He was too much alive.

'At least we know Christina's clear.' His cheeks were suddenly very hollow.

Izzy's voice was small. 'That's good then.'

'They can do genetic tests, and she tested negative, before she had the kids.'

Izzy couldn't believe he sounded so matter of fact about it, when her own heart was suddenly banging but this time with the adrenalin of anxiety.

'What about you?' Her voice was a croak.

Xander narrowed his eyes. 'That's the rub. I've had all the counselling, but they suggest you only take the test if there's a really important reason to know. So long as you don't test, there's half a chance you're clear, whereas if you test for no reason and get a positive result, people find that hard to live with.' He gave a low laugh, and tapped his fingers on the table top. 'Everyone presents differently with this disease, the age of onset varies tremendously, and so do the symptoms. Until you get it, it really is a case of the less you know the better.'

'I don't know what to say...' The fact she said it so quietly, meant she might as well not have said it at all.

He was bashing on. 'I've had no reason to test. I'm a natural optimist, and I've got my money on my coin falling on the good side too.'

Izzy hugged her chest. Locking her eyes on the back of Xander's hand, and focussing on that tanned skin, and the dark hairs, she was filled with a sudden sense of desperation at the thought that she might lose him. She knew she couldn't bear to lose him. She fought the instinct that was driving her to grab hold of him, fling her arms around him, and never let go, ever again. One horrible thought passed through her mind. Love. She swallowed it back, along with the huge lump in her throat. Love didn't have anything to do with how she was feeling now. The sooner she kicked that thought into touch the better. It didn't explain this at all. This wasn't her Xander. Her first thought, and this one wouldn't go away. Except he definitely wasn't hers to lose. And if the wrenching in her gut was anything, it was simply concern for another human, who was up against it. End of story.

'But how do you...?' Her question dwindled to a halt. She wasn't quite sure what she was even meaning.

He was straight back at her, shrugging it off. 'When you've known about it for a long time, like I have, you just put it out of your mind, and get on with your life.'

'I see.' She didn't at all. She had no idea how he could be so calm and cool and collected and casual about something so monumental and huge. I mean, she was feeling devastated, and shocked, and ill, and it wasn't even her it was happening to.

'So, moving on...' He eyed her squarely, but he was still biting his lip.

Moving on? How could he? Except he'd already picked up his

spoon, and now he was slipping a dribbling spoonful of mocha ice cream into his mouth.

He pushed on. 'Moving on, and more to the point, much more important – what about your immediate cash flow problems?' Complete change of subject there, and the way Xander was looking at her through his thatch of dark eyelashes turned her frozen tummy to hot raspberry sauce, in one slow blink.

He was waggling his spoon at her now, as he swallowed. 'I thought we might try the Moulin de Roc restaurant. I booked for Friday, I was hoping the food will be spectacular enough for us to come up with some amazing solutions to your problems over dinner.'

'What?' If she was opening and closing her mouth here, it was only because she didn't know how he'd skipped from a devastating genetic outlook, to dinner, all in the course of three seconds.

'Look at your wrinkled nose.' His voice rose in mock indignation. 'I might as well be suggesting four courses of poison, not dinner at some place with enough Michelin stars to light up the night sky.'

Izzy found she was shaking her head again, not in response to the question, just in reaction to the man. She forced herself to drag herself together, and tried not to feel quite so faint and floppy.

'I thought making it work related would sway you.' His eyes were fixed on her face now, and damn that he was so bloody determined. She knew he wasn't going to back off. And damn too, to the way she was going to feel so scared of losing him, that she was going to agree to everything he suggested from now on, until forever. She was going to have to get to grips with that one, or she was going to be in all kinds of trouble here.

'Okay, just the once, I'll be swayed.' She gazed at him, and narrowed her eyes, and tried to sound gracious. 'Thank you.' She drew in a long breath. 'Dinner on Friday, to discuss work, would be lovely.' She tried to ignore the rivers of perspiration running down her back, and posted him a smile. 'But don't think I'm going to give in so easily every time.' Because if she did, the next ten days were going to be hell.

The grin that stretched across his face, wider than she'd seen before, made her heart falter. That recurring thought, that this guy who was so full of vitality, and so alive...She gave another deep sigh, and tried to push that one away before her throat went wobbly.

He was hassling her again. 'Come on you, eat your sundae, or it'll be a smoothie in no time in this heat.' This time Xander was right. Despite the shade of the red and white stripy awning overhead, here in town, with the heat coming off the buildings all around, it was baking.

If she needed proof that he wasn't going to back off on the commanding any time soon, she had it there. Meantime she was just going to have to grow some backbone, and be strong. For herself, possibly, as much as for him.

58

Friday Evening, 18th July

IZZY

In the shower, Les Cerisiers, France

A drench and a strategy

'Okay, dress code is smart.' Xander was standing by the door to her bedroom, rapping out those orders he was so good at. 'We need to leave in an hour, Nico the owner gets very upset if people turn up late. Do you think you can manage that?' Still nailing condescending here, no mistaking it, that glower of his was entirely superior.

Izzy, barring the door in a way that was a lot more fierce and business-like than she really meant, when, for two pins and an ice cream sundae she'd have hoiked him straight over the threshold, took a deep breath. 'I'll do my best.' Sometimes he was disgustingly patronising, even if...She stopped herself there. Since Monday she'd been training herself to do the blocking thing with Xander and his outlook. Either not to go there at all, or else to stay firmly in the fifty per cent green zone, he claimed to inhabit himself. Otherwise it was just too upsetting. As for ice cream sundaes, in reality she didn't think she could ever face eating another one of those again.

Xander gave a grimace. 'There's a lot to live down at this restaurant. Christina's husband took her there the night he proposed. They'd only known each other a few weeks, and Christina was so shocked she passed out, very spectacularly, and caused total mayhem in the dining room. Nico has never forgotten, and I'm not sure he has ever forgiven either, come to that.'

'Again, I'll do my best not to...' Izzy was coming on strong with the reassurance, in the hope that she could dive straight into the shower, and not waste any of her allocated preparation time. She might not ever look that polished, but even this look didn't happen without a shit load of effort on her part.

She dug deep to harden herself enough to sound like she shouldn't be messed with. 'Go on, shoo. Go and get ready yourself.' She added a mocking grin, to give him a taste of his own medicine. 'If you think you can manage it, in the allocated time.' Closing the door looked like the only way to get rid of him here.

Izzy, standing in the shower shortly afterwards, stared up into the shower head, and let the water pelt into her face. Right now she'd have given anything for a chin wag with Luce, just to work out if there was anything strange going on with Xander. He may have been looking at her weirdly the last few days, but there again, maybe it had simply been her imagination. Hell, there was no reason on earth to think Xander was going to go all soppy on her, and maybe ask for something more than they had. Whatever, perhaps she needed a strategy. Strategies were good. And suddenly it was obvious. She'd get in first, and say something that explained, simply and clearly, why she was welded to her single life, just to be sure he didn't have other ideas. And if she made a complete fool of herself, or ended up saying more about her dad than she usually would, then too bad.

Now all she needed to decide was what to say.

59

Friday Evening, 18th July

XANDER & IZZY

At the Moulin de Roc Restaurant

Lobster and tantric sex

Xander was only a breath behind Izzy as he followed her through the restaurant, and out towards the riverside terrace. He was close enough to be enveloped in the sweet tantalising smell of her, to see the downy hairs on the nape of her neck. One small view that sent a thousand shivers through his torso. He'd been hoping to become inured to the strange sensations he'd been having ever since she arrived here. Maybe even before that. But inured hadn't happened yet.

He knew there was a logical explanation, and the one he'd come up with had a lot to do with the explosive sex they'd had, and then, hadn't. Everyone knew that if there was huge chemistry with someone you were in close contact with on a daily basis, it was best expressed. In fact, he'd only ever heard this from other people, because he'd personally made it through his thirty four years without experiencing off the scale chemistry. Until he'd met Izzy. But with Izzy, the chemistry had hit him like a thunderbolt, and sent his whole hormone system haywire, and blown his entire periodic table skywards.

His theory was that being close to someone for whom you had a chemical attraction, and not expressing it, was hard enough. If you slept with that person, and then backed off, and then spent a week hanging around with them, it had to blast your brain chemicals out of the park. It was a bit like Sting style tantric sex. A kind of orgasmic deferral, where extended arousal could lead to sex that lasted for days, and an orgasm that blew off the roof. And being in this off limits yet oh so close situation with Izzy was leading to a kind of extended arousal, with no end game in sight. And instead of blowing off the roof, it was blowing his rational mind. This was his theory, and he was sticking to it.

After twenty four hours of concentrated soul searching, he'd finally pulled the pieces together. The tightness in his chest, his whole life feeling like it had been turned upside down and shaken, that high octane accidental snog that blew his mind at the pizza place, his round the clock hard on. And once he'd worked it out, he'd realised it was nothing new. In fact it had been hanging around him, wrapping him up, and taking him over for weeks. And now he'd accepted it was there, he definitely couldn't fight it. He'd simply have to do his best to work with it.

This evening Izzy's curls were somehow all caught up on top of her head, leaving her throat and neck deliciously naked. Tonight she looked totally, dizzily beautiful, her black dress skimming her hips, and bad luck for him that the more elegantly she dressed, the more vulnerable she appeared, because vulnerable smashed his heart to smithereens, every time.

Izzy glanced over her shoulder at him. 'Did I tell you how great you look in that tux?'

Xander swallowed hard. Was she fiddling with her tongue?

'Please tell me you aren't eating bubble gum.' Being in a state of prolonged sexual over excitement was one thing, tolerating a chewing gum habit was something else entirely.

'Disgusted much?' She returned his frown with a snort, and an indignant hiss . 'It helps when I'm nervous, and I'll obviously get rid of it as soon as we get to the table, so stop stressing.'

Xander, watching the defiance skim across her broad cheekbones, and sweep her lips into that familiar berry pout, readjusted his collar, as his temperature shot up.

'It feels like we're on our own island here.' She slid into the chair which was being held out for her by the waiter who had shown them across the picturesque main terrace to a small peninsula. 'It's amazing, with the table balanced between the mill wheel and the river.'

The garlands of tiny lights on the pergola above their heads, swung gently in the twilight breeze, sending tiny dappled shadows across her face. And there went the bubble gum, into a tissue. Result.

A smile played at the corners of Xander's lips. Thinking back now, he couldn't remember a time she hadn't made him dizzy. The way he'd caught her looking at him lately, almost like she was going to burst into tears, only wrung his heart out more. Traipsing around the markets, when they'd been buying towels. When they'd made love, that night so long ago at The Pink House, the sex had been explosive. The day he'd told her he couldn't do a relationship had almost made him sick, and the way he hadn't been able to stop looking at the photo he'd taken when they were in her bedroom, looking at her bed, was simply an earlier manifestation of the same syndrome. Even the first time he'd touched her, when he'd hauled her out of the skip, he'd kind of known. That strange, gut wrenching, primitive reaction he'd been having all along, had been there from day one. How the hell had it not dawned on him before?

He slipped his hand into his pocket, and closed it around the box. Another impulse buy, fuelled by that same driving force as all the rest. Small silver cherub earrings, once they'd caught his eye in the window, he hadn't been able to walk away and leave them in the shop. Just because he knew they'd be perfect for her. And somewhere along the line he needed to talk to her about all this, and work out where the hell they went from here, because if it was coming to an end in a week's time, he was going to feel like he'd jumped off a cliff. He was hoping the earrings might be a way in.

'Everything okay?' Izzy looked up at him quizzically.

As he lowered himself onto his chair, he took a deep breath.

'Izzy, I've been thinking...' Xander heard his voice, a ripple over a moment of hesitation.

'Me too.' Izzy narrowed her eyes as if she was concentrating, then she cleared her throat. 'My dad used to bring us to places like this, once he made it.' She was talking faster than usual, almost as if she was trying to stop him getting a word in. 'Did I ever tell you that basically he was the biggest bastard out there? When he left us, he took everything. Everything. The only way I know to be happy, is to make the best of very little. My mum taught us how to live with no money, and I'm glad she did, because now I know what's important in life. And that's why I hate to see good things thrown away, and why I'm desperate to make the vintage cinema work, so I can be independent, and on my own – so I only have to rely on myself, and I never have to depend on anyone, in case they turn out to be a bastard like my dad.'

Xander raised his eyebrows, and sighed inwardly. He had no idea where all that had just come from, but it had put the brakes on any talk about where they might be heading. He closed his fingers over the box he had cupped in his palm one last time, then released it, and slid his hand out of his pocket.

Time for a change of tack here. As Xander sat back, the hovering waiter took his chance, and slid in with the menus.

Ignoring the menu, Xander looked Izzy straight in the eye.

'That's exactly why I've been thinking...about your business difficulties. You mentioned that you're short of cash for quality pieces for the load, so I've got a business proposition for you.' He watched her expression change from panic to bemusement, and knew he'd got away with it.

'Okay. I'm listening.' She tilted her head on one side. 'Business proposals are always best discussed under fairy lights.' Her breathless tone had gone strangely flat now.

'I've got a little bit of cash left over from my building project. I could always back you, and loan you the extra money you need.' What he was offering now was simply an extension of how he'd been helping her so far, and an expression of how much he was willing her to do well, because with the effort and commitment she put into her work, if anyone should succeed, she should. The last thing he wanted to do was let her think he was throwing money at the problem. He sat back, and waited to gauge her reaction.

'You're suggesting that you lend me the money, and become a backer?'

'Something like that. We can sort out the details later.' He tried to sound detached and business-like. The last thing he wanted was to sound patronising, by suggesting she took the money without obligation.

She scrunched up her face, and shook her head. 'Nope. Out of the question.'

He took in the jut of her chin, the flash of her eyes, and gave a hollow, disbelieving laugh. 'It's a no-brainer, why would you refuse?'

'You muscle in and take control? Thanks, but I'm not interested.'

Xander wasn't sure if the prickles needling at the back of his neck were because she'd refused his offer, or because the evening was veering so far away from how he'd imagined it.

'It's up to you. When your chin is at that angle, I know there's no point discussing anything.' He watched her jaw shoot up another ten degrees, as his words hit home. It was true, the tilt of her chin

306

showed a direct correlation with her mood. His lips twitched with satisfaction. He'd nailed step one of understanding Izzy, and on his newly calibrated flip-ometer, she was entering the red zone. Time to back pedal, and salvage something before the whole damned show went belly up.

'Fine. Forget it, and let's order.' He turned on her with a slow burn smile. 'How about lobster with ginger to start, or would you prefer artichoke and truffle tart?'

*   *   *   *

Xander, swirling his brandy around his glass, some three hours and six courses later, couldn't help thinking that he was the one baring his soul here, whilst Izzy had told him approximately zilch, or at least, nothing she hadn't said before. For someone who never opened up, he found sharing stuff with her very helpful. It was almost as though the more he let her get to know him, the more he was coming to understand himself. Maybe it was possible to open up to her, because she was so uncalculating he knew he could trust her. Although Izzy hadn't spent the evening spilling secrets, that was possibly because she didn't actually have them. She was so damned transparent, she didn't seem to hide anything at all, but he liked the way she was so straightforward. And even if she bowled her home truths with a speed and accuracy that meant they invariably knocked him for six, in the end he found her unguarded honesty completely refreshing.

'So how do you reckon people see you, and do you think they're right?' One last chance to draw her out here, and he was going to take it.

That made her smile. 'Even though I'd love to be seen as powerful, driven and successful, I probably come across as a bit ditsy. Creative but fiery.'

The way she took his affirming nod the wrong way, and shot

straight onto the defensive, only went to prove the point.

'Are you implying I overreact?' She was suddenly all shouty and frowny.

He couldn't help but laugh. 'There you go.'

Then her expression softened, as she shuffled in her seat, and took time to rearrange her skirt. 'Flaring up is something I'm working on. Mostly I try to see people for who they are too.' She laughed too. 'How about you?'

He'd take it that her foot, lightly grazing his shin, and sending electric shocks straight to his groin, was accidental.

There she went again, turning it straight back onto him. Maybe that was why she always got so much out of him.

Swishing his brandy, he pondered. 'It always annoys me that my dad saw success as a bottom line thing, whereas my mum was pleased with anything we did. She just wanted us to be happy.' He grimaced at how he'd totally failed at the happy part. 'My dad dismisses anything I achieve in film, because that isn't an area he values.' Xander was veering onto dangerous territory now talking about money defining success. If Izzy had a whiff of how wealthy his family was, like her father had been, he was pretty certain she would leg it before the coffee arrived.

Across the table from him Izzy was revving up. Xander braced himself for the familiar metaphorical smoke, that he knew was about to come out of her nostrils.

'Just don't get me started on my dad.' Her voice had lowered to a growl. 'He was fine until he hit the big money.'

'New money can be hard to get used to...' Alarm bells clanged in Xander's head as that slipped out, but she hadn't picked it up.

Under the straight line of her brow, her eyes flashed. 'My dad thought running a mistress as well as his family was fine, and when my mother wouldn't play ball he went apeshit. And to punish her, he emptied the bank accounts, and whipped the whole lot off to The Cayman Islands, where she couldn't touch it. I mean what kind of person does that to their family?'

Xander took a deep breath. Three hours, and she'd finally cracked. 'I'm guessing that's why you're so obsessed with control then?'

'What, me?'

The half tilt of her head, and the octave her voice jumped, told him she really hadn't made the connection here.

Xander rested his chin on his hand, and took in the smudgy rose of her lips. Every day since the kiss at the pizzeria, it became harder to stop himself from crashing his mouth over hers. But given he'd made a promise to stick by her conditions, so long as she kept her distance, he had to keep his.

60

Saturday Morning, 19th July

IZZY

On the terrace, Les Cerisiers, France

Skipping breakfast

'Luce?' Izzy dived into her dungaree pocket as her phone rang.

'I was trying to get you all last night.' Her friend sounded peeved.

'Sorry, I was out for dinner with Xander, I left my phone at the house.'

Luce softened. 'Nice. How did that go?'

'Fine, it wasn't a big deal.' Missing out the Michelin stars, and the whole perfection of the place seemed a good idea. Izzy wouldn't want Luce to get the wrong impression. 'We ate then came home, end of.'

'So, nothing romantic happened, you didn't even get a good-night kiss?' Luce's snort registered her utter disapproval.

'Nope. Nothing like that at all. Xander offered to bankroll me, but I had to turn him down.' Izzy stared into her half empty cup, and prayed that the flatness in her voice didn't give away her own flood of disappointment. It was too irrational to admit to herself, let alone discuss with anyone else. She sent silent apologies to Luce and Dida, for stuffing up their chances too, because she had an awful feeling that she was letting her personal feelings get in the way of business. But she couldn't get any more entangled with Xander. If it came down to it, she was sure Luce and Dida could have another whip round the crew for cash and come up with some other money-making schemes.

Last night she'd come over all furious with Xander for being arrogant, and trying to take over her life, when really she suspected she'd just been smarting because he hadn't come through with the speech she'd deluded herself into thinking he was going to make. Just when she'd thought he was going to suggest they maybe reassess their ground rules, he'd veered off and offered to take a controlling interest in the business. And then later, he'd had the cheek to imply her control issues were all about not trusting her dad. Huge eye rolls to that one, especially when it came from someone as determined to stay in control as Xander. Just when she'd totally revised what she thought about him, he'd reverted to type.

'Do you need us to send you more cash?' Luce was straight onto it.

Izzy explained. 'The bigger, statement pieces we were hoping for are coming in expensive, but I'll let you know.'

'Well I'm only ringing because there's something urgent I need to check.' Luce's voice was strangely breathy.

Something was definitely up here, given they'd agreed not to rack up the mobile roaming charges gossiping, and had been texting and emailing instead.

Izzy barely dared to ask. 'Urgent bad?' Dida getting a "no" from the bank was the first idea that came crashing into Izzy's head. Then although she'd barely thought of them for days, Izzy's mind fast forwarded to the twins. Crashing their cars, flooding the basement...

'Urgent good.'

Luce's voice so high now, it was almost strangled. 'So you remember Mr Browntree? Well yesterday I took him up to see that art deco table in the outbuilding at your place. The one Ollie and I pulled out of that house just before he went away.'

Nothing too exciting about a table that Izzy could see. 'The one Ollie was going to repair when he came back?' Izzy still had bruises on her hips from squeezing past that thing. 'Mr Browntree can definitely take that if he wants it.'

Luce broke in. 'He does, but whilst he was there he saw the pile of pictures that came from that same clearance.'

Izzy put her hand to her head. Home might feel light years away, but she knew those pictures. There was a huge pile of them, stacked on the roof ties. 'The horrible brown dowdy Victorian ones with animals on, that we thought wouldn't sell?'

'Mr Browntree thinks they might be worth something, possibly quite a lot. So much in fact that he made us take them into the house for last night, just to be on the safe side. Is it okay if he takes them for an expert valuation?'

'Yes, of course.' Izzy tried to get her head around being excited, and at the same time not getting her hopes up. 'This is just like the Antiques Road Show.' And it might even be enough to save the cinema, but it could just as easily come to nothing.

'A lot of the time the stuff on there doesn't turn out to be worth anything.' Luce gave a sigh. 'He said there are a lot of Victorian fakes about, so not to get our hopes up. I'll let you know the minute we hear anything.'

Izzy tried not to smile too much. 'Fingers crossed for The Vintage Cinema Club then.'

'Better go. Be good.' Luce replied.

'I will.' Izzy gave a grin.

Luce was right back at her. 'I really don't mean that.' And then she rang off.

And Izzy didn't think she meant it either.

61

IZZY & XANDER

On the terrace, Les Cerisiers, France

Skipping at breakfast

It was eleven o' clock when Izzy finally made coffee, and she still had no idea where Xander had disappeared to. She hesitated, as she heard an engine behind the barn, and the clatter of a slamming door.

Izzy watched as Xander emerged from the house, and crossed the terrace towards her. At least he'd be in jeans this morning. There'd been something so exquisitely enticing about him when he'd worn a tux that had whisked away every shred of her resistance, and left her folding into a helpless mess. Yet another reason why she hadn't been able to sleep afterwards, and had tossed and turned, beating herself up over everything that hadn't happened as much as the things that had. Despite having lost the suit, in his faded jeans and flip flops, sex-appeal still sizzled from every pore of that body of his, and his smile was electric.

She tried to steady her voice. 'Someone looks happy this morning.' With any luck he wouldn't notice she was personally looking only slightly more healthy than a corpse.

'Yep, I am happy, because I've solved the problem of the extra furniture there's no money for, and all at a bargain price you can afford.'

Izzy's eyes widened. There had to be a catch here. But Xander didn't pause for breath.

'I've sorted a house clearance for you, down in the village. Nicolas, the local Notaire, put me onto it earlier.' So that explained why Xander was flying.

'Wow, that's amazing.' Izzy stemmed her immediate impulse to jump up and down, high fiving the air, and made do with a full on grin instead. A house clearance in France was beyond her wildest dreams.

'It's an old man who has died, the house is crammed full, and the family want rid of the furniture. We've got a key for the house, for today and tomorrow, and we can take whatever we want. And I've drafted in some local muscle from the farm next door to do the lifting. There's some class one junk in there for you.'

'Thanks so much, that's brilliant. Thank you so much.' Izzy didn't quite know how to react to Xander in whirlwind form, standing in front of her now, with his hands in his pockets, and a grin that pretty much stretched from the walnut tree to the barn. She fought her instant reaction to throw her arms around his neck. Talk about getting things moving. As for snogging the socks off him...

'You're welcome. Anytime.' He gave a shrug, as if it were all in a day's work for Superman.

And with one completely unexpected move, Xander had turned the tables on her again. Not only had he taken on board her distress at his offer, he'd gone all out to find a way to make things work for her, on terms that she was comfortable with. Every time she thought the worst of Xander, he proved her wrong, and he came through for her. She was here, being paid a bomb to style his sister's villa, and at the same time put together a furniture load that could well get The Vintage Cinema Club off the hook. Now he'd just ensured that she landed a load of terrific pieces that she could afford with the small amount of cash she had left from the cinema fund. Not to mention how much work he brought in for them at The Pink House. She owed him so much. Izzy couldn't help but think he was obviously an awesome guy who loved helping people.

'I'm so grateful for this.' Now she stopped to think, he went that extra mile with everything in his life. His building projects were top flight, and no doubt he applied the same workaholic dynamism and talent to his film career too. And suddenly the penny dropped. Was this his reaction to the threat he had hanging over him.

'That's nice of you to say, but honestly don't mention it.'

'The way you make the most of every opportunity, and really go for it, is spectacular. It's a total lesson for me in getting the most out of life. I'm really going to do that in future. In fact that's going to be my new mantra.' She took a few moments to move the words around in her head to form a snappy sound bite. 'Grab the moment, and go for it. From now on, that's going to be what I do too. Thank you, Xander.'

'As I said before, you're welcome. Anytime.' And he inclined his head, and slid her a lazy, come-to-bed smile, that blew all thoughts of house clearances out of her head.

62

Sunday Lunchtime, 20th July

IZZY & XANDER

In Brantome, after the house clearance

Tied up with pink ribbon

Xander had not been exaggerating about the amount or the quality of what was on offer in the house clearance. When she had walked into the half light of the shuttered house, Izzy hadn't been able to believe her eyes, or her luck. The place was stuffed full, yet apparently abandoned by the distant family members, who had neither the time, nor the interest to clear out what was there. Along with stacks of everyday household paraphernalia which always sold well, there were also armoires, and chiffonnières, and desks, not to mention a stack of lovely beds, and a whole variety of garden furniture and ornaments. As her jaw dropped, and her excitement rose further, with each subsequent room she went in to, she was thanking her lucky stars she had Xander going all out on her behalf.

Xander had apparently been able to pull off the deal, because he'd played tennis together with Nicolas the Notaire, every summer since they'd been ten. Advantage Xander.

'I taught him every English swear word he knows.' Had been Xander's explanation. 'What's more I always used to let him win, because it was hellish hot on those courts in August, but I knew that compromise would come in handy one day.'

They had agreed to store everything in Christina's outbuilding, until it was picked up by the removal company, and delivered to the cinema in manageable loads, later. With the help of some burly local farmers, who came with two tractors and trailers and their own bottle of home distilled spirits, they'd worked solidly, transferring the furniture from the village house to the barn, and by mid-morning the next day they had loaded their last van-full.

Xander waited until Izzy slammed the van door, and then set off, to drive slowly through the village. 'There should be enough beds here to keep Derbyshire going for a few months. We'll call by the Notaire's in town on the way back, to drop the key off, and we can collect some bread for lunch.'

'I'll go to the bakery whilst you take the key back, if you like. It's usually heaving in there at this time.' Izzy brushed the dust streaks off her legs. 'I'll get you some strawberry tarts, as a thank you.'

'I don't need any more thank yous.' He sent her a reassuring smile, but the way he inadvertently licked his lips showed he was a hundred percent in favour of the idea. 'Watch out, you sound like a long-stay prisoner.' He flashed a grin at her, then let his gaze drop to her knees. 'Even your freckles are joining up into a tan.'

She let that go without protest, idly watching his lean forearm, as he pushed the gear lever into place, wishing she didn't want to run her finger along it. She leant back into her seat, and let the warm breeze from the window blow over her. It was true. She had settled in. After ten short days, the country lanes, the local towns, and the routines felt comfortingly familiar. And so, unnervingly, did Xander, when he wasn't either annoying the shit out of her, or making her stomach do somersaults. Hard to think that in a couple of days it would all be over.

When she arrived at the bakery, the queue stretched out of the shop and along the cobbled street. She took her place at the end of it, breathing in the smell of freshly baked bread, hardly noticing the two women, who arrived behind her. English, and ex pat local, she gathered, from their animated chatter, which she couldn't help overhearing. She turned and tried a smile, to indicate that she could understand what they were saying, but they were oblivious.

She shrugged and couldn't help but listen to the buzz of their chatter. Pool liners, barbecue engagements, champagne offers, all helped to make the time pass, as the queue inched forward. Then Izzy froze. One minute she was hearing about arguments over who was doing what at a flower festival in St Jean, and the next she heard the name Blackman.

Blackman? Her spine went rigid.

'That poor boy's still on his own, all these years later. He gave her everything too.'

'It's not as if they can't afford it. The vineyards at the Chateau are what they play at.'

Which Chateau? They had to be talking about someone else.

'Apparently he's desperate to take her back, always has been.'

An ice-shiver jived through Izzy's body. She'd have run, but her feet were superglued to the pavers. She tried but failed to block out the words.

'Astrid's a high flyer, but now they're working together again, it'll only be a matter of time.'

Astrid. It had to be Xander they were talking about. But was he desperate to take her back?

Her ears rang, the street was spinning around her as the images from the last ten days fell like a series of dominos in her head. As each memory thudded down like a tombstone, she reassessed her take on events. It was obvious when she thought about it. This explained why he'd seemed so happy since they had arrived in

France, because he'd known the woman he'd been waiting for all this time, was finally free, and that he could have her back again. That kiss in the pizzeria was probably to fast-forward proceedings. Nothing like a snog with another woman to make the jealousy kick in, and bring the ex-wife off the fence. And he never hid how highly he thought of Astrid. As for taking Izzy out for dinner, again that would have been so they'd be seen in public, to encourage Astrid to rush in and re-stake her claim. As soon as she'd seen Astrid, Izzy knew she shouldn't ever have registered on Xander's radar. Izzy had no one to blame here, except herself. Small and ashamed didn't begin to cover it.

Words from behind floated over her shoulder. The chatter behind had moved on to firemen's dances but Izzy was lost in her own thoughts.

Then she was into the shop, and back out on the street again, with a crusty French loaf, and a perfect box of strawberry tarts, tied up with pink ribbon.

63

IZZY & XANDER

Out haymaking in France

Long grass

'So are you quiet because you wanted to sort out the barn, and I took us haymaking instead?'

However fast Izzy was hurrying home across the prickly grass of the hay meadow, Xander was managing to keep up with her, firing questions over her shoulder.

'Who's quiet?' She was almost gasping now, because the rushing was making her breathless. 'It was great throwing bales around, and riding back on top of the loaded trailer was fun. I loved having plums in eau de vie in the farmhouse afterwards, and I don't mind that we're all sweaty and covered in hay seeds...' All she wanted was to get back to Christina's place, and she hoped that gabbled speech would be enough from her until they got there.

In fact haymaking had been an ideal diversion, when all she had bouncing around her head was what the women had said at the bakery.

'You disappeared into the barn as soon as we got back from town, and barely ate any lunch either. Are you still cross I offered you money on Friday?' He was very persistent.

She rolled her eyes, exasperated, trying to find a reply that would bring this to a close. 'It doesn't always have to be about money.'

A debrief from Luce would be so useful here. What the hell was she supposed to do, when she found out the guy she wasn't supposed to care about anyway, but still fancied the pants off, was very likely still in love with someone else? She simply had to block out the attraction she felt for him, and try to get through the next few days with her dignity intact. He had made it clear from the start she was a one night stand he'd fallen into against his better judgement, and if she'd read anything more into it than that, it was her own fault for being so stupid.

'Believe me, if anyone knows that, I do.' Xander's voice was grave. 'When you watch someone die of a debilitating illness, you learn there are times when money is no use at all. It changes how you look at life. I'll never argue about money again.'

Shit. 'I'm sorry. I should have known better.'

She slowed to a walk, and he fell into step next to her, and glanced at his watch. 'You know, if we get a move on sorting the barn, we can go out for ice-cream afterwards.'

And just like that, he'd moved on to somewhere else she didn't want to go. For her own self-preservation, she was done with hanging out in cafés with Xander. And she wasn't going to pussy-foot about with vague excuses, and get into more trouble. This time she was going to man up and come clean.

'You know, I think I'd rather give that one a miss – I'd rather not upset what's going on with you and Astrid.' She tried to sound matter of fact, but her voice wavered more than she'd planned. That was a diplomatic reply. It brought the Astrid thing out in the open, without bigging it up too much.

'What?' Xander stopped, and for a minute all she could hear was the sound of the crickets in the grass, and the buzz of bees, as they dipped in and out of the wild roses in the hedge.

'I know you've been trying to get her back, and I really appreciate everything you've done for me personally, but if it's alright with you, I'd like to stop being paraded in public to help your cause.' She gave a dismissive sniff, to show she didn't give a damn. 'I heard all about it in town, the women behind me in the bakery queue were very enlightening.'

Xander spat out the words with a curse. 'You surely can't think...? Me and Astrid?' The beads of sweat were standing out on his forehead, in between the hay seeds sticking to his skin, as he screwed up his eyes against the beating sun. 'Is that why you're quiet?'

Izzy fixed her gaze on the pulse in his dirt streaked neck. 'Maybe.'

'Jeeeeesus, some things I don't believe.' He ran a hand through his hair and shook his head. 'Come here...'

One broad hand landed on each of her shoulders, and he spun her around to face him. 'Let me show you who I want.' His voice was gruff as his stubble rubbed against her cheek, and somehow she caught a glimpse of his eyelashes, closing against his tanned cheekbones.

As she opened her mouth to take a breath, his lips brushed across hers, sending a convulsion of shivers through her body, then with a low growl in his throat, his tongue pushed through and she tasted the whole glorious velvet of him. Dark, sensuous plum, mixed with salty sweat from the hayfield.

'A skirt for haymaking is nice...' The burr of his voice blurred back into the kiss again.

Then his hand was feathering under the soft gathers of her dress, and she was pushing herself towards him as his hand slid up between her thighs, slipping his fingers into the warmth between her legs. She gave a sharp cry as his fingers found her clit, and leaned into him, groaning as her hip hit the bulge of his dick, straining against his jeans.

She gave a moan as he tugged away, but it was only to peel off his shirt. Then a moment later her back thudded against the ground, and he landed beside her in the long grass of the field edge.

'Okay?' He bundled his shirt under her head, and smiled down at her.

A twig pricking the back of her knees, grass sticking in her hair, and Xander's body, hot and heavy, half on her, half off her.

'Are we okay here, will anyone come?'

He gave a low laugh. 'With any luck, only us.'

Then as she laughed back at him, he crashed his mouth onto hers again, and tumbled her into another amazing kiss. By the time she remembered to breathe again, his fingers were pushing up into her, and she was hot and wet and dying, as, without taking his mouth off hers, he jerked and unzipped his jeans, then pulled off her panties with one swift tug. Her snatched breath of surprise, descended into a low, satisfying moan of recognition as he moved against her, and she bent her knees, aching to have him inside her. One fleeting thought of a condom, pushed away. Thank Luce she was on the pill. One thrust later he was there.

This was fast, furious, desperate lust. She tugged on his hair, writhing against him now, and he was taking her with him every inch of the way. Savage, deep. Closing her eyes tightly, the deep blue of the sky above blurred and disappeared, and all she knew was the greatest need she had ever had, and she heard her own cries far away, as the roar of a distant tidal wave came thundering to sweep her away. And then all hell broke loose, and it was all too late, and her whole body exploded.

*   *   *   *

'God, I'm sorry about the condom. Didn't even have one.' Xander smacked his hand to his forehead, as he zipped up, then dragged her body tight against his. 'Weeks of pent up lust. I've wanted this on an hourly basis, ever since the last time.' He tried to push away the thought that now they'd done it, all he wanted was to do it again.

Her whisper tickled his skin, where her face was tucked in the crook of his neck. 'It's okay, I didn't want to stop either. I'm on the pill, so it's all good.'

Xander kissed her forehead. 'I'm guessing you can tell I didn't plan this...but I'd really like to carry on...maybe somewhere less prickly.' He peeled away the grass seeds from her cheek one by one. 'But I don't want to force you into anything. Or make you decide too quickly. There's definitely no pressure...but having said that, there's a very private corner beyond the pool, which would be way more comfortable than here.' Maybe it was unfair to ask her, while she was still basking in the afterglow.

Despite the heat Izzy snuggled into him. 'I'll have a think.'

Her breathing, regular against his chest, went on for five minutes. Five minutes had to be enough time. He decided to press her. 'And?'

'You know I don't do relationships, or one night stands, or casual sex...' She tapped his chest ominously.

'I know all of that.' He shifted his shoulder, stiffening now, under the weight of her head, and sent a silent prayer to the god, of whatever that list of hers hadn't covered. 'I was thinking more of what we were talking about yesterday? All that grab the moment, and go for it stuff.' He watched her bite her lip. 'I just think we should.'

'I'm guessing grab the moment, and go for it kind of overwrites all the other rules?' Her lips twitched into a smile. 'I'll think of it as a kind of "one off" prize for all the hard work we've put in.'

If she hadn't been lying on his arm he'd have punched the air.

'That's good by me.' He'd go with whatever she said, and now might be a good time to slip in where he stood in all this. 'I've got to go to America for a while soon, that's why I can't promise anything much in the way of a relationship, like I said before.'

Xander knew he might be twisting the truth here. For a start this was nothing like he'd meant before. The words were maybe the same, but the order was different, which changed their meaning entirely. Before when he'd been running scared, he'd said, no commitment, full stop, and meant it. Whereas "nothing much in the way of a relationship", in his book, was a hell of a lot more than no relationship at all. Back then he'd been a messed up guy, who'd just spend eight years in hell, and had no reason on earth to expect that hell to end. But somewhere along the line he'd changed. Going head to head with Izzy, day to day, had knocked the sense into him, and knocked the sadness out. When he stopped to think, he felt like a different guy entirely now.

And then there was the whole America thing. Did he really *have* to go? Well, maybe he did for a bit, especially the way his project with Astrid was moving forwards. But it might also be just a very convenient get-out clause, because he couldn't face everything ending up like it had done last time, with Astrid. America – that great big, all encompassing, elastic, safety-net.

America was one big word. It was easy to say. He tried not to think of the bit about Izzy not being there, and how it would feel, to wake up to every empty day, knowing that he wasn't going to see her.

Xander rolled over and buried his face in the nape of her neck. He tried to soak it all in. Toffee waves spilling across the dry grass, the freckled softness of her cheeks, the indefinable sweetness of her smell. As for the "wired and dizzy" he felt whenever Izzy was around, he'd been taking that out of his pocket and examining it almost as often as he had the earrings he'd bought her. And he had the strangest feeling there was more to it than lust. Somehow, finding Izzy was like coming home, for the first time since longer than he could remember.

'We've got two days and three more nights before you fly back.' He gave a low laugh as her leg wriggled against him, and his erection sprung to life again. 'I suggest we make the most of them. Grab the moment, let's go for it.'

64

Monday Morning, 20th July

IZZY & XANDER

Les Cerisiers, France

In Xander's bed

'Xander?'

Izzy was lying on her back, head resting on Xander's chest, staring up at the beamed ceiling, as the dawn light seeped through the gauze drapes.

'Mmmm...' He squirmed, and swallowed.

Despite his regular breathing, she could tell he was still awake, his tanned limbs splayed, muscular and beautiful, across the sheet, after yet another bout of delicious sex. Only her second morning of waking up in his bed, and this time he hadn't done a runner, and given his contented grunts, he wasn't having any regrets. Turning over and curling in, her face nestling close against his neck, she dragged in a breath. That was a scent that she knew she would never get tired of, however many mornings she woke up breathing him in. Two short days, then they'd have to move on, but for now, she was trying to concentrate on the moment she was in, and how fabulous it was to be here beside Xander. It seemed totally unreal, and yet at the same time it felt so right, that it was hard to think it could be any other way. She was screwing her courage up in the half light to ask him the question she'd been trying to ask for days. Not that she knew what answer she was expecting, but she was hoping it might help her sort out the issue she was finding impossible to get her head around. If she didn't do it now, she might never get the chance.

'Do you ever worry about getting ill?' Her voice came out small and scratchy, three inches below his ear.

He shifted under her, and screwed his head round to look down at her. Definitely awake then. He took time to consider. 'Sometimes I worry more than others. It depends.' The sigh he let out was pensive. Resigned.

As much as she blocked the illness, and rammed it to the back of her mind, it just kept bouncing right back out, and bobbing around right in front of her eyes.

'I hoped you might have some pointers for me.' She left it deliberately vague. How to blank it would be a start.

He reached up, tousled his fingers through his hair, and sighed again. 'At first I used to think about it a lot, but once my mum died, it wasn't there to see every day. It kicks in quite young in some cases, and it's easy to get into a mind-set where you're looking for signs in yourself all the time. Every time you trip over, or drop something, or can't remember a word, you think you're starting, but you have to be strong, and get that under control, or it drives you insane. Basically, it's a total head fuck.' He dragged down the corners of his mouth.

'I can imagine.' Except she couldn't at all. She had the idea she was going to hear a lot of sighs from both of them. It was hard not to sigh about it. It was hard not to cry if you thought of it actually happening to Xander, rather than in the abstract. Since the day they had ice cream sundaes, she'd often woken up with her pillow wet with tears. And yet if it didn't ever happen at all, think of the energy wasted in worrying. Scrunching up the end of the sheet in her hand, she tried to put herself, in his place, but she didn't even get half way there.

He went on, his voice matter of fact, yet determined. 'There's two ways to deal with this. You can either crap yourself, and let it beat you, or you can come out and fight it, in the best way you can. Humans are programmed to be strong, we survive as a species because we're tough. Think of you, and your Vintage Cinema Club.'

'What?' Izzy failed to see where that came in.

Xander's voice was patient. 'When The Vintage Cinema Club came under threat, you didn't wimp out and give up, you came out fighting on all fronts, with every bit of strength you had. What you've got is brilliant, and you're determined it won't be taken away.'

'Yes, that's so right.' The adrenalin rush those few words kick started translated into an immediate urge to leap off the bed.

He grinned at that. 'You see it's not all gloom and doom. The other positive thing I've done was to sign up for the main research project, where people who are at risk of the disease get tracked. Once a year I go for an afternoon of tests, and all the data is stored, so they'll have detailed records of how the disease develops from very early on, if I do have it. It's a worldwide project, so although the disease is rare, they can collect a lot of information, and compare it. And because of having all their data, the patients on that project will be first in line, if they eventually find drugs to treat it. On that one afternoon, when I go and do all the tests, I think about it. Otherwise, I try my hardest to forget.'

The vibrations of his voice reverberated through her fingers as they sat lightly on his chest. She couldn't see his mouth, but she knew it was one straight, teeth clenched line. Izzy had no idea how Xander could be so brave, but she seized on the mention of treatment.

'Are they hopeful they'll find a cure?' She forced herself to sound casual, and laid back, rather than desperate and frantic. She had to tell herself it was fine now. Xander was fine. It was a matter of getting her head around the unknowns of the future. It wasn't even as if she knew she was going to be with him, but she knew she wanted this wonderful guy to grow old, and live the amazing life that was due to him.

Xander sniffed, and shifted again, pulling a rope of twisted sheet across his thigh. When Xander was so fit and bursting with energy, Izzy found it hard to envisage him being anything other than strong and healthy.

'Different labs are working on it all the time. It's very complex, but in theory they're only one molecule away from a treatment. Optimistically, it might happen tomorrow, but there again, it may take decades. You've got to hit this thing taking an upbeat view, and imagining the best case scenario, which is not having it at all. There's no point letting it kill off your life with worry, before it even strikes.'

'Right.' All so far out of her experience, and yet he spoke about it as if he was chatting about something completely normal. She tried to get as upbeat as him, and got about a tenth of the way there.

'In the meantime, all we can do…' he nuzzled the top of her head, and gave her a wink. 'Is to grab every moment.' He twisted her around, and his mouth, when it traced across hers, was warm, and soft. 'And I've got a very good idea, about how I'm going to do that.'

Despite the knot of worry gnawing at her inside, Izzy's lips twisted into a smile. The next second she was hurling herself into another of Xander's hot chocolate kisses, and suddenly that was all that mattered.

65

XANDER & IZZY

On the love swing, Les Cerisiers, France

Some little flowery bits

Although it was twelve long days since Izzy had arrived, in some ways her trip had only started for real the afternoon in the hayfield. In which case this was only day three, and having their last day so soon after their first had definitely come too fast. Somehow they'd both been reluctant to acknowledge that "the end" was actually happening. Making "last day" plans had been beyond both of them, even if Izzy had got all the work with the furniture for the cinema finished yesterday. It wasn't that Xander regretted wasting the days before, because he didn't. A lot had changed in the nine days between her arrival and them getting together. The woman who'd finally got into bed with him was very different to the person who'd got off the plane. Whether it was Izzy who'd changed, or him, he wasn't sure, but he was different too.

'Still in your jimjams?' He couldn't resist the tease about the skimpy shorts and hardly there cami he loved so much, as he came out into the midday sun. Almost lunchtime, and sex had figured high on the day's activity list so far, with a hurried breakfast, and now, a quick link up with the outside world.

She pushed back the swing seat, and then gave him the pout he'd been hoping for, along with a sniff. 'I'm catching up on emails, and finishing some little flowery bits to hang on the door latches.'

She waggled a stuffed heart at him, and readjusted the laptop on her knee. Even though she was sitting in the shade, under the swing seat canopy, the freckles he loved so much were coming out more every day.

His chest constricted at the mention of emails. He'd just had one through from Astrid he'd rather not have opened. Dinosaur vampires were apparently going down well with the Paris backer. So well, that the major big gun meeting he was heading for tomorrow had been brought forward, and Astrid was shouting, no, pleading for him to get himself up there for this evening. They both knew how massive this was. Pleading didn't come easy to Astrid, the words simply weren't in her vocabulary, but she was backing him into an impossible corner here.

'So, what's new...?' He snuck in next to Izzy, and closed his teeth on the skin below her ear, nuzzling her neck.

Izzy clutched at her laptop, as she recovered herself. 'It's mainly Dida, saying the experts are all over the pictures from Ollie's shed, but once they start using doubtful words like provenance, you know the game's up. So don't hold your breath over that one, we won't be millionaires this week.'

Sad, but only what he'd anticipated. And damn that his stomach dropped on her behalf. He so wanted this to come right for her and the rest of the cinema club.

She chewed at her lip, and scratched the haystack of hair and ribbons on the top of her head. 'And the bank have come back too.' Izzy wrinkled her nose. 'Dida copied in what they wrote, but it's hard to decide exactly what they mean.'

He went in carefully. 'Definitely not wanting to butt in, and really not trying to take over, but I could take a look...' He probably had the experience to decipher, but it was up to her.

'Would you?' The way her face lit up had his heart melting to hot butter. 'Here...' She leaned back, and tilted her laptop towards him.

He dodged his head, to get the light in the right place, and skimmed the sentences.

'There's a lot of hot air here, but basically the first guy is saying no to the loan, but he's passing the file on to someone else, which means you're still in with a chance. So all good.' He'd gloss over his own doubts, if only so she could stay happy for today. As he posted her what he hoped was a suitably optimistic smile, his eyes flicked back to the screen, and as he automatically took in the next line of the email, an iron hand gripped his gut.

Are you sleeping with the enemy yet? So important to stay close. We owe you big time for all of this ;) ;)

What the hell?

Now he'd seen it, he couldn't let it go.

'What's the bit at the bottom mean exactly?' His words shot out, hard and accusing and bitter. 'The bit about sleeping with the enemy?'

For a second Izzy's face went blank, then her eyes went wide.

'Let's get this clear, the enemy is me isn't it?' If someone had thrown a champagne bucket of icy water over his head, he couldn't have cooled down faster.

'Yes, you were the enemy, but...' One squeak.

He rounded on her. 'Why the enemy?'

Her face blanched under her tan, and her voice was a squeak. 'Because we thought you were buying the cinema.'

One disgusted snort from him was more than that deserved.

'But look at the emoticon, it's got a winky eye.' Her voice was shrill and almost indignant, but the flash of fear in her eyes didn't reflect the jokey tone she was going for.

Xander was first in line to accuse Izzy of overreacting, and fleetingly, he wondered if he wasn't doing the same. He spoke through gritted teeth. 'You've got one chance to tell me what this is about...'

Izzy squirmed. 'It's complicated.'

If she thought she could skim over this by coming on all vulnerable, she could think again. Vulnerable was what he'd fallen for. To think she'd been with him, listening to him, letting him pour his secrets out to her, not to mention screwing him, and all because she wanted to keep tabs on the developer who might buy their building. Although what had he been saying in bed yesterday, about fighting off threats in whatever way was possible. Desperate to save the bloody cinema. It all tied in.

He turned on her again. 'It's not complicated from where I'm standing. In fact it couldn't be more simple.'

Sleeping with the enemy. Although maybe that explained a lot. Thinking about it, no wonder she'd been holding off. She hadn't meant to sleep with him at all. Hell, she'd kept him at bay for nine days, until she really couldn't avoid it any longer. He'd pushed her that far? If he hadn't been biting down his anger, he might have felt worse about that.

'So?' Even if it was going to twist the knife that was stabbing through his chest now, he had to push her. And knowing Ms Transparent here, she wouldn't be able to lie. It would all come pouring out. 'Did you do it, or didn't you...' He braced himself. 'Keeping close to the enemy?'

She closed her eyes, and her voice flattened to a whisper. 'It was mentioned, yes.'

And now he had her. 'I knew it.' As for where her fight had gone, that had to be a defeated whisper.

She stared at the ground. 'It came up really early on. If it was mentioned in relation to this trip, it was only to force my hand

335

when I was trying not to come.'

Worse and worse. Forcing her hand? That's how reluctant she'd been?

'I don't know why it came up again. I promise it isn't like that Xander, not any more. Luce and Dida are just being silly.' Her bottom lip jutted and her voice was wobbling horribly. 'You have to believe me...'

If she thought tears were going to work...he shook himself to his senses...she was probably right. He needed to get out of here fast, before he fell for any more of those promises. That was the trouble, she sounded so damned sincere. Maybe that had been the trouble all along. He'd been so damned dysfunctional, and so damned needy, and he should have known better than to let her in.

At least it was easy to know what he had to do now. The difficult choice about his priorities for today had been made.

He steadied the swing seat, and pushed himself up to standing. 'This fits right in with my plans. I just got an email saying I'm needed urgently in Paris.'

Backing away towards the house, he tried to ignore that her crumpling face was ripping his heart out of his chest at the same time.

'Don't worry, I'll arrange a taxi to take you to the airport tomorrow. But right now I need to pack.'

If there was the smallest shadow of doubt in his head, that he was doing the right thing here, he needed to stamp on it. She'd backed right down when he'd turned on her. If he'd got any of this wrong, if what they had was of value to her, she'd have been out there fighting for what she wanted to keep. As it was it looked like she was able to let him go.

66

Early hours of Wednesday Morning, 23rd July

XANDER

Hotel Lancaster, Paris, France

'Have a good flight'

'Izzy...'

Her voice was full of sleep. 'Xander?'

Bleary. He'd woken her up.

'Xander? What time is it? Where are you?'

Shit, three in the morning. Bad timing. 'I'm up in Paris, the meeting just ended, I wanted to call.'

He wanted to call so he could hear her say she wanted him, that he'd got her completely wrong. To hear her say come back. He paused, to let that sink in. Gave her the space to reply...but when she didn't he carried on.

'I just wanted to tell you, I'll be flying straight out to the States from here...in the next few days.' So much for dystopian vampire

337

dinosaurs getting wings. He had to go and tie up that deal, which was so huge, and he really should be high fiving the whole of Paris for the way he tipped the balance on that one. But it also fitted in very conveniently with his own escape, because he couldn't handle the possibility that Izzy had used him, and had only been with him because she'd been told to. And if that wasn't the case, she'd have told him, clearly, because that's how she was. Bolshy and ballsy. She'd have fought her corner.

How the hell did he ever get around to convincing himself he was relationship material when there wasn't even a relationship there?

Silence.

'So...have a good flight back.'

More silence.

'Goodbye Izzy.' Was there anything more to add? 'And thanks.' Was that it? 'For everything...and sorry I got you so wrong.' He did mean that. More for him than for her perhaps. He clicked on "end the call".

All wrapped up. So that was that.

67

Wednesday Afternoon, 23rd July

IZZY

At home in Matlock

Happy landings

By two the next day, Izzy was home again, and trudging along Albert Street, past a mud splattered Chou-fleur. Not so many Corsas lined up along the kerb today either. Turning in at the gate, the path was damp, and the pink geranium blooms in the pot by the door were mostly brown and withered. She was already missing the sun. Not to mention everything else.

As for Xander, she'd been half asleep when he'd phoned. At least he had phoned, even if it was the blurry middle of the night, but she'd got the gist. He was going to America. Like, deep down, at the very bottom of her heart, she always suspected he would, however much he'd been making his staying noises. She was kicking herself for that horrible last argument. How had it only been yesterday?

It had spun out of control so fast, she hadn't been able to pull it back. Because in the end, although Xander had got it so wrong, she couldn't deny he was partly right. She was guilty. The words sleeping with the enemy, referring to him, were up on that screen in black and white. It might have been written tongue in cheek yesterday, but there was a time when that concept had been an integral part of their strategy. Even if things had moved on, she couldn't argue with that.

It was so like him to have phoned too. The Xander she'd come to know always did the decent thing. And this time he'd rung, to make sure she understood, to confirm it was over, make sure she knew he was going. She supposed he was saving her from hanging on, snuffing out the vague hope he might reconsider with a meticulous finality. That call was to underline, in bold, that this was his definitive position. i.e. Gone. Out of the picture as of now. And it was horribly, horribly sad that she wouldn't see him again.

So that was that.

She presumed he'd be flying off with Astrid, but that was immaterial now. Izzy couldn't begin to understand why she felt so numb, when she should have been completely prepared for this outcome. After all, he had never pretended he was offering anything more than seize the moment fun. She had fully accepted that, even welcomed it. But when he'd driven away from Les Cerisiers yesterday, she felt as though she'd lost a limb. Somewhere along the line, she'd got all entangled with that lovely man, and then completely failed to refute the allegation, and reassure him, when he assumed she'd been using him. But although she'd always said she didn't want anything more herself, now it came down to it, she was aching to know someone she cared for so very deeply had slipped away.

So now the fireworks were over, and she was as free as she had always wanted to be. Free to do all the things she needed to do, to be who she needed to be. Great. Not.

She'd stalled all the offers of lifts back from the airport, because it was comforting to sit in a seat on her own, as the airport bus hurtled along the A52 into Derby, and then take the slow single carriage train back to Matlock. On her own was good. It was how she wanted to be. If, after two weeks of bumping into Xander at every turn, she was now feeling like she'd chopped off her leg, or even worse, hewn out her soul, that was too bad.

A branch of the blowsy pink climbing rose had fallen down across the doorway, scattering petals across the door mat. She dipped underneath it and let herself into a hall that smelled less fresh than she expected. Stuffy even. A stack of mail in the hall, pushed up against the skirting board. She went down to the kitchen. Piles of pizza boxes. Beer cans. Guitars. Burned saucepans on the hob. Sauce up the wall. She was definitely regretting the home made spag bol suggestion now.

Up in her room, she crept into her bed on the floor, and pulled the cabbage rose quilt tightly over her head. Something about the cabbage roses made her feel sick though. They were going to have to go. Then remembering, she leapt up, and dashed over to where the cut out wooden letters spelling LOVE stood on top of the chest of drawers. She swept them together, slammed them into her knicker drawer, then dived back into bed. She stuck a hand out and fumbled in her bag until her hand closed around the roughness of the small plaster cherub that had come out of the skip, and shuddering, she held him tight against her chest.

A while later she heard the slam of the front door, footsteps on the stairs, voices. Then, minutes afterwards, she was assaulted with enough noise to break the sound barrier, as the twins launched into band practice.

68

Text from Izzy to Dida and Luce:

Back in town, fab loads to follow shortly, missed you all like crazy, off to sleep now, will catch up tomoz, big love xx

*

Text from Luce to Izzy:

Can't wait 2 c u, missed you 2 XXXXXXX

*

Text from Dida to Izzy:

You are going to save the cinema, you are SO AWESOME. Vive Le Vintage Cinema Club xx

*

Text from Luce to Izzy:

**Shall we do breakfast, or I cd come at 11? Hugs til tomorrow
xx**

*

Text from Izzy to Luce:

Let's do 11 :) xx

69

IZZY & LUCE

On Izzy's doorstep

Not cracking open the champagne

The clang of the doorbell jangled Izzy out of a deep, yet uncomfortable, doze. Despite being knackered, she'd slept fitfully, but it had to be late, because she never usually got to see the shadows of the slatted blinds on the floor. They were faint, but at least they showed there was a bit of sun outside, not like yesterday's grey drizzle. Prizing herself out from under the quilt, she crawled to the window, dipped behind the blind, and pushed up the sash.

'Luce...?' How had eleven o'clock happened already?

It was Luce, but she was out in the road, talking to a guy with an Interflora van. As the driver slammed the back door, Luce turned and grinned up at Izzy, clutching at least half a flower shop in her arms.

'Izzy, lovely to see you, get your bum down here and let me in.' Luce staggered towards the gate.

Izzy dragging on a sweatshirt and joggers, catapulted down the stairs. First thought: Ibuprofen. Her head was banging. Second: Who knew she'd love bright pink flowers? She had to rule Xander out on that one, but her heart had got there ahead of her, and had already started to race. Bloody hell. As she flung open the door, the scent of lilies and roses wafted straight up her nose, and there was Luce, warm and smiling, and wonderfully familiar, giving Izzy a big lump in her throat.

'Come here.' Luce dropped the huge arrangement onto the seat of a wide chair, and dragged Izzy into a huge hug. 'Look at you, all sun tanned and pretty.'

Izzy, catching a glimpse in the hall mirror, of her hair sticking out in a hundred different horizontal directions, couldn't go with the pretty. She squinted at her arm critically. 'This tan took a lot of work.' Even if the rest had been a disaster, she could live with skin the colour of pale honey.

'As for the flowers, my sister's bunch wasn't even that huge when she got Topshop Face Of 2004.' Luce sniffed them. 'Your favourite colour too, do you want the card?'

Izzy wasn't sure she did, but nor did she want to take Luce down to witness the wreckage in the slum-dog kitchen either.

'Here.' Luce handed it to her anyway.

Izzy scratched it open, hoping her friend didn't notice she'd stopped breathing. 'Ahhhh...' Izzy skimmed the superlatives. Stupendous...amazing...talented...then, as she saw the name, she exhaled, and her body deflated under her sweatshirt. She dragged her lips into a smile, and made her voice as bright as she could. 'Christina, saying thanks. She loved the pics I sent. They're down there next week.' Izzy gave another tight lipped beam, to emphasise how "over the moon" she was. In what world might she have imagined that Xander would have sent flowers?

'That's lovely of her.' Luce gave Izzy another squeeze. 'You are such a star for going, tell me all about it over coffee, and I'll bring you up to speed on Vintage Cinema Club developments.'

Izzy swallowed hard, and hung onto her mouth to stop it stretching to the odd place it went when she was about to cry. Then, bracing herself for Armageddon, she followed Luce down to the kitchen.

70

LUCE & DIDA

At St Nic's end of term Fun Run

The Healthy Drinks Stall

'We have so screwed up here.' Luce, standing behind the drinks table, was almost wailing. 'Izzy is heartbroken, Xander's across the Atlantic, and all because of our desperation to save things here. I should so not have persuaded her to go to France.' Luce had never seen Izzy in pieces like this before. Awful Alastair had left her spitting tacks, but this time Izzy wasn't angry. Izzy now, anguished and hopeless, had Luce shivering with worry, and beating herself up.

'And I so regret that "enemy" email.' Dida pursed her bright red lips, and shook her head hard. 'This is a right royal Vintage Cinema Club stuff up.'

Luce scoured the sky for signs of rain clouds. 'Izzy wasn't even enthusiastic about the paintings being checked out, but she's probably right there, I'm sure it's a false alarm.'

Dida put her fists on her hips, determinedly. 'We need to make this up to Izzy. I'm not sure how, but I'm damned sure we will.' She staggered, as her wedge heeled trainer toppled down a divot. 'Shit, where did all the customers come from?' A circle of kids around their stall were soaking up the juicy bits of their conversation, as only seven year olds can. Treating them to a withering smile, she waved a hand across the jugs. 'Carrot juice, apple and elderflower, or homemade lemonade, which isn't actually fizzy.'

The kids let out a plaintive collective groan. 'Haven't you got any pop?'

'Sorry, this is it.' Luce mouthed at Dida over their heads. 'So much for the PTA getting politically correct with the drinks.'

Dida laughed. 'I'd rather be here though, than standing on the finish line, as a spotter.' She rolled her eyes. 'Fun and run are words that shouldn't appear in the same sentence.' She looked up from her muttering, and saw that the children were still there. 'If you'd rather have a smoothie, there's a man with a pedal-powered smoothie maker across the field. He's gasping, with a purple face, you can't miss him.'

The kids wandered off, still clasping their money.

'At least Aidie turned up.' Luce gazed at the little crowd across the field gathered around Aidie's machine.

Dida gave a dismissive snort. 'Apparently it's a man thing, he's doing a favour to the Chair of Governors, who's a big gun at the Chamber of Commerce. It must be ten years since I last saw my husband home on Friday afternoon.'

'He's certainly looking slimmer.' Luce wasn't sure where Dida stood on this, but Aidie was like a shadow of his former self.

'The weight has dropped off him.' Dida gave another sniff and dropped her voice. 'He's still obsessed.'

Luce raised a querying eyebrow. 'With his personal trainer?

'That's the one.' Dida shook her head, and gave a shrug. 'It's worrying. He's never restricted himself to one at a time before, and he's lost all interest in the kids and home. I can't help wondering if it's why he's put the cinema up for sale.'

'You mean he's on his way out?' Luce frowned. This was huge.

'Possibly. Men like him move on to have second and even third families.' Dida shrugged. 'So long as I overlooked his infidelity this far, the kids and Alport towers have been enough of a pull to keep him coming home. Basically I always knew I could manage Aidie's lust, but if he ever falls in love, that's another ball game.'

Luce crumpled her face. 'You think Aidie might be...?' In love? Highly unlikely, given all the signs indicated that Aidie didn't have a heart.

'Who knows?' Dida simply shut her eyes and shuddered, as she leaned in to Luce. 'Put it this way, this last week I have been trying to mentally rehearse living somewhere other than Alport Towers.'

Shit, this was serious, given that Dida was welded to that house. 'Did you make any progress?' Luce wondered where the hell Dida might go.

Dida sniffed, and hugged her arms around her. 'The kids and I could possibly manage in one of those penthouses overlooking the park. Thank heavens I didn't give way on Lolly's falabella demands. We couldn't possibly keep one there, even if the balconies are big.'

The penthouses were lovely, and a lifetime away from where Luce could ever imagine getting to, but they were a quantum leap downwards for Dida.

Luce wasn't used to seeing her friend at such a loss. 'So have you heard from the guy from the holiday?'

'No.' Dida tossed her head. 'I didn't expect to.' She ran her fingers through her hair and tugged hard. 'It's not important.'

Luce knew the hair pulling was a dead giveaway. Dida cared a lot more than she was letting on.

'Does he have your number?' Stupid question from Luce, but kind of crucial.

'We swapped mobile numbers when we went to Assisi.' Dida shrugged again.

Luce pursed her lips. 'He won't contact you, if he doesn't know you're thinking about him.'

Dida blew out a long sigh. 'He was just a nice guy, nothing more. Sane and uncomplicated, easy to be with.'

'You could always text him something small and insignificant, as an opener.' Luce shot Dida a grin. 'Like "miss you so much it hurts".'

'Bloody hell, nothing as full on as that!' Dida let out an appalled squawk.

'Joking there, obviously.' Luce knew Dida's sense of humour going AWOL was another sign how much this mattered. 'If he isn't interested, he won't text back.' Luce softened the grin to a smile. 'It seems a shame to throw it away. I mean, how many other people like opera?'

Dida picked up the paper cups that had fallen over, and sent Luce a sideways glance. 'So what about you? I take it Ollie hasn't emailed back yet?' She gave a thoughtful frown. 'We could both text. Or we could both do nothing...'

Luce sighed. If Ollie still had his phone, a text might reach him, when an email wouldn't. She'd had six long weeks with no reply from Ollie, although no one else had heard from him either. He still didn't know about the pictures, which were half his and half Luce's, but she'd face that in the unlikely event they came good and were proven to be originals. But maybe a text couldn't hurt...

'Customer alert – those children are back.' Dida picked up a jug, and waved it at the approaching group. 'Four lemonades?' She turned to Luce, talking through the clenched teeth of her smile. 'You know, every time I look at Aidie, all I see is bloody Elvi, and her bloody minute tits, and personal trainer abs, and the "For Sale" sign over the cinema. Damn it, that settles it, let's text.'

71

Friday Evening, 25th July

LUCE

In her flat

A second thought

Luce, curled up on her bed, late at night, clicked her phone on. She flicked onto messages, and began to tap on the screen.

Wish you were here, Luce x

That summed it up. Small, but perfectly formed. That was all she needed to say. She held her finger over "send", and let it hover there for a second or two.

What the hell was she thinking? However much she was missing Ollie, and however much she'd changed the way she was thinking, she refused to be "Ms Desperate of Matlock".

She moved her finger, and tapped delete.

72

Sunday Evening, 27th July

*

Text from Dida to Hamish:

Had any nice gelato lately? Dida

*

Text from Hamish to Dida:

**Gelato in Morpeth is sadly lacking. Making do with Lidl
Chocolate chip. Hamish**

*

Text from Dida to Hamish:

Eating Ben and Jerry's Baked Alaska as I text. Tosca and the

PIazza del Comune seem very far away.

*

Text from Hamish to Dida:

The oregano isn't the same here either. Ever tried Ben and Jerry's Strawberry Cheesecake?

*

Text from Dida to Luce:

Whoop. I did it, he replied! Now we're talking ice cream and oregano. Thanks for pushing me over the cliff. How about you? XXXXXXXX

*

Text from Luce to Dida:

Yay, brilliant news on H, see, I told you. I chickened out. Hugs on the H thing. Xx

*

Text from Dida to Ollie:

When did you last check your inbox? You have v IMPORTANT email!!!! xx

*

Text from Hamish to Dida:

Can definitely recommend Haagen Dazs salted caramel. Having Tosca withdrawals, so thinking of going to Arias in the Park, in York.

*

Text from Dida to Hamish:

Sounds amazing. How wonderfully civilised. Haagen Daz mint leaves and chocolate is worth a try, if you haven't already.

*

Text from Hamish to Dida:

9/10 for HD mint leaves and choc. Short notice, but you could always come to York a week on Saturday. What would you give HD pralines and cream? If you're free that is.

*

Text from Dida to Hamish:

HD pralines and cream get a straight 10 :) Yes to York, but need to sort child care etc. – will get back to you on that. HD Baileys?

*

Text from Hamish to Dida:

HD Baileys – will defo try that this week. York news: 12/10. Text me your email and I'll send more details.

*

Text from Dida to Luce:

You will not believe this...H asked for a) my email b) opera appointment in York!!!!! :D XXXX

*

Text from Luce to Dida:

Whoop, you got a date. XXXX

*

Text from Dida to Luce:

It's an appointment, not a date. There's a big difference. H is a friend X

73

Monday, 28th July

Subject: Back in the room

Hi Luce and Ruby,

Great to hear from you, pleased you like the cards. I have got lots of panda ones you'll like too. Pleased to hear you like falabellas Ruby. I made a little metal pony the other day. Been hanging round the local forge – can't keep away and the craftsmen here are incredible. I'll give the pony to you when I come home

waving from Koh Samui Ollie x

p.s. sorry it took so long to reply - was off the radar for a while, but I'm back online again now

74

Monday Morning, 28th July

LUCE & DIDA

At the St Nic's holiday club

Only a friend

'So, you got your date then, Mrs Compton?' Luce who always ran two minutes later than Dida in the mornings, regardless of whether they were heading for school or holiday club, did a mad dash across the playground, and caught up with Dida by the kissing gate. Getting Ollie's email had supercharged Luce's legs, and pushed her face into a full time insane grin, which she attempted to minimise.

'It's definitely not a date.' Dida's nose in the air went with an aloofness that exactly matched the pale teal linen trouser suit she was wearing this morning. 'We're simply two opera enthusiasts, going for an afternoon in the park.'

If that was her story, good on her.

'Brilliant.' Luce was still surprised how up front she was being.

'But aren't you worried about Aidie?' Who would no doubt spin off the proverbial fan with all the decorum of an inflight cowpat, when he found out.

Dida's nose flared as she drew in a long breath. 'I've nothing to hide, I'll tell Aidie nearer the time. Thanks to Ms Spicy Sport AA Cup, he's only gracing us with his presence here every other weekend, and then only for a night and usually, a fight. Still not wanting sex at home. He's hardly in a position to complain.' She jumped in her car, and whizzed down the window. 'And thanks for saying you'll have the kids for me. The kids and Alport Towers are way too precious for me to get into adultery, but this is simply civilised company. Life with Aidie is such a cultural desert.'

Luce, realising her beam was too radiant for the comment, toned it down. 'Mrs GI Joe is coming in on Saturday morning to pick up her dress, but she can come to the flat.' Seeing as Jules had been round before, Luce knew it wouldn't be a problem. 'And then my Mum's volunteered to take all the kids for a picnic up at Carsington Water in the afternoon.'

'I owe you for this, Luce. Hamish is only a friend, and it's still twelve days away,' Dida scrunched up her face, 'but bloody hell, my heart is banging every time I think about it – which is a lot.'

Luce nodded enthusiastically. She knew all about thumping hearts. 'You need to check this out.' Luce had to agree, and damn that the elation from one little email from Ollie had her encouraging Dida for all she was worth.

Dida's bright red lips pursed, then she tapped her tooth with one peachy nail. 'So is it my imagination, or are you looking extra happy this morning?' She tilted her head, narrowing her eyes at Luce. 'Have you heard from Ollie?'

Luce might be transparent, but there was only one reason why Dida might be straight onto that. 'Did you text him?'

'I might have done.' Dida's lips spread into a smile. 'Step one of The Vintage Cinema Club, getting us all back on track. The whole disaster with Izzy has made me realise it isn't only the business we need to strive for. We need to look after ourselves too.'

'That's so true.' Luce gave a grateful shrug. 'And thanks for starting with Ollie and me.' Since the email this morning, alongside the elation, a strange calm had spread through her. Only a few words on a screen, and not many lines to read between, but the break between her and Ollie had somehow been mended. Suddenly, after six weeks of silence, the idea of emailing their news to each other across the world wasn't so bad.

'February isn't so long.' Luce's smile wasn't out of control any more. If she said it fast, she could pretend she wasn't feeling like her chest was full of stones, because when she thought about not seeing Ollie until then, February seemed like a lifetime away.

Dida's eyes wrinkled with her smile. 'That'll be one big home-coming. Checking out the sparks and all that.'

Luce's stomach hit the pavement, and at the same time her cheeks began to burn.

But Dida was straight onto her. 'Oh my god, you already did, didn't you?'

'If Izzy knew any of this, she'd throttle me.' Luce was sure of that. She'd throttle herself too, if she were in Izzy's shoes. Messing her brother about, hurting him to the point she'd driven him away. That's exactly why best friends' brothers should stay off limits.

'When was this?' Dida's surprise sent her voice and eyebrows skywards.

Luce was dying here. 'Only the once. Completely by accident.'

From the times had she replayed it in her head, her mental tape should have worn out by now. Ollie coming round to say goodbye to Ruby the night he left, but Ruby was asleep, and Ollie wouldn't let Luce wake her. How Ollie's one goodbye peck on Luce's cheek had ended up in bed, with the most explosive chemistry ever, and the sex had been incredible, as if everything they'd put off for months had ended up in one humungous orgasmic hour of bliss. And then he'd left for the airport. Except it had been more than bliss. Bliss was too gentle for what she'd been trying to blot out of her head ever since. And when he'd sent her an email to talk about it, she hadn't been able to bring herself to reply.

Luce turned back to Dida with a long sigh. 'It's so damned stupid that you only come around to realise what you want when it's too late to have it.'

'It's never too late.' Dida stuck her hand through the car window and gave Luce's arm a squeeze. 'We'll make sure Izzy only gets to know the good bits, and then only if she needs to.' Dida wrinkled her nose, and gave a smile. 'On balance that stint on the healthy drinks stall didn't work out too badly did it?'

75

Wednesday Morning, 6th August

Subject: ALL HANDS ON DECK

THE SECOND DELIVERY FROM FRANCE IS COMING
MONDAY AFTERNOON 2PM.

PLEASE BE THERE TO HELP IF YOU CAN,

Dida x

76

Thursday Afternoon, 7th August

Text from Ollie to Luce:

Fancy a walk in the park?

*

Text from Luce to Ollie:

Which park?

*

Text from Ollie to Luce:

Matlock park?

*

Text from Luce to Ollie:

What, are u booking early for next February?

*

Text from Ollie to Luce:

No, I mean now ;)

*

Text from Luce to Ollie:

OMG is this a joke?

*

Text from Ollie to Luce:

Meet you by the swings in seven...minutes not months :)

*

Text from Ollie to Luce:

Is that a yes?????

*

Text from Luce to Ollie:

Oooops, YES YES YES YES

77

Thursday Afternoon, 7th August

OLLIE & LUCE

By the swings in Matlock park

Wind, puffa jackets and straggly hair

In his head it hadn't been pouring with rain, it had been sunny. For twenty six solid hours, since he left Bangkok, Ollie had been imagining lounging on a park bench, his rucksack thrown on the ground, the sun beating on his face as he waited. Hell, for the best part of five months he'd imagined watching the kids splashing in and out of the fountains as he searched the horizon to see Ruby and Luce running towards him, their dresses streaming out behind them, all set against an orange sunset, not an iron grey sky. And in his head he'd forgotten the noise of teatime traffic too, and the lone duck, strutting under the slide.

As it was, he was under the eaves of the toilet block, squatting on his bag, with the rain sluicing down in a sheet over the edge of a blocked gutter, counting down the minutes, and suddenly they were there, struggling with the latch on the child proof gate. Ruby in wellies, stomping in the puddles, galloping from one to the next shouting, her yellow cagoule shorter than it was when he'd left, with that spotty ladybird umbrella he'd bought her, looking up at Luce as she ran. And Luce. Luce in her puffa jacket and jeans, with the hood up, hands thrust deep in her pockets, shoulders shrugged against the wind squalls, and her hair all wet and straggly, blowing across, sticking to her cheeks. Suddenly he knew it was good it was raining, rain was the best weather he could have hoped for, because tears were streaming down his cheeks.

And then they saw him, and Ruby was shrieking, and running towards him across the tarmac, hurling herself at him as he stood up. 'Olls? Mummy, is it really Olls?'

He winced as Ruby thumped into him, and accidentally elbowed him in the groin as he scooped her up.

'Hey you.' Luce arrived next to them, smiling, putting a hand up to his cheek, and making his shivers turn to shuddering.

His gut contracted like a spring, as she held his jaw between her splayed thumb and finger, then her lips landed on his, and for a split second his mouth burst like popping candy, as her lips brushed over his. Then, she pulled away gently, leaving her taste behind. Just like he'd imagined. Just like he'd remembered, every single day since he left.

'Hey, you're soaked through, and you're so thin – I can feel all your ribs.' She stood back and gave him the once over. 'No wonder you're freezing, in a T shirt. You aren't in the tropics now you know.' She shot him a grin.

'Just a minute.' He dug into his pocket, almost losing his denims. 'I brought you something, Ruby.' When the hell had his jeans got so slack? He'd dragged them on in the toilets at Heathrow, it had to be five months since he'd last worn them. His fingers closed around something small and hard and spikey, and he pulled out the tiny horse that had brought him all the way around the world, and shown him the way back home.

'It's a pony.' Ruby's lips curved into a smile, and she settled herself onto his hip. 'How did you know I liked ponies Olls?'

'Good question, Rubes. I'm guessing I just kind of knew somehow.' He'd made the pony for her the week before he picked up the email about falabellas.

As she squirmed against his grip to be free, he let her slide down to the ground.

'I'm taking him for a gallop.'

As Ruby belted off, Luce's hip bumped against his, as she slipped her arm around his waist. 'Rubes and I were just about to have tea, you look like a good meal would warm you up.' She looped a finger through his belt loop. 'Beans on toast okay for you?'

Beans on toast, like he'd never been away. Except he already knew it wasn't the same as before, it was definitely very different. There was something about the way Luce had held his chin, and something about the way one of her hands was touching his chest, the way her shoulder was wedged under his armpit, and her other arm was wound around him. Maybe she was pleased to see him, but the way her fingers had locked onto his belt like she was never going to let go, made him feel it was more than that. Whatever, now he'd been without her, and found her again, he was happy to take whatever she was offering, big or small, however she wanted to offer it.

'Sounds great.' Beans on toast? If he'd thought of that when he'd been sitting on a tropical beach, he might have come back sooner. Beans on toast with Luce and Ruby? 'I can't think of anything I'd rather have.'

78

Friday Lunchtime, 8th August

IZZY & OLLIE

In Izzy's kitchen

Is there any flapjack?

'Ollie?'

Izzy, stumbling across a rucksack covered in Far Eastern airline stickers in the hall, on her way downstairs, belted down into the kitchen and did a double take. 'What the hell are you doing here? I thought you were away until Christmas at least.'

'Nice to see you too.' Ollie looked up from his bowl of crunchy nut cornflakes, and inclined his head to the pizza boxes and piles of washing up. 'So, what happened here, a zombie apocalypse?'

Izzy shook her head, and tried to get her brain around the shock. As for a male in their family, commenting on a messy kitchen, that had to be a first. 'I haven't caught up after France yet. You know I've been to France?' She watched him nod and wave his spoon. 'So how come you're back so early?' France was a long time ago now, but her house cleaning fetish had been lost in transit. Since she'd been back she hadn't had the energy or the heart to sort out the house. The mess was just a blur on the edge of the confusion in her head.

Ollie grunted into his cereal. 'Turns out I'm less of a globe trotter than I thought. I decided there was more for me here than there.' He gave a wide grin. 'Don't look so worried, you can use Chou-fleur, and you can keep my space so long as the cinema lasts.'

Izzy shuddered to hear him talking about the cinema as if it was already lost, but given her fast come backs were yet another thing that had deserted her, she simply stared at him.

'So what's new here, apart from Vintage at the Cinema being under threat, and battleship grey being your new favourite paint colour, which matches the circles under your eyes by the way?' Ollie got up, and threw his dish into the sink, but left the cereal packet on the table. Brothers knew just how to flatter a girl, didn't they?

'Nothing much.' Izzy didn't have the energy to tell him off.

'Don't worry about the business side of me coming back home again.' Ollie swung around on the bannister, as he started up the stairs two at a time. 'I'm thinking of concentrating more on the metalwork side anyway, maybe we can look for a shared space in Chesterfield? You sound like you've found your niche doing interior styling. By the way, is there any cake to eat?'

'Six thousand miles away, and you haven't missed a thing.' Izzy couldn't quite believe how he'd kept up. 'And sorry, we're fresh out of baking.' Because baking was beyond her too.

*　*　*　*

'Izzy, someone's at the front door.' Ollie's voice bellowed down, from two floors up.

Izzy yelled back. 'Will you get it?' Worth a try at least, given they were both a floor away from the door.

Ollie's reply wafted down. 'I'm supposed to be in Thailand, it won't be for me.' Good point well made.

Izzy got up, securing her slipping dungaree strap, and idled upstairs to the front door. These days hurrying was beyond her. Pushing her hair out of her eyes, she inched the door open. 'Yes?' As her eyes slid into focus, her heart gave a jump strong enough to propel her whole body half way up the street.

'Xander? What are you doing here?'

Leaning on her door frame, all faded denim, cheekbones, and choppy hair, with an anxious smile that still had enough sexy in it to give her tingles all over. Izzy grabbed her stomach with one hand, and the wall with the other. She looked beyond him, past the blur of the roses round the door, and saw his ancient blue convertible, parked outside the gate. For a moment she couldn't decide whether to grab him, and give him the snog of the decade, or keep her distance. In the end she simply stood still, blinking.

'And?' Part of her wanted to see him so much her body was already thrumming – seeing being a euphemism for jumping on him and shagging the life out of him, obviously – and part of her was beating away the hurt of the last two weeks, since he'd driven out of her life, leaving her a taxi ride from the airport. It wasn't even as if he'd dumped her, because they weren't actually going out. But however responsible for the argument she'd felt, him buggering off to America had been pretty damn final. Final enough to leave her in bits she knew she had no right to be in.

'I was wondering about that lunch we never had?' Xander rubbed a thumb across the stubble of his chin and then gazed at her face intently. 'You've got really dark circles under your eyes. Have you lost weight?' If he expected a response to that, he didn't give her time to say it. 'Maybe dinner...or a drink?' He raised one eyebrow. 'Or have you gone all quiet on me again?'

Quiet? That was rich. He was the one who'd decided to drop out of her life, acting like she'd pushed him. And he'd maintained radio silence for two weeks.

Izzy scrunched up her face. 'I'll have to think about it.' Total confusion didn't begin to cover it. Two weeks down the road of getting on with life after Xander, she had no idea what to say.

'Well how about you invite me in for juice and flapjacks whilst you mull it over?'

'There isn't any flapjack.' She took in the softness of his eyelashes, the scar on his cheek, and her stomach went into freefall.

'But you always have flapjack.' How could he sound so miffed? 'You even made it in France.'

'Don't you start.' Everyone had been bemoaning the lack of flapjack since she'd been back. As if that was all they relied on her for. She gave a long sigh, and sidled towards the stairs, knowing she was heading in completely the wrong direction, given she should be going to work.

So, he must have taken the fact she hadn't slammed the door in his face as an invitation, because he was following her towards the stairs now, except he'd already veered off to peer in through the open door to the living room. Obviously still not found his manners then, and just as much at home as he had been that first day he came to see the bed. She gave a mental head shake to the different, carefree, shouty person she'd been that day. She so needed to reconnect with her shout again.

'That chest looks great painted dark blue. I'm thinking of maybe getting a few more pieces.' Xander's words came down after her as she trudged down the stairs. He could only mean for The Pink House. Somehow she wasn't sure she could face another shopping list, given where the last one had got her.

She ignored that, reached the kitchen, slid a glass onto the table, and slopped juice into it from a carton. Thank you Ollie for leaving that out.

There was something so confusing about Xander, and his on/ off intentions.

'I thought you were in America.' She squared up to him across

370

the corner of the table, and gave a mental curse to how edible he looked, now he was down here.

'Obviously not, given that I'm here. I wanted to talk. About how maybe I jumped to the wrong conclusions...and overreacted.' He tried to meet her eyes, but she looked away.

'What about it? It's in the past, I'm in a hurry, and I've got a shift at the cinema. I think I might be way past giving a damn anyway.' That just about summed it up. Sulky wasn't a good way to be, but she was wrung out. If he'd let her explain properly two weeks ago, she'd have been up for it, but at this stage she was bordering on past it.

'I bolted to America, because I was annoyed and hurt when I thought you'd used me. It hit me in a sensitive place. The worst bit was thinking you didn't care about me at all when I...' He broke off. 'I know running was the wrong thing to do, I'm sorry for that. I know I've messed you about.'

'Fair enough. And so...?' Izzy filled her lungs, not that oxygen would help, because this was impossible. Two people, neither of whom knew, or were able to express what they wanted, hedging around each other. She stared at the crumbs on the floorboards.

Xander gave a grimace. 'It was Astrid who finally kicked some sense into my butt.'

Izzy couldn't hide her surprise. 'Astrid?' That was one name she'd thought she'd heard the last of.

He went on, hurrying past what should have been elephant in the room, not the second thing he mentioned. 'If I hadn't been so hung up and blinded with my own issues, I'd have worked it out a lot quicker. And if I hadn't cared so much I'd have got there sooner, because caring made it so much harder to see straight.' He gave a long sigh. 'You weren't faking that kiss at the pizza place, or any of the rest, I know that, and I shouldn't have doubted you. I'm so sorry for stuffing up. And for the record, I've hated being without you.'

He was waiting for a response, but she couldn't think of anything to say. Biting her lip filled the gap. Somewhere all tied up in the middle of that, did he say something about caring?

He wrinkled his face, and stared at her, as if he was trying to peer deep inside her. 'I was hoping we could talk. That's if you're still talking to me.'

Moving towards her, he stretched his hand towards her chin, and tilted it, so she was forced to look at him. Take in the flecks in those grey brown eyes she'd missed so much. She could hear his voice, that familiar cross between gravel and chocolate, but somehow she couldn't take in the words.

'So what do you think?'

Not sure what to say, she opened and closed her mouth, but nothing came out. A rush of tears welled in her eyes, as her face crumpled. Damn. What a time to cry. She couldn't help it, and she couldn't stop. Why the hell was she crying?

He reached out and clasped her to him, raking his hands through her hair, drawing her body to his, folding his arms around her as she shook. She buried her face in his chest, and he carried on holding her, as the tears seeped through his shirt to his skin. He held her for what seemed like forever, rubbing his face against the top of her head until her jerking sobs slowed.

Even the smell of him was too much. This beautiful man, who'd wrung out her heart enough to make her completely debilitated, was here. Maybe not wanting her specifically, but wanting to talk, and she had to decide if she could go there again. She had to give herself some space to consider. At least at work she could think. When she finally got it together to move her mouth, the croak that came out was pathetic.

'Okay, I'll come for a drink with you. Ring me later, we'll sort it out.'

79

Friday Lunchtime, 8th August

IZZY & OLLIE

In Izzy's hall

Notes on an engine and ringing bells

'What the hell was he doing here?'

Izzy, hurrying along the hall five minutes later, collided with Ollie, who was barring her way, and staring down at her accusingly.

'There's no time for an inquisition Ollie, I should be at the cinema to take over from Dida...like now.'

'I'm not moving until you tell me.' Ollie put his hands on his hips, spreading himself across the hall. 'What the hell was he doing here?'

Izzy rolled her eyes that at the age of thirty he was using tactics this childish, but she knew she wasn't going to get past without replying.

'Nothing much.' Now he'd gone she wasn't even sure herself why

Xander had come. What with the shock of him appearing, and the roundabout way he'd talked, he'd left her not quite knowing why he'd been there at all.

Ollie choked in mock disbelief. 'It didn't look like nothing much when I walked into the kitchen.'

'Sorry. I didn't even see you.'

He sounded triumphant. 'My point exactly. You do know who he is, don't you?'

No need to admit she hadn't always known his name. 'Yep. I do know, I've been in France, working for his sister.' If he wanted names, he could have them. 'He's Xander Blackman, is that a problem?'

Ollie shook his head. 'I never thought you'd be with anyone so loaded, not after what we went through with Dad.'

She stared at Ollie.

'First I'm definitely not *with* him, and second, he's not loaded. He works in development – and most developers owe as much as they own.' She tossed that nugget in. 'Otherwise he works in film production and drives an old banger. Nothing too loaded with that is there?'

He gave her an incredulous stare. 'You are so wrong, how can you not know?' And he was shaking his head, as if he really didn't understand. 'That's Xander Blackman, of Colewell Blackman Morgan fame. Ring any bells? Private bankers, family seat not far from Ashbourne, they own half of Hong Kong, probably a good section of London, and more than one chateau in France? He just plays at the film thing. It was the car I recognised first, out in the street before – that old banger you talk about is a rare Aston, worth a cool half million, and he simply knocks about in it. You must have noticed the engine note?'

She let out a long, low groan.

He couldn't keep the scorn out of his voice. 'How did you not realise?'

She stopped and thought, and tried to steady her voice. 'I knew

374

his sister had the most gorgeous place in France.' Which someone had stumped up completely silly money for her to style. She gave a mental head shake to that. This was her own fault entirely. The signs had all been there, but she'd let her view be clouded. But now Ollie had been kind enough to point it out, she must have been bloody blind.

'So how deep in are you?' Ollie noted her flinch at that.

She sighed. Did she even know that? Failing to function because she'd been so upset he'd gone, she'd practically swooned when she'd opened the door to him, as for the rest...

Best to gloss over the gorier details, for Ollie. 'I said I'd go for a drink with him. That's all. It's fine. I'll sort it.' Because if Xander was from serious money, even though he'd come back from America claiming to be missing her, however much she might think she cared about him, she was going to have to put the brakes on whatever this was or wasn't. Ollie was right about that. She could never have a relationship with anyone who had the potential to treat her just as badly as her money-obsessed father had done.

'Something else...' Ollie was staring at her, waiting for her attention. 'I'd like you to hear it from me first.'

More news? Izzy leaned against the radiator for support, and prayed Dida wasn't in a rush to get off. 'Yes?'

He started tentatively. 'I'm not sure how you're going to take this...'

'But...? Izzy prompted.

He gave a nervous laugh. 'I've come back to be with Luce.'

Izzy shook her head, and tried not to overreact. 'You and Luce?' That definitely came out as a screech. Talk about a morning of shocks. She hadn't seen that one coming.

Ollie nodded. 'Yep. Me and Luce.'

'Why, when, what, where, how the hell did that happen?' Somewhere, a very long time ago, she remembered warning him to stay away from Luce. Very fiercely.

But suddenly none of that mattered, because Izzy caught sight of his grin – it was a grin that stretched at least the width of the house. She pulled her brother into a huge hug.

80

Friday Lunchtime, 9th August

XANDER & IZZY

Amandine's Patisserie and Coffee Shop

Feathery hearts and favourite Ferraris

'Two lattes.' The waitress put them down in front of them and hesitated. 'Are you sure you won't change your mind about a cake or a tart?' Two gloomy head shakes later, deciding she was onto a loser, she turned away to find more receptive customers.

This was a million miles away from what Xander had in mind when he'd first mentioned dinner. Across the table, despite her tan, Izzy was ashen, and flatter and tenser than yesterday, if that was possible. He'd been hoping for a chat to find out where they both were, where they might go from here.

In a way he was glad he'd gone away. If he hadn't he might not have realised how much he had to be with Izzy. Quite how bad he'd felt when he was without her had come as a shock, but he was back, and he was determined to make things right. It was only when he'd seen Izzy again yesterday that he'd realised that he wanted much more than just carrying on from where they left off. And wanting more changed everything.

Today the blank stare on Izzy's face was very different from yesterday's wounded reticence, and thinking he was responsible for her downward spiral, made the tourniquet he'd had around his chest since France, tighten another twist. As for feathery hearts in the coffee froth, he couldn't help his toes curling at those.

He tried for a jokey opener. 'Did you know you've got paint in your hair?'

If he hadn't known before, the way she chewed her lip, and closed her eyes was a final giveaway that something had changed. A second later she launched.

'Why didn't you tell me you were loaded, Xander?'

He reeled. Overnight he'd mentally talked himself through a lot of scenarios and awkward questions, but this one hadn't come up. Her chin wasn't jutting, and her eyes weren't flashing, but her dead stare and cold words struck harder for that.

'So how has this come up now?' Only fair he should ask, but knowing about her issues with her father sent his pulse into instant, thumping overdrive.

'My brother Ollie came back from travelling. He recognised you yesterday.'

Xander sighed. Talk about bad timing. Just his luck. 'Well you knew I wasn't poor, Izzy.' That much was true.

Leaning forward slightly, she was straight back at him, hissing. 'How exactly does the largest private bank in London, half of Hong Kong, a large swathe of Derbyshire, not to mention a castle or two, fit in with "not poor"?'

'Okay, I hold my hands up, you've got me there.' His dry throat made his voice grate. There really was no place to hide. 'I never tell anyone about my money, and there's a good reason for that. If they know I'm rich it stops them seeing *me*, because most people

378

can't see past the cash.' That was one of the things in life he hated most about being wealthy. It shifted the balance time and time again. 'When we talked in France, you were right in there saying how important it is to see people for who they are, not what they are.' She couldn't deny that.

Her voice was level, and strangely stark, as she came back at him. 'Maybe so, but we both know there's been an element of deception here.' Not actually accusing him straight out, but she was right.

'Deceived is a bit strong.' It was his only defence. 'Once I knew you had issues with rich guys, I didn't deliberately lie, but I admit I didn't want you to find out, because I knew you'd run.'

For the first time, she smiled, a very small bunched up smile. It could only be in triumph. 'There you go. Proves I'm right. Rich guys are bad news every time, because they don't know the meaning of playing straight.'

Small and so awesome he couldn't bear to be without her, yet she still had the ability to drive him around the bend every time, with her full on bloody mindedness.

'It's ridiculous to write off a whole section of society like that Izzy, anyway you should know me better than that. You've spent time with me, you've seen my integrity, and as you get to know me more, you'll learn you can trust me.' Even as he said it he could see the catch.

He'd pretty much admitted he'd lied to her. Maybe it was time to go on the offensive. The way this was going, he had nothing to lose.

'If we're pointing fingers here, you're hardly squeaky clean yourself are you?' He rounded on her, and watched her mouth drop open.

'What?' Her voice rose to a shriek.

'Coming to France to keep tabs on "the enemy" wasn't exactly honest.' It still needled him, even though he'd rationalised it. 'So you can drop the self-righteous act.'

'That was completely different.' She recovered fast, scowling across the table. 'And you know it.'

'Doing one thing while implying you're doing something else doesn't count as deception, so long as you're the one doing it?' His tone was scathing.

The slow way she dragged in a breath suggested he had her on the ropes, but she was straight back at him, with a maddeningly inscrutable look. 'I explained about the misunderstanding in France at the time.'

That wasn't how he remembered it. 'So how come your explanations wipe out the wrong, but mine don't count?'

'Because...because...'

He turned on her. 'Because you have double standards. Simple as that. So get down off your bloody high horse, and face up to the truth.' In a flash it was obvious to him what was at the root of her attack. 'You've come here, guns blazing, and firing them at me but it's actually all about your dad isn't it?'

Her flinch told him he might be right.

'You talk about trusting people, but the one person in the world I should have been able to trust was my dad.' Her voice was bitter. 'He used to read us stories, and tuck us up in bed, and when I had bad dreams, he used to hold me when I cried, until I went to sleep again. But in the end, even after all that, he screwed us over. I can't put myself in that position again. Trusting someone with money is not an option for me. That's why it's so important for me to be independent.'

This was Xander's last chance. Despite the way she drove him round the bend, he didn't want to lose her. He could feel her slipping through his fingers. 'But your dad wasn't always wealthy was he?'

'He was an engineer with a small business, but when some of his designs went global, the money poured in, from the patents.'

Xander blew out his cheeks. 'Look, my mum brought us up to put people before money, every time. For me, it's inbuilt.' He had to make her to see he wasn't anything like her dad at all, or his for that matter.

Izzy shook her head, apparently deaf to everything he said. 'I didn't plan to be with anyone, but I just assumed if ever I was, I'd be safer with someone ordinary, someone who wouldn't ever have the power to control me.'

'So that's not a post I'd fit the job spec for?' Obviously. Unless he became a Buddhist monk. This sounded like her winding up speech. She was two seconds away from the Goodbye Xander part.

'I'm sorry, Xander. You're an amazing guy, and part of me knows you are everything you claim, but we're miles apart, both financially and in our backgrounds. I'd find it impossible to trust you, and without trust, I'd never feel safe.'

There it was. His dismissal. He had one final, fleeting, thought. 'You're desperate to be in charge, but hanging on to what your father did means he's still the one ruling your life. You'll only be in control when you let this go, and move on.'

He dragged in a breath. 'Thanks for being honest.' He wouldn't have expected anything less, despite what he'd said earlier about her double standards.

He hadn't lost this fight, and nor was he finished. In fact she'd given him a huge amount to work with. It was important to make it out of here before she went any further, and blew him out of the water for good.

'I'm the one who has to run now.' He glanced at his watch. 'I'm off to the hospital for the annual afternoon of tests.' He'd been hoping she might want to come with him, but that was out of the question now.

Her expression changed. 'That's why you came back?'

He hadn't meant to play the pity card, and worse, the devastated look on her face was wrenching his heart.

'That's one of the reasons I'm back.' The biggest one of all though was sitting across the table from him, her brow crisscrossed with deep furrows, and it was taking every bit of self-control to stop himself dragging her against his chest, and never letting go.

She pushed back from the table. 'Don't let me hold you up.'

Apart from the way she'd obliterated the frothy heart in the foam, her coffee was untouched, but she was already up out of her chair, one hand landing fleetingly on his shoulder. 'Think about what we said about The Pink House, Xander, you belong there, and you do need a home.' The slightest squeeze of her fingers. 'And be careful what you haul out of skips in future.' So maybe she did have a bit of bossy left, even if her voice was cracking. 'I'll see you then.' She turned away, hiding her face behind her hand, and made a dash for the door.

Xander locked his eyes onto the pale slice of skin at the base of her T shirt, as she disappeared around the end of the glass patisserie case. He rubbed his neck where she'd touched him, and focussed on the gaping hole in his chest that appeared like a chasm the moment she wasn't there.

As he eased to his feet, the waitress came along, sending a sympathetic eye roll in Izzy's direction, and then turned into a narrow eyed stare.

She came in close, with a hushed whisper. 'You aren't in that Poldark programme are you?'

'What?' If his stomach hadn't been so knotted he'd have gone for an inward groan.

'It's just your hair, and your beard makes you look a lot like...'

He let out a hollow laugh. 'They wanted me for a body double, but I was too ripped.' The waitress gawped. 'Do you have the bill, please?'

She gave him a beam. 'Already paid thanks, your friend gave me ten pounds on her way out.'

'Of course she did.' He shook his head, for what she'd done, but also to try to shake away the dizzy sense that this morning wasn't actually happening.

So like Izzy, teeth grindingly stubborn and independent to the end.

His phone beeped, and he glanced at the screen. A message from the estate agent.

We have strong interest in the cinema building. Please get in touch if you wish to be included further.

Izzy was at rock bottom, and this could only make things worse.

81

Saturday Afternoon, 15th August

IZZY & LUCE

At the cinema

All the way from Lithuania

'The customers can't get enough of the French antiques.' Luce was pouring over the sales ledger, writing in the codes and prices. 'I just sold another two christening gowns there, and the person before bought a whole stack of wire baskets.'

Izzy, unrolling a sheaf of posters along the counter, blanked that her stomach had curled up like a cabbage at the mention of wire baskets.

Izzy tried for a smile. 'We'll be bursting at the seams when the next load comes in, and there's still another delivery after that.'

In fact it was hard to look at anything remotely France-related, when every piece came with its own agonising memory welded to it. Whether it was Xander's easy, teasing laugh, echoing from when she'd bought yet another set of candlesticks, or the way he'd come to kiss her, when she was half way through wiping cobwebs off a bedside cabinet. Xander was clinging onto every goddam item that had arrived.

Luce looked up, and peered at Izzy. 'It's been a total coup for The Vintage Cinema Club, but every time I see how pale you are, I wish we hadn't made you go.'

Izzy knew however bad she was feeling, she had to man up here. 'Don't feel guilty. Xander turned out to be amazing, and he helped us a lot. It's not your fault there were just too many obstacles.'

'And the money issue is totally non-negotiable?' Luce kept on trying to talk her round.

'My final position.'

Luce's face scrunched in concern. 'Still crying yourself to sleep?'

Izzy gave a rueful nod. As for the exhaustion and lethargy, some days she couldn't even bring herself to crawl out of bed, and clearing up at home was a thing of the past. Her clothes were still in a pile on the floor where she'd tipped them out her first day home, and somehow she couldn't bring herself to move them, let alone wash them.

'I try to put off going to bed, and paint furniture instead.' Izzy tried to smile. Even painting hadn't cheered her up. She'd found herself painting one huge chest a deep dark dusky blue, and another in battleship grey, then asked herself what the hell that was about. But Izzy needed to move the conversation away from herself here.

'How are you and Ollie getting on?' Izzy sent Luce a grin. 'He always liked you didn't he?'

Luce laughed. 'You made it clear he was off limits from the first day I came home with you. On the up side, twelve years on, I think we both know what we want now.' Luce's eyes twinkled. 'You may have done us a favour in keeping us apart.'

'Back then I didn't want my best friend and my brother hurting each other, or squeezing me out.' Izzy did feel slightly guilty. 'Now is different.' Especially since Luce had pointed out that she hadn't had one of her famous one night stands since the month after Ollie left. 'Let's hope you have better luck trying to domesticate him than I have.' Izzy gave a laugh. 'He still hasn't learned to put the coco pops back in the cupboard at home.'

Luce's cheeks were a very pale shade of pink. 'It's strange, because now Ollie's back, it feels like we couldn't be any other way than this, and Ruby's happy too. It's early days, but we're all homey.' She gave her own contented smile. 'Ollie's sorting out his costume for the Fancy Dress Vintage Film Evening, even though it's ages away. There's a picture of him as a hound dog, back in nineteen eighty eight, so he's recreating that, and dressing up as one of the hundred and one Dalmatians. He wanted me to be one too, but I'm not that couply yet, so I'm going as Pocahontas.'

Izzy's mind boggled at what love could do to people. 'What the hell happened to the vintage part of the fancy dress theme? I thought we were aiming for classy.' Someone had to make a stand. She might be way floppier than usual, but she wasn't letting this through.

'Pocahontas was historical, before she signed to Disney.' Luce was unapologetic. 'Anyway Dida's coming as Bridget Jones the bunny girl. She's definitely post Pocahontas.'

Izzy gave up on that with a sigh. 'Still no news on the paintings then?'

Luce gave a grunt. 'Nope. Which is a shame as Ollie and I discussed it – we'd definitely buy the cinema building if we hit the big time. LOL to that one.'

Izzy couldn't help smile at the new, extra happy Luce. 'It's cool. Do you realise you and Ollie are the Vintage Cinema Club's first couple.' She chewed her nail as she thought. 'Dida and Aidie don't count, because even if he does own the building I totally refuse to include him.'

But Luce didn't reply, because she was taking more notice of something out on the street.

'Major shit alert, we're about to get a visit from that very man.'

Izzy gawped. 'I thought he's supposed to be in Lithuania this weekend?'

'He is.' Luce hissed through teeth clenched into a smile. 'Leave this to me. We can't risk you shouting at him.'

Izzy hated to say there was no chance of that happening. These days she was too exhausted to be cross. She watched Aidie stop to dip into the basket of rusty tools outside the shop.

Izzy couldn't help her observation. 'Is it just me, or is he looking ancient?' She didn't see Aidie that often.

Luce was hissing under her breath. 'Dropping a few stones can make you look very haggard.'

Despite the weight loss, Aidie hadn't lost his waddle. Luce made her voice bright. 'Hi Aidie, anything we can help with?'

Aidie clunked a wood plane down onto the counter. 'I'll take this please.'

'Great.' Luce kept up the brightness, as she located the stock ticket, and peeled it off. 'That's ten pounds fifty please.'

Aidie gave a guffaw. 'Stick it on Dida's tab will you.'

'If you're sure.' Luce exchanged a "cheeky sod" eye roll with Izzy.

'So Dida's in York then?' Something about Aidie's swagger made it clear he already knew the answer.

Luce flicked back her hair, and carried on smiling. 'And, in case you're wondering, the children are up at Carsington with my mum and Ruby, having a picnic.'

Izzy sent Luce a nod of encouragement and an insane grin, for that inspired retort.

Aidie's dismissive snort suggested that the children weren't upper most in his mind. 'Opera with a gay Geordie...rather her than me.'

Luce beamed, and picked up the plane. 'Shall I wrap this, or will you take it as it is?'

'Or maybe not so gay after all, if you read his emails...' Aidie gave a grimace. 'Someone should tell her she needs a password

387

on her laptop.'

Izzy stood her ground, and held her fixed grin tightly in place, even though her stomach had dropped through the floor on Dida's behalf.

'Passwords are for people with something to hide.' Luce's expression was inscrutable, and she held Aidie's gaze manfully, for a few seconds. 'I'll get you a bag.' She dipped behind the counter.

Izzy gave Luce a "good point well made" thumbs up, at low level, as Luce bobbed back into view, popped the plane into a Sainsbury's bag, rolled it up, and stuck some sticky tape on.

'There you go, Aidie.' She pushed the parcel across the counter, still showing enough teeth to be on a toothpaste advert. 'Enjoy your afternoon.'

Aidie took the plane, stepped back, and rolled backwards and forwards on the balls of his feet.

He leaned forwards, and narrowed his eyes. 'This isn't the end of it.'

Then he spun around, and waddled out of the shop.

'Bloody hell, pick my jaw off the floor time, or what?' Luce's eyes were wide, and perplexed. 'He was practically snarling. Maybe I should have given him a proper carrier bag.'

Izzy rushed to reassure Luce. 'I'm not sure a bag would have helped. You nailed the rest brilliantly.' She hesitated. 'I wouldn't like to be in Dida's shoes. We'll have to hope that Hamish and hunger don't push him over the edge.'

Luce rubbed her nose. 'You know he didn't even bother to turn up when Lolly was born. I shudder every time I remember that The Vintage Cinema Club is completely in his hands. The way he looks today, anything could happen.'

Text from Luce to Dida:

**Aidie just dropped in at the cinema, not a happy bunny, said
he'd read your emails**

:(Hugs xx

*

Text from Dida to Luce:

Thanks, Aidie is full of shit. There's nothing in them xx

82

Subject: More GI Joe's news

Hi guys,

The future Mrs GI Joe has been to pick up her wedding dress today. Fab news – GI Joe's has run into problems with their shipping, so the launch has been put back. She showed me round the shop, and the spaces are amazing. Big hugs to Izzy for her trip to France – the first load arrived and is AWESOME. See you Monday to unload the next. I heart armoires :)

Love Luce xx

83

DIDA, IZZY, LUCE & THE CREW

At the cinema

I don't like Mondays

'So, Henni's got the cones out on the road and he's waiting for the lorry.' Dida marched through the cinema, talking to anyone who would listen as she passed. 'We've cleared space at the far end to unload into, I've got four more lemon drizzle cakes here for the cafe, and some Prosecco for when we've finished, so it looks like we're all set for a great start to the week.'

It could be the new red Michael Kors pumps she'd treated herself to for Saturday, or the fab swishy skirt from Mint Velvet that practically made her hips disappear, or maybe it was a hangover from the brilliant day in York with Hamish. Three good reasons – all of which led back to Hamish – which meant, this afternoon Dida was literally waltzing on air.

Izzy gave her a knowing wink as she passed. 'I take it York went well then?'

'It was amazing, thanks.' If she closed her eyes, she could re-play every second of Saturday. Wandering along the white stone city walls, picnicking with champagne, being blown away by the music...

Izzy leaned in. 'So was there "a connection" then?'

Dida tried to explain. 'It's a cerebral thing.'

In the right context there'd be sparks. If they ever actually got to kiss, the voltage would probably equal the output of Ferrybridge power station. But this wasn't just about her. Every tiny decision she made could have a huge knock on effect on the children's lives. Getting entangled would only weaken her position. She needed every ounce of her active brain operational, when it came to considering and negotiating her future, with the family and Aidie.

'And what about Aidie?' Izzy asked, pulling a face summed that one up.

Dida shrugged. 'I arrived back to a takeaway, then he left the next morning. He knows he's in no position to talk about adultery.' The very bumpy sex that had come later was about territory marking not lust, but the way he'd ground her into submission was something else. She rubbed her wrist as she remembered.

Izzy gave a sympathetic glance, then did a double take. 'Are those bruises on your arm?' Her voice rose as she leaned in to see better. 'What happened there?'

Dida rubbed at the marks on her skin and sighed. The colour had come out a lot since Saturday night. 'Basically my first ever attempt at withholding sex from Aidie ended in a big argument.'

Izzy hissed at her. 'Shit Dida, we can't let this go, he's hurt you.' Her forehead wrinkled with concern. 'Does Luce know? It's not on, it's...'

Dida cut in. 'I know what it is. I'll get an appointment with the solicitor.' She'd put off ringing this morning. 'I'll do it once the delivery's done. We'll talk later. And thanks, Izzy.' The thing was, Dida was reluctant to call the solicitor, because, however like a coward it made her seem, she didn't want to inflame Aidie any further. Solicitors might jump in and force her hand. But so long as there was a chance to save the cinema building, she didn't want to take steps against Aidie.

Ollie was by the door shouting down the cinema. 'Big blue truck pulling up outside, this could be it...'

Luce hurried past them, almost running towards the door. 'Right guys, we're on, I can't wait to see what's coming.'

For the next hour they all rushed in and out, with boxes and smaller bits, while the muscle guys did their man stuff, shoving the bigger pieces around.

Dida handed a chunk of cake in a serviette to Izzy. 'Here, have some lemon drizzle to keep you going.' Dida was circulating. It was essential to keep the crew's energy levels high, and Izzy was definitely in need of a calorie boost, given how pale she was this afternoon.

'Cheers.' Izzy took the cake, and slid it into the pocket of her dress. 'It's funny how it takes ages to load up, and yet it comes off the lorry really fast. There are only a couple more things to bring in now.'

That was Dida's cue. 'Right, time for a celebratory drink.'

'Are we raising a glass to opera in the ruins too?' Izzy shot her the briefest smile, over the box of linen she was carrying.

'Maybe a private one.' Dida swept off towards the kitchen. 'If you get everyone to gather round the counter, I'll grab the Prosecco out of the fridge.'

Two minutes later, she was back, sliding the wine and glasses onto the counter. No way was she risking a toast after the last awful showdown at the birthday party, but the way things were panning out, it was important to mark the day.

One by one the crew took the last of their boxes to add to the chaos at the back of the cinema, and sidled up. Only Luce was left outside on the pavement, talking on her phone. Dida watched her through the shop window, flapping her hands, as she often did, but today they were on overdrive. A second later Luce ran in, letting out a scream loud enough to make ear drums bleed, and hurled herself at a sweat streaked Ollie, knocking him against the chiffonnière he'd just put down.

Totally breathless, and pink and incoherent, Luce was hurling random words into the air. 'Pictures...worth a bloody fortune... auction six figures...maybe three hundred thousand...all for some brown paintings...'

Dida blinked, barely taking it in.

Then Luce whipped around, grabbed the bunch of tulips from the counter, and hurled them into the air, and as water and petals rained down on their heads she stopped hyperventilating long enough to take a big gulp of air and shout, 'Omigod, the pictures are worth a bomb! Ollie and I can buy the cinema!'

Then, tears streaming down her face, silky hair flying in all directions, Luce dragged Ollie across to Dida and Izzy, and hauled them all into a huge sweaty hug.

'We've bloody done it, The Vintage Cinema Club can save the cinema, how bloody brilliant is that?'

Everyone was patting everyone on the back, and cheering too, then Ollie grabbed a bottle, popped a cork, and began filling glasses.

Eventually, they all had a glass in their hand, and the mayhem had subsided to an excited flutter. Dida, propping herself up against the counter because her legs were in danger of giving way, cleared her throat.

'Well guys, the second French delivery is here, sales are at an all-time high, and now, thanks to an amazing stroke of luck with some pictures, it looks as though Ollie and Luce are going to be in a position to buy the building. This really is a good news afternoon.'

'Gut, is verrry gut.' Henni waved his glass at her, and reflected her full on beam back at her.

Outside on the pavement, Dida noticed a ladder appearing from a van. Didn't the window cleaner usually come in the mornings?

She carried on.

'Our "Vintage at the Cinema say Bonjour" adverts are all over the local papers. A huge thank you to Izzy, and Luce, but thank you to everyone for pulling together, for all your support.'

There were a chorus of shouts of 'Yay!' and 'Vive La Vintage at the Cinema!'

Beyond the high fives, Dida focussed on the ladder, now propped up in front of the door, and her stomach clenched as she saw a horribly familiar guy, foot on the bottom rung. Déjà bloody vu or what?

'Excuse me, one minute.' As the crew parted to let her through, she bustled out of the shop, and onto the pavement, barely believing this was actually happening.

'Watch it love, it's unlucky to walk under ladders.' It was the same guy as before, drill in hand, stepping forward, barring her way.

The tiny prickles bristling on the back of Dida's neck turned to damn great spikes. 'What the hell are you doing this time?' He surely couldn't be...could he? As if his belligerent grin wasn't enough, worse still, was the long narrow strip of red plastic he had in his hand. Despite her spanx, her stomach began to travel towards the ground at a rate that made her groan.

Dida gave a large gulp, and from somewhere found her voice, which came out as a squeak. 'That can't be a "sold" sign?' Her voice rose to a volley of panicked cries. 'This building isn't sold... it can't possibly be sold...I'd have heard if it was...' Bloody Aidie. Dida, shaking her head, scraped a finger nail under each eye, and bit her lip as she tried to stop her mouth from contorting. She was the last person in the world to cry. She could sit through Children In Need without even getting a lump in her throat, let alone crying. She stayed dry eyed right through school concerts, when parents around her were sobbing buckets. She wasn't going to bloody give in now. She dragged in a breath and cursed that it made her shoulders shake. That fucking arsehole of a husband. Surely he'd have let her know if he'd sold her dream.

The guy shook his head. 'Once again love, I only put up the signs, you need to check back with the agents.'

The same conversation they'd had before. If last time was bad, this was a thousand times worse. 'Stop calling me love.' Dida heard her voice morph into a roar.

With a grimace, the guy gave a shrug, pulled a crumpled piece of paper out of his pocket, and waved it at her. 'There. Email, came through this morning. Sold subject to contract. You can't argue with that.'

And in that one awful, earth shattering moment, Dida realised he was probably right.

All this time she'd thrown herself into Vintage at the Cinema, it had given her an amazing purpose in life, and a sense of achievement, and fulfilment, and pride. What's more, it had taken her mind off the awfulness of her marriage, and somehow made it possible to carry on, where she otherwise wouldn't have done. If Aidie truly had let the hatchet fall on the cinema, she was one hundred per cent finished with him too.

84

Tuesday Morning, 19th August

Subject: Talking Italian

Amore Dida,

Thinking about our chat last night... So sorry to hear about your deep shit, and for my part in it. Take your time, do whatever is best for you, I'll wait for as long as it takes,

Tante bellecose, Hamish

85

Friday Afternoon, 22nd August

LUCE & IZZY

In Luce's bedroom

The scent of raspberries

'So here's your tea. How's it going, is there anything I can help with?'

Luce popped her head around her bedroom door, to see a view that hadn't changed for days. Izzy bending over the sewing machine, with the ironing board covered in fabric triangles. All that room at Izzy's house, yet here she was holed up in Luce's tiny flat, to make sure Xander wouldn't find her. Not that he was looking for her any more. Luce suspected that it was more because Izzy couldn't face being home alone with her memories.

Izzy bobbed her head up. 'Would you believe I'm almost finished? Hearts and cherubs, and enough bunting to deck out the whole of Matlock Park. This happy couple aren't doing things by halves, but they've saved my sanity, as well as my bank balance with their last minute order – I haven't had time to think about the cinema, or Xander.' Izzy gave a shudder. 'So, any news from Dida?'

This was how it had been for days now. Izzy here, Ollie doing Izzy's shifts, Luce bringing Izzy the news from the outside world.

Luce pondered. 'Hamish is still happy to wait for her to sort herself out.'

'That man sounds a seriously nice guy.' Izzy snipped off some cotton ends.

Luce rescued a stray flag from the floor. 'And Dida's finally been to the solicitors to get advice on a separation. She held off until now, hoping that Aidie would reconsider the sale of the cinema, and hang on until our money came through from the pictures, but he wouldn't.'

'There are no words bad enough to describe Aidie are there?' Izzy gritted her teeth.

Luce knew Izzy was talking more about Dida's bruises than the cinema.

She gave a shrug. 'Aidie's gone too far this time, but Dida thinks it's because he wants out. He was always a nightmare to live with, his bank balance was never a compensation.'

Izzy gave a faint grin. 'So, talking of insanely rich people, has anyone seen Xander?' She might be looking drawn and ill, but she hadn't lost her sense of irony.

Luce kicked herself for letting that particular Aidie comment slip. 'No idea where Xander is. Maybe he's respecting what you want, and staying away.' Luce caught Izzy's expression falling, and knew she was still hurting.

Izzy forced a smile onto her face, and changed the subject. 'So any news on places to move to?'

Luce pulled a face. 'There's nothing out there at all.' The first time in her life she had the promise of a substantial wodge of cash coming her way, and she couldn't believe it wasn't helping them at all. 'Ollie's rushing around, and he's seen a vacant garden centre and an out of the way barn, but neither of those were workable. It's hard to think there were so many empty shops here when we started, and now there aren't any.'

Izzy scrunched up her face. 'We all love what we do, but it isn't just the income, we rely on the cinema for our whole social structure. Popping to work isn't going to be easy for any of us if we have to move away, not to mention all the trade we'll lose when we leave vintage central.'

Luce, very aware of that, gave a sigh. Being anxious was so tiring too. 'Are you back here again tomorrow?'

'Not if I can help it, I'm almost finished.' Izzy posted her a grin. 'I'm delivering this in the morning, meeting the couple half way to Sheffield, and then I might just dare to pop in at the cinema. I want to be there to help when the last load from France arrives.'

Luce's chest tightened. 'Better make the most of it while you can. Dida thinks we've got two months, maybe less. Apparently the deal's moving very fast.'

'I hate it, I hate it all.' Izzy raked her fingers through her hair, and the faint scent of raspberries drifted across the room. 'But I love that we put up a fight. Aidie can take the building, but we'll always be The Vintage Cinema Club. He can never take that away from us.'

86

Saturday Morning, 23rd August

IZZY

A car park near Curbar Edge

A stiff breeze and a following wind

'Damned bloody sold sign.' Izzy, having got an eyeful as she passed the cinema was still muttering to herself six miles later as she swerved around three sheep wandering across the road as she drove past Chatsworth House. 'It's just all so unfair.' As she drove up the hill out of Baslow, the meadows turned to birch woods, and then to moorland.

There was nothing fair about this situation at all. They'd all worked their butts off to make the business work, they loved what they did, and they'd all come to rely on it for a lot more than just the income. For now she was blocking out that last part, because the thought of being without money was just too scary. They had mountains of stock now, but what good was that if they didn't have anywhere to put it? At least this mega order of bunting gave her the cushion of some immediate cash. The buyer had paid up front, and Izzy had made it in record time because, really, there was no point in going to bed when she couldn't sleep.

She checked the map on her iPhone, turned left, and half a mile down a bumpy road that ran between heather covered banks, she came to a wide car park entrance. A moss covered sign saying Coppice Wood confirmed this was the place. Izzy wrestled Choufleur across the loose gravel and pot holes, and then pulled in by the wall. At the far end of the car park, beyond the scattering of randomly parked cars, she spotted an ice cream van. The only good thing on the horizon this morning. Izzy checked her phone. Ten minutes was enough time to finish an ice cream, and still look professional when the customer arrived.

Izzy crossed to the ice cream van, as cloud shadows raced across the car park. Good thing she'd worn her thick cardi given the gale that was blowing up here, but the wind tearing at her full skirt was a wardrobe malfunction waiting to happen. Approaching the van, she waved at the hunched teenager inside, who put down his phone, and pushed the sliding glass open.

'Yes?'

Tucking her skirt firmly between her knees, and pulling her cardi closer around her, Izzy pondered over the pictures in the window.

'You might like to try the bubble gum cone.'

Izzy jumped at the gruff voice, next to her shoulder. Looking down, she took in scuffed leather deck shoes, tanned feet, and her heart gave a lurch. Faded denim. She hardly dared hope, hardly dared go further. Thumbs, hooked through the belt loops, pretty much gave it away. A T-shirt, flapping in the breeze, and no one else she knew would hang out in a T-shirt with holes, saying Cannes Film Festival 84...

'Xander?' She flinched as a flash of abs made her look up sharply, and as her eyes locked with his dark brown gaze, her heart jumped and lodged right in her throat. She missed furious

402

by a mile, almost hit angry, and ended up with a shocked gulp. Stalking, following, tracking her down, whatever, the two weeks since she'd last seen him had been like an aching lifetime. 'What the hell are you doing here?'

*   *   *   *

Xander stared at Izzy, huddled against the wind. Every time he saw her, it felt like coming home.

'I'm passing through, getting an ice cream, just like you.' The hair he brushed out of his eyes had started to curl at the ends. 'What are you having?'

She bit her lip. 'Actually I think I'll leave it now.'

She backed away from the ice cream van, and propped herself against a nearby dry stone wall instead. 'I'm waiting to meet someone.'

Xander dragged in a breath, and nudged his bum against the wall beside her. Knowing how big she was on honesty, he needed to come clean fast.

'Yep, that's me.' He watched her face scrunch.

'You're here to collect the bunting?' Her voice rose in disbelief. 'So that means you're the one who made the order?'

He shuffled, wishing he didn't feel so guilty. 'Indirectly. It was the only way I could think of to get you to meet me.' He'd miss out the bit about wanting to take the financial pressure off whilst he'd been getting the rest of his side together. And it had worked hadn't it? How else would he have got to see her when she'd blocked his calls, refused to answer her door, and gone AWOL from the cinema?

'Right.' She shook her head, and squinted at the sun. 'I suppose you heard the cinema's been sold?' Still staring into the blue yonder, her shoulders heaved with a huge, heartfelt sigh.

He had to get straight in here, and do what he had to. He

braced himself, and threw out the words. 'I know you hate people meddling with your life, but I've a confession to make…I bought the cinema.' A hard hat for the fall out might have been a good idea.

'What?' Izzy's screech was even more ear piercing than he'd expected. 'The cinema's going to be yours?'

He kept his own voice level. He really hoped she wasn't going to go apeshit about this. 'The paperwork was finalised this morning. I'm sorry, there was another buyer, and Aidie was hell bent on selling. Stepping in and hiking up the price was the only way I could save it. It all happened very fast, and I'm sorry I couldn't tell you before, but the deal was on a knife edge.'

'Shit, Xander.' She put her hand to her forehead, and brushed away her hair.

He waited for more, but it didn't come. So that went well. With Izzy, it was hard to predict how she was going to take things. He screwed himself up for the next bit, which was way bigger.

'I've got some papers here I'd like you to take away and read.' He slid an envelope out of his back pocket. 'Basically, they outline an agreement to pass the cinema building to you, in trust.' A lot of work had gone into the planning here. Hopefully she'd find this easier to accept than an outright gift. 'Once you sign the papers, the building is yours to use as you want to.' He held his breath, waiting to see her reaction.

She chewed her thumb hard, and for a moment he thought she was about to cry. The knot in his chest tightened. God, he loved this woman so much, he couldn't believe it had taken him quite so long to see it for what it was. He bit back the lump in his own throat, and willed himself not to wrap his arms around her, and wreck everything.

'Why Xander?' Her two scratchy words made his lips curl into a smile.

'Well, there are lots of reasons.' Loving her as if his life depended on it was only the start. 'Most important, I want you to have your independence.' He paused. 'I've made my money, we both know money isn't what's important in life, but just occasionally I can use it for something that will make a huge difference to someone, and this is one of those times. That's going to make me happy. You're so talented, but I've never met anyone as selfless as you. I was pretty jaded, but seeing the way you always put everyone else in front of yourself, made me feel good again. You helped me see things differently, and come to terms with a lot of things. I guess in return, I wanted to buy you your freedom. This way you'll never have to rely on anyone else again, you'll always be the one in control, and you'll always have an income.'

Izzy sniffed beside him, and when she spoke her voice wobbled. 'I don't know what to say. Every time you surprise me, every time you come up with something new and amazing and awesome.' She hugged her arms around her chest, and seemed to be tugging her skirt a lot.

Xander turned a small box over in the pocket of his jeans. Cherub earrings. He'd almost given them to her once before. Looking back, that was the night he finally recognised the huge and major feeling of being in love with her. He just hadn't quite got the vocabulary sorted at the time to put a name to it, given it had never actually happened to him before.

Izzy carried on. 'I was so wrong the other day Xander, when I implied you were like my dad, because when I actually thought about it, you're different on every level. You are good, and kind and you have every bit of the integrity you claim.' Her voice was soft and warm now, and she leaned towards him. 'Thank you Xander, this is the most thoughtful, awesome thing anyone has ever done for me.'

For a minute it felt like his heart was going to burst in his chest. 'You have no idea how much I want to make you happy.'

'That's the other wonderful thing...' Her hand wavered next to his knee. 'You understand me, and you know me so well. The one thing in the world that would make me secure, and you found it.'

He let his gaze play across the freckles below her eyelashes, and land in the dimple in her left cheek. 'I'm glad I got something right.'

Wrinkling her nose, she sent him a smile that turned his insides to hot toffee. Then, as her face fell, she looked suddenly serious. 'You did this so I could feel safe enough to be with you, didn't you?'

He dragged in a breath, not knowing how to answer.

She carried on. 'It's not only about the money any more.' She looked right into his eyes. 'You thinking about this at all, and understanding me, makes me know I can trust you enough to be with you.'

His voice was low and close to cracking as he spoke. 'I'm so sorry Izzy, I've done all this for you because I want you to have the life you deserve.' He'd said this over and over to himself so many times, but still, he didn't know how to say it now. 'You're wonderful, you're the most amazing woman I've ever met, but in the end this is what this was about. I'm not going to be able to be with you, because I can't let you throw all that away, on me. On someone with my genetic outlook.'

'What?' Her voice rose again, and she stared at him as if she didn't understand.

This was the hardest thing he'd ever done in his life. It was so complicated, and yet so clear.

'I can't take the risk.' His words were almost a whisper now, and he raked his fingers through his hair. 'If I do end up ill with what my mum had, at some time in the future, I love you way too much to lay that on you. I came back because I wanted to be with you, desperately, but the longer I thought about it, the more I know you deserve more than I can offer. You need to be with someone who will put you first, but I can't guarantee that, so I can't be that person. Now the cinema is yours I'm leaving so you can move on.'

'No Xander, no.' Izzy was in front of him now, tears streaming down her cheeks, winding her arms tightly around his neck, her sweet scent enveloping his head as he tried to wrestle back his own sobs. 'I won't let you do this. You mustn't.'

His fingers wound under her jacket, digging into the muscles beside her spine, his chin resting on the soft raspberry tangles of her hair. If he closed his eyes really tight, for a minute he could pretend this wasn't happening, that he was never going to let go, and that he could hold her here forever. He could rock her crying, convulsing body against his, and pretend he didn't ever have to let go. Pretend that he could wake up with her every day, and go to sleep beside her every night. Soak up all her goodness and strength, and let it make him the guy he'd never imagined he could be until he met her. When he looked into buying the cinema, he had been hoping to set her free to be with him. But now he knew, after all she'd been through with her dad, and always being there for her brothers, he couldn't let her give everything up for him, if or when he would need 24 hour care. He was setting her free to go on to a new life, which would have to be without him. It was the only way for this to end.

He drew in one last lungful of her scent, disentangled a hand, and dug into his pocket.

'Here, I want you to have these.' He flipped off the lid, and held out the box.

'Silver cherubs?' The words came through the last breathy gulps of her sobs, as she took them and held them in the cup of her hand. 'They're beautiful. Thank you so much.' Then she stared up at him, shaking her head, and bereft. 'What are we going to do Xander?'

He bit his lip hard, and drew every bit of strength in his body. 'We're going to go back to our lives, and live them the very best way we can. And you'll be able to do whatever you want, and be whoever you want, because you'll be strong and you'll have your independence. And the first thing you're going to do is to go back, and tell everyone that the cinema is safe.' He was talking her through every step here. Missing the bit about being with someone else, but she would be, eventually, because she deserved that too.

'And the bunting?' She shook her head, as if it was a random thing she'd just remembered. 'There's so much of it...'

'You keep it.'

Bending down, he picked up the envelope from the ground, disentangled her arms from around his neck, and taking her by the hand, he led her back to her van, and pulled open the door.

'Get in, Izzy.'

He almost shouldered her up into the driver's seat. Bossy and forceful didn't begin to cover how he was being, but it was the only way. There was a volcano pushing up in his thorax, and he wasn't sure how long he could hold it back.

Handing her the envelope, he couldn't meet her eye. Quite how he was keeping his voice low and collected he had no idea. 'The solicitors will be in touch with you on Monday. You need to go now.' For both their sakes this parting had to happen at the speed of light, or he might never do it. 'Now drive away, and don't look back.'

Saying goodbye was beyond him. He took a step back, as the engine spluttered into life, and he remembered another time, what seemed like a lifetime ago now, when he'd been praying for this same engine to fail. He heard the gears grind, and then the tyres were crunching across the pebbles. Catching a last glimpse of her hair as she turned into the lane, the ache in his chest racked off the scale. Then he made a dive for his car, slammed the door, and only then did he let himself cry. And for half an hour he sobbed for everything they had, and for everything they didn't.

87

Saturday Lunchtime, 24th August

DIDA, LUCE & IZZY

In the Bridal Suite

Red eyes and coffee cake

'Well, talk about quick changes. Five minutes ago we were unloading a van in silence, with long faces, now there's a full blown celebration, and it's all down to you.' Dida eased her way past the long rail of floaty lace dresses, and threw her arms around Izzy, who was snivelling into her sleeve. 'You've saved the cinema, but what about you?'

Dida threw a desperate querying glance at Luce, over Izzy's shoulder. Luce had dashed after Izzy when she'd bolted upstairs moments after coming in with her stupendous news, but Luce was shaking her head at Dida now.

Sinking onto the chaise lounge, Dida pulled Izzy down beside her.

'Here, my special mother of the bride's tissue box.' Luce pushed some hankies at Izzy, who blew her nose loudly, and dabbed her bloodshot eyes. Izzy's sunken cheeks were blotchy, and behind the sleeves of her denim jacket, huddled across her chest, her body shrank to nothing.

Finally, Izzy gulped in some air, and then her words came out in a rush. 'You know Xander bought the cinema, so I could be independent.' Throwing up her head, she battled to push away the ragged curls falling across her face. 'That's not all though. His mother died from a horrible, debilitating genetic disease, which he might have. But even though he doesn't know for sure, he's decided he doesn't want to be with me and that's why I'm...' Izzy's bottom lip went again, and she collapsed into a shaking mass of sobs.

'Oh shit, I'm so sorry.' While Dida gave her another long hug, patting her heaving shoulders, Luce knelt on the floor, and rubbed Izzy's knee.

Once Izzy's tears had subsided, Dida eased her grip, and carried on talking. 'So what do *you* think about this?' From where Dida was sitting, this sounded like a good man, being selfless, and no doubt about it, Xander was that.

Izzy considered. 'I'm gutted that he's got the disease hanging over him.'

Dida couldn't begin to imagine how Izzy must be feeling. 'I can see why he would want to save you from that too, especially if he loves you, which he obviously does, very much.'

After another nose blow, Izzy managed to croak. 'I sound like I'm changing my mind a lot, but I do know for certain I want to be with him...I can't actually imagine living my life without him.'

Luce's frown was indulgent. 'At last. You have no idea how glad I am to finally hear that. We've known you and Xander belonged together since day one. It was completely obvious to everyone but you.'

'I was hung up on the money part, but once I saw how he'd handled the cinema, I realised how well he understands me. I knew in that instant that I want to be with him, and his potential for illness doesn't change that at all.'

'It might be a very big commitment.' Great, Luce was playing devil's advocate here.

Izzy's voice was quiet. 'In the long term it might not be easy. But I want to be with Xander, whatever.'

Dida narrowed her eyes. 'I thought you might say that, in which case you can't hide away here. You're going to have to go and tell him this.' There was no other way forward. 'It's up to you to persuade him this is right for both of you.'

'And it might not be easy.' Luce chimed in.

Izzy gulped again. 'I don't even know where he is.'

Dida was already on her feet, heading for the door. 'I'll bring you some tea, and coffee cake, you're going to need every bit of strength you can get.' If this was the only thing they did for Izzy, they had to pull it off, after everything she'd done for all of them. 'As for tracking Xander down, The Vintage Cinema Club is on the case. We owe you on so many levels Izzy, and we're here for you. Xander's a strong guy, and I suspect you're going to have to fight hard to win this one. But we're right here, fighting with you.'

88

Saturday Afternoon, 24th August

IZZY

At The Pink House

Kitten heels

'Here goes, wish me luck.'

As she knocked on the front door, Izzy slipped the plaster cherub she'd been talking to back into her bag, wrenched in her stomach to stop it lurching off down the drive, and gave a last chomp on her gum. Much as she needed it, on balance it was crucial she did as little as possible to annoy Xander. This time the bubble gum had to go.

The sound of her own heartbeat banging in her ears was loud enough to drown out the birdsong, as she waited for what seemed like forever. Luce had insisted she wore her lemon kitten heels but as Izzy peered down at her feet, she knew it was going to take more than lucky shoes to pull this off. And then he was there, peeling back the door, all stubble and cheekbones, but the two lines between his eyebrows deepening as his frown descended told her he was less than happy to see her.

'Not disturbing you I hope?' She threw out the remark anyway, even though it couldn't be more obvious she was.

'I've got a stack of scripts to read, but I hear you're insistent...' His shrug was gruff.

He shook his head as he stood back to let her in. 'This isn't a good idea, Izzy.'

Expecting her, already primed, his mind already firmly made up then. Leading her along the hall, he sent a grimace of complaint over his shoulder as he shuffled her through the kitchen to the snug. One uneasy nod at a sofa told her where to sit, and underlined exactly how delighted he was to see her, i.e. Not at all.

She tried for a watery smile, and wished her full skirt didn't take so much tucking into place.

Xander, still standing, stretched one arm across his body, and the corners of his mouth pulled down in recrimination. 'Saying goodbye once was hard enough. I was two hours into my life without you, now I'll have to start all over again.'

As she dropped her bag and perched on the edge of her seat she couldn't help biting her lip. She took a breath, wished her voice hadn't disappeared quite so completely, and desperately tried to nail the first line she'd rehearsed. Luce and Dida had talked her though it. The key was to put forward all the arguments, logically and calmly. But if she couldn't remember the start, how the hell was she going to get to the end? She'd counted on resistance from Xander, but his cold detachment was making her more twitchy by the minute.

Under his ferociously dark brow his eyes narrowed. 'Are you wearing lipstick?'

Izzy sighed, and pushed back an escaping strand of hair. She'd resisted Dida's insistence on sending her into battle slicked up with bright red Ruby Woo, and compromised. 'Crushed strawberry

413

gloss.'

'Right.' Just for a moment the granite in his eyes blurred. 'Your cherubs look nice.'

'I love them.' She instinctively grabbed her ear, and then hurled herself in. 'That's the whole point of why I'm here, you're the only person in the whole world who would know these are the perfect present for me. How the hell can you expect me to let you go when you know me so well? Just tell me that.' Her words dwindled, as his scowl deepened.

He advanced a step, and then jerked to a halt, sending her a grave warning stare. 'You have to stop this Izzy. I understand it's been a shock, but you'll get used to it in time, we both will, we have to. We've got to do this, and the sooner we start the sooner we'll get...' He tailed off.

Something about the way he rubbed his chin spun her straight back to the day they were eating their sundaes, and she'd broken her heart at the thought of him ever getting ill. Then she'd cried because she was hurting and sad, but now the thought of Xander, not only the possibility of him getting ill, but wrecking his life and hers because of it, sent a volcano force of anger rushing through her chest.

'This is so not fair Xander.' The quiet she'd intended went out of the window. 'It's not fair that one day you might get ill, but it's really not fair the way you're just giving in, and letting it ruin both our lives.' Somehow all the pent up pain and stress and hurt she'd been holding in since France was exploding out of her like a bursting damn. 'Yes, I'm sorry for you, but I'm also furious. You think you're being so damned selfless saving me, but actually all you're being is bloody selfish, because you're not thinking of what I want at all.' Her howling accusations bounced off the walls, and she wasn't sure if she was yelling, or crying now, because her face was wet, and she was gulping back sobs. 'How exactly am I meant to cope with this?' As her wailing rose to a scream, Xander moved towards her, and suddenly she was beating her fists on his chest.

'And what the fucking hell happened to seizing the moment?' A whole tumult of love bottled up inside her, and her whole body ached, because it had nowhere to go. So much for being a calm woman, arguing her case. She was howling like a banshee, with snot running out of her nose, her face probably looked like a raspberry sundae, and she didn't give a damn, because all she wanted was to be with the man she loved. How the hell could he deny her that? 'This isn't grabbing life, it's lying down to bloody die, and I refuse to let you do it.'

Xander's arms closed around her back, and as her ribs collided with his stomach, her face was crushed against his chest. As her hands wound up under his T shirt, his scent engulfed her, as she fought to get her breath back.

'I'm sorry.' She scraped her nose on her sleeve, kicking herself for being girlie enough to cry. 'I didn't mean to lose it...' The last thing she wanted was to use tears to manipulate him.

His voice reverberated through his chest. 'Maybe I should have guessed you'd fight me on this.' He tugged her towards a chair, flopped down, and one twist of her hand later, she landed on his knee. 'Now we're here, we might as well talk rather than fight. Are you going to tell me about it quietly?' He raised one eyebrow expectantly.

'I know I've been inconsistent, but since France I've been completely screwed up and miserable. Then this morning, when I thought you'd bought the cinema as a way that we could be together, there was this amazing moment when all the pain dropped away, and everything was suddenly clear. In that split second I knew that all I want is to be with you.'

'Oh, Izzy.' He propped his chin on his hand, and shook his head. 'It can't happen.'

'It's because I love you.' She scratched her head, and puzzled. 'When we're apart I get this awful dragging emptiness, and it hurts so much, but as soon as we're together I feel amazing.'

'Right.'

She told this guy she loved him, and he looks pained and says right? 'Well do you get that too or what? We've never talked about this before.' Lately all she'd done was hide from him. Knowing he was about to leave, she couldn't believe she'd wasted so much time running away.

'I told you the day I came back from America – I hate being apart from you.' He cleared his throat. 'When I came back it wasn't because I wanted to see you again, it was because I knew I loved you so much I wanted to spend my life with you. But I've had time to think and I can't live with myself if I put you in this position.' He gave a guilty grimace. 'When I look back I loved you long before that. Really, I knew there was something going on as I hauled you out of the skip, I just didn't recognise what it was.'

Another time Xander saying all that would have had her melting into a pool on the woodblock floor. Hearing this, but knowing he was still holding back, saying he couldn't be with her, made her stomach wrench.

Raking his hand through his hair, he went on, his voice so low it almost cracked. 'It's because I love you so much that I know you deserve much more than a life with me.'

She screwed up her face. Somehow talking about the illness made it seem more real and threatening, not less. 'I know what might happen. I read a lot about these kind of illnesses when I came back from France. And I'm strong, and ready to face it, if...' She had to throw in everything she could here.

'I know how strong you are Izzy, but after what I went through with my mum, I don't want to put you through the same. If it happens, when it happens, it's not pretty, it's not good.'

Izzy drew in a breath. 'I'm sorry, but I should be the one who decides what I deserve here. I've thought about this a lot since this morning. Losing you some time in the future is something I'm prepared to live with, and I'm ready to support you through whatever illness you have to go through.' Even as she spoke, silent tears were running down her cheeks again at the thought of Xander being ill. 'But I'm sorry, I love you too much to let you go now.'

Xander's face came towards hers, and his stubble pricked her cheek as he rubbed against her. She clung onto him and felt his chest shuddering.

Eventually he swallowed loudly. 'You aren't supposed to say that. Holding you here, every bone in my body is telling me to keep you with me, and never let go, but deep down inside I know that's not fair. It's too selfish of me.'

Brushing her wet cheek on his T shirt, she gave a sniff. 'Xander, we love each other so much, we need to stop obsessing about the future, and make the most of whatever time we have. With luck, we may have years and years. Even if we only had a few months, I'd still choose the option that meant I was with you, every time.' Izzy took his hand in hers and squeezed it very tight. 'I know what I want Xander. I want to be with you, whatever happens. If I'm strong enough to fight you on this, I'm strong enough to face the future with you. What I don't think I can face is being without you.' Looking deep into his eyes, she saw his eyelashes, clumped with tears. 'So that's settled then?'

His face slid into a half smile. 'I'm guessing it could be, if that's what you really mean. And if I really am going to get to keep you, I might just be able to risk a kiss.'

As he slid his mouth gently onto hers, all soft heat and tenderness, the tears poured down her cheeks again, for everything she'd almost lost, and everything she was about to have.

When they finally broke apart, with long, lingering sighs on both sides, she knew there was something else she needed to do. She was miles away from the step by step guide they'd made on Dida's spreadsheet, but somehow she had to find her way back.

'I was thinking about that wedding bunting...' She looked down at Xander. Somehow knowing how very much she loved him, and how committed she was to the future with him, binding it all up with wedding bunting wasn't at all scary.

He shook his head and gave an eye roll. 'Another mistake I'm

417

never going to live down.'

She knew she was pushing him here. 'Had you earmarked it for anywhere special?'

His chest expanded underneath her, as he drew in a long breath. 'I'd thought maybe the garden here...' His shrug was wistful. 'But that was before I decided I shouldn't.'

'Wow, wedding planning now, and a perfect suggestion. You have come a long way.' She flashed him a grin, then she took her courage in both hands and jumped off the proverbial cliff. 'I'd still like to use it, if it's alright with you that is.' She waited to give that bombshell time to fall. 'To me, making a commitment to each other is more important than ever. It's what I'd love to do, if you would too.'

She watched Xander's Adam's apple bob as he swallowed, praying to the god of leap years that she hadn't gone too far here.

'This I do not believe.' He raised his eyebrows at her. 'Did you, the most determinedly independent woman in the world, just ask me to be Mr Izzy Mellor?' There was laughter in his voice, but his eyes shone very brightly.

She laughed back at him. 'Contrary to every opinion I may ever have expressed in the past, I did, and I completely mean it. So what do you say?' Now she'd dared to do it, she knew it was what she wanted. Xander was the man she loved, and the man she trusted, and the man she wanted to spend her life with, and there was no better way of showing him.

His face broke into a smile that sent creases up his cheeks. 'I can't think of anything I'd love more – so long as you'll be Mrs Blackman in return.'

'Definitely, yes.' She gave a shiver of anticipation as Xander's fingers traced a sinuous path up the inside of her thigh.

His tongue tickled the base of her neck, and his voice was breathy in his ear. 'So, getting in practice here on all fronts, does the future Mrs Blackman agree it's a good idea to grab the moment, and consummate the engagement?'

'I do, I do, I do.' Izzy stifled a giggle, as his mouth crashed onto hers.

And this time when he kissed her they didn't stop for a very long time.

89

IZZY, XANDER, LUCE, OLLIE, DIDA, & THE CREW

At the cinema

Ninety nine toasts

'Bringing the ice cream van back with you was a total coup.' Dida was reclining in a deckchair she'd pulled in off the pavement. Beyond the shop window, the ice cream van was doing a great trade, with a queue of customers stretching along the street.

Izzy, propped against an armoire, wedged closely against Xander, barely looked up from her own cone. 'I had to bribe him out of the layby we found him in, but it was worth it.'

'Better than a hijack.' Luce casually rested her elbow on Ollie's shoulder, as they perched side by side on the counter edge.

Dida took an extended lick of her ice cream. 'I know we had cake earlier, but this double ninety nine is hitting the spot. What a day, but it's all working out in the end.'

'So much for your coffee cake.' Izzy flicked a grin in Dida's direction. 'I doubt I'd have got anywhere near getting engaged without it.'

As Izzy gazed up at Xander, standing beside her all hunky and beautiful, and hers to grab whenever she wanted, a warm tingle started at her stomach, and radiated through her whole body. Even a glimpse of him was enough to make her knees go wobbly, every time.

She still couldn't quite believe they were actually together, let alone engaged, but as he'd told her on the drive back to Matlock, once they moved into The Pink House, which he wanted to do straight away, it would begin to feel real. As for getting married as soon as they could, at least they had the bunting. A whoosh rushed through her every time she thought about becoming Mrs Blackman, and riding yet another wave of excitement, Izzy waved her cone in the air.

'Let's do ice cream toasts. I have to have some good reason for justifying that this is my third.'

Dida jumped straight in. 'No way will I ever risk a toast with fizz again. One wave of a bubbly glass in here brings that damned man with his ladders and his signs and his bombshells.'

Izzy laughed. 'That Sold sign takes on a whole new meaning now the cinema's coming to us. It used to send me cold, but now it gives me a thrill. I keep nipping out to look at it.' She flashed a look at Luce. 'By the way, Xander heard GI Joe's might not be opening after all so he's all for us moving into that building. Then he can re-open this as an independent cinema. Joking aside, it would be nice to work next door to him.'

'And GI Joe's building is a great retail space.' Luce sounded very enthusiastic. 'Well, here goes my toast. Yay to the Vintage Cinema Club we all love so much, and which is so much more than the sum of the parts, wherever we are, and here's to everyone who helped to save the business!' Wow, Luce getting all philosophical too. 'But I'm also celebrating having my Friday night dates sorted for the foreseeable future.' She gave a nod to Ollie, whose smile was blissful.

Dida joined in. 'I bet Ruby's happy.'

'We're giving it a few more weeks before Ollie stays over full time.' After so long on her own, it was only natural that Luce was going to be careful, and take things a small step at a time.

Ollie chimed in cheerily. 'That's in case Luce can't cope with the couple bit, and runs for the hills...'

But from the way Luce was leaning into Ollie, and gazing down at him as if she could wolf him down along with her magnum, that wasn't going to happen.

Izzy laughed. 'And don't forget, there'll be more excitement for you two, once the pictures go to auction.'

'That's what's officially known as having my ice cream, and eating it.' Luce grinned at them all.

Dida pulled a flake out of her cone, and bit into it. 'Since Ollie came back with his panda postcards, the falabella craze is fading. Lolly and Ruby want to be zoo keepers.' She waved what was left of her flake at Luce and Izzy, her voice thick with chocolate. 'As for my ice cream toast, here's to the next wave of our small, but perfectly formed Vintage Cinema Club, to all the crew, and also to revenge, which I swear will be served to Aidie and the future Mrs Crompton, ice cream cold.'

Izzy knew Dida's solicitors were picking their way through the separation, and that Dida was bluffing it out here. With the children and Alport Towers to think about, not to mention Aidie in full on fight mode, Dida was in for a difficult time.

'It's a kind of ongoing, daily revenge that we'll still be here.' Luce gave a happy sigh and wafted her ice cream again. 'And a huge thank you to Xander, for making it happen, but even more, for finally persuading Izzy off the singles fence.'

Xander pulled Izzy so close, her hair was catching under his chin, and his low laugh resonated in her ear.

'He's definitely worth the wait.' Izzy smiled up at him. 'Two new couples for The Vintage Cinema Club, but don't they say things happen in threes?' Izzy sent Dida a wink. 'So I'd like to make my toasts, first to my truly amazing Xander who makes me the happiest woman in the world, over and over again, second to grabbing every moment and going for it, and third, Vive La Vintage Cinema Club!'

Izzy knew Dida wasn't too happy about public displays of affection in front of customers, so who knew where she stood on PDAs *with* customers, but just for once, Izzy didn't give a damn. She moved her face upwards, rubbing her cheek across Xander's jaw, searching for the slide of his lips, and the heat of his mouth, and there it was again. One teensy kiss, this one all velvety and dreamy, and it had to be the best in the world, even if it did make her dizzy every time.

And as the room began to spin for Izzy, everyone laughed, and started to clap and cheer.

Acknowledgements

Huge thanks... To my wonderful, talented, amazing editor Charlotte Ledger, who has put so much effort and flair into this book. To her great team at HarperCollins, for making this book real. To the fabulous and tireless bloggers who spread the word.

To Debbie Johnson and Zara Stoneley, and all my other writing friends, for being there with round-the-world, round-the-clock support.

To my children Anna, Indi, and Max, for constantly cheering me on, for the fab techie support, for understanding when I'm not quite here, and that dinner's burned again. And to my own personal hero, Phil, for everything else, which, as he knows, is quite a lot.